Sara Kea   the
West Cou   on
High Scho   e
House of   European
Commission   She has published a
political me... , *A Question of Judgement*; *The Black Book* is her first novel.

THE BLACK BOOK

Sara Keays

CORGI BOOKS

THE BLACK BOOK
A CORGI BOOK : 0 552 14397 9

Originally published in Great Britain by Doubleday,
a division of Transworld Publishers Ltd

PRINTING HISTORY
Doubleday edition published 1996
Corgi edition published 1997

Set in 10 on 11.5 point Sabon by Falcon Oast Graphic Art

Corgi Books are published by Transworld Publishers Ltd,
61–63 Uxbridge Road, London W5 5SA,
in Australia by Transworld Publishers (Australia) Pty Ltd,
15–25 Helles Avenue, Moorebank, NSW 2170
and in New Zealand by Transworld Publishers (NZ) Ltd,
3 William Pickering Drive, Albany, Auckland.

Reproduced, printed and bound in Great Britain by
Cox & Wyman Ltd, Reading, Berks.

THE BLACK BOOK

PROLOGUE

'You don't look very happy, my dear, not your usual self at all. Are you all right?' the old man asked.

'I'm worried and I've not slept too well these last few days. When I leave here I'm going home.' She sighed. 'I suppose the truth is I'm a bit scared.'

He pushed her cup nearer to her. 'You haven't touched it. Have some, you might feel better.' They sipped their coffee in silence. The room was full of shadows and dark corners, with a single bright space between them from the green-shaded brass reading lamp on his desk.

'I expect there've been many people who've sat here and confided in you,' she said.

'Quite a few. But no-one ever brought me anything like that.' He looked at the bulky brown envelope on the table next to her. Her forearm rested across it, protecting it, her hand curled around one corner. She wasn't quite ready to part with it.

It was cool in the little room. Looking through the doorway she could see specks of dust floating in the sunlight which slanted down into Peers' Lobby, pale shafts

7

which illuminated the russets and blues of the tiled floor like spotlights on a waiting stage. There wasn't a sound to be heard. It was as if the Houses of Parliament were deserted, though she knew that there were people at work – Members' secretaries and Parliamentary officials – in various parts of the Palace of Westminster and its outbuildings. The Recess had begun and Members and Peers had departed for their holidays. Immediately the place was transformed. Where yesterday there had been crowds of people, now it was empty and silent. She noted, as she had on many occasions before, the curious fact that the traffic which she knew must be roaring along the Embankment only a short distance away, was inaudible here. It was an unchanging, centuries-old silence. For a moment she heard the distant sound of footsteps in the corridor leading to the Commons Chamber. Then silence again. The stillness was complete. The big man sitting opposite her was a part of it; serene, rock-like, unshakeable. His eyes had the misty look of old age.

'Well, here you are.' She gave him the parcel. 'You won't leave it here will you, George? You'll keep it safe?'

'Don't you worry. It'll be safe with me.'

'Thank you very much.' She picked up her bag from the floor beside her chair and stood up. 'I hope it's not too much of a chore. I think I've got it all down, the most important points anyway. But will it do any good? I've a horrible feeling that without any hard evidence, no-one will believe it. Before deciding who to give it to, I'd like to know what you think – your candid opinion.'

'You can count on that, my dear.'

CHAPTER ONE

The young woman turned gratefully out of the crowded street, through an archway into a cobbled mews. Immediately the deafening roar of the traffic was diminished. No longer did she have to screw up her eyes against the enveloping spray from the rain-soaked road. She hurried on, her head down against the wind, umbrella sloping forward.

There had been no particular purpose to her expedition. She had walked for miles, looked at some galleries, at endless windows, had thought, remembered. She was hurrying now not to an appointment, but to the sanctuary of the apartment and tranquillity. When she reached the front door and stepped inside, she seemed to bring with her a miasma of damp, penetrating cold from the street. She walked through to the kitchen and dropped her dripping umbrella into the sink, then slowly returned to the living room, switched on a table lamp, and sat down on the sofa. She had forgotten to remove her coat. Droplets of moisture glinted on the surface of the dark-green wool. She removed her navy beret with one hand and scooped her hair out from inside her coat collar with the other. She dropped the beret beside her. Her soft black boots were stained from the slush on the pavements. Her eyes were dark with an inward gaze, as if she were working on a difficult mental puzzle.

She tipped her head back and closed her eyes. If only she could get the images out of her mind: the figure flying forward, crashing to the ground, arms spread out; the feeble attempt to crawl away; then stillness. How long had he gone on living, lying amongst the shellholes and debris in that desolate road? How long had he suffered? What were his thoughts in those last moments?

How she longed for him. If only he hadn't gone back. If only she'd gone with him. Sometimes the images were so sharp in her mind, she felt as if she had been there, as if she herself had been shot, felt the hard cold ground beneath her.

She kept her eyes closed, trying to remember his face and his voice. Would she always be tormented by those images of his death? She was gritting her teeth and frowning slightly. Her thick coppery hair was pushed up behind her head like a ruff by the back of the sofa. Her brows and lashes were very dark. Her skin appeared slightly suntanned, but was in fact covered with a fine, barely perceptible dusting of tiny freckles. She was very still. Her hands were limp in her lap. Only her brow and jaw revealed her tension.

Sometimes she thought she'd never be able to remember his face again, only the image of him lying in that road. It was if seeing it had robbed her of her memories of him as well as of his life.

She became aware of the physical effort she was making and relaxed, remaining perfectly still and hardly breathing. She felt as if everything within her and beyond her, time itself, had stopped. Gradually the images faded and she became aware once more of her surroundings, feeling the weight of her inertia and the impossibility of making decisions. Everything seemed so pointless. She felt that it made no difference whether she lived or died. She remained motionless, her eyes closed.

She was constantly encountering reminders of Donald's death and none, it seemed, of their happiness together. She could hardly turn on the television without reliving that moment. The film clip of the shooting was shown frequently in programmes about the fighting in the Balkans and Eastern Europe, but with fewer and fewer mentions of who he was and why he had died. He had become just another casualty of war.

The first time she had seen the film she had been totally unprepared for it and had been prostrated by the shock. Afterwards the images would return without warning and with devastating force. They overlaid all her thoughts of him. A few days ago, with friends who were watching a rugby match on television, the sight of a player falling forward had reminded her so vividly that she had felt faint.

She knew little of the events of the last day of Donald's life. He'd telephoned her the previous evening but hadn't talked about himself, or his work, only about her and how much he missed her. All she knew of his last day was what she'd been told by his colleague and great friend, Etienne Bernhardt, who'd called at their flat to break the news to her: that Donald, as the senior UN official in his region, had been supervising the hand-over of refugees when he was shot by a sniper. No hand-over had taken place. Heavy fighting had broken out again and large numbers of refugees had been slaughtered. NATO and Russian forces were now caught up in the fighting.

She'd remained in Geneva, waiting with Etienne at Donald's office, not knowing what else to do. A call came in at last. Where did she want his body to be taken? She rang his family in England, only to find that they had learned of his death from the media. She regretted not

11

having telephoned them sooner and felt she had let them down. She rang her mother in New Zealand. Then she cleared her desk and got ready to return to England.

She had been taken by surprise by the media onslaught. Reporters had turned up in droves to interview her and Donald's colleagues. She had escaped most of them by staying with Etienne and his wife, Lucia, but a man had called to see her at her office, a friend of Donald's he had said, who'd served with him in the army and had been intending to visit them on his way through Geneva. He'd been so plausible, so sympathetic. She knew little of Donald's army days and had been tricked into talking about him. Only after her return to England had she seen the newspaper articles and learned that the man she had thought was a friend was a reporter who'd never even met Donald, let alone been in the army.

The reporting of Donald's death had caused her great distress. She realized with a shock that, for the press, his death was simply a commercial asset to be exploited. For them his life was of no interest, but his death was a sensational story: good copy with dramatic photos which would make lots of money. How they had relished the fact that she and Donald had been married for only ten days. What dedication and heroism, they said, to sacrifice their honeymoon in order to return to the war zone. What might they have written if they had known his feelings about the whole operation? His work with UNHCR had brought him feelings of deep despair. He'd said the UN was being manipulated by the Security Council and was scathing in his condemnation of America and Britain for their part in the betrayal of helpless people.

'They pass high-minded resolutions and get away with doing nothing. They weep crocodile tears over the slaughter and suffering of millions while weighing up what military or trading advantage they can gain from the situation.'

He'd had enough and wanted to get away from it all, but had been asked to go back. Only the UN could provide people whom both sides would trust to supervise the hand-over of prisoners and refugees and the collection of evidence of war crimes. But he'd been uneasy, believing that a peace deal built on ethnic partition was doomed to failure. He was deeply depressed by the mounting xenophobia and nationalism throughout Europe. 'It's a powder keg, waiting to explode,' he'd told her gloomily. 'Just one major incident could set it off and embroil us all in war.' And he had died in just such an incident.

Donald's family had made the arrangements for his funeral. It had been a bleak, comfortless day for her. She had experienced a curious feeling of detachment, her grief suspended. His family were deeply sympathetic but she did not know them well and found it difficult to talk to them about her life with him, most of which had been spent abroad. She wished she'd brought them some photographs and some of his possessions. She would send things to them when she got back to Geneva. She hadn't gone back immediately but had been staying in London, glad to be alone, to do as she pleased and postpone decisions.

She felt leaden, the sofa beneath her seemed to press against her. She was no longer aware of her own body, only of external sensations.

Suddenly, like a bright light, a vivid memory flooded her mind: the lake, the shimmering water, the mist obscuring the far shore, Donald holding her hand. They had stopped for a picnic on their way to Montreux and had gone for a walk by Lake Geneva. There was a thin layer of mist rising from the water and, in the distance, they could just make out the towers of the Château de Chillon. The air was cold and smelled faintly smokey, as if from burning leaves. Their breath steamed in front of them, but the sun was warm on their backs.

He'd asked her to marry him. 'We've been together now for nearly four years. Isn't it about time we got married?' She could hear his warm, humorous voice and remembered how they'd talked of all the places they still wanted to visit, of where they might settle down. She begged him not to take another assignment but to let someone else from the team go in his place.

'Don't worry, Jo,' he'd said. 'It'll only be for another month, I promise. I'll be home for Christmas and after this, I'm going to pack it in. Let's make a change. We've both had enough of the UN, haven't we? Let's go away, go off round the world. Start making a list of all the things you'd like to do, the places you'd like to see.'

He'd been anxious that they should get married before he went back. Had he had a premonition? The warm memories vanished and she was back once more in the darkness of her grief.

The sound of the telephone put a stop to the treadmill of her thoughts. She got up and crossed the room to answer it.

'Joanna? It's Laura here. I'm glad I've tracked you down at last.'

'Was it so difficult?'

'Well you haven't exactly broadcast your whereabouts. I should have asked you after the funeral, but you were surrounded and looked to me as if you'd had enough. Where are you staying?'

'Do you remember Lydia Rowe? She was at school with me and stayed with us occasionally.'

'I can't say I do. I remember the name.'

'I'm staying in her flat. She works for an airline and is away at the moment.'

'I gather from the family that you're thinking of going back to Geneva. Is that right?'

'I haven't made any firm plans yet. Perhaps I'll go back. I don't know. I can't stay here indefinitely.'

'How are you getting on, Jo? Are you all right?'

'It's not easy, but I'm OK.'

'Are you on your own?'

'Yes, but that's fine.'

'You could always stay with me. I'd love to have you here, Jo. Do come.'

'This is OK, really Laura. It suits me to be on my own at the moment. D'you understand?'

'Of course I do.'

'And you, Laura? How are you? What's your news?' asked Jo, anxious to change the subject.

'I'm fine. Things are pretty much as they always are. I was wondering whether we could get together. It would be good to see you and I've a proposition to put to you.'

'What kind of proposition?' Jo propped her head with her hand and tried to sound interested.

'A job. Here, in the House of Commons. It just happens that a friend of mine has had an accident and is going to be away from her job for two or three months. The chap she works for needs someone to stand in for her while she's away. I thought you might like to do it. Just to fill in some time while you decide what you want to do. What do you think?'

'I'm finding it quite difficult to decide what to do. The trouble is I don't feel like doing anything.' Jo sighed. 'In any case, I'm hardly qualified for it, am I? I can't say that I know anything very much about British politics these days, except for what a mess the Government seem to be making of everything, especially foreign policy.'

'You'd find it a breeze. It couldn't be more demanding than the jobs you've done at NATO and the UN.'

'But I haven't done any secretarial work for years,' Jo said wearily. 'And my typing was never too hot. I've kept up my shorthand but I never much cared for sitting in an office all day, pounding a keyboard.'

'Well obviously there's a certain amount of typing

involved, but there's a lot more to the job than that. In any case, the secret is to choose an MP with the right kind of constituency – far enough from London for you not to be plagued with visits from constituents, in an area that doesn't generate a huge case-load, so that when he's in his constituency he won't feel inclined to keep popping back to the House. This chap fits the bill beautifully.'

'Who is it?'

'The Government Chief Whip.'

'Surely he'll want someone terribly high-powered, smart and on the ball?'

'Exactly. I told him I knew just the person.'

'Come off it, Laura,' Jo protested. 'I'm hardly the right person for that kind of work and you know it. I vowed years ago that I'd never do the PA bit again, toiling away for some ambitious creep who takes you for granted and gets all the credit for your efforts.'

'I can't say that doesn't happen in this place. It certainly does. And there are plenty of creeps, I admit. But this chap's really not bad, and working here is different from any other kind of secretarial job. I think you'd find it quite intriguing and it would take your mind off things.' Jo didn't respond, so Laura continued enthusiastically, 'Also, quite a lot of the work involves trying to help people with problems. I know that's important to you. I think you'd find it quite worthwhile. And it would only be for a short time, until his regular girl gets back. Why don't you come and have lunch with me and I'll tell you more? And you can meet Harry.'

'Harry?'

'Harry Hunter. The Government Chief Whip.'

'There you are,' said Jo. 'That shows you how clued-up I am about British politics. I've never even heard of the guy. I don't think it's on, Laura.'

'Nonsense. You'd have it all at your fingertips in no

time. And it would only be for a short time, after all. About ten weeks, I should think. I don't want to press you, but please come and have lunch with me and give him the once over. Will you?'

Jo hesitated, 'Well, I'd love to see you, Laura. But I'm not sure about the job. And I will have to go back to Geneva at some stage to sort things out. I've left my job but they say they'll take me back if I decide that's what I want.'

'Well don't make up your mind yet. Let's get together. Could you make it on Monday?'

'I suppose so,' said Jo, then realized how churlish she sounded. 'Yes, of course I can. I'm not doing anything and it would be really good to see you. Thanks, Laura.'

As she put the phone down, Jo became aware that she was still wearing her coat and wet boots. I must pull myself together, she thought, as she slipped them off, and I ought at least to consider Laura's suggestion.

CHAPTER TWO

Laura manoeuvred her car through the dense traffic of Parliament Square and turned in at the gates to New Palace Yard, slowing to wave to the police officer on duty, who smiled back at her. She drove down the ramp into the underground car-park, continuing on down to a lower level where she reversed quickly and easily, with the skill of long practice, into a space near the stairway. She got out of the car and stretched. She was tall and shapely, with the steady, confident gaze of a mature and experienced woman. Her skin was smooth and creamy, with the well-nurtured look of an easy life. In fact she had had to work hard to achieve the luxuries she enjoyed: her own house, a car and exotic holidays. She was lightly made-up, her fair hair sleek and shiny. Her eyebrows and lashes were dark, her eyes a greeny-grey, with a faint puckering of tiny creases at the corners and beneath the lower lids. The slight upward slant of her eyes, high rounded cheekbones and the little double crease at the corners of her mouth gave her the appearance of being on the brink of a smile.

She leant into the car to pick up her handbag and

briefcase, locked the door and left the car-park, taking the stairs two at a time.

She made her way through a network of corridors and staircases to Members' Lobby, her footsteps striking a brisk, rapid note on the stone floor. She turned aside, into the Members' Post Office where she collected two large bundles of mail.

Next she stopped at the Vote Office window beside the doorway to the Commons Chamber and collected *Hansard*. Finally she put her head round the door of a small room at the side of Members' Lobby and said 'Morning, Fred,' to a man sitting at a desk, who was unable to respond as he was talking on the telephone but who nodded and smiled at her. Having taken some papers from a pile behind him, Laura withdrew from the room and left Members' Lobby, hurrying up a flight of stairs and turning into a long corridor. Here the floors were carpeted and her footsteps were inaudible. The oak panelling, thick green carpet and heavy oak doors, each one closed, gave the place an almost claustrophobic feel after the echoing Lobby below. She stopped at a door bearing a card in a small brass frame, inscribed 'Mr Ian Swift MP'. She opened the door and stepped into a small room. It was stuffy, having been closed up for the week-end. No sunlight reached the leaded window, which looked out onto an inner courtyard of the Palace of Westminster, giving a vista of mellow stone and slate. The room contained a desk, three filing cabinets, a swivel chair, two green covered armchairs and a low table. It was already crowded without anyone in it. Laura stepped across to the desk and dumped her briefcase and one bundle of mail. She picked up the phone and dialled a number. When there was no answer after five rings, she replaced the receiver, retrieved her briefcase and left the room, retracing her steps, through Members' Lobby, Central Lobby and St Stephen's Hall to the public entrance to the Palace of Westminster, St Stephen's Entrance.

It was a bitterly cold morning but the sun was shining and Laura felt content with her lot. She had worked in the House of Commons for most of the past twenty years, for a number of Members of Parliament and Peers. From time to time she would get an urge to leave Westminster and do a job totally removed from politics, but, after combing the advertisements she would decide that she was better off where she was. She had once made the break and had worked in Paris for a couple of years, but after an unhappy love affair had returned to London where, for want of any other ideas, she had gone back to the Commons. Now she worked for two MPs. One was a somewhat tiresome young man, Ian Swift, one of the new intake from the last General Election who had received rapid and surprising promotion to a Junior Ministerial post and was altogether too pleased with himself as a result. Laura told friends that she put up with him believing that he would improve with time, after the initial anxiety to make a good impression had worn off. Charles Donaldson, on the other hand, was amusing, kind and appreciative. He was fond of her and more dependent on her than he realized. They had an easy, affectionate relationship that had grown out of their long association. Laura had worked for him for years and would probably continue to do so until he quit or dropped. He was Deputy Speaker and would probably eventually become Speaker.

Laura worked in Ian's office in the House, which he used only rarely, generally in the evenings after she had gone home. It was close to the Chamber and just a few doors along the corridor from Charles's room. She enjoyed working close to the hub of Parliament and being able to keep in touch with events.

Various MPs and other friends dropped in regularly to

see her, to gossip, or invite her down to the bar for a drink. She was a mine of information, but very discreet. She was attractive, cheerful and undemanding and men poured out their hearts to her. She would listen with a sympathy and attentiveness that made each feel that he was her most valued friend, but it never occurred to any of them, even to Charles who thought he knew her better than anyone, that he might not be her only confidant.

She crossed the road and walked briskly to the out-building not far from Parliament which was used as office accommodation for a number of MPs and secretaries and where Ian still had the desk allocated to his first secretary, who had quit after only a few weeks, and where he kept his constituency files. Laura enjoyed going over and sometimes working there as it gave her the opportunity of seeing various friends. It was here that she had arranged to meet Jo.

She pressed the doorbell and looked up at the closed-circuit television camera above the doorway, wondering which attendant was now inspecting her and what kind of greeting she would get when the door opened.

'Lost our card again, have we, Miss James?'

'Sorry, Vic, it's buried somewhere in my bag and with this lot to carry, I couldn't face the struggle of digging for it.' She liked Vic. He was always cheerful and helpful.

'You've got a visitor, Joanna Delvere. I put her upstairs and gave her a cup of coffee.'

'Thanks.'

She went on past Vic's office and opened the door on the other side of the passage. As usual the room was crowded, noisy and untidy. 'Morning all,' she said. One or two of the women looked up. 'Hi, Laura.' 'What time d'you call this?' Most of them continued working. There was a humming noise from the word-processors and computers, printers and fax machines. Already the air had a baked, stale smell to it. She was, as always, glad that her desk was nearest to the door. For the moment it was clear of papers and tidy, although her filing cabinets, against the wall behind her chair, were piled high with papers and files waiting to be put away. She dumped her bag, briefcase and bundle of mail on her desk, picked up her telephone and dialled. After letting it ring for a few moments she hung up and went out to Vic's room. 'Vic, I hate to ask, but would you do me a favour?'

'Another one?'

'I can't get Sir Charles on the phone. If he rings, tell him that I had to go over to the House to meet a visitor. With a bit of luck he'll think I'm looking after a constituent. I want to spend some time with Jo. She's probably taking over Lois's job for the time being.'

On the first floor she flung open the door of the reading room. Jo was sitting in an armchair opposite the door. She came over to Laura and they embraced.

Laura looked round the room. There were two men sitting in the far corners, reading newspapers. A third man was standing at the table in the centre of the room, leafing through a pile of newspapers and magazines. He glanced up at them.

'Hello, Laura. Good of you to show up.' He smiled as he said this. 'Are we going to do any work today?'

'Ian! Vic didn't tell me you were here. I thought you didn't want to see me until this afternoon. I've got to see Charles shortly.'

'That's all right. I wasn't expecting to see you, but I'll leave the constituency case notes from the weekend. There's rather a lot I'm afraid. You might look through them, if you have a moment and get out any files we need. I'll see you in the House at about five.'

'Sure thing. Ian, this is Joanna. She's probably going to be working here. Jo, this is Ian Swift, one of my long-suffering employers.'

Jo thought he looked very young to be an MP,

probably in his early thirties. He had a good natured, rather self-conscious smile. He shook hands with Jo. 'I'll see you this evening then, Laura. Bye. Bye, Joanna.' He picked up his briefcase and left the room.

Laura lowered her voice, not wishing to be overheard by the occupants of the far end of the room.

'It would be really good having you working here. I think you'd enjoy it.'

'You're talking as if it's a foregone conclusion that I'll get the job, when I'm not even sure I want it. I don't know how you can be so confident that he'll offer it to me.'

'Oh don't worry about that. He'll be glad to have you after everything I've told him.'

'What have you told him?'

'That you're clever, reliable, hard-working, discreet, sexy—'

'What?'

Laura held up a hand in a placatory gesture.

'Joke. Of course I didn't. He'd see that for himself anyway.'

'What are you saying? Is it a requirement?'

'Don't be daft. I'm just trying to cheer you up. You're looking terrific, you know, and I'm envious.'

One of the men got to his feet, returned his newspaper to the table and left the room.

Laura flopped into an armchair. Jo sat down again next to her.

'Seriously, what have you told him about me?' she asked.

'Just what I said.' Laura glanced across at the occupant of the far corner. As if prompted by her gaze, he too left the room.

'Don't worry,' said Laura, speaking normally once more. 'I did as you asked. I gave him your maiden name and I haven't told him about Donald. And I didn't tell

23

him you're my cousin. That's what you wanted, wasn't it?'

'Yes. It's just that I can't face talking about what happened to Donald. And if people know I'm your cousin they may ask you about me. The next thing is they'll be treating me as if I'm an invalid or something. That's what so often happens.' She sighed, then added, 'And I don't want the press after me again. You understand, don't you, Laura?'

'Of course I do,' said Laura, leaning forward in her chair. She was twelve years older than Jo and had always felt protective towards her. After Jo's father had died when she was still in her teens and her mother remarried, Laura had become more like a sister to her.

'All the press reports referred to me as Joanna Hammond, so I thought I might have a better chance of escaping their attention if I used my maiden name,' said Jo. 'And my passport still says Delvere rather than Hammond.' She sighed. 'The thing is I still quite often get people saying, "Don't I know you?" or "Haven't I seen you somewhere before?" and if they hear the name Hammond they tend to make the connection. I just don't feel equal to any more of that at the moment.'

'You poor thing,' said Laura sympathetically. 'Don't worry. There's no need for Harry or anyone else to know. And in any case, he hasn't asked what my connection is with you, so why should I volunteer it?'

'Thanks, Laura.'

'Just take it one day at a time,' said Laura. 'Who knows, you may decide you like it here and want to stay. Just try to show a little enthusiasm when you meet Harry, OK?'

'Of course I will, though to be honest with you, nothing fills me with enthusiasm at the moment. But I do appreciate you doing all this for me, Laura, really I do.'

Laura reached across to pat Jo's arm. 'Don't be silly. I

know you'd have done the same for me.'

'I don't rate in the Palais des Nations the way you do here. In any case I can't imagine you'd ever want to work there. It's pretty dull. It must produce more cynics and unread documents than any other organization on earth, except perhaps the European Commission.'

'I'm afraid some of the work here is pretty boring at times, but the place is interesting. Learning about the way Parliament works is quite a revelation.'

'In what way?' asked Jo.

'The inmates are a bit of a mixed bag,' said Laura. 'On the one hand you've got the politicians and their hangers-on: on the other, the permanent staff. The relationship between the two groups is a bit like a rocky marriage: the face they present to the outside world is rather different from what they get up to behind closed doors.' Laura warmed to her subject. 'They live together for their mutual benefit – each needs the other for the institution to continue but when something goes wrong, it's always the other lot's fault. They don't like to do their dirty washing in public and there are usually things happening behind the scenes they'd rather weren't found out.'

'Like what sort of things?'

They were interrupted as the door opened and a man came in.

'Hello, Laura. How's tricks?'

He was tall, immaculate in a dark suit, exuding self-confidence. His black hair was thick and glossy, his skin glowed with a ruddy tan.

'Hello, Randall. I'm not as well as you by the look of things.'

'Who's this?' he said, eying Jo. 'Aren't you going to introduce me?'

'Jo, this is Randall Myers. He's a researcher for a group of YTs.'

'YTs?'

25

'Young Thrusters.'

'Must you, Laura?' he said, but smiled as if entirely pleased by her remark.

'This is Joanna Delvere. She's probably going to be working for the Chief Whip – if he comes up to scratch, that is.'

'Well, hello there,' he said with exaggerated enthusiasm as he shook hands with her. 'I can see you're someone I'm going to want to get to know. Perhaps you'll let me give you lunch some time.'

'Not until I've briefed her thoroughly first,' said Laura. 'Come on, Jo. We've got places to go and people to see. Catch you later, Randall.'

When they were outside, Jo said, 'What's wrong with him? Are you trying to tell me I should avoid him?'

'Not a bit of it. I always tease him. I just thought I'd warn you that he'll pump you for information, any chance he gets. He's very good at that and people don't always realize what he's doing until it's too late. I wonder sometimes if he isn't a fearful gossip although he's very secretive about himself. Good-looking, too, don't you think? He's amusing company and he's a mine of useful information. He hangs out in this building because the Members he works for have offices here.'

Laura looked at her watch. 'We'd better go on over to the House and meet Harry.'

They walked over to St Stephen's Entrance where Jo, not having a pass, had to go through the security check. They walked across the end of Westminster Hall, and on to Central Lobby, Laura talking all the time, giving a little history here and there and explaining which parts of the building Jo'd be likely to visit regularly and why. Jo was struck by the number of people Laura knew. Almost everyone they passed greeted her. They reached Members' Lobby. 'There's the Commons Chamber,' said Laura and took her in. 'Government benches to the

26

right of the Speaker, Opposition to the left. Strangers' Gallery up there,' Laura pointed above the door. 'Press Gallery the other end.'

'Why "Strangers"?' asked Jo.

'The public. You and me. Anyone who's not an MP is a stranger.'

'How ordinary it all looks,' said Jo.

'Everything here is more ordinary than you'd expect, including the MPs,' said Laura. 'Of course there are good people here, trying their best, but the system doesn't exactly promote brilliance and courage.'

'Why not?'

'It's dependent on tradition and ritual. If you don't conform, you won't get on.'

'Aren't large institutions often like that?' said Jo.

'Maybe. Televising the proceedings seems to have made it worse.'

'I've seen it on television and I find it a total turn-off,' said Jo.

'I am sure most people do. The system promotes aggressive and adversarial behaviour, rather than sharing and compromise. Every decision is the result of contest rather than a meeting of minds.'

'Perhaps that's why there are so few women MPs,' said Jo.

'Could be,' said Laura, 'though people usually blame the long hours.'

They had advanced further into the Chamber and were standing by the Table.

'You see the red line on the carpet on each side of the Chamber?' said Laura. 'Well, there was a time when if you stepped over that while speaking, you'd be ruled out of order. The lines are exactly two swords' lengths apart and the rule was imposed to prevent Members running each other through with their swords in the heat of debate. Amazing, isn't it?'

Jo smiled. 'It seems to me the way they behave hasn't changed very much.'

'Too true,' said Laura. She looked at her watch. 'Come on, we'd better go and see Harry.'

She led the way across Members' Lobby, into the Government Whips' Office, a large room with desks arranged in pairs, back to back, along three sides and a single desk at the far end. As in the Chamber, the colours everywhere were brown and green. Light-green carpet, dark-green leather chairs, brown oak panelling, doors and desks. Two of the desks were occupied. I suppose those men are Whips, thought Jo. I wonder what they do? There was a sofa and some armchairs in the middle of the room. On the sofa sat a lean, grey-haired man with very blue eyes and a heavily lined, almost leathery complexion. He was holding a glass of orange juice in one hand and a cigarette in the other. He greeted Laura heartily and smiled at Jo. 'You can go on in, Laura. He's expecting you.' He had the grainy voice of a heavy smoker. They went through a door at the far end of the room into a smaller room. The man who got up from behind the desk looked surprisingly young. He was about the same height as Jo and his close-cropped curly dark hair was only slightly greying at the temples. She had expected someone older, taller and more imposing.

'Good morning, Laura,' he said. 'How are you?' He smiled at Jo. 'And you must be Joanna.' He stepped forward and shook her hand. 'Do come and sit down.'

'I'll leave you to it and come back later, shall I?' said Laura.

'Fine,' said Harry. 'Joanna can give you a ring when we've had a chat.'

Laura took a piece of paper from her bag, scribbled her number on it and handed it to Jo. 'I'll come back for you and we can have some lunch.'

'Thanks, Laura,' said Harry. He leant back in his chair and smiled at Jo. 'Well Joanna, I expect Laura has told you what the job entails.'

'Not in great detail.'

'I need someone who's pretty much a self-starter, you know. Lois, who's worked for me for years, takes care of the constituency side of things for me to a great extent, drafting letters for my signature, organizing my diary, liaising with my agent, and so on. I think you'll find she's kept things pretty well organized, though there's a bit of a backlog of mail accumulating.'

He patted a pile of papers on his desk. 'I've got some of it here and there's nothing too awful but obviously I want to get on top of it again as soon as possible.'

'Of course.' He seems to have taken it for granted that I'll do the job, she thought.

'Laura tells me you've done plenty of PA work, is that right?'

'Yes, in the City originally. Then I decided on a complete change and went abroad, Brussels first – NATO – then the Middle East, working with aid agencies and the UN, then Geneva. Chiefly administrative.' She was being deliberately vague, preferring to wait for specific questions. But apparently he didn't want to ask any.

He continued, almost talking over her words: 'Impressive. In fact you're probably too high-powered for the job.' The compliment was belied by the little laugh which accompanied it. 'As I was saying, there's a bit of a backlog, but once we're on top of that I don't think you'd find it too demanding. The hours you work are pretty much what suits you, provided I can see you at certain times – Monday mornings, for example, to go through my surgery case notes from the weekends when I have surgeries in the constituency – and provided you get the work done of course!' He chuckled. He proceeded to tell her about the constituency and the kind of

29

work that arose from it and about his weekly programme in the House. He talked easily and with a practised rapidity. He was resting his elbows on the arms of his chair, holding his hands up in a tent shape in front of him, the tips of his thumbs and fingers touching. He wagged his hands back and forth, thumbs pressed together, so that his fingertips made a distinct tapping sound.

'I'd usually want to see you here, with the mail and any accompanying files we may need. Sometimes you might have to come over to Number Twelve Downing Street, though not very often.'

He swung his swivel chair slightly back and forth as he spoke, pushing on the floor with one foot. She noticed that his feet were small, encased in very expensive-looking laced shoes with unusually thick soles and heels. It occurred to her that he was self-conscious about his height and she felt sorry for him.

He seems almost nervous, too, she thought, then decided he must be merely preoccupied. The telephone rang and Harry picked it up. 'Yes,' he said and listened attentively to his caller. 'Oh, he does, does he? We'll see about that.' His tone was unpleasant and there was a hard edge to his voice. Jo was taken aback by the change in him and watched him surreptitiously as he listened again to his caller and scribbled notes on a pad in front of him. He seemed oblivious to her presence. 'I'll fix him,' he said to his caller, frowning at the notes in front of him. 'Don't worry. I'll come up with something.' He listened again, then gave a short, humourless laugh. 'Yes . . . yes. I see . . . Leave it to me. OK. Bye.' He hung up.

'Sorry about that, Joanna. I have to go over to Number Ten shortly. Is there anything you want to know?'

'I thought it would be the other way around,' she replied.

'Oh, Laura's filled me in. If anything, you're too highly

qualified, but if a temporary assignment would suit you, it would help me out no end.'

He smiled. A warm, apparently sincere smile that dispelled her doubts of a moment ago. She found herself smiling back and saying, 'I think it would be interesting.'

He got up to leave and she followed suit. He said, 'When can you start?'

'Straight away, if you like.'

'That's great,' he said. They shook hands and he led the way out of the room. In the outer office, the leathery man was still sitting on the sofa, glass in hand, listening to something being said by one of the other men.

'You can ring Laura from here, Joanna,' said Harry. Addressing the man on the sofa he said, 'Joanna's going to be working for me until Lois gets back. Look after her will you, Jack? I've got to go over to Number Ten. Thanks for coming, Joanna. Laura will fill you in about passes and so on and show you where your desk is. I'll see you tomorrow, I expect.'

He left the room and she suddenly realized that she had not asked him what salary the job carried. The same thought must have occurred to him because the door opened and he reappeared. 'I'll pay you the same as I pay Lois. Will that be all right?'

She felt unable to ask, in front of these strangers, what he was paying Lois, so she said, 'I'm sure that will be fine. Thank you.' He left again. 'May I use this telephone?' she asked of the man called Jack.

'You certainly may.' She dialled Laura's number. 'Care for a drink?' asked Jack.

'Well . . .'

Laura answered and said she'd be with her in a moment.

Jack stood up and went over to the far side of the room. There was a jug of orange juice and glasses on a sideboard. He poured out a glassful.

One of the other men called out, 'It's not orange juice, you know.'

'What is it?'

'Buck's Fizz,' said Jack. 'Champagne and orange. Most refreshing. Try it.' She took a sip. 'So you're going to be working for Harry,' he continued. 'Have you worked here before?'

'No. Why?'

'Your face is familiar. Where have I seen you before?'

'I don't think you have. I've been living abroad for some years. I shall only be filling in here before going back – until I decide what I want to do next.'

'Well, it'll be good to have you with us, Joanna. I expect we'll be seeing quite a lot of you. Hey, Steve! Roy!' he called across the room to the other two men. 'Meet Joanna. She's going to be working for Harry till Lois gets back.'

The man at the nearest desk was talking on the telephone. He gave a slight wave of acknowledgement and looked down once more at the papers in front of him. The other looked up from his work and smiled at Jo. 'Hello, Joanna. Welcome aboard.' He leaned back in his chair, looking at her. 'Aren't I going to get a drink?' he said, presumably to Jack, but without taking his eyes off Jo.

'Help yourself, Steve,' said Jack. 'Jo's not going to wait on you.' Steve was prevented from replying by having to answer his telephone. Jack said to Jo, 'It's every man for himself here, in more ways than one.' At that moment the door opened and two men came into the room.

'Is Harry here?' said the first, a big, burly ginger-haired man, who was followed by a lean, dark, anxious-looking individual.

'Not at the moment. What's up, Eddie?' asked Jack of the big man.

'We've got trouble looming.' Eddie glanced round at

Jo. He and his companion moved to the other end of the room where Jack joined them and an earnest conversation in lowered voices ensued. Feeling that she was definitely surplus to requirements, Jo moved a little away from them and studied her surroundings. There was a large white plastic board on one wall of the room with lists of names printed on it in alphabetical order in black lettering, with numbers and letters written alongside the names in different colours. She sipped her drink. There were framed photographs on one wall. She supposed they must be MPs, probably former Whips. She recognized one of them as a former Prime Minister. Had he been a Whip? she wondered.

The door opened and Laura came in. 'Oh, I see he's got you on Buck's Fizz already. You'll be getting bad habits if I don't keep an eye on you.'

Joanna took some more of her drink, then decided she didn't want to appear to be swigging it and put it down half-finished. They left the room.

Jack refilled his glass and sat down again on the sofa. The two recent arrivals were still in conversation at one side of the room. Jack looked across to the other two men sitting at their desks and said, 'Well what did you think of her, Steve? A cracker, wouldn't you say?'

'You're telling me. Lucky Harry. She can stand in for my old bat any day.'

'She's not going to be around long enough for any chance of that, fortunately for her. Mind you I don't think she'd stand any nonsense, somehow. She looked pretty shrewd to me. Nice eyes too.'

The door opened and Harry reappeared, accompanied by another of the Whips.

'Are we meant to be having a meeting now?' asked Jack in a tone of surprise as he glanced down at his watch.

'No,' said Harry. 'Charlie just intercepted me to say that

we've got trouble brewing on tonight's vote and I want you all to double check the figures.'

'That's just what I wanted to see you about,' said Eddie. 'Drew and I've been hearing the same thing.'

'I thought we had a clear margin,' said Harry, 'but if Charlie's right on the number of rebels, we could be in trouble.' He sat down in an armchair next to Jack. The others followed suit.

'I think Dick Brandon is the ringleader,' said Charlie.

'I wouldn't be surprised,' said Harry. 'We could be in difficulties in all the coastal resorts, where the new anti-pollution regulations are really going to hit hard. It's infuriating, because we did our bit and got the right question planted, but those stupid bastards at Environment cocked it up so that the Minister's answer was inaccurate.'

'What a balls-up,' said Roy.

'I dare say it was deliberate,' said Jack. 'The usual technique for breaking bad news. Give the public the worst case scenario and when they're reeling from shock say, "Sorry! Typo! The actual figure is only X," and they might think it's not so bad after all. They should have left it a bit longer before announcing the correction.'

'No chance,' said Harry. 'When Brussels spotted the error they issued an announcement of their own immediately and forced our hand. Anyway, enough of that. No good crying over spilt milk. The worry is that with all the anti-Europe feeling over the last lot of health measures, there could be more rebels than we think.'

'This is just what Drew and I were saying,' said Eddie.

'What I need to know,' said Harry, 'is exactly who the troublemakers are. I want you each to check your people thoroughly. Jack, get on to the others and make sure they get the message. Then get hold of Dick Brandon and say I want to see him. Be nice to him but make sure he comes and I want to see him *before* PM's Questions, OK?'

'Shall be done,' said Jack. 'D'you think you can turn him around?'

'We did once before, remember? I'm not worried about him. All we've got to do is scare the shit out of him sufficiently to make him persuade his little band of followers to fall into line too. Until we know exactly who they are, we can't be sure they will. So report back to me at two-thirty.'

'Well?' said Laura.

'Well what?'

'Don't be perverse. How did you get on?'

'He offered me the job and I took it,' said Jo with a nonchalant shrug. Then she turned towards Laura and added, 'And he was so casual about the whole thing, I was staggered. He didn't want to know anything about me! It's obvious you had the whole thing organized before I even crossed the threshold.'

Laura looked smug. 'Come on, let's get some lunch.' They were walking towards Central Lobby. 'I'm really glad you're going to be working here. I hope you won't be disappointed.'

'As you said, it will be different from anything I've done before. By the way, who was the man who gave me the drink?' asked Jo.

'Jack Bendall, the Deputy Chief Whip. He'll make a pass at you at the first opportunity, but he's harmless and quite fun. A terrible old soak, though. He starts on the Buck's Fizz as soon as he gets in. They say he's been a Whip for so long that he's forgotten how to speak in public – Whips never speak in the Chamber – and was made Deputy Chief Whip as a reward for long and faithful service, but will never get any further.'

Entering Central Lobby they turned into St Stephen's Hall which was crowded with visitors.

'The others you saw are a different kettle of fish,'

Laura continued. 'Let's see, there were two sitting down: Steve Lisle and Roy Phillips. Steve is incredibly pleased with himself and chats up every woman he meets. I can't imagine him ever getting anywhere but it doesn't seem to get him down. He's a bit of a bore. Roy is clever and funny. Always cracking jokes. Good company but I wouldn't trust him an inch.'

'What about the other two – one was called Eddie – who were talking to Jack?'

'Eddie Mallins. He's the big ginger-haired man, a comparative newcomer to the Whips' Office. I seem to recall there was some surprise that he was made a Whip. Don't ask me why. The other chap is an eager beaver called Andrew Oxley. Whenever you see him, he's either hurrying along, like a dog on a scent, or deep in earnest conversation with someone in a corner somewhere. But I suppose that's his job.'

'What is?'

'Keeping on the scent and rootling about for information which might be of value to his master, the Chief Whip.'

Working here is certainly going to be an education, thought Jo.

CHAPTER THREE

'I want to introduce you to my friend Ann Fenchurch and we're meeting her in the Westminster Hall canteen. That all right with you?' asked Laura.

'I'm sure it'll be fine,' said Jo, who had not had any breakfast and was beginning to feel somewhat light-headed. 'What have you been up to while I was with Harry?'

'I had a sherry with my adorable boss, Charles, whom you'll meet in due course. He's feeling tremendously pleased about his eldest daughter doing so well in her music exams and we had a little celebration. Since his wife died he needs someone to share these things with.'

They reached the steps at the top of Westminster Hall, a great empty stone chamber with a lofty roof supported by massive wooden beams. The pale winter sunlight which they could see beyond St Stephen's Entrance, and which illuminated the tall stained glass windows above them, made no impression on the great hall, which looked chill and grey. Beyond the doors of St Stephen's Entrance they could see a queue of people. Laura explained that they were visitors hoping for tickets to the

Strangers' Gallery who would have to wait at least another two hours before any likelihood of admission.

They descended the steps into Westminster Hall and walked over to a doorway set into the far wall, a few steps down from the hall.

'You must learn something of the history of this place while you're here, Jo. It would be such a shame not to, while you've got the chance.' Laura checked herself. 'That's if you'd like to, of course.'

'I would, but I think I've reached saturation point for today.'

'Oh, I wasn't going to try to fill you in myself. What I had in mind would be much better. I want to introduce you to George. He used to be in the police and has worked in the House of Lords for years. You'll love him and what he doesn't know about Parliament isn't worth knowing. He showed me round the place many years ago, when I first worked here.'

The canteen was hot, crowded and noisy. They collected their trays and joined the queue at the counter.

'There's Ann.' Laura waved to a fair-haired girl who was sitting at the far end of the L-shaped room.

When they joined Ann she held out her hand to Jo. 'Nice to meet you,' she said. 'Laura's told me a lot about you. What did you think of Harry Hunter?'

'I found it rather hard to tell what he's like,' said Jo. 'He was pleasant enough I suppose,' she said somewhat doubtfully. 'He didn't really want to know very much about me. It seemed to be a foregone conclusion that he'd offer me the job – and that I'd take it.'

'That's because Laura recommended you. She's very highly thought of you know. And you've done some high-powered jobs, I gather. I expect he was a bit intimidated by you.'

'I don't know what line Laura's fed him, but I fear he's going to be sadly disappointed!' said Jo.

Laura turned to Ann. 'I've told her she'll pick it up quickly enough and that we'll help her out whenever she needs it.'

'Certainly.' Ann looked very youthful, almost schoolgirlish. She was wearing a blue denim skirt and a cardigan of a similar colour, with the collar of an open-necked pink checked blouse showing above it. She had the soft, even, rosy complexion of a teenager and her fine blonde hair was drawn back from her face in a single, thick plait. Jo wondered whether, if she looked under the table, she would find Ann was wearing white ankle socks.

'Have you worked here long, Ann?' asked Jo.

'Nearly two years. But I shall be leaving in a year or two when Tim, my husband, is posted overseas again. He's in the Foreign Office.'

Jo felt sudden despair. My husband. I would have been saying that about Donald. She felt homesick for Geneva and an almost overwhelming sadness.

Laura said, 'Jo, you remember I was telling you how there are two distinct groups here: the politicians and the permanent staff. Well, Ann is on the permanent staff, part of the establishment of Parliament. She can tell you all about that side of things. This is actually a royal palace and her boss is the Serjeant-at-Arms. He's the link between the House of Commons and the monarch.'

'My office is near Central Lobby,' said Ann. 'If you want to ask anything you can always look in on me. I'll show you where I hang out.'

'Thanks. I can imagine you have to work here for ages to grasp the way the place works,' said Jo. She had her feelings back under control.

'Not really. You'll pick it up very quickly if you're interested,' said Ann.

'And it will all make more sense when you've been here for a while and know your way around,' said Laura.

'I don't even know what a Whip is – or does,' said Jo.

'All the parties have them,' said Laura. 'The term comes from fox-hunting. The whipper-in keeps the hounds under control. That's pretty much what the party Whips do: make sure that their people go into the right Division Lobby on crucial votes. But they also keep tabs on everyone,' she added. 'They're on the lookout for anything that might embarrass the Party. And it's said they bully people unmercifully if they step out of line. All that's always denied in public, but there's no doubt the Chief Whip is very powerful.'

'I got that impression this morning,' said Jo. 'I don't know who he was talking to, but you should have heard the way he said, "I'll fix him". I'd say he had something like bullying in mind,' said Jo.

'Well, well,' said Laura. 'I wonder who he was talking about?'

'You said it would be a revelation working here,' said Jo. 'I can see what you mean.'

'It's a pity Barbara couldn't be here today,' said Ann.

'Who's Barbara?' asked Jo.

Laura answered for Ann. 'Barbara Wallingbury. She's worked here for a long time too. Her husband's an MP. Michael. He's a good sort. Terribly keen and determined to change the world, but really nice with it.'

Ann said, 'Laura and Barbara and I get together for lunch every two or three weeks—'

'And we usually eat somewhere rather better than this,' interrupted Laura.

'Barbara isn't in today,' Ann continued. 'I said we'd get together tomorrow. Is that OK with you, Laura?'

'I won't be able to manage it I'm afraid. I shall be showing Jo the ropes. I think it would be better if Jo and I skipped it tomorrow and joined you next time. That's if you'd like to come too, Jo. We usually go to an Italian restaurant not far from the House.'

'I'll look forward to it.'

Jo found herself enjoying her lunch. Laura and Ann entertained her with gossip about the Palace of Westminster, their fellow secretaries and the people they worked for. She was pleased that Laura had got in touch with her. The job was a good idea. It would fill in her time while she decided what she wanted to do in the long term and would be interesting into the bargain.

CHAPTER FOUR

The following morning Laura met Jo at her office as
before. She took her down to the basement. 'This is
where you'll be working. I'm afraid it's a bit of a dump,
but then the whole building is like that. Parliament treats
its women workers like battery hens. They seem to think
that the more of us they stuff into these rooms, the more
work we'll produce.'

'Is the whole place like this? It's very overcrowded,
isn't it, and rather shabby.'

'Yes, it's a bit down at heel and it's certainly crowded.'

They were standing in the doorway of a room in the
basement which was crowded with desks and filing
cabinets. A printer was working in one corner, but there
was no-one in the room.

'My desk is in the room directly above this. I'll show
you in a minute. I prefer this building to any of the
modern accommodation myself and I think you will too.
Most of the time I work in Ian's room in the House. I'll
explain later when I show you round. That's Lois's desk
over there,' she pointed to a desk in the far corner, by the
window.

'Harry'll be too busy to come over here,' she continued. 'You'll have to go over to his room in the House to see him. You'll find the Whips' Office very traditional, very hierarchical and very secretive. I know, I worked for a Chief Whip once, a long time ago.'

At that moment a small, grey-haired woman with her arms full of files appeared beside them.

Laura smiled. 'Hello, Mary meet Jo. She's going to be working for Harry Hunter, standing in for Lois until she gets back. She hasn't worked in the House before so I'm just filling her in.'

'Good to meet you, Jo. Laura's an expert all right. She's been here even longer than I have. But if she's not about and I can help at all, just say the word. We'll be in the same room. That's my desk over there.' She pointed to the opposite corner, where the printer was churning out pages of text. There was a desk next to it piled with papers. Mary went over to it, dumped her armful of files, and went back upstairs.

'How long *have* you worked in the House, Laura?'

'I don't like to remember. Too long. Most of the past twenty years. I was in Paris for a couple of years.'

Laura took her over to the Pass Office in the House, where Jo filled in various forms and was photographed for her security pass. Then they called at Members' Post Office to collect the bundle of mail addressed to her new employer and returned to her office with it. Laura sat with her while she opened her mail, explaining to her how to deal with the huge range of issues and problems the job would entail.

They went over to the House for lunch, calling in at the Serjeant-at-Arms's Office to see Ann and then at the Admission Order Office where Laura explained the complicated procedure for the allocation and booking of tickets for the Strangers' Gallery.

In the afternoon, Harry rang to ask her to go over to

his office. There were a lot of men in the Whips' Office, talking earnestly in small groups. There was a feeling of tension in the room. From the looks she received, Jo felt they disapproved of her presence. Jack came over to Jo and told her that Harry was in a meeting and it would be better if she went away and came back in half an hour. When she did so, the room was deserted but she could hear a heated conversation going on in Harry's room. She waited and after a few minutes the door opened and four men emerged looking annoyed.

'Sorry to have kept you waiting, Jo,' said Harry. They made a start on the work but were soon interrupted by the division bell and Jo waited alone in the main office for about a quarter of an hour. Then Harry, Jack and two of the Whips reappeared and disappeared into Harry's room, closing the door behind them.

When their meeting ended and Jo went in at last, Harry was evidently preoccupied. He tapped continually with his pen on the side of the table as he looked through his correspondence. They had been working for only a few minutes when the door opened and Jack looked into the room.

'Trouble!' he said to Harry. Jo could hear the sound of voices in the outer room.

'I'm afraid we'll have to leave it there, Jo,' said Harry. 'I'll see you tomorrow.' Jo gathered up her papers and made her way through the outer room, which was full of people arguing vociferously.

When Laura came over to see her at the end of the afternoon, Jo asked her if she knew what all the fuss was about.

'It's all to do with this European peace conference. Having persuaded all the participating nations to have it in the UK, the government now find the thing threatened by some of their own MPs. All the anti-European Union MPs are claiming it's going to be manipulated by

Brussels and Bonn and used as a platform for European federalism.'

The next day, Laura again met Jo at her office. They walked over to the House together.

'Before we collect our mail, I'll show you the main Vote Office downstairs, where you have to go for Parliamentary papers when the House is sitting,' said Laura and led the way to the Interview Floor, where MPs were sitting at tables in the alcoves, working with their secretaries.

They came to a corner where the corridor turned at right angles. 'That room there is the Transport Office where you can get travel tickets for your boss. Or make any travel arrangements for yourself, for that matter.' They continued on their way, Laura pointing out features of interest. 'You see that chap over there,' she whispered. 'He's got hardly any toes.'

'Now that's what I call a really useful bit of information,' said Jo.

'It's the most interesting thing about him.'

'The interesting thing is how you know,' said Jo. Laura chuckled. 'Hearsay, of course. They say he was an explorer in his youth and got a bad case of frostbite. No, the interesting thing concerns the woman with him. The redhead with the tired expression. Her previous employer died on the job, so to speak.'

'What do you mean?'

'He was on top of her at the time, so they say. Gave her the fright of her life. It was a Saturday morning. They were in their office in one of the outbuildings. Not many people about. She had a terrible time extricating herself and trying to get some clothes on him before the ambulance arrived.'

'You know, Laura, I've as much difficulty knowing whether you're telling the truth now as when I was a child. We used to hang on your every word. I remember you had us all petrified with a story about gangsters para-chuting into the field behind the house and hiding in that old barn, waiting for nightfall to execute their deadly plot.'

'Do you mean to say you don't believe me?' said Laura, in mock despair. 'It's true, I tell you,' she added. 'In fact, it's a good example of the power of the Whips that they managed to keep it quiet. You'd think that something like that would have become public, wouldn't you? They have ways of covering these things up.'

On their way back through Members' Lobby, Laura introduced Jo to Fred, who ran the Whips' Messengers' Office. He was sitting in his little room just off the Lobby, talking on the phone. He hung up as they came in.

'Fred is responsible for seeing that the Whip gets sent to all our MPs. Can I have a copy to show Jo, please, Fred?'

He handed her three sheets of paper. The top one seemed to be a mass of black underlining.

'This is the Whip,' said Laura. 'Confusing, isn't it? There are Members called Whips and there is this docu-ment prepared each week also called the Whip. You'll see that it lists the business for each day of the week. The number of underlinings indicate whether or not Members absolutely have to be present or whether they can make arrangements to be away. A three-line Whip means they have to be here, come hell or high water.' She handed the papers back to Fred.

'And Fred also has copies of all the briefing notes pre-pared at party headquarters, if you need them. They write them on every subject from seal culls to the Social Chapter, so that MPs know what to say to their con-stituents. Thanks, Fred.' They left the room and took a side corridor towards Central Lobby, so that Laura could show Jo the way up to the Strangers' Gallery.

'Do you mean to say they have to be spoonfed with the

right answers to give to their constituents, rather than researching matters themselves and making up their own minds?' Jo was incredulous.

'Well some of them think for themselves,' said Laura. 'They don't all use the official handouts, although they all receive them. The official excuse would be that MPs have such vast quantities of mail nowadays that they couldn't cope with it all without that kind of help, poor dears. The cynics amongst us say it's just that they're all too busy earning fat fees from their outside interests to do the work themselves.'

'You said it would be a revelation, Laura, but it's rather depressing,' said Jo.

'It's not all bad,' said Laura. 'The system's long over-due for radical reform, but there are still a lot of people trying hard to do a good job. You'll see. I think you'll find it entertaining and it's only for a short time, after all,' she added reassuringly as they made their way back to Central Lobby.

CHAPTER FIVE

Jo's nights were long and full of desolate, fearful dreams. She felt exhausted each morning and had to force herself to get going. Her days, however, were comfortingly busy and demanding.

She found the Palace of Westminster confusing. There were too many new names and places to remember. She was forever being introduced to people and realizing too late that she had not been concentrating and had forgotten their names almost immediately. This was embarrassing because most of them seemed to have grasped her name without difficulty and greeted her like an old friend on chance encounters. She liked this friendliness and the feeling of having been admitted to a rather exclusive club.

Most of the time, she shared her room with only two other people, Mary and Bella. Laura's room, on the ground floor, seemed always to be full of people and Jo was glad to be in more peaceful surroundings. Mary was friendly and helpful but seemed always to be under frantic pressure. It was hard to know what to make of Bella. She said very little to either of her companions, so there were long spells when they didn't talk at all. Bella did not appear to Jo to have a huge quantity of correspondence to deal with but was always typing, apparently copying some lengthy document. She came in early and often left at lunch-time. Sometimes her husband would call for her in the afternoon. He would poke his head round the door, nod at Bella and withdraw into the passaage outside to wait for her. He rarely spoke to Mary or Jo. Jo thought she'd never met a more reserved couple. Mary explained that Bella worked for a former Cabinet Minister who was now a Peer and was typing up the manuscript of his autobiography. Her husband, Frank, was a former racing car driver who had had an accident which had left him deaf. 'They're quite wealthy and Bella does the job for pleasure rather than the money.'

'You could have fooled me!' said Jo. 'She never looks as if she's enjoying herself. And he's painfully shy, it seems.'

'Bella does let her hair down sometimes. And Frank is still getting to grips with lip reading and doesn't like meeting people. I'm afraid it's you he's shy of, Jo,' said Mary.

There were times when Jo had the room to herself, which she preferred, and like a number of other secretaries she took to working into the evening, when she could get more work done because there were fewer phone calls.

A regular caller was Harry's wife, Patricia, a forceful and energetic-sounding woman, who rang her frequently. She sympathized with Jo over her work-load. 'Do ring me if you think I can help with anything,' she said. 'I'm usually in London, at Number Twelve, but I'll be spending a bit of time in the constituency as we're having the house redecorated. But next time I'm in London, perhaps you'll have lunch with me.' Then there was the constituency agent, who was helpful in explaining how to deal with various constituency enquiries.

The atmosphere in the Whips' Office ranged from easygoing, casual routine, livened by bouts of intoxicated hilarity, to hectic activity, with mounting and ominous tension. On such days, the Whips' Office would be thronging with Members talking to their Whips, or having private meetings with Harry, and Jo would have to wait outside or kill time by going down to the cafeteria. At such times Harry would be preoccupied and irritable. On one occasion when Jo walked into his office, he was poring over some book, which he hastily covered up and snapped at her, 'You should knock before you come in!'

The time passed quickly and work kept her fully occupied and for much of the time she was able to shut out the thoughts that defeated her elsewhere. If she was at a loss about how to deal with an enquiry or letter she would telephone Laura, who always had the answer and usually illustrated it with an amusing anecdote.

She got to know the secretaries in the adjoining room, all of whom worked for Opposition MPs and Peers. One of them, Andrea, put her head round the door of Jo's room one morning, looked at the huge pile of papers, booklets and magazines on her desk and said, 'I strongly advise you to chuck a lot of stuff straight out. We all do. You'll drown in paper here, if you're not careful.'

'I see what you mean,' said Jo, who was beginning to feel swamped.

'I'm rather fortunate in my employers,' said Andrea and explained that she worked for an Opposition Peer, Lord Hemsley, who didn't have a particularly heavy work-load, and a Member of the European Parliament called Tom Henchard.

'He has a secretary in Strasbourg so I don't have too much to do for him. How are you getting on?'

'Not very well, as you can see,' said Jo. 'A huge pile of

correspondence on one side of my desk and about half a dozen replies on the other.'

'I came to ask if you'd like to play tennis on Saturday,' said Andrea. 'I've got a court booked for doubles, and one of our foursome has had to go away. How about it?'

'I'd like that. Thanks.'

As she left her office that evening, Jo thought about going to Geneva. It was time to straighten things out there, let the flat, put things into storage. Or should she give it all up, move everything back to England? For the first time, she found she could think calmly about it. Maybe I'll go at the end of next week. Perhaps I could take an extra day and make a long weekend of it, she thought. I'll ask Harry. No, on second thoughts, I'll just go. I'll pick a weekend when he's coming back late from his constituency.

She returned to the flat to find a note from Lydia on the hall table, explaining that her flight schedule would keep her away for most of the next month. Jo felt relieved. Although they got on well enough when their paths crossed, the fact that this happened infrequently suited them both. Lydia was glad to have someone keeping an eye on her flat and Jo was pleased to be able to be on her own, although she was looking forward to her game of tennis with Andrea.

Saturday morning was bright and cold, with a thin sparkle of frost on the pavement. Jo had got up early and had so much time to spare that she decided to walk to the tennis courts, which were on the other side of the river. The sky was a distant pale blue, the air sharp in her lungs. As she approached the tennis courts she could see Andrea standing with a tall, tousled-haired man in denim shorts and a black pullover and an athletic-looking girl in a pink track suit. The man was leaning heavily on his tennis racket, yawning uninhibitedly. The girl was eating an apple. Andrea waved to Jo. Her companions turned to look.

51

'Hi, Jo. How are you? Our court will be free in a few minutes. Meet Geoff and Alicia Harper. Alicia works for an Irish television company with an unpronounceable name. Geoff's a Lobby correspondent for the *Daily Enquirer*. Perhaps you know each other?'

'No, we haven't met,' said Jo and shook hands with Alicia, who gave her an appraising but friendly look. Geoff was evidently having difficulty stifling another yawn. He put a hand up to his face in an attempt to conceal it, nostrils flaring, then decided there was no point, yawned noisily and had a good stretch into the bargain.

''Scuse me. Very late night.' He shook hands with Jo. 'Can't say I feel much like tennis, but 'Licia says it'll do me good.' He was unhsaven and bleary-eyed. 'I've seen you going into the Government Whips' Office. Andrea tells me you work for Harry Hunter.'

'What does a Lobby correspondent have to do exactly?' asked Jo.

'Are you winding me up? You really don't know?' said Geoff.

'I've got a rough idea, but perhaps you'd like to explain it to me,' said Jo, 'if you're not too tired, that is.'

He gave her a searching look, unsure whether she was being sarcastic, then launched into a somewhat pompous explanation of the privileges and function of journalists such as himself. 'We're allowed into Members' Lobby while the House is sitting.'

Jo couldn't resist saying, 'So am I.'

He smiled at her, 'So I've seen. I lurk there to pump unsuspecting MPs and get them to divulge their inmost secrets.'

'And do they?' asked Jo.

'Most of them love talking about themselves, haven't you noticed?' said Andrea.

'And about other people,' said Geoff. 'The Whips do it all the time. You ought to bear that in mind, Jo. I wouldn't let them know anything about your private life, for example. They're dreadful gossips, especially Harry. I wouldn't trust him an inch.'

'Just listen to him,' said Alicia. She had a soft, slightly husky voice. 'One of the biggest gossips in the place.'

'Me? Gossip?' said Geoff in mock horror. 'Perish the thought.' He smiled at Jo again. 'I just listen while they talk.'

Jo could readily believe this. There's something about him, she thought. He'd be easy to talk to and confide in. She found herself smiling back at him.

Alicia said, 'What he hasn't explained is that Lobby correspondents are told things on "Lobby terms" which means that they're not allowed to divulge their source. As they say of parasites and their hosts, they live together for their mutual benefit—'

'Just like us, me darlin',' said Geoff, leaning on his racket again. She ignored him. 'Lobby correspondents feel *terribly* important because they have the ear of Ministers and can drink with MPs in Annie's Bar,' she continued. 'When they're told things on "Lobby terms" they have to say "Sources close to the Prime Minister revealed that . . ." or "A Westminster source said . . ."'

'What's the point?' asked Jo.

'It enables them to ensure that ignorant hacks like me write informed articles, that we get things right,' said Geoff.

'What it actually means,' said Alicia, 'is that your boss and his colleagues can leak things, soften up public opinion, try to manipulate the views of members of their own party and use the media to do hatchet jobs on people they don't like.'

'She's right of course,' said Geoff, 'that's Harry's speciality. But we're not all so gullible. We don't all allow ourselves to be used like that. But that's the system and we have to work with it.'

'No we don't,' said Alicia. 'Some of us manage to get the stories without being Lobby correspondents.'

'That's because you've got me.' He gave her a playful pat with his tennis racket.

Seeing Geoff and Alicia together made Jo think of Donald. Our marriage would have been like that, she thought sadly. We had the same comfortable, happy companionship and shared interests.

Their court came free. As they walked on, Geoff said, 'How do you like working for Harry?'

'So-so,' said Jo.

'What do you think of him?'

'It's a bit early to say.'

'You always this forthcoming?'

'This is one of my better days,' she replied with a smile. They were prevented from further conversation by Andrea starting play.

Geoff played effortlessly good tennis. He was lean and wiry and it was hard to tell how old he was. He could have been in his thirties or forties. His hair was very dark, almost black, with flecks of grey at the sides. His face was thin and he had a somewhat careworn look, but his voice was youthful and attractive. He ran about as little as possible, but nevertheless managed to return the ball devastatingly whenever it came his way. Alicia partnered him. She was lithe and graceful and partnered him well, seeming always to know where and which shots to play. Andrea took her tennis rather too seriously for Jo's liking and Jo, who was not a particularly good player, had to work hard not to let her down.

When they were changing ends between games, Geoff said to Jo, 'Seriously, I'd be interested to know what you think of Harry.'

'I have to say I don't like him much,' said Jo, 'but perhaps it's not fair to form an opinion of someone after such a short time.'

'What's it been like in the Whips' Office this week? I should imagine they've been pretty busy, haven't they?'

'You can say that again,' said Jo. 'And there's been such a lot of ill-feeling too. The atmosphere was absolutely poisonous at times.'

'Well you've got to hand it to Harry,' said Geoff. 'We thought the anti-Europeans would split the conference issue wide open, but he seems to have kicked them into line. I'd love to know how he did it.'

'Don't ask me,' she said. 'I'm afraid I'm still learning the ropes.'

Jo had enjoyed her morning far more than she'd expected and was disappointed when Geoff and Alicia turned down Andrea's invitation to lunch. She walked with Andrea to her flat, where she too excused herself from lunch and set off across the river. In the afternoon she walked for miles across London, taking a bus home when it started to get dark. On Sunday her sense of well-being deserted her and she felt lonely and depressed. She was glad when Monday morning came and she could go to work.

CHAPTER SIX

Laura had arranged for George to give Jo a tour of the building. She met Jo in Central Lobby but instead of walking towards Members' Lobby and the Commons, they headed in the opposite direction, to the House of Lords.

'Everything is much grander at this end of the building,' said Laura as they arrived in Peers' Lobby. Jo was struck by the contrast with the House of Commons. Where Members' Lobby was pale creams and browns of stone and oak, here the colours were rich and warm: reds, blues and black in the polished tiled floor, massive gleaming brass doors to the Chamber, dark wood panelling.

'Take a look at this,' said Laura and she swung open one of the great brass doors. They stepped inside, out of the ringing space of the Peers' Lobby into the carpeted silence of the Chamber. 'Television simply doesn't convey the opulence of this place, does it?' Jo was amazed. The room glowed with colour, from the ranks of red leather seats, the red and gold of the throne at the far end, the gleaming brass rails and the brilliance of the colours of the coats of arms of all the hereditary peerages arrayed along the walls. It was magnificent.

'I'll let George tell you all about it. Let's go and meet him.' They withdrew from the Chamber. As Laura led her across Peers' Lobby a man emerged from a doorway facing them. He was big and heavy-looking, with a thick neck, a double chin and very short hair which was almost completely black, save for a few grey hairs at the temples, although Jo thought he looked at least seventy. He greeted Laura in a soft, slightly breathless voice. He had a delightful smile.

'You must be Joanna. Nice to meet you,' he said, shaking her warmly by the hand. 'I gather you'd like the full tour, one of my specials.'

'That would be very kind. Whatever you've got time for,' said Jo, who'd always loathed visits to museums, stately homes and other historic places as a child and found herself automatically resisting the idea of having to absorb a stream of facts and figures. As if he could read her mind, he said, 'Not a list of kings and queens and dates, more your inside story, if you know what I mean. Then you'll be able to take visitors round yourself and impress them with your knowledge.' He gave a chuckle.

'I don't think I'm going to be working here long enough to do that,' said Jo.

'It'll stand you in good stead, all the same. You'll see,' said Laura, unaware of the prophetic nature of her words. 'George did the same for me when I first started working here, all those years ago.' She smiled at him. 'I'd better be going now, if you don't mind, and I'll meet you in Central Lobby in about an hour.'

Jo was surprised to find how much she enjoyed her tour. George led her slowly round the building, explaining what happened in each part of it, telling her about the rules of both Houses, their customs and traditions. She was amused by his proprietorial manner. He loved the place as if it were his own and when, towards the end of their tour, she said as much, he said, 'Well it belongs to all of us, doesn't it, and we've got to look after it. It's our Parliament. What happens here affects all of us and it's up to all of us to see that it's what we want it to be.' She was surprised to realize that she had never thought of Parliament and Government as belonging to the people, but only as something imposed from above. Our Parliament. How strange. She looked around her with a sudden feeling of intimacy and enjoyment. I'm not just a visitor passing through. I ought to try to understand it all, to learn as much as possible.

Jo found she wasn't bored or tired for a moment and she was charmed that George should willingly give up so much time to do this for her. She found herself infected by his love of the place and he was gratified by her enthusiasm.

'I'm not really supposed to show you half these things,' he said conspiratorially, as he led her down a back staircase and pointed out the corridors to the Serjeant-at-Arms's quarters and the Speaker's House, 'but nobody stops me. I've been here too long.' He took her down into Star Chamber Court, showed her the series of connecting courtyards running through the centre of the Palace.

They went out onto the terrace, which was deserted, and stood in an icy wind gazing at the river while a string of sand-filled barges chugged by.

'I've worked here over thirty years now,' said George, 'and it's all changed enormously in that time, not always for the best. It seems to me there are different kinds of folk here these days, the Members I mean, and they don't have the same values as in the old days.' They returned gratefully to the warmth of the Terrace Corridor.

'No offence, George, but isn't that what people always feel as they get older, that it wasn't like this in the old days and that everything's going to the dogs?'

He chuckled. 'You're quite right, my dear, but what I'm saying is true, even so. You take that, for example.' He pointed to a gift and souvenir shop which they were passing. 'When I first worked here, neither their lordships nor the Members would have dreamed of allowing such a thing. Then the Refreshment Department started buying in whisky with their own label, then it was chocolate mints and now there's a whole stack of things with the Palace of Westminster portcullis on them.'

'Is that so awful?' asked Jo. 'Does it matter if tourists buy a few Parliamentary knick-knacks?'

'They're not for the tourists, do you see. It's the Members and Peers who buy them, to impress their friends. And so do lots of the people who work here. I don't like it myself.' She was prevented from enquiring further by a Badge Messenger waylaying George. She occupied herself with an examination of the cartoons which were hanging in the Terrace Corridor.

After a few minutes the messenger continued on his way and George and Jo left the terrace, climbed the staircase to Lower Waiting Hall and turned into the corridor by the Commons Library. Halfway along this they turned back towards the Chamber and then into what looked like another corridor but was in fact the No Division Lobby. George explained that the Aye, or Yes Lobby lay on the other side of the Chamber. When they reached the far end of the lobby Jo was surprised to find that they were standing at the back of the Commons Chamber, just behind the Speaker's Chair. George talked about the role of the Speaker, the ancient traditions of the Commons, and the archaic wording of prayers and petitions, pointing out the Petition Bag hanging on the back of the Speaker's Chair. He was just telling her about the Table Office, where Members handed in Parliamentary Questions for oral or written answer, when Laura appeared suddenly round the Speaker's Chair.

'She's looking a bit wan, George. I think she's had enough.'

'I think she has too,' he replied.

Jo thanked him warmly. She had enjoyed her tour far more than she could have imagined at the outset and had developed a great liking for George. She asked him if he were free to join them for lunch.

'I can't today, my dear. But if you'd like to buy me a drink one day, we'll go to the staff bar in the Lords. That's one place I forgot to show you.'

The three of them walked back together to Central Lobby where Jo thanked George again and he left them.

'What can I give him by way of a thank-you, do you think?'

'I can't think of anything offhand. What he would like is for you to be a friend. Have that drink with him and keep in touch. He's been a widower for many years and his work here is his life. Of course he's got lots of friends here, especially amongst the police. He really likes to be with people who care about the place and are involved with it. I'm very fond of him. He's a lovely person.' Jo felt that it would be no hardship at all to keep in touch with George.

CHAPTER SEVEN

When Jo arrived at work the following morning she could hear laughter from the room above hers. She looked in to find Laura sitting at her desk looking up at a worn-looking middle-aged man wearing a smart grey suit with a silk waistcoat and fob watch, who was perched on the corner of her desk, holding forth in a loud voice, evidently regaling her and the other women in the room with an amusing story. He stopped in mid-sentence and looked at Jo. 'Well what have we here? You're a turn-up for the books.'

'If you sit any closer to me, Jimmy, I'll be intoxicated by the fumes,' said Laura, waving him away from her. Jo glanced at the man and could see that his eyes had the swimmy look of a drunk. He rose unsteadily to his feet, smiling at Jo and extending his hand towards her.

'This is Jo,' said Laura. 'She works for Harry Hunter.' The enthusiastic smile on the man's face faded and he withdrew his hand, putting it in his pocket.

'Well I'd better go and peruse the papers, keep abreast of developments,' he said to no-one in particular and walked carefully out of the room.

'God, he gets worse every day,' exclaimed one of the women.

'Who is he?' asked Jo.

'Jimmy Underwood,' said Laura. 'A rather sad case. He's never got over the fact that the PM didn't include him in his last reshuffle. He was absolutely convinced he'd get an appointment. I think he'd been promised something by the Whips. He used to be a terrible thorn in their side, a real maverick. Rumour has it that they bought him off by promising him a job, then punished him by making sure he didn't get it. When that happened, his wife was so disappointed that she left him and he's been hitting the bottle ever since.' Laura stood up. 'I'm off to see Charles.'

'What a foul story. So they didn't like him because he wouldn't co-operate with the Party line? A rare man of principle and they did for him? How sickening,' Jo exclaimed.

'Yes, isn't it. But you could argue, of course, that he wasn't so highly principled after all, or he couldn't have been bought off with the promise of rewards later,' Laura replied. 'I think there's a bit more to it than that, though what exactly I've never been able to find out.' She put on her coat. 'I'm meeting Ann and Barbara later for our regular lunch date. I was going to leave a note for you asking if you'd like to join us. How about it?'

'I'm so swamped with work that I'm not sure I'll have time,' said Jo.

'You've got to eat and the break will help. The work can wait for an hour, surely.'

Jo agreed to meet her at St Stephen's Entrance at a quarter to one so that they could walk over to the restaurant together. When they reached it, Ann and Barbara were already at a table.

Barbara was tall and slim, with glossy black hair that hung in a smooth curve to her jaw line. It was slightly shorter at the back, so that the nape of her neck just showed above the collar of her pink silk blouse. She was leaning back in her chair and laughing at something Ann had said. She had a wide mouth, even teeth, and a big laugh. Everything about her appearance looked perfect, from her expensive-looking dark-blue suit to her heavy gold bracelet and rings. She leant forward in her chair as Laura introduced Jo, held out her hand and said, 'It's very nice to meet you,' with warmth and pulled out the chair next to her. Jo sat down, opposite Ann who poured wine for her and Laura. 'We started without you. How's it going, Jo? Are you enjoying the work?'

'I'm enjoying the place, the new people and so on, but I can't say I'm wild about the work. There's so much, I'll never get on top of it.'

'Didn't Laura tell you, no-one ever does?' said Barbara. 'The backlog goes with the territory nowadays. You just learn to carry it along with you and to recognize which things need to be given priority.'

'Which constituents are desperately in need of help and which can wait another month for a reply,' said Laura.

'It's not that bad,' said Barbara defensively. 'Michael deals with his surgery cases immediately.'

Laura and Ann exchanged smiles. Barbara said, 'But he does!' somewhat indignantly, then smiled sheepishly.

'He'll get like the rest of them in time, don't you worry, dearie,' said Laura. Then to Jo she said, 'We give Barbara a hard time but actually Michael is a really nice, genuine guy, hard-working and clever.'

Barbara looked pleased. 'Well he must be to have married me,' she said smugly.

'They carry on like this a lot, Jo,' said Ann. 'Just ignore them.'

A waitress came and took their orders. The restaurant was almost full by now. The room was large and high-ceilinged. There was no piped music, just a cheerful hubbub of conversation. The sun was shining outside and Jo felt a pleasant inner warmth from the wine and the company. Ann, Barbara and Laura had the comfortable relations of friends of long-standing, but they did their best to include Jo in their conversation.

'There is quite a lot of drudgery to the job, I must say,' said Barbara.

'There's quite a lot of drudgery to being an MP's wife, I should think, isn't there?' said Ann.

'Too right. But I don't mind it too much if Mike and I are doing the work together. We can have quite a laugh about it some of the time and also we manage to do quite a lot to help people. But I think you'll find, Jo, that you're better off than many of us because your man's got a quiet constituency.'

'What do you mean, quiet? It seems pretty busy to me,' said Jo.

'Well it's far enough from London for most people to be reluctant to spend the money and the time involved in a train or car journey to London to see their MP. So you don't get hordes of constituents coming here to lobby Harry and asking for guided tours and tickets to the Gallery. Also you'll get a lighter post than a lot of us.'

'You could have fooled me!'

'Anyway, just think what scintillating company you have, what dazzling new personalities you'll meet while you're here,' said Laura.

'Like that poor sod this morning.'

'She met Jimmy Underwood,' Laura explained to the others.

'That must have been a treat for her,' said Barbara.

'I felt rather sorry for him,' said Jo.

'You'll notice after you've been here a while that the place is full of oddballs and misfits,' said Laura. 'I've a theory that it's often men with some kind of hangup who

64

go into politics to make themselves feel important. Either they become more sympathetic to the lot of others as a result, or they end up as arrogant little shits.'

'Honestly, Laura!' exclaimed Jo. 'You sound so cynical about it all, I wonder why you carry on working here.'

'She's always been like that,' said Barbara, 'but beneath that tough exterior beats a heart of gold.'

'You don't change anything by walking away from it,' said Laura, 'and I think these things should be said.'

Ann tried to change the subject. 'Barbara and I were talking about what a frenzy everyone's getting into over this European conference crisis, when you two arrived,' she said. Barbara leaned forward and lowered her voice, 'Michael says things are really tense. They really think the European Union could disintegrate. NATO too.'

'Tim says the problem is that what should be a peace conference is being turned into an argument about the European Union,' said Ann.

'Dayton Ohio comes to More Wittering, Wilts.,' said Laura.

'Greater Slaughter, Glos., is more like it,' said Ann.

Barbara looked serious. 'They really seem to think it could all fall apart.'

'With the tabloids and the anti-Europeans teaming up to play the xenophobia card, it could easily happen,' said Laura.

'How's Tim enjoying life, Ann?' asked Barbara. 'When do you expect to be posted overseas again?'

'Oh they never tell us until the last moment. Probably not for another year. Tim's OK, working very hard as usual. Which reminds me,' she turned to Jo, 'I was wondering if you were free the Saturday after next, Jo. Tim and I have to entertain a chap from the State Department. We're giving a drinks party for him and it would be lovely if you could come.'

'I'd like that very much. What time?'

'Seven-thirty.' Ann got out a piece of paper from her handbag and wrote on it. 'Here's our address. Do you know the area? We're quite close to Pimlico tube station.'

'I'll find it,' said Jo. 'Thanks for asking me. I look forward to it.'

Laura and Barbara were engaged in a heated discussion about the news reports over the weekend concerning one Heyton Mowberry MP, whom Jo had never heard of but who was embroiled in a financial scandal.

'If the money's not good enough, he should go and work elsewhere,' Laura was saying.

'Michael says the press are on a witch-hunt, that they've always had it in for him,' said Barbara.

'It looks like he's given them the chance they were looking for then, doesn't it?' said Laura. 'The trouble with so many of them nowadays is they're plain greedy. And arrogant too. They really think they can get away with murder.'

'What a set-up!' exclaimed Jo. 'Anywhere else they'd get the boot, or the police would be called in. Why doesn't the Opposition demand it?'

'If the Opposition were to start crowing over scandals in the Government, they would risk having their own skeletons brought out of the cupboard,' said Barbara.

'That's the real work of the Whips, as you'll discover,' said Laura, 'their unofficial, secret role: covering all these things up and keeping the skeletons firmly locked away.'

'Parliament doesn't like its dirty washing done in public,' said Ann.

'It seems to me it's about time it was,' said Jo.

CHAPTER EIGHT

When Jo got back to her office after lunch she was surprised to find a woman sitting at her desk: a smartly dressed, rather too made-up looking woman with short, stylish blond hair sprayed into immobility in a gravity-defying upward sweep at the sides. She had sharp blue eyes that showed just a little too much of the whites and gave her a slightly startled look which was enhanced by her hairstyle. She looked as if she were ready to leap to her feet. There was no-one else in the room.

As Jo was taking all this in she was thinking: who the hell's this? What a nerve to be sitting at my desk. I wonder whether I left anything out that I shouldn't have. Then it dawned on her that this was Harry's wife. Somehow she matched the voice Jo had heard on the phone.

'You must be Jo.' She stood up and stepped forward to shake hands. 'I'm Patricia Hunter. I hope you don't mind me sitting at your desk. I really didn't think I could sit at anyone else's and I'm dead on my feet.' She had a natural, whole-hearted smile which banished the too wide awake look of her eyes and Jo was momentarily disarmed. Then it occurred to her that the woman could have sat in the reading room upstairs, as all other visitors did. Just protruding from beneath Jo's desk diary lay the letter she had received that morning from Etienne. She thought, this woman is just the kind who'd have looked at it.

'I thought it was high time I came over and introduced myself,' said Mrs Hunter. 'I've an ulterior motive, I'm afraid. I'm going to be away quite a lot in the next few weeks and I was wondering if you'd mind keeping an eye on things at our flat for us. Our son and daughter use it when they're here. Harry never has time to go round there. It would be a great help to me if we could go round there this afternoon so that I could explain what's what.'

Jo could see that there was no question of her being able to refuse to undertake this extra chore so she said, 'Of course. We could go straight away if you like.'

'Thank you, Jo. It won't take long, I promise.'

As they left the building and set off in the direction of Victoria, Mrs Hunter said, 'I'd rather you didn't mention it to Harry, if you don't mind. He'll be annoyed if he thinks I'm taking you away from his work.'

Their destination was a mansion block in Ashdon Gardens. The building was luxurious, with thick carpeting and gleaming brass fittings in the hallway and a handsome staircase, which they ascended to the first floor. After the rather dimly lit stairway, the apartment was bright and welcoming. The sitting room was spacious, with French windows opening onto a balcony.

Mrs Hunter said, 'All I want you to do is come here when I'm away, say, twice a week, and pick up the mail and make sure that there's nothing left rotting in the fridge. Johnny will be back briefly and then off again and he's absolutely hopeless about clearing up. When Alison's here she's pretty good about it but she's in America for several months.' She took Jo into the kitchen. 'Don't get me wrong. I'm not asking you to do housework or anything like that. Just to check the place out. Once I came to check everything when the flat hadn't been used for a few weeks and found that the people above had had a flood, let their bath overflow or something, and one of our rooms was ruined. So if you could just cast your eye over it once in a while when I'm away that would be a great help.'

'That's quite all right,' said Jo. 'I don't mind.'

Mrs Hunter put the kettle on. 'Would you like some tea? Or coffee?' Jo opted for tea and they took it into the sitting room and sat down in comfortable armchairs. Jo noticed a large desk and two filing cabinets at the end of the room facing her. Mrs Hunter must have been watching her.

'That's Harry's desk. He doesn't use it much now, of course. We live at Number Twelve but have kept this on for the family – and for ourselves, of course. We'll need it again one day. Maybe sooner than we think.' Once again, she gave a natural, pleasing smile and Jo thought perhaps there was a rather nice person concealed beneath the busy, too dynamic manner.

'If there's any mail, messages on the answering machine, or any faxes – there's a machine on the shelf there behind the desk – would you mind very much taking it over to Number Twelve for me?'

'Not at all,' said Jo.

'Well I think that's about it,' said Mrs Hunter, eying Jo's cup.

Jo finished her tea. As soon as she put the cup down, Mrs Hunter stood up. She took their cups into the kitchen and washed them up, dried them and put them away. Then she wiped the kitchen worktop with the drying-up cloth and pushed the kettle back to its original position as if she wished to eradicate any trace of their visit. Jo walked out into the hall. She turned back to see

Mrs Hunter look carefully round the sitting room, then bend over the sofa to plump up the cushions. She left Jo in the hall, presumably to check the other rooms and returned a moment or two later. They left the apartment, Mrs Hunter locking up behind them. She handed the keys to Jo.

'You'll be sure to double-lock the door behind you, won't you?'

'Of course,' said Jo.

When they reached the street Mrs Hunter said that she wouldn't be walking back with Jo as she had to do some shopping.

'It's been nice to meet you, Jo,' she said warmly, 'and I'm so glad you're going to be keeping an eye on things for me. I'll give you a ring to let you know when I'm going to be away.'

Jo returned somewhat reluctantly to her office and the mountain of paperwork. Before settling down to it she reread Etienne's letter, wondering as she did so whether Mrs Hunter had also perused it. She wouldn't have gleaned much information from it if she had:

Dear Jo,

I haven't heard from you and I am anxious. We miss you. I would like very much to receive your letter or call. What are your plans? All is the same here as always and our programme continues with the same difficulties and worries. Maybe I too shall be going into the field but hope to see you first. Please call me or send me your number.

I embrace you.
Affectionately,
Etienne

Jo looked at her watch. She would get some of her work done first before telephoning him. Mary came in carrying a mass of papers and looking harassed. They worked in silence for the next hour. Then Mary tidied her desk and left. 'See you tomorrow, Jo. Don't work too late,' and she was gone, carrying an armful of mail to be posted.

Jo made her call to Geneva and in a moment she heard Etienne's familiar tones. She spoke to him in French and he replied in English. They often did this: each speaking the other's language out of politeness. If they were at work they usually spoke French. At home it was usually English. Sometimes they spoke in Arabic. They had met in Lebanon, years ago. Etienne's Arabic was excellent. Jo's wasn't bad considering how little formal tuition she had had in it. She could understand it quite well and could get by in simple conversation.

'Jo! It's so good to hear you. How are you? We've been thinking about you so much.'

'I'm all right. Just about. I got your letter this morning. Thanks. I meant to ring you before now, but I hadn't made up my mind what to do. In fact I'm thinking of coming to Geneva this weekend. Will you and Lucia be there?'

'Certainly. Will you come and stay with us?'

'I'm not sure. Can I ring you when I've checked plane times and so on?'

It was a spur of the moment decision to go to Geneva on the weekend but now she'd made it she felt cheered and confident. With a bit of luck Harry wouldn't need to see her until Monday evening and she could come back that morning. She would go on Friday, as early as possible and sort things out about the flat, tell Etienne what she was doing and make some firm plans. If they'd keep her old job open she'd go back to it. If not, well perhaps it was time for a complete change and she'd have time to think of something during the next couple of months.

CHAPTER NINE

Jo continued to fall prey to morbid thoughts when alone. Nevertheless she preferred being on her own in the evenings after work and felt a pang of disappointment when she arrived home from work the following day to find Lydia had returned. Lydia radiated health, thanks to a rich, almost burnt suntan which she had acquired on a few days respite in Australia and which looked scarcely credible in London's grey wintry light. She wanted to share her feeling of well-being with Jo and persuaded her to go out for dinner. A week or two earlier Jo couldn't have faced such an evening. Now she found it quite enjoyable and was pleasantly distracted by Lydia's account of her trip.

'Would you mind if I stayed on a bit longer, Lydia? I would have asked you before, but you were away.' Jo explained about the job at the Commons. 'Could you stand it, do you think? And of course I must pay you rent. I should have been contributing from the outset.'

'Of course you can stay,' said Lydia. 'It's nice to have you. In fact it's rather reassuring you being there, keeping an eye on things for me while I'm away.'

'Thanks very much. The girl I'm standing in for should be back early in April. I haven't decided quite what to do after that, but I'm going to go back to Geneva this weekend to sort a few things out.'

'I expect I could get you a cheap ticket. Check out the flight times and let me know when you're going and I'll see what I can do.'

'That'd be great, Lydia. Thanks very much.'

'I'll be off again myself this weekend, but back for a couple of nights next week. After that I won't be around again much until the end of February, so you'll have the flat pretty much to yourself.'

Lydia was as good as her word and left a note for Jo the next evening saying that she'd arranged a cheap fare for her and she could pick up the ticket at the airport on Friday.

She saw Harry briefly the following morning, when he hastily ran through some correspondence with her. Her spirits rose when he handed her a letter and said, 'I'll accept this one.' It was an invitation to a meeting and lunch in the constituency. So Harry would be leaving early and she would be able to do the same.

She rang Etienne and told him her flight times. He said he would meet her at the airport. That evening Jo worked until after seven, determined to try to get on top of her work before going away. She packed up her papers, cleared her desk and hurried over to the House to leave a folder of letters for Harry to sign.

There was no-one in the Whips' Office. The door of Harry's room wasn't quite closed and Jo could hear him speaking.

'If that got out he'd be done for.'

'And how would it make the rest of us look? If—' Jo knocked on the door and pushed it open. It was Jack who had been speaking. He and Eddie Mallins were sitting with Harry. Eddie scowled at her and Harry said sharply,

'Not now, Jo! Just leave whatever you've got there with Fred.' As Jo started to turn away, Jack caught her eye and gave her a rueful smile.

She shut the door behind her, relieved not to have to stay longer. If Harry hadn't been in a meeting, he might have given her some task for the following morning and she didn't want anything to interfere with her plans for the weekend. She left his folder of letters in the Whips' Messengers' Office, with a note asking Fred to put it on Harry's desk later and left the building. She wondered what Harry had been discussing with Eddie and Jack but these thoughts were soon banished by feelings of anxiety about her trip to Geneva.

Friday morning was brilliantly sunny, the air crisp and invigorating. There seemed to be a change in the air, a hint of mildness, a reminder that spring was not far away. Jo was shocked to realize how much time had elapsed since Donald's death and how quickly it had passed; how completely life had moved on without him.

In her anxiety to be in good time for her plane, she arrived at Heathrow much earlier than she needed. She had only hand luggage in the form of a large shoulder bag that was big enough to double as an overnight case. Having picked up her ticket and checked on to her flight she browsed at the bookstall and bought herself a coffee before going through to the departure lounge. She was unaware of being observed, as she was going through passport control, by Geoff Harper who, only moments before, had seen Alicia off on a flight to Paris. Geoff called out to her, but his words were drowned by an announcement over the public address system and Jo passed through the barrier, oblivious to his presence. Her flight was already boarding, so she went straight through the main departure lounge to the gate for her plane and did not see Alicia, who was by then strolling through the duty-free shop.

Jo began to feel apprehensive as the plane approached Geneva. Looking down from her window on what had long been familiar territory, she had the strange sensation of coming to it afresh, like an outsider, whereas for several years Geneva had been the centre of her existence, from which she looked out on the world. It no longer seemed as welcoming to her as it used to feel whenever she had been away. It was disturbing to find that her feelings about everything had changed so profoundly and so rapidly.

Not only was Etienne there to meet her, but Lucia and their two small children as well. The sight of them waiting for her was too much for Jo. Her eyes filled with tears. She hadn't cried at the funeral or at any time since then in the presence of other people, though she had done so many times at night, tears of rage and desolation. Lucia put her arm through hers and bore her away, signalling to Etienne to take the children and head for the car.

'Jo, I'm sorry. Shall we go and have something to drink? Or just go for a little walk?'

Lucia was petite, dark-haired and vivacious. She held Jo's arm, looking up at her with concern and sympathy in her eyes.

'It's good to see you, Lucia. I'm glad you came. It's just that there are a lot of things I've not been allowing myself to think about and they all came rushing back into my mind when I saw you. I'm all right really. Let's join Etienne.'

'Are your sure?' Jo nodded. 'OK. Will you stay with us, Jo? We want you to so much.'

'Not tonight. Perhaps tomorrow? I'd love to come back to your house for a little while, but I must go back to the flat. I need to sort things out.'

They caught up with Etienne and the two children. Jo

took their hands, 'Hello, Rosa, Philippe. How are you?' she asked them in French. 'Have you got something for us?' asked the little girl. 'When we get into the car, we'll look in my bag, shall we, and see what we can find?' said Jo. She smiled at Etienne and Lucia. 'It's good to see you all again. Thanks so much for meeting me.'

'Let's go home,' said Lucia to Etienne. 'Then later on you could take Jo home, maybe take her somewhere for an early supper. Then, Jo darling, you come and stay with us tomorrow night. Yes? Good idea?'

'Fine, Lucia. That would be great. Thanks.'

So that evening Jo and Etienne went to a little restaurant near the UNHCR building where they ate a little fondue with a lot of white wine and Jo finally gave vent to her feelings of anger at Donald for going back to the Balkans and getting himself killed. 'He didn't want to go back you know, Etienne. It was as if he had a premonition of disaster. And if I'd really begged him not to he wouldn't have gone.' She put her elbows on the table and rested her head on her hands, feeling drained and exhausted. 'It's all so pointless. That's what I can't stand. He died for nothing. What good has he or any of us done? What's the point? The whole place has fallen apart.'

'It's terrible, Jo, but we must always try to do something to help, mustn't we?'

She didn't answer immediately. She picked up her fondue fork and prodded a piece of bread. 'So long as it's the right thing that we're doing,' she protested. 'I know what you're saying, but that's what it all boils down to: is anyone doing the *right* thing to try and help? The answer is no.'

Etienne eventually managed to steer her away to other topics, finally bringing up the question of the flat. What was she going to do with it while she worked in London? How long was she going to be away? It transpired that

Etienne and Lucia had come up with a plan, with which Jo was only too happy to concur: Etienne knew of someone at the World Health Organization who needed accommodation until he found somewhere permanent and who would be very pleased to rent the flat for a while.

Going back to the flat wasn't as painful as Jo had expected. Perhaps she was over the worst now. She gazed about her at all their possessions, mementoes of their earlier, separate lives and the treasures of their life together: reminders of how the threads of their separate lives had been woven into the rich fabric of their shared existence. She sat for a long time in the sitting room, with the window open so that she could hear the noise from the cobbled street below. Suddenly she realized that she was frozen. She closed the window and ran a hot bath. Finally she got into bed and lay still in the dark, listening to all the old familiar sounds. Her rage at the futility of Donald's death was subsiding, being replaced by an awareness of the lonely burden of her sorrow, of the relentless continuity of the universe and its harsh indifference. She thought about her own life. When I die, what difference will I have made to anything? Etienne was right. We must each of us try to make a difference, to do some good with our lives, otherwise there's no point in being alive.

When she awoke on Saturday morning she felt listless, leaden with sleep, but calm. She spent the morning sorting out their belongings, piling up on the bed all Donald's clothes and shoes and making a separate collection of the things that she thought she should give to his parents. Everything else, her clothes and things she didn't need in London, their books, CDs, tapes and the remainder of their shared possessions, she packed up into two large trunks, leaving just the things that would be needed by the tenant.

Etienne arrived with a box for the things to be sent to Donald's parents. The clothes would go to a charity and Jo's trunks would be stored at Etienne's and Lucia's house.

At the last moment, Jo removed Donald's favourite sweater and scarf from the bundle of clothes and put them into her bag. Then they packed everything into Etienne's car and he departed, promising to return in a couple of hours. By the time he got back Jo had cleaned the flat and rearranged the furniture. She took a last look round as they were leaving. There was a lingering aura of their life there, but it was fading. She wondered if she would ever live there again. They went out and she locked the door behind her.

CHAPTER TEN

Jo's plane landed late at Heathrow and she had to hurry
to the underground. The airport was very crowded, the
train even worse. She supposed Monday mornings were
always like this and was glad she didn't have to make
such a journey regularly. It would have made more sense
to come back the previous evening, but she had had such
a good day with Etienne and Lucia, playing in the snow
with the children and lounging in front of a roaring log
fire after lunch, that she had not been able to tear herself
away. Now she was anxious lest Harry should be wanting to see her that morning.

She needn't have worried. When she reached the
Commons she went straight to the Whips' Office. Eddie
Mallins, Steve Lisle and Andrew Oxley were talking with
another Whip, Charlie Culver. They all stopped talking
as she entered the room.

What is it about this place? thought Jo. Why do I always
get the feeling there's something unpleasant going on?
Aloud she said, 'Is Harry about?'

'No,' said Charlie. 'Will I do?' He gave her a knowing
look.

'Definitely not,' said Jo.

'Any time you get tired of Harry, you come and see me!' he called after her as she left the room. She heard one of them snigger.

There were several little knots of people standing about in Members' Lobby when she came out of the Whips' Office. She glimpsed Barbara talking to someone near the doorway to Central Lobby. There was a group of people sitting on the benches in one corner of the Lobby talking. The Badge Messengers were busy at the letter and message boards. Sunlight streamed down into the Lobby from the leaded windows high above. Jo saw Randall Myers, the researcher she'd met on her first visit, and a man she didn't know with their heads bent over a newspaper Randall was holding. They were deep in conversation. She went past them into Members' Post Office and joined the queue of Members and secretaries collecting their mail. When she emerged Barbara spotted her and waved.

Randall called out, 'Good morning, Jo,' as she walked past. She stopped. Randall's companion said, 'See you, Randall,' and walked away.

'How goes it, Jo?' asked Randall.

'Fine thanks.'

'I'm going down to the Strangers' Cafeteria,' said Randall. 'Care to join me?'

'Not this morning, thanks,' said Jo. At that moment Geoff Harper joined them.

'Morning Randall, morning Jo,' said Geoff. He smiled at her. 'Good weekend?'

'Not bad, thanks.'

'Did you do anything special?'

'No,' she said. 'What about you?'

'Me? Oh, I just loafed about. No tennis this weekend.'

'I must be going,' said Jo, who could see Barbara still standing near the doors to Central Lobby, looking in her direction as if waiting for her. 'Bye.'

Geoff watched her walking away from them.

'Strange,' he said.

'What is?' asked Randall.

'I saw her at Heathrow on Friday morning,' Geoff was following Jo with his eyes as he spoke. 'She was going into the departure lounge for an overseas flight.'

'So?'

'Oh, I don't know, I just think for most people taking a long weekend and going abroad would count as "doing something special". She's dressed as she was on Friday morning, so I'd say she'd just come from the airport. And when I ask her about it she rushes off.'

'I fear you overestimate your appeal, Geoff. Doesn't it occur to you that she just might not want to tell *you*?'

Barbara was standing with a tall, good-looking man. 'Hello, Jo,' she said enthusiastically as Jo approached them. 'I want you to meet Michael. Mike this is Jo, Laura's friend I was telling you about.' Michael had a high forehead and receding hairline, but a youthful, pink-cheeked complexion and a boyish smile. He shook hands with Jo enthusiastically. 'Good to meet you, Jo. I hope you're enjoying it here.'

'I am, thanks to Laura and Barbara, who've been showing me the ropes. It's interesting, but by the time I've got the hang of the job it will be time to leave, I expect,' she replied.

'Then we'd better find you another Member. There's always someone looking for a secretary, isn't there?' He turned to Barbara.

'Yes, but she can't take just anybody. There are some you wouldn't touch with a bargepole. They're not all like you.' She put her arm through his, clasped her hands in front of her, and smiled broadly at Jo.

Ann appeared in the Lobby, saw them and came over. 'Morning everybody. How are you, Michael?'

'Not as well as you by the look of things, Ann. How's Tim enjoying working in the Cabinet Office?'

'He *loves* it,' said Ann with heavy exaggeration. 'Personally I can't wait to go overseas, preferably somewhere hot. It's freezing in our office this morning. God knows what's happened to the heating system.'

'Well, I can't stand here gossiping with you girls all day,' said Michael. Barbara withdrew her arm from his. 'See you later,' he said to her and departed.

'Those two were talking about you, Jo,' said Barbara looking across at Geoff and Randall. 'You want to watch that Geoff Harper. You can't be sure with some of these journalists whether they're chatting you up because they fancy you, or whether they're trying to extract information.'

'Either way, they're trying to take advantage of you, hey Barbara?' said Ann with a laugh. She turned to Jo, 'What you've got to understand is that a long time ago Geoff pursued Barbara—'

'In vain, I might say,' said Barbara, still looking in Geoff's direction. Geoff smiled at her and gave a little salute, almost as if he knew what she were saying. She smiled back at him. 'That was before I met Michael. By the way, are we getting together next week for lunch?'

'Tuesday suits me,' said Ann.

'Me too,' said Jo. 'That's if you mean me too, of course,' she added hastily.

'Of course we do,' said Barbara. She looked at her watch. 'Duty calls. Bye.' And she left them.

Ann and Jo walked through to Central Lobby together. 'How's it going, Jo? You look a bit tired, if you don't mind my saying so.' Jo did indeed look rather pale and exhausted.

'I had a tiring weekend,' said Jo, 'but I'm fine thanks, Ann. And I'm looking forward to coming to your party on Saturday.'

When Jo reached her office, she received a friendly greeting from Vic, who was standing in the doorway, propping the front door open, as he gazed out at the weather and the passers-by. The building was a hive of activity.

In the basement, she found Mary hard at work, but not too busy to stop and chat for a moment, while Jo made them both a cup of coffee. A little later, Andrea put her head round the door and asked Jo if she'd like to join her for lunch. Outside the sun was shining and Jo felt happier than she had for weeks. She settled to her work with energy and an enthusiasm which might have been dampened somewhat had she known that Randall Myers, having noted her name and Friday's and Monday's dates in a notebook, had gone down to the Transport Office, where he said she had asked him to check the price charged for her airfare. When they told him that she had not bought a ticket from them he said, 'Silly of me, of course she said she collected it at the airport,' and left. He then made a brief call from a nearby phone, hung up and waited. A few minutes later the phone rang and he picked it up. 'I see,' he said, jotting something down in his notebook. 'Right, thanks. Bye.'

Before she went home in the evening, Jo rang Etienne.

'Thanks so much for everything. I can't tell you how much it helped being able to talk things through with you on the weekend.'

'It was good to see you, Jo. I hope you'll come again soon.'

They talked about mutual friends, about work and what Jo could do if and when she went back. Jo was speaking in French. She was immersed in her conversation with Etienne when she thought she heard soft footsteps on the stairs outside her room. She lowered her voice. Whoever it was on the stairs had stopped. She switched into Arabic and said to Etienne, 'I'm not alone any more. I'll talk to you again another time, perhaps from home. Thanks for everything and please give my love to Lucia.'

'Don't forget: we're always here for you.'

'I won't. Thanks. Bye.'

She put the telephone down and Randall Myers came into the room. She wondered what had possessed him to stand outside the door of her room while she was on the phone.

'You're working late,' he said.

'I've got a bit of a backlog,' she replied. 'In fact I've got such a big backlog I wonder if I'll ever get on top of it.'

'Don't worry about it. Everyone feels like that. How are you enjoying it here?'

There was something about him that she couldn't identify but which made her feel uneasy. Had he really been listening at the door? Why had he come down to her room? He looked attractive, sympathetic, but there was something about him she didn't care for. He perched on the corner of the desk next to hers, one foot on the floor, the other leg swinging, revealing a crimson sock, with a little pattern in it that matched the pattern in his crimson tie. A self-conscious and snappy dresser, she thought.

'It's all right. I enjoy it well enough when I'm not going flat out. I'm afraid I'm going to have to get my head down and toil now, if I'm to get finished soon.'

'I can take a hint,' he said amiably and stood up. 'One of these days perhaps I'll find you free to come and have a drink. Or a meal. I'll look down again some time.'

'Thanks, Randall.'

'See you,' he said and left the room.

CHAPTER ELEVEN

Jo's life was settling into a routine which she found comforting, although she was developing serious doubts about Harry's activities. The feeling of having been admitted to an exclusive and somewhat secretive club persisted, but Jo didn't feel she really belonged. She felt like a bird of passage, forced by unexpected bad weather to put down in unfamiliar territory. She could stop a while and recuperate, but would probably never pass this way again.

The enthusiasm aroused by her tour with George was being replaced by scepticism, a feeling that the arcane customs of Parliament were irrelevant, its deliberations a hypocritical sham. These feelings were heightened by her encounters with the Whips who seemed, with their ribald, schoolboy jokes, to behave as if life in the Commons was simply an extension of public school. The Whips' Office was an all-male preserve where women were clearly regarded as intruders, useful but not to be treated too seriously or allowed to linger too long.

At the same time there was a murky undercurrent to their activities, a feeling of something unpleasant going on that stopped as she entered and resumed as soon as she left.

She was becoming increasingly aware of Harry's affectations and mannerisms. She soon realized that he was not much interested in knowing anything about anyone, except in so far as it concerned his job. He would listen to what people said with a manner which she thought most people would find disconcerting. His attitude and expression generally suggested that he was thinking of something else. He would fold his arms across his chest and look at the floor. From time to time he would bring his right hand to his face, index finger to cheek, his thumb supporting his chin and his other fingers covering his mouth; a contained, even defensive pose. Periodically he would look up at the other person and switch on a warm but artificial smile by way of momentary encouragement then revert once more to his attitude of detached attention. She noticed that no matter whom he was talking to, he could not put up a convincing show of interest except momentarily. If someone was telling him something, especially if it appeared from the lowered voice or inclination of the speaker's head to be something confidential, he would respond as if he were mentally writing down the conversation. If he happened to be sitting at his desk, he would make brief entries on a notepad in front of him.

Harry was like a syphon, sucking up information wherever he could find it. He was indeed constantly making mental notes of everything that he heard, but he did not care to rely on his memory and at the first opportunity he would hurry to the privacy of his office, where he could sit down and make a lengthy and careful record of every useful piece of information he had acquired.

Sincerity was a quality Jo valued highly and she found Harry's manner singularly off-putting, to the extent that she would lose the thread when telling him something, for example about a constituent's telephone enquiry or a message from an MP, because she would feel that he wasn't paying attention. 'Go on,' he would say sharply, as if she were the one at fault.

Once again, Jo had had to work late. She was looking forward to going home but first she must take the work over to Harry. She assembled it all in folders: replies to constituents, letters to Ministers, and letters and telephone messages for Harry. She put them all into a folder and put on her coat. She was on the point of leaving the room to walk over to the House in order to put the folder on Harry's desk, when the telephone rang.

'Hello.'

'Hello?' said a woman's voice, an urgent, excited voice. 'Oh, that's not Lois, is it?' The caller was disappointed, anxious.

'No, Lois is away. I'm Joanna. I'm standing in for her.'

The woman continued, her voice hurried, with a hint of breathlessness: 'Oh, I hope you'll help me. I've written to Mr Hunter but he hasn't answered my letter. Do you know anything about it?'

'Can you give me your name?'

'Rita Hanssen. H-a-n-s-s-e-n.' She spelled it out for Jo. 'He'll know all about it. I've been to see him and written to him. Lois was going to ring me but she never did and I'm getting desperate.'

'I'm afraid Lois is off sick and I don't know anything about the matter. I haven't seen your letter or file. I can have a word with Mr Hunter and call you back, but I don't think I'll be able to speak to him until tomorrow. Can it wait till then?'

'Oh God!' the woman exclaimed. 'I suppose it'll have to, but I'm so worried. I know he's going to take my kids away and I'll never see them again.'

'Who is?'

'My husband. My ex-husband. I don't know what to do. Please speak to Mr Hunter for me and ring me as *soon* as you can. Please.'

'Of course, I will, Mrs Hanssen. Give me your number.'

The woman sounded increasingly overwrought: 'You'll ring me then? Definitely? In the morning?'

'Yes. I promise.'

'I don't know what to do. You must help me.'

'I'll do my best.' Jo had difficulty bringing the call to an end. At last she was able to hang up and set off for the House.

As she entered Members' Lobby she saw Geoff Harper standing just inside the door. He had his back to her and was deep in conversation with two men. They switched their gaze from him to Jo as she entered the Lobby and Geoff looked round to see what had caught their interest.

'Hi there, Jo,' he called out to her. He looked as if he wanted to break away from his companions to talk to her. She smiled back at him, but did not give him any opportunity to talk. Instead she hurried past and went straight into the Government Whips' Office.

She must have opened the door very quietly because Jack Bendall and Eddie Mallins, who were at the far end of the room, did not turn round and appeared not to have heard her. Eddie Mallins was saying '. . . so we'll put him on the shit list and let him know he's on it. We'll see how he likes that.' She turned the doorknob noisily as she closed the door behind her. The men turned round. Jack Bendall smiled at her; Eddie Mallins scowled. She didn't care for him and suspected the feeling was mutual. He had never exchanged a single pleasantry with her, unlike most of the others. Roy Phillips, for example, was always polite and friendly.

Jack said, 'Hello gorgeous,' to Jo. She had heard him say that to other secretaries and knew that it was an automatic and, for him at least, meaningless salutation. 'Harry's not here at the moment. Can I help?'

Jo liked him because he was always the same: relaxed, easygoing and undemanding. He never looked or sounded self-important and was always good-natured. Eddie Mallins, by contrast, was still frowning at Jo, with a hard, disapproving stare.

'No thanks. I'll just leave these things on his desk.' She went into Harry's room. As she placed the folder on his desk she noticed what she thought of as his scribble-pad, beside his desk blotter. She glanced at it. There were various indecipherable words but two caught her eye. One looked like 'Parrie'. Beneath it was another word which looked like 'Kistringham'. She felt she shouldn't be looking and straightened up. As she turned away from the desk, the door opened and Harry came in.

'Hello, Jo. What are you up to? I'd have thought you'd have gone home hours ago.'

'I was just leaving various things for you to sign,' said Jo.

'Well if you can hang on a moment, I'll deal with them now and you can take it to the post.' Just as he was about to turn to the letters for signature she said, 'There was another phone call just before I came over here. I didn't type out a note of it. Mrs Rita Hanssen. She sounded terribly upset. She said you'd know about it. She's written to you and is hoping to hear from you.'

'Oh God, not her again. She's a pain in the neck.'

'She sounded desperate. She talked about her husband taking her children away.'

'It's for the court to decide. There's nothing I can do.' The phone rang and Harry picked it up. He kept looking at Jo as he listened to his caller. She looked away. Harry was saying 'Yes' and 'No' and 'I see' at intervals and scribbling on his pad. Jo got out her notebook, hoping to get him to dictate a letter to Mrs Hanssen. 'Right. Well, we'd better lay on something special for him. The usual arrangement? With bed and board, if you know what I mean?' He smirked as he said this, listened for a moment longer, then said, 'OK, Bye,' to his caller and put the phone down. He closed Jo's folder, pushed back his chair and stood up.

'Those will have to wait. You can pick them up in the morning.'

'What about Mrs Hanssen? Have you got time to dictate a reply to her?'

'No, I haven't.' He was decidedly annoyed. 'You'll have to speak to her and tell her that there's nothing more I can do. It's a legal matter and if she wants to take it any further she'll have to consult her solicitor.' He looked at his watch. 'The rest'll have to wait.' He left the room.

Jo closed her notebook and put it in her bag. She did not look forward to ringing Mrs Hanssen. She had a feeling the woman would react very badly to Harry's message and wished she did not have to be the one to deliver it. Although she knew nothing of Mrs Hanssen's problems, she felt concern for her. She had heard those anguished tones before, from other desperate people, in very different places and circumstances: refugees who were at their last gasp and had nowhere to go and no-one to turn to. The work had taken such a toll on her that eventually she had had to give it up. Something about Mrs Hanssen had brought it back to her now.

She stood up and was about to turn away from Harry's desk when a thought struck her. His phone call had been so much more important to him than Jo's message. What had he been jotting down? She leant forward and looked again at his scribble-pad. The two words that had intrigued her before had been heavily scored through and were no longer recognizable. There was a new entry: 'Wesker'. She wondered idly who Wesker was. The person for whom Harry was going to lay on 'something special'. Harry Hunter didn't give a damn about Mrs Hanssen, that was clear. He wasn't the slightest bit interested. Why hadn't he answered the poor woman's letter, or telephoned her?

She left the room. Jack was sitting at his desk, reading something. Roy Phillips and two other men were deep in conversation at the other end of the room. Jack looked up at Jo. 'Care for a drink, Jo? You look as if you could do with one.'

'No thanks, Jack. I've got rather a lot to do.' Perhaps her anger with Harry was showing in her face. She made an effort to overcome it. She smiled at Jack and said, 'Can I take a rain check?'

'By all means. I won't let you forget.' She left the room. As she entered Members' Lobby again she saw Geoff. He was in almost the same spot as before, talking to a middle-aged woman. He glanced at Jo. 'Well that's most helpful. Thanks,' he said to his companion and turned away from her, clearly intent on waylaying Jo.

'Don't rush off,' he said to her. 'Where are you headed?'

'Back to my office.'

'Can I buy you a drink? Or a coffee, or something?'

'People keep trying to give me drinks. No thanks.'

'There's no need to make it sound like an insult.'

'I'm sorry. I didn't mean it like that.'

'You look fed up. I thought you needed cheering up.' What a pathetic line, he thought as he said this. I ought to be able to do better than that. He wanted to delay her, to make her face him. He was thinking, I wish she'd look at me. How lovely she is. But she's annoyed about something. Perhaps it's me.

'Well I don't,' she said. She knew she sounded rude and cross. 'Thank you,' she added.

'What can I offer you instead of a drink? Dinner,

perhaps?'

She had continued walking, trying to get past him, but he had accompanied her, holding the door open for her to leave the Lobby.

She stopped and looked at him. She was tempted to ask, 'With or without Alicia?' but instead she said, 'No thanks. I really have got an awful lot to do. I want to get it finished and go home. I really must go.'

She turned away, hurrying towards Central Lobby. She glanced at her watch. It was late, after seven o'clock. If she had packed up her things she could have gone straight home after leaving the Whips' Office. What she ought to do was ring Mrs Hanssen, get the call over with instead of leaving it until tomorrow.

It was raining slightly as she left St Stephen's Entrance, and the night was bitterly cold. She hurried back to her office and had her security card at the ready, pushed it into the machine on the wall and opened the front door. She stepped gratefully inside to find Vic, the doorman, talking to an elderly man she had not seen before. 'Hello, Jo,' said Vic. To his companion he said, 'Have you met Jo, Dave?'

'No, I haven't. Hello, Jo. You new here?'

'Yes, I am, and only temporary. I'm standing in for someone else.'

'Dave does night shifts here,' explained Vic. 'You working late tonight?'

'Yes,' said Jo, 'but not much longer. I'm just going to make a phone call and tidy up. Is that all right?'

'You can stay here all night if you want to,' said Dave, 'but I wouldn't advise it. You girls mustn't work too hard.' He had thinning grey hair and a white moustache. His eyes were a faded blue-grey with dark hollows beneath them. His face was pale. The skin over his temples looked fine and taut, the blue of the veins showing clearly through it. Jo thought that he looked as if he rarely saw the light of day.

'I'll be putting the kettle on shortly to make myself some soup. Would you like some?' She was about to give an automatic refusal when she was suddenly struck by a feeling of sympathy, a recognition of something in him. Was it loneliness, or sadness? Loss perhaps? 'I'd like that very much,' she said.

A few minutes later Dave came downstairs and put a mug of soup on the desk next to her. She thanked him.

'How do you like working down here?' he asked.

'Oh it's fine. Nice and peaceful and not too crowded. Just right for me,' she replied.

'It's a funny old house this,' he said, looking around him. 'I've known it for years. I've been doing this job a long time, you know.'

'Have you?'

'Years.' He smiled at her, revealing several gaps in his teeth. 'I was batman to the last Deputy Serjeant-at-Arms. That was a long time ago now, before he came here of course. He got me the job after my wife died. He was always good to me.' He was silent for a moment, remembering.

'Do you like working here, Dave?'

'It suits me,' he said.

'Do you always work the night shift?'

'Yes. Have done for years.' He paused again. 'Soup all right?'

Jo hadn't tasted it yet. She picked up her mug and sipped it.

'It's very nice thanks. Especially on a night like this.'

'What was I going to say?' Dave asked himself. 'Oh yes, this building. As I say it's a funny old house. Seen a lot of things I can tell you. If you knew some of the things that had happened round these parts it'd make your hair curl.'

'Like what sort of things?'

93

Dave put his finger to his lips. 'You know what they say: walls have ears.'

Jo smiled at him.

'Sometimes I come down here in the middle of the night,' said Dave, 'when there's no-one around and I just sit here, in the dark. Well, not totally dark. The door's open of course and there's a little light from the passage there. And sometimes I could swear there's someone in here with me. How about that? Isn't that something?'

'It certainly is. Do you mean a ghost, Dave?'

'Well, it depends what you mean by ghost,' he said and rocked with inward laughter, his eyes shining. 'Look at you. Have I frightened you?'

'Not a bit of it,' said Jo, laughing. 'It doesn't bother me. But I think it's funny to think of you sitting down here in the dark, waiting for ghosts.'

'I can see you don't believe me,' he said, wagging a forefinger at her. 'Just you wait and see. Maybe there's somebody watching us even now.' He gave her a little wave and headed for the door. 'See you later.'

'Thanks very much for the soup,' Jo called after him as he went out of the room.

Jo leaned back in her chair and drank her soup. She wondered how much Harry had done to try to help Mrs Hanssen. She got up and went to the filing cabinet but could find no file marked Hanssen. She must take the plunge. She checked the number in her notebook and dialled. The number rang and rang. No answer. Jo was disappointed. She was about to hang up when a woman's voice answered, 'Yes?'

'Hello. Is that Mrs Hanssen?'

'Yes it is.' Her voice sounded different from before.

'It's Mr Hunter's secretary here, at the House of Commons. You rang me earlier.'

'Oh yes.' She sounded more alert now. 'Have you

spoken to him?'

'Yes. I saw him a little while ago, but I'm afraid there's nothing more he can do to help you.'

'Nothing? Nothing at all?' She was agitated, her voice rising. 'Why didn't he tell me straight away then? Why've I had to wait all this time to hear from him?'

'I'm afraid I don't know. I'm sorry. He said that you should talk to your solicitor.'

'A lot of good that'll do. He doesn't believe me either. He says I've just got to wait and see what happens. Isn't anyone going to help me?' She was shouting, furiously angry. 'He's going to get away with it. What about my children? Doesn't anyone care what happens to them?' She was crying now.

'I'm sure they do, Mrs Hanssen. Have you spoken to your solicitor?'

'I've tried. So that's all he said then? Speak to my solicitor? Thanks for nothing.' She hung up before Jo had a chance to say anything else. Jo sat at her desk, waiting, wondering whether Mrs Hanssen would ring her back. Perhaps Harry really had done all he could and the woman was just refusing to face facts. What was it she'd said? 'My solicitor doesn't believe me either' Maybe she was deranged. Jo had been ready to talk to her but the woman hadn't given her a chance. Well it was done now and Jo was glad to have got the call out of the way. She felt too tired to do any more work, so she packed her things away, and left, stopping at the attendants' room by the front door to return the soup mug to Dave. He was nowhere to be seen so she left the mug on the desk with a note saying, 'The soup was great. Thanks. Jo' and departed.

CHAPTER TWELVE

Jo was determined to get away from work early on Friday so that she could buy something to wear to Ann and Tim's party the next day. She worked fast and at three o'clock decided that she had done as much as she needed for the day.

When she entered the Whips' Office it was deserted. She walked through to Harry's room and knocked on the door.

She heard his peremptory 'Come!' She always found the single word irritating, an imperious affectation. She opened the door to see Harry slouched in an armchair with a glass in his hand and a good-looking fair-haired woman in an equally relaxed attitude in the armchair next to him. They had their feet up on a low table. Harry took his feet off the table and sat up slightly. The woman followed suit. She must have been in her mid-thirties, or older. She was carefully made-up. Her thick hair was pinned up, but a few strands had escaped. She had long, shapely legs and gave an ineffectual tug to her tight straight skirt, a gesture which was more effective in drawing attention to her thighs than in concealing them.

'I thought you'd gone,' exclaimed Harry. 'I tried to ring you just before lunch.'

'I went out for a sandwich,' Jo said. 'Sorry. Were you wanting me to do something?'

'No. I was ringing to tell you to go early if you wanted to.'

'Thanks. As a matter of fact, I'm on my way home now.'

'Do you know Jane?' asked Harry. 'She's worked here for years. Often looks in here for a drink on Fridays.'

'No, we haven't met,' said Jo. 'Hello, I'm Jo. I'm standing in for Lois for a while.'

'Hi,' said Jane. 'Pleased to meet you.' Pleased was not what she looked. Jo could read in her expression the careful assessment of one who senses a possible rival.

'Care to join us for a drink?' said Harry. Another pleasantry. Harry couldn't wait for her to leave.

'That's very kind of you,' said Jo, 'but I want to catch the shops before they close. I'll just leave these and be off.'

By the time Saturday evening came, Jo was having second thoughts about Ann's invitation. She came close to telephoning to say she couldn't come after all, then thought better of it. It would be churlish to cry off now. And she'd bought a dress the previous afternoon, on her way home from work; a spur of the moment purchase. It would be a pity not to wear it. She went to some trouble getting ready and on checking her appearance in the mirror, decided that, all things considered, she looked quite good. She treated herself to a taxi. Spring wasn't far off, but the weather was unpredictable and windy.

'Hello, Jo. How nice to see you.' For a moment Jo didn't recognize Ann, she looked so different from the unsophisticated girl she had seen at the House of Commons. She was wearing a filmy painted-silk jacket over a close-fitting sleeveless black dress. Her hair hung over one shoulder in a heavy plait entwined with sparkling multi-coloured ribbons. Her very high-heeled shoes and the narrow dress made her look several inches taller.

'You look wonderful, Ann,' said Jo.

'Thanks. Come on in.' Ann led her to a bedroom where she took off her coat.

'Am I the last to arrive?'

'No, I'm sure you're not. A whole lot of people arrived together. We had a bit of a jam in the passage there. I hate it when that happens, don't you?'

'I know what you mean.' Jo inspected herself in a mirror.

'You look great, Jo. Come and meet some people.'

'How many have you invited?'

'I thought it was fifteen, but I think Tim must have asked a few more at the last moment. He has to look after this chap David Wesker from the State Department in Washington so I suppose it's chiefly for his benefit.'

'Wesker. Where have I heard that name before?'

'On the news perhaps. He's over here to discuss arrangements for the peace conference.'

'Oh yes,' said Jo. She'd remembered where she'd encountered the name: not on a news programme but on Harry's notepad.

Ann got Jo a glass of wine and led her through the throng to two men who were talking earnestly. The older of the two, a big man with grey hair, had his arms folded across his chest and was looking down, with his head at an angle, listening attentively. His companion turned as they approached and his eyes lit up as he looked at Ann. This must be Tim, thought Jo. What a nice-looking man and what incredibly blue eyes he has. Tim stepped forward as Ann said, 'This is Jo Delvere, Tim, Laura's friend I was telling you about.' He shook hands with Jo and gave her a warm smile.

'I'm very pleased to meet you, Jo.' He sounded as if he meant it. 'Laura's a great friend of ours. Ann tells me you've been working at the UN. I'd like to talk to you about that some time. I did a spell there for the Foreign Office, a long time ago.'

'I'd like to hear about that too,' said Ann. 'That was before I knew Tim,' she said to Jo. 'There are still so many things that he's done that I know so little about. I want to learn all about the places he's visited.' Jo understood what she meant. She had felt like that about Donald. She had wanted to know everything about him, his younger days, his childhood, the things he'd liked doing, his adventures.

'How long have you been married?' she asked. Tim's companion was talking to him again and Tim had to turn away.

'Two years. We met – oh dash it. I'll have to get that,' said Ann, as the doorbell rang. She went to answer it.

Tim introduced Jo to David Wesker. 'Jo works for the Government Chief Whip,' said Tim. 'Really? How interesting,' said Wesker. Jo asked him how long he was expecting to be in London. 'A week or so,' he said, looking at a point above her head. He resumed his conversation with Tim.

'Don't I know you?' said a voice with an American accent. 'Where have we met before?' Jo looked round to see a middle-aged man with a crew-cut and horn-rimmed glasses smiling at her, 'Hi, Jo.'

'Hank! What a surprise. How fantastic to see you.'

'You two know each other?' asked Wesker. Jo had become interesting.

'Sure, from Brussels. It's been a long time mind.'

'What are you doing now?' asked Jo.

'I've gone up in the world, you might say. I'm working in the White House these days, as an adviser to the President on European security matters.'

'Sounds impressive. Spookier than ever, no doubt.'

He laughed.

'You don't deny it, so you're still in the same line of work?'

'What can I say? You never did quite approve of me, did you, Jo, no matter how hard I tried to impress you.' He laughed heartily. 'I can see you haven't changed. What are you doing these days?'

'I'm working at the House of Commons. Only temporarily. For the Government Chief Whip. Does that mean anything to you?'

'Harry Hunter. Yes I met him at a reception at Ten Downing Street not long ago.'

'Do you know him, Mr Wesker?' Jo asked.

'No, I've never met the man,' Wesker drawled. 'I'm here for meetings with your Foreign Office. Talking of which, we shall have to be going shortly, Hank. I'll just have a word with Fenchurch about tomorrow.'

He moved away to find Tim, who had been drawn into another group of guests.

Out of the corner of her eye, Jo could see someone watching her. She decided not to look round just yet but continued to talk to Hank. She was beginning to enjoy herself. After a while she glanced round. It was Randall who was inspecting her and he had moved closer. He looked away but she felt certain he had been listening to their conversation. Not that that would have been particularly difficult as Hank had a voice that carried all too well.

She turned back to Hank and found that Geoff Harper had joined them. He smiled at Jo and ignored Hank. Hank said, 'Any chance of our meeting up again? Can you give me a number where I can reach you?'

'Certainly,' said Jo. He got a card and pen out of his pocket and she wrote her office number down for him.

'That's great. I'll give you a call. I'll be in town for

another week. You can get hold of me at the Embassy if you want to.' Hank moved away.

'At last I get a chance to talk to you. You look terrific,' said Geoff who believed in getting straight to the point.

'Thank you,' said Jo, feeling pleased. 'How is Alicia? I don't see her here.'

'Alicia?' He sounded puzzled. 'Oh, she's fine. She's in Paris at the moment.'

Jo sensed she was being watched again. She glanced round. Randall was still in position. He appeared to be talking to someone but Jo was convinced he was listening to her conversation.

'Am I right in thinking there's food over there?' she asked Geoff.

'You are. Would you like some?'

'I certainly would.' They walked across to the buffet at the far end of the room and helped themselves to food, then went and stood near the fireplace, where they could put their glasses on the mantelpiece.

'Tell me something,' said Jo, 'do the names Parrie and Kistringham mean anything to you? Or maybe its Kisington. I'm not sure.'

'Kisington. No, I don't think so.' Geoff put a forkful of food into his mouth and ate. Jo looked around the room. Oh God, she thought, that ghastly man's still at it. Randall was once again within earshot. She turned towards the fire so that her back was to the room. Geoff turned too.

'Wait a minute,' said Geoff. 'Kistrington. Could that be it? There's a place called Kistrington. A kind of stately home. I think it's used for judges' lodgings.'

'Really?' said Jo. She was about to ask what judges' lodgings were when Geoff said, 'Parrie. Come to think of it there's a High Court judge called Parrie. Perhaps that's it. Parrie. Kistrington. Why do you ask?'

'Oh, I can't think where I heard them now,' Jo lied,

'but Kistringham seemed such an odd name. Perhaps it's Kistrington.'

'Now it's my turn to ask you a question,' said Geoff. 'Where—'

But Jo had glanced round and seen Randall approaching. She interrupted Geoff. 'What is it with that fellow Randall?' she asked, lowering her voice. 'He's always listening in to other people's conversations. I can't stand it!'

'Hello,' said Randall and they turned to find him smiling at them. 'What are you two discussing so earnestly?'

Geoff was about to speak but Jo cut him off by saying, 'Hello, Randall. Tell me, what is it that you do?' There was an unpleasant edge to her voice. Geoff noticed it but Randall was oblivious, apparently. 'Laura did tell me, but I've forgotten.'

'Research work mainly and some speech writing for various Members,' he replied smoothly.

'How interesting. Where do you do your research as a rule? *Do* tell me how you go about it,' she asked.

'Libraries, at the Commons and elsewhere. Interviews, phone calls.'

'Phone calls? Really? Your own or other people's?' said Jo nastily. Randall's eyes narrowed. Jo had noticed Tim talking to Michael Wallingbury and looked round for Barbara, but couldn't see her.

'Excuse me, Geoff,' she said, ignoring Randall, 'I must go and speak to Ann and Tim.'

'Did I hear Jo talking about Kistrington?' asked Randall.

'I think if she'd wanted you to know what she was talking about she'd have told you, don't you?' Geoff looked smug. 'Can't stop, I'm afraid.' He was determined not to let Jo get away from him. He left Randall standing by the fireplace looking thoughtful.

Geoff was waylaid by another guest before he could

rejoin Jo. He kept looking in her direction until he was able to extricate himself. Jo was standing with Tim, listening to Michael Wallingbury talk about the deteriorating situation in Eastern Europe when he rejoined her.

'Can I get you a drink?' he asked her.

'No thanks.' Jo looked at her watch. 'I'm going in a moment,' she said.

'Can I give you a lift? I've got my car outside.' She hesitated.

'I'm only offering you a lift for God's sake, not that I wouldn't love to give you dinner. But I have a feeling you'd say no.'

She couldn't help laughing. 'A lift would be great, thanks.'

Jo went to find her coat and met Ann in the passage.

'I've enjoyed your party very much, Ann. Thanks for asking me.'

'I'm glad you could come. How are you getting back? Do you need a taxi?'

'No thanks. Geoff Harper is giving me a lift.'

'It's just as well Barbara isn't here or she'd be uttering all sorts of dire warnings. I think he's rather nice myself,' said Ann. 'See you, Jo.'

On the way home, Jo plied Geoff with questions about his career. He'd done a number of overseas assignments in various war zones, he explained. It was evident from the way he spoke that he didn't wish to talk about them. Perhaps the memories are too upsetting, thought Jo, which might account for his careworn expression. In fact Geoff was wondering whether he could ask Jo all the things he wanted to know about her, like where she'd been going the previous Friday morning. However, he'd seen her reaction to Randall and decided against this. He didn't want to put her off. A more subtle approach was called for.

'I'd much rather talk about you,' he said. 'Why don't

you let me give you dinner?'

'You don't give up, do you?' she said, with a smile. They reached her street and she opened the door to get out.

'Another time then?' asked Geoff. She looked at him. If he weren't married, I'd say yes, she thought. I like being with him. Instead she said, 'Maybe,' and got out of the car. 'Thanks for the lift.' She shut the door and waved goodbye.

CHAPTER THIRTEEN

When she arrived at her office on Monday morning, she found Laura sitting at her desk, writing. There was no-one else in the room.

'Hello, Jo. Excuse me making myself at home.' She stood up. 'I never seem to see you these days so I thought I'd scribble you a note about lunch tomorrow.' She crumpled up the piece of paper and dropped it in the waste-paper bin.

Bella came into the room, with a bundle of mail in one hand and a bunch of snowdrops and crocuses.

'D'you pick the flowers in the park?' asked Laura. Bella gave her a despairing look and went out of the room in search of a vase.

'No sense of humour, that girl,' said Laura. 'Even when spring's in the air and the snail's on the thorn and all that carry on.' She looked critically at Jo. 'Do you know, you're looking great? How's everything going?'

'I have to admit that I'm enjoying it all much more than I thought I would. That's largely due to you, thanks, Laura.'

'Nonsense,' said Laura, looking pleased. 'I'm glad

things are working out all right.' She stooped to pick up her bag from the floor. 'I'd better get back to my labours. I only came to see how you were and ask if you were going to join us for lunch tomorrow.'

'I'd love to. What time?'

'Why don't you meet me in Central Lobby at about ten to one and we'll go over together?'

Not long after Laura left, Harry rang and asked Jo to go over to his office immediately. She knocked and went in without waiting. He was sitting at his desk, his swivel chair turned so that his back was to the door, putting something away in a cupboard. As he closed the door Jo saw that it was a kind of safe, with a combination lock. The outer door which closed over it made it look like a plain office cupboard. Harry swung round in his chair and smiled at Jo. 'Good morning, Jo,' he said enthusiastically. 'I trust you had a good weekend.' He reached over to draw the upright chair nearer to his desk for her.

'Thank you.' She sat down. 'Yes, I had a good week-end, thanks.'

He was in an expansive mood. 'I hope you're enjoying it here. You're doing a great job.'

'I'm glad you think so.'

'You'll be pleased to know that I won't be giving you a huge amount today. I've made notes on a few things for you to deal with.' He passed a pile of letters over to her. 'Perhaps you'd look through the rest and deal with anything you can.' He gave her a condescending smile, 'You know how to deal with a lot of them, I'm sure. Anything else will have to wait until later. Any messages?'

She handed him the message folder and he went through it, giving her instructions from time to time. The door opened and Jack Bendall looked in. 'Coming?' he asked. Harry stood up. 'OK, Jo, I'll see you later.'

On her way back through Central Lobby Jo saw George. He waved and she went over to him.

106

'Hello, Jo. How are you getting on? Are you enjoying it here?'

'Very much thank you, George. How are you?'

'Mustn't grumble, my dear. Would you care to join me for a cup of coffee? I put the kettle on a few minutes ago. It should be boiling now.'

'I'd love one.' She wondered where he made it. He led her towards the House of Lords Chamber, to a small, windowless room at the side of Peers' Lobby. It contained a desk with a reading lamp, some cupboards, on one of which stood a kettle, and three upright chairs.

'Have a seat,' said George. He made two cups of coffee and sat down opposite her.

'Laura told me you used to be in the police. Do you miss it?' asked Jo.

'Oh not now. I'm too old for that kind of work. In any case I've got a lot of mates in the force here. Did you know we've got our own Chief of Police for the Palace of Westminster? You've probably seen him. Commander Bowerbridge. A big bloke.'

'Can't say I have,' said Jo.

'Things have changed a lot here, over the years,' said George wistfully. 'It was nicer in the old days when it was more informal. And the politicians weren't so self-important then, they were more down on our level.'

'How do you mean?'

'Well they used to walk to their meetings in Whitehall, for example. Now they go everywhere in cars. Even the Prime Minister would walk over from Number Ten. You take Sir Alec. I remember he used to walk in, just like a member of the public. And he'd always get his pass out for us, as if we didn't know who he was. "Good evening, George," he'd say to me, as he walked through.'

He sipped his coffee in silence for a moment or two then said, 'It doesn't do to make too many trips down memory lane.'

'I know what you mean.'

He gave her a shrewd look. 'Yes, I think you do. But if you don't mind my saying so, you look a lot better than when you came here. This place must be agreeing with you.'

Jo laughed. 'I think it is, but there is a lot I don't understand.'

'I wonder. You don't give much away but you take it all in. Am I right?'

'Maybe. What about you, George?'

'I certainly hear a lot. You should hear some of the things people tell me. One of the Government drivers, for example, comes out with amazing stories about the things he's heard – and seen – in his job.' He bit into a biscuit and chewed a while, looking at Jo thoughtfully. 'There's a whole army of people working behind the scenes here that you probably never meet: the catering and kitchen staff, the staff in the Vote Office and Journal Office, all the places like that, the maintenance staff, the cleaners. That's what makes it so interesting. If you've got your head down over a typewriter all day, you might just as well be working somewhere else.'

'Well I won't be working here for very long. Just till Lois gets back. But I'd love to hear some of your stories, George.'

'One of these days, when you've got more time, I'll tell you some.' He drank some more of his coffee. 'I think you could tell *me* some stories, couldn't you?'

'I could at that.'

'Well then, we'll make it a swap. I'll tell you some of mine, if you'll tell me a bit about yourself.'

'It's a deal,' said Jo and stood up. 'I'd better be getting back to my desk. Thank you very much for the coffee, George.'

'I hope you'll come again, my dear.'

'I certainly will. I've enjoyed it.'

As she walked back to her office she passed throngs of visitors in Central Lobby and St Stephen's Hall. Outside on the embankment, rows of coaches were disgorging their passengers. The streets seemed to be suddenly crowded as if people had been lured out of hibernation by the brilliant sunshine.

Jo worked hard for the rest of the morning, heartened by having a smaller workload from Harry than usual.

At lunch-time she decided to go out for a walk in St James's Park. It was a beautiful day. Amongst the trees the air was cold and invigorating, but the sunshine was warm enough to arouse memories of the luxurious heat of summer, now only a few months off. There were crowds of gold and purple crocuses under the trees and daffodils just opening. It was the kind of day to bring hope to the most despairing heart, thought Jo. Although she felt that her sadness would never leave her, it was a burden she now felt equal to carrying. It would always colour her feelings about everything, but it would enrich rather than destroy each new experience. She felt strong. She would find worthwhile work to do, where she could help others and feel fulfilled. She walked back to her office, feeling optimistic and at peace with herself.

Bella was typing fast, a thick pile of manuscript lying next to her word-processor. She looked up and nodded at Jo.

'I love the flowers, Bella. It was such a nice idea to bring them in.'

'Thanks. Glad you like them.' She carried on typing.

Jo had bought herself a sandwich on the way back from the park and was eating it when the phone rang. She swallowed her mouthful and picked up the receiver.

'Hello, Jo. Patricia Hunter here. I was just ringing to let you know that I'm going to America to visit my daughter and I'd be grateful if you'd keep an eye on the flat for me until the end of the month.'

'Is there anything in particular you want me to do?'

'Just give the place the once over and bring any post and messages over to Number Twelve, unless it's for Johnny, of course. You may find he's been there. Was there anything last week?'

'Not a thing. No problems. No mail or messages.'

'Thank you so much, Jo. I'll be in touch when I get back.'

Mary came into the room, carrying a large bundle of files. She was followed by a tall, distinguished-looking man, with thinning grey hair and a small moustache. His eyes looked pale, as if sun-bleached. He was lean and dapper and had a kindly expression.

'Hello, Jo,' said Mary. 'You haven't met my boss, have you? Arnold Hobbs. Arnold, this is Jo Delvere, who's standing in for Lois.'

'Hello, Jo. Hello, Bella. Will it be all right with you ladies if I do some work here with Mary? The rooms upstairs are all full. We'll keep our voices down.'

'That's fine by me,' said Jo.

'Of course,' said Bella, who scarcely paused in her typing.

Jo settled to her work again but couldn't help listening to Mary and her boss. He had borrowed a swivel chair from an unoccupied desk and placed it next to Mary. Jo looked up from time to time and studied his profile. He was quite old, she decided, perhaps in his late sixties. She was struck by how much trouble he took with his constituency case work. He would pick up a letter and read it carefully and then discuss it with Mary.

'What do you think about this one, Mary? She wrote to us before, d'you remember? It doesn't look as if the Council have helped her at all. We must do something about it.' And of another one, 'This is appalling. I'll speak to the Minister myself. It's about time we lit a fire under the Department.'

He seemed to be genuinely concerned about his constituents and anxious to try to help them. He took care with each letter that he dictated. And Jo noticed that he extracted one or two and put them to one side, saying that he would write the replies to those himself.

What a contrast with Harry, thought Jo. He never seems to care about anyone or anything.

When Arnold Hobbs had gone, Jo said, 'Your boss seemed like a really nice person, Mary.'

'He's a pet.'

'Have you worked for him for long?'

'Years.' She thought a moment. 'I don't know what I shall do when he retires and I have to find someone else.'

'I couldn't help noticing how much trouble he took with his constituents' problems.'

'He really cares. He's one of the old school, the kind of MP who believes in public service. Contrary to what Laura may have told you, there are still quite a few of them about. In fact she works for one, Charles Donaldson.'

'I know, she's told me. I don't think she thinks they're all bad, by any means, but she loathes phoneys.'

'Don't we all.' Mary leant back in her chair, warming to her subject. 'I think the trouble is the old-fashioned type don't seem to get so much media attention as some of the others. Perhaps it's because they're less concerned with PR than the younger ones, who've been brought up to think about their image more than their actions.'

'That's what Laura was saying to me the other day, more or less.'

'Oh Laura's all right,' said Mary. 'Her heart's in the right place, but she's got a sharp tongue at times.'

Jo suppressed a smile. She knew all about Laura's acid wit, but she also knew better than anyone that Laura had a heart of gold.

CHAPTER FOURTEEN

Jo's newfound feeling of well-being did not desert her the following day, even though it was bitterly cold and the spring-like balm of the previous day had been banished by a hard, sleet-laden wind. When she and Laura set off for the restaurant at lunch-time the street was almost deserted and they hurried along, heads bent, holding their coat collars up to shield their faces from the cold.

'We should have given it a miss today,' said Laura. 'How I hate this weather.'

'Yesterday you were telling me spring had arrived,' said Jo, glad to be wearing boots, but wishing she had thought of a scarf or beret.

Once again, when they reached the restaurant, Ann and Barbara were there before them.

'You two look as if you've been here all morning,' said Laura. 'Evidently you don't have enough work to do.'

'We like to get here early so we can talk about you before you arrive,' said Barbara.

'Then you must have been having an enthralling conversation,' replied Laura. 'Tell me all.'

'For starters, our Joanna is a dark horse,' said Barbara. 'Mike said that at Ann's and Tim's party for visiting

American bigwigs, Jo was hobnobbing with the President's adviser on European security, who turns out to be an old flame of hers.'

'Slight exaggeration,' said Jo. 'We only spoke for a few minutes. I knew him years ago.'

'Ah, but what we want to know is whether he's an old flame,' said Ann.

'Not really. He could turn up the gas, but never find the matches, if you know what I mean,' said Jo, looking demure.

'I'm really disappointed I wasn't at this party,' said Barbara.

'She's just jealous because Mike told her you left with Geoff Harper,' said Ann.

Jo smiled and said nothing.

'Well, Jo,' said Barbara when their food had arrived, 'what do you think of it all so far? Are you going to take root in the House?'

'I doubt it, for all sorts of reasons. I'd only stay on if I could work for someone nice. I can't say Harry fits the bill.'

'Why not?' asked Ann.

'Because he's self-seeking, calculating and devious,' Laura answered for her.

'I thought you approved of him,' protested Jo.

'I never said he was a particularly nice person. I said he was a better choice than many as an employer because your work-load wouldn't be too heavy and you could organize your life around the work rather better than with a lot of them.'

'What is it that you don't like about him?' asked Barbara. 'I've met him a number of times and he seemed OK to me, though not the most lovable type I suppose.'

'I can think of one person who'd disagree with you,' Jo replied.

'Who, Patricia?'

'No, but talking of Patricia, when I got back to my room after our last lunch, I found her sitting at my desk, cool as you please, and I'd a feeling she'd been reading a letter of mine. A private letter, I mean.'

'What cheek,' said Barbara.

'Of course I don't know for sure, but you know how it is. She had that look about her.'

'Guilty, is the word you're groping for,' said Laura.

'Why was she there?'

'She wanted to rope me in to keep an eye on their flat for them when she's away.'

'She was probably wanting to cast an eye over you, to see whether you needed watching,' said Barbara.

'I'm not the one that needs watching. She ought to have her eye on our Harry. I found him in his office on Friday afternoon, drinking with a woman called Jane. They were both so laid back they were practically horizontal.'

'That must be Jane Templeman,' said Laura. 'Perhaps Patricia is using you to keep tabs on Harry.'

'He'd hardly get up to anything at their flat with his son living there,' said Jo.

'I feel a bit sorry for her,' said Barbara.

'Perhaps I'm being rather unfair,' said Jo. 'I could be completely wrong about Harry and this woman, Jane.'

'Oh no, you're not,' said Laura. 'It's an open secret that she and Harry are having an affair. David probably knows about it too.'

'Is she David Templeman's wife?' asked Jo.

'She is indeed, but they separated about the time he became Defence Secretary.'

'That's right,' said Barbara. 'She's tried out quite a number of Members, if you see what I mean.'

'Does she work in the House?' asked Ann.

'You could put it like that,' said Laura. 'She's a freelance journalist. I suppose you'd call it political research.'

'I think she writes rather well,' said Barbara. 'But forget about her, tell me why you don't like Harry, Jo. I'm intrigued.'

'It's a lot of things, really. He's insincere. He can turn on the charm when he wants to, but it's phoney. I don't like that. But I suppose the thing that I dislike the most is that he can make time for the things he wants to do, like boozing with his girlfriend, but he hasn't got time to telephone or write to a constituent who's feeling really desperate.'

She proceeded to tell them about Rita Hanssen.

'Poor woman,' said Ann. 'But if he says there's nothing more that he can do, maybe he really can't do anything.'

'But she'd written to him again and he hadn't replied,' Jo protested. 'If he couldn't do anything, he should have told her, not left her waiting and hoping. That's what's so heartless.'

'I'm afraid you'll find that there are some constituents who hang on like a ferret and just won't let go,' said Laura. 'Sometimes you simply can't do anything for them, but they won't take no for an answer.'

'That's true,' said Barbara. 'We have a regular at Michael's surgeries, a really sad case. He's convinced he's being spied on from outer space. Mike says he's just a terribly lonely guy who needs someone to talk to from time to time. So he sees him and writes to him occasionally.'

'Michael's a nice man,' said Ann, 'and he's got you to keep him human.'

'Harry wasn't remotely interested in Mrs Hanssen. His exact words were "She's a pain in the neck".'

'Perhaps he's got good reason. You ought to look at the file,' said Barbara.

'I tried to, but I couldn't find it. Anyway,' said Jo defiantly, 'whatever the rights and wrongs of the case, it wouldn't have cost Harry any great effort to talk to her or write to her and say why he couldn't do anything more for her, would it?'

They were all silent for a while. Then Jo said, 'Anyone know what the "shit list" is?'

'Never heard of it,' said Ann. 'It sounds revolting.'

Barbara looked puzzled. 'Is it something to do with the Whips' Office?' she asked.

'It must be,' said Jo. 'I heard Eddie Mallins say to Jack Bendall, "we'll put him on the shit list and see how he likes it."'

Laura said, 'It's a list – not very long I think – of those MPs the Whips regard as troublemakers. You can rock the boat once or twice maybe, but more than that and you risk getting put on the shit list.'

'What happens then?' asked Jo.

'I think eventually you get punished in various ways, some subtle, some very obvious. Once they've decided you're a shit, you get treated like one.'

'Like Jimmy Underwood?' asked Jo.

'I suppose so. I wouldn't know whether he was ever on the list,' said Laura, a trifle defensively. She had recognized a dangerous look in Jo's eye.

Barbara put in, 'I seem to remember hearing something about him being mixed up in some financial malpractice, but I can't remember what.'

'Supposing they'd been unfair to him and had got it wrong in some way?' said Jo. 'What would you think about that?'

'I would think it pretty awful. But I wouldn't like to judge unless I really *did* know all the facts,' said Barbara.

'I don't suppose anyone does, except perhaps the Whips,' said Laura.

CHAPTER FIFTEEN

When Jo got back to her office she was intercepted by Vic.

'Your boss rang while you were out. Sounded a bit annoyed to me.'

'You'd think I could go out for some lunch!' said Jo crossly.

'They're all like that sometimes,' said Vic. 'He wanted to know where you were. I said you'd gone for lunch and he said, "Tell her not to bother to come over this afternoon. I'm going to be very busy. And she needn't bother bringing anything over unless it's urgent. I'll see her tomorrow."'

'Did he say what time he wants to see me tomorrow?'

'No. I didn't think to ask, I'm afraid. Don't worry. I expect he'll ring you tomorrow morning.'

'Oh, I'm not worried,' said Jo. Two glasses of wine with her lunch had given her a more relaxed view of work. 'Thanks, Vic.' She went downstairs. To her surprise, Randall emerged from her room as she reached the bottom of the staircase.

'Afternoon, Jo,' he said. 'How are you?' and went on past her up the stairs.

'I'm fine thanks,' she called after him, wondering whether it was Mary or Bella he'd been visiting. But the room was empty. She remembered that Mary had come in early because she had to leave early and Bella hadn't put in an appearance yet. What was Randall up to? she wondered. She looked at Mary's and Bella's desks thinking that if he'd been visiting either of them he'd probably have left a note, but there was no sign of one. Remembering Patricia Hunter's visit, she wondered if she'd left anything of her own lying about. She hadn't, of course, because she hadn't had any letters recently and anyway she'd had her handbag with her. Everything looked just as she'd left it. She considered running upstairs and asking Randall what he'd wanted, then thought better of it. I'm being ridiculous. He'd love to have provoked me into such a question. And then he'd start asking some of his own. Then it occurred to her that he'd probably been to Andrea's room. She sat down at her desk, but her doubts persisted so she went to see Andrea.

'Have you seen Randall?' she asked as she put her head round the door. Andrea and the two secretaries who shared a room with her were all hard at work.

'Who?' said Andrea.

'Randall Myers.'

'We never have anything to do with *him*,' replied Andrea disdainfully. 'What on earth do you want with him?'

'Nothing. But I was told he was looking for me and I thought perhaps he'd come this way by mistake.'

'He only makes those kind of mistakes when no-one's here. He's a snoop. Isn't that right, folks?' said Andrea. The others agreed. 'I would give him a wide berth, if I were you,' she added.

'Oh, right,' said Jo, feeling embarrassed. 'Thanks for the advice.' She didn't have to act on it, however, because Randall did not reappear and was nowhere to be seen when she went upstairs later.

The following morning Harry rang to ask Jo to come over. There was an air of tension in the Whips' Office. Some of the Whips were sitting at their desks, others were with Jack at the other end of the room. He said, 'Good morning' to Jo, but without his usual cheerful tone. When she entered Harry's room, he was too preoccupied to greet her, it seemed, but said simply, 'Sit down, Jo. I've got a lot to get done this morning so let's get this lot out of the way quickly.'

He rattled off instructions, asking her to compose most of the letters herself. 'You know what to say to Mrs So-and-So. Thank her for writing. Sympathize with her views and will pass them on to the appropriate quarter.' He pushed the letter across the desk. 'Next one. Take that up with the Housing Office. Next one. See if you can get them some tickets for the Gallery. That should make their day,' and so on. He raced through the pile of work then stood up. 'I've got several meetings this afternoon. If I'm not free when you bring the letters over you can leave them with Fred.'

As she walked back through Central Lobby she met George with a party of visitors and greeted him cheerfully. As she hurried away she heard him saying to his visitors, 'That young lady is a Member's Private Secretary, one of the many people who . . .' but she didn't hear the rest.

Her work-load was daunting, but she set to with a will, determined to keep on top of it. She didn't go out for lunch, but ate a sandwich she'd had the foresight to buy on her way to work that morning. Mary did the same. During a brief break, Jo said, 'Is Randall Myers a friend of yours, Mary?'

'No. I don't know him at all. I mean, I know who he is, I see him upstairs in the reading room sometimes, but

I don't think I've exchanged two words with the fellow, except perhaps to say "Good morning" once in a while. Why?'

'Oh, he was down here yesterday and I thought he must have been looking for you.'

'Not me. It's rather more likely it was you he was after,' she said mischievously, 'I'm a bit old for him.'

Jo smiled and let the matter drop.

It was nearly six when she decided to call it a day. She packed everything up, put on her coat and assembled her folders of work for Harry and was about to walk over to the House when the phone rang.

It was the police officer in Central Lobby. 'Mr Hunter's secretary?'

'Yes.'

'The police at the barrier here. There's a constituent of Mr Hunter's here in Central Lobby who wants to see him. A Mrs Rita Hanssen. She sent a green card in and it's come back marked for your attention.'

'For my attention?' said Jo, puzzled.

'Mr Hunter's in a meeting and can't come out, so he's asked us to ring you and ask you to see her.'

'Oh, I see,' said Jo. 'Well, I'm coming over in a moment. Where will I find her?'

'Just come to the barrier in Central Lobby and we'll point her out to you.'

The barrier was a railing at the side of Central Lobby near the corridor to Members' Lobby. Behind it stood a tall desk, the top of which was illuminated by a small lamp. Standing at the desk were a police officer and a Badge Messenger. Although the Lobby was crowded with visitors, Jo was surprised to find that the police officer knew who she was and picked her out immediately. He beckoned to her. She went over to him and he said, 'Mr Hunter's visitor is sitting over there on the other side of the Lobby.' Jo looked round and saw a fair-haired young woman in a long black overcoat and black boots sitting on a bench on the far side of the Lobby. She was hunched forward, staring at the floor. 'I explained to her that Mr Hunter couldn't see her and she got very upset, really worked up,' the officer continued. 'I said that I would try to get in touch with you. But I haven't told her I've spoken to you, so if you don't want to see her, I can say you've gone home if you'd rather.'

'Oh I couldn't do that. I shall have to see her,' said Jo, 'but I'd better just go and leave these things for Mr Hunter first. I'll be back in a minute.' She hurried through to Members' Lobby and left Harry's folders in Fred's office with a note asking that they be put on Harry's desk when his meeting ended. Then she returned to Central Lobby and walked over to where Mrs Hanssen was sitting.

'Mrs Hanssen?' The woman looked up. 'Hello. I'm Mr Hunter's secretary, Joanna. We spoke on the phone last week.'

Mrs Hanssen stood up and Jo shook hands with her. We're probably about the same age, thought Jo, but she looks worn out, finished. Mrs Hanssen was thin and very pale. The mascara on her eyelashes had run slightly in places, emphasizing the dark shadows under her eyes. Jo wondered if she had been crying.

'I wanted to see Mr Hunter but the policeman said he was in a meeting and couldn't come out.'

'Yes, I'm afraid so. Can I help at all?'

'It seems no-one can help me. My solicitor says he's done all he can. Mr Hunter was the only person I could think of.'

'Would you like to tell me about it?' asked Jo. 'We could go to the canteen downstairs and have a cup of tea if you liked and you could tell me what the problem is.'

'All right. Thanks very much.' Her voice was slightly hoarse. Jo took her downstairs to the Strangers' Cafeteria

121

where they queued for a cup of tea. Jo thought Mrs Hanssen looked half starved and persuaded her to have a buttered teacake with her tea. She picked up their tray and led the way to a table in the far corner of the room. Mrs Hanssen took the seat facing into the room and sat down.

'I'm afraid I'm not familiar with the details of your case, Mrs Hanssen.' Jo stopped herself from saying that she couldn't find the file. She thought this would only undermine the poor woman further. 'Don't feel you have to tell me about it if you'd rather not. I probably can't do anything myself, but of course I can speak to Mr Hunter again for you, though I have to say he was quite emphatic that there was nothing more he could do.'

Mrs Hanssen looked down. Her jaw trembled. She kept tugging at a strand of hair behind her right ear and when, a moment later, she turned her head slightly, Jo could see a bald patch behind her ear where some hair had been pulled out.

'I've had to talk to so many people,' she began. 'I'm worn out with trying to get people to understand.' Nevertheless, once she started to explain, it all came pouring out. She told Jo about her marriage to Robert, how it had all started to go wrong soon after their second child was born. Robert had become more and more cruel, ridiculing and belittling her all the time and terrifying her with his shouting, his uncontrollable rage if she didn't meet his demands: if the food wasn't cooked to his liking, or she mismanaged the shopping and forgot some little thing, or spent too much money. He checked up on everything she did. He seemed to be insanely jealous of her. The children were frightened of him and were always trying to please him, to keep him happy. No-one else ever saw the way he behaved at home. To the oustide world he was apparently a normal husband and father. He was popular at work, enjoyed a drink or two with the lads at his local pub but never got hopelessly drunk, only a little merry, his barrister said during the custody hearing.

It had never occurred to her that her husband could get custody of the children and when she had realized what was happening, it was too late. She had been dumbfounded, horrified. The judge had awarded him temporary custody, pending his final decision. She couldn't understand this. She had expected the children to stay with her. Her solicitor had tried to reassure her, saying that the judge would look at everything very carefully before deciding finally who should have custody, but she could see that he wasn't confident about the outcome. And now the children had been with their father for months while her husband and his lawyers had dragged things out with all sorts of applications to the Court and adjournments and things she didn't understand. They'd run rings round her lawyers.

She had not told the Court at the outset about Robert's violent temper and cruelty. She hadn't even told her solicitor, for the same reason that she had never told anyone else. She was afraid that she would be seen as somehow responsible for it, as having provoked him in some way. She was afraid people would believe that she was what Robert accused her of being: an inadequate wife and mother who drove her husband to fury. She hadn't said anything about his behaviour until a later hearing when she was driven to it in frantic self-defence by his overbearing barrister.

In Court, Robert had been cool, articulate and reasonable: the model parent. He had produced statements from witnesses to support his claims that he was the better parent and that Rita was incompetent, inadequate and unpredictable. Rita, giving evidence, had fallen apart, become tearful and incoherent. There was no-one who could testify to Robert's rages because no-one else had experienced them. At the end of a gruelling cross-examination by his barrister about her performance as a mother, she had blurted out that she was afraid of her husband and afraid that he would abuse the children.

The judge had made no secret of his feelings. He had asked sarcastically why she hadn't said something much sooner. 'You had plenty of opportunity to say something about this at the outset. I rather think it's news to your solicitor and counsel as well. Such a revelation at this late stage will need to be supported by some evidence.'

But there was no-one she could ask to testify to his behaviour because no-one had ever seen it. He was only like that in the privacy of their home.

'It's terrible not to be believed,' said Rita with tears in her eyes. 'It's the worst kind of nightmare and you can never get out of it. Never.' She looked down and swallowed hard, but a single tear trickled slowly down each cheek. Jo reached across and stroked her hand.

'Don't talk any more for a moment. Have a little rest and drink some tea.' But Rita couldn't stop now. She had to tell it all.

'To have people say you're no good as a mother – I can't tell you what it's like. I love my children more than my life. I'd do anything for them. And I'm a good mother. I've protected them from his rages as best I can. I gave them fun even when things were desperate. We used to go places together and have a nice time. And they were happy, except when he got into his rages. And they've been with him now for months . . .' She stopped for a moment exhausted. But she wasn't crying any more. Her face was paler than ever. There was a hot look in her eyes. Her hands shook.

'I was so nervous. Robert's barrister, Mr Marchander, kept on and on at me until I was exhausted. And Parrie made me nervous too, the way he looked at me and interrupted me.'

'Who?' asked Jo.

'The judge.'

'Is that P-a-r-r-i-e?' asked Jo.

'Yes, I think so. Why?'

'I've come across his name somewhere before.' How strange, thought Jo. The name on Harry's notepad. I wonder who had he been talking to about Parrie? Perhaps he'd been discussing Rita Hanssen's case? No, he'd made that note while Jo was sitting in his office, waiting to tell him about Mrs Hanssen's phone call.

'You could tell from the way he spoke that the judge was impressed by Robert,' said Mrs Hanssen, 'but he didn't like me from the start. When I was giving evidence he interrupted me, told me to get on and answer the question, things like that. He was horrible. He kept looking round the room in a self-important way, as if he wanted to see the effect of his words. You should have heard the way he and my husband's barrister talked to each other. Sucking up. The judge chatted to Robert's barrister like he was an old friend or something. He even started talking about another case to him. "Do you remember that boy, Child Q, Mr Marchander?" he said. "A sad case: the parents refusing him a blood transfusion on religious grounds. I made him my personal Ward. I don't remember his name. Do you know what became of him? Oh, he died did he?"' Rita looked at Jo. 'How about that? His own Ward! He couldn't even remember his name! He didn't even know the boy had died! And a man like that can take my children away from me!'

She paused, exhausted, then continued: 'The judge renewed the order, saying he didn't accept my evidence, that I'd dreamed it up at the last moment as a desperate attempt to discredit my husband. He said that because I'd had a nervous breakdown years before, when I was arrested for shoplifting, he was worried that I was unstable. And now he'll make a final, permanent order and I'll never get my children back.'

'I'm so sorry,' said Jo. She believed Mrs Hanssen and felt deep sympathy for her.

'What is it that you wanted Mr Hunter to do? How do you think he can help?' asked Jo.

'I thought he would know what I could do to get the Court to look into my husband's behaviour, to prove that he shouldn't have custody. He ought to be examined by a psychiatrist or something. I thought Mr Hunter would know what to do. But the hearing's next Tuesday and you said he couldn't do anything about it.'

'That's right. He said he couldn't intervene and that you should speak to your solicitor.'

'My solicitor won't do anything about it. I'm on legal aid and he says I can't ask for another adjournment. It's all dragged on too long already. And I can't go to another solicitor because I won't get another legal aid certificate. And the solicitor says he can't do any more work than he's done already unless I can produce the money to pay his fees in advance.'

'I take it you can't?' said Jo.

'No. I was on income support until my husband got custody of the children. Now that's been taken away from me too.'

'I don't know what I can do, Mrs Hanssen, except speak to Mr Hunter again,' said Jo. 'I'll tell him what you've told me, I promise, and ask him if there's anything at all that can be done. Then I'll ring you. All right?'

Mrs Hanssen's gratitude was embarrassing. 'Don't thank me,' said Jo. 'And please don't get your hopes up too high.' She was feeling very uneasy already about what Harry would say and do. 'All I can do is speak to him and see what he says.'

Mrs Hanssen seemed calmer. Jo asked her if she

wouldn't rather have a fresh cup of tea as her first one had got cold. She hadn't touched her teacake.

'No thank you. You've been very kind and I've taken up a lot of your time.' She looked at her watch. 'I expect you've got to go home, haven't you?'

'Some time soon, yes,' said Jo, 'but I haven't got anything in particular that I've got to rush away for, so please don't feel you have to go.' But Mrs Hanssen stood up. 'I'd better be going now,' she said. She looked exhausted. Jo took her upstairs and walked with her to St Stephen's Entrance where she shook hands with her and said, 'I'll telephone you as soon as I've had a chance to talk to Mr Hunter. Good luck.'

'Do you know, you're the first person I've talked to about this who's believed me,' said Mrs Hanssen. 'Other people have made the right noises, said how sorry they are, said they'd do what they could to help – like the children's teachers and my doctor – but they didn't do anything. But I can see you believe me and that you care.' Jo felt slightly uneasy. Was she really the only person who believed this woman? Could she be wrong about her? Mrs Hanssen thanked her again and walked away. Jo returned to Central Lobby, deep in thought. As she passed the police officer at the barrier he said, 'Were you able to sort her out, then?'

'I doubt it,' said Jo. 'She's got terrible problems and I haven't got a magic wand, unfortunately.'

'I've seen her type before,' said the officer reflectively. He was tall, with a weather-beaten complexion; a big, handsome man. The look in his eyes was partially obscured by the shadow from his helmet, but Jo thought she could see a kindly expression, the look of detachment of a long-time observer, for whom life holds neither surprise nor disappointment.

'Have you?' said Jo. It was on the tip of her tongue to ask, 'And what might her type be?' but she decided against it.

'Yes. People who've run out of help, who come here because they've got nowhere else to go.'

'Do you see a lot of people like that?' asked Jo, depressed by this remark.

'You'd be amazed. We get them here all the time. Some of them get helped. For some there just isn't anything anyone can do,' said the police officer matter-of-factly. 'Your visitor looked to me a bit like one of those, as if she's about to crack up. She was in a right state when she arrived.'

'She's got good reason,' said Jo with feeling.

'There now, you mustn't upset yourself. You can't always help. Sometimes it's a job for someone else.'

'Just so long as there is someone else,' said Jo. 'It's too easy to pass the buck.' She remembered her dinner with Etienne. 'People ought to try to help one another, to make a difference.'

The policeman looked at her with interest. He liked what he saw and smiled at her. She thought he was being condescending, humouring her. She was about to turn away when he said, 'You know, we've got our own share of oddballs right here.'

'What do you mean?' asked Jo.

'Some of the Members,' he said, lowering his voice. 'Do you mean to say you haven't noticed?' Jo decided he was just trying to delay her, enjoying having someone to chat to. 'Why we've even had some of the Members come to blows. I remember two of them having a punch-up right here in front of me.'

'That can't have increased their standing with the public,' said Jo, imagining the scene. 'I'd better be on my way. It's time I went home.'

'It certainly is. Well it was nice talking to you. Come and see us again.'

Jo walked through to Members' Lobby and looked into the Whips' Messengers' Office. Fred was sitting at his desk with what looked like a glass of white wine in his hand. Jo's folders were no longer in front of him.

'So you took the work in to Harry? Thanks.'

'Oh yes, I gave it to him ages ago.'

'His meeting finished early then?'

'Meeting? I don't know about any meeting. They've been having a drinks party in the Whips' Office this afternoon. Weren't you invited?' he asked in a sympathetic tone.

'No. I'd have been much too busy anyway.' She tried to conceal her anger. 'What time did the party start?'

'Oh about an hour and a half ago. You ought to go in. They're having a right carry-on.'

'No thanks. I'd better be going. See you tomorrow, Fred.' She turned and hurried out of the Lobby, heading for the stairs and the exit to the underground. She heard a man's voice call, 'Jo! Wait!' She stopped and half turned on the stairs. Geoff Harper came running down after her.

'Where are you off to?'

'I'm going home.'

'I was hoping you'd got time for a drink, maybe a bite to eat.'

'I'm afraid I haven't.' Her voice was cold. She couldn't stop thinking of Rita Hanssen and her terrible despair.

'What's the matter?' said Geoff, his voice full of concern. He came down another step to stand closer to her.

'I'm sick of this place,' she said furiously, 'and all the hypocrites in it.' She turned away. 'I'm going home. Bye,' and she ran down the stairs. 'Suit yourself,' he said. He didn't call after her, but said it almost to himself, in a puzzled tone. She heard him, however, and called back, 'I will, don't worry.' She regretted her words as soon as they were out of her mouth, but it was too late. There was no point in turning back, he'd have gone by now. In fact, he had stayed where he was, hoping she would have a change of heart. Something told him that her anger wasn't really directed at him. Perhaps he could have helped her. He felt deep disappointment when he heard the sound of her footsteps as she reached the stone passageway at the foot of the stairs, turned out of the building and hurried away through the courtyard.

CHAPTER SIXTEEN

Jo's anger had cooled somewhat by the time she arrived at work the following day. Perhaps it was significant that she should be, according to Mrs Hanssen, the only person who had believed her story. Perhaps she had missed something important, or was being naive. Nevertheless she was sickened by Harry's heartless refusal to see the woman. She waited all morning for his phone call asking her to go over to his office. When eleven-thirty a.m. came and he still hadn't called, she rang him to ask if he wanted to see her, saying that she had some messages for him.

'Oh, you'd better come over now,' he said, 'I won't be able to see you this afternoon.'

She waited until he had dealt with the mail and messages. He said, 'Right, Jo, that's all, thank you. I'll see you later,' and stood up.

'It's not all, actually,' she said. 'Mrs Hanssen came here yesterday, as you know.'

'Oh yes, I sent her card out with a note for the officer at the barrier to call you. Did you deal with her?'

'What do you mean, "deal" with her? How could I

131

deal with her?' said Jo, not bothering to conceal her anger. 'I did see her. I took her downstairs and gave her a cup of tea as a matter of fact, and listened to what she had to say.'

'Well?'

'She's very upset because her case has been mishandled and she's lost custody of her children to a violent and abusive husband.'

'I told you last week that I can't get involved in it. It's purely a matter for the court.'

'But that's the point, the final decision is being made next week and she's convinced that the judge is prejudiced against her and that she won't get a fair hearing.'

'I can't interfere with the judicial process. It's not an MP's function.' He was getting annoyed now. 'And you've no business encouraging her to think that I can.'

'I didn't,' said Jo icily. 'I heard her out and said that I would speak to you about it. That's what I'm doing.'

'Then you'll just have to go back to her and say the same thing as before. If you'd worked here a bit longer you might have a better grasp of what an MP can and can't do,' he said sarcastically. Jo had kept her cool until now. This last remark was too much. She could be sarcastic too.

'It's a pity you had a drinks party yesterday and weren't able to spare a few minutes to see her yourself,' she said and stood up. A change came over Harry. She was surprised to hear a placatory tone in his voice.

'Now, now, you mustn't upset yourself. Laura will explain to you, I'm sure, that one of the difficulties about this job is that people expect and hope for much more of you than you are able to give.' He got up to accompany her to the door and opened it for her. 'Also, you must realize that the Courts wouldn't deprive a mother of custody without very good reason.' He gave an ingratiating smile and said, 'I'll see you later.' She did not reply and walked through the outer office aware of the presence of a number of the Whips, including Jack, but determined not to let any of them catch her eye. As she entered Members' Lobby she saw Geoff walking in her direction. She started towards him, intending to speak to him, but a man hurried up and engaged him in conversation. She would have liked the chance to apologize for her rudeness the previous evening. He looked at her intently as she walked away.

Jo dreaded having to speak to Mrs Hanssen. She decided to ring her immediately. She imagined the poor woman waiting to hear from her, hoping for help. She was surprised to hear Mrs Hanssen's voice on an answering machine, sounding calm and efficient. Was this an old recording or a recent one? she wondered. She tried several times during the day, with the same result. She didn't leave a message, however. Somehow it didn't seem the right thing to do; she felt she must speak to her in person. However, when she rang the following morning and once again got the answering machine, Jo decided she had no choice. She floundered a little, not having prepared a message in advance, and repeated herself, but Mrs Hanssen would have been in no doubt about Harry's response: there was nothing further he could do. Jo dressed it up a little, saying she had 'discussed' the matter with him and that he was 'very sorry' he couldn't help. She tried to soften the blow with her own words, wishing Mrs Hanssen luck and saying she would be thinking of her.

For the rest of the day, every time the phone rang, Jo expected to hear Mrs Hanssen's voice. However, she didn't call. Nor was there a call from her the next day. Jo decided that no news was good news. Perhaps Mrs Hanssen had found someone else who would help. Perhaps her solicitor had come up with something after all. Jo put the matter out of her mind without too much difficulty, being burdened with a huge amount of work.

On the Friday morning, she remembered Mrs Hunter's request, but decided she could get away with leaving the visit to the flat until the following week. After all, who was to know that she hadn't been round?

When Tuesday came, Jo found she couldn't get Rita Hanssen out of her mind. She imagined her in Court, waiting to know her fate. Would she have to give evidence again, or was it just to be a pronouncement by the judge? How would Mrs Hanssen cope if she had to give evidence again? Would she become overwrought, or confused? Would she become incoherent, unable to answer questions? Of course she'd have her solicitor with her. He would explain what was required of her and be on hand to reassure her.

Jo was surprised Mrs Hanssen hadn't telephoned. She'd been convinced she would. Would she telephone to let her know the outcome? When would the hearing end? Jo had forgotten to ask her these questions. But she heard nothing from her that day or the next.

On the Thursday morning, Jo decided she could no longer put off going to the flat. Although Mrs Hunter was safely out of the way in America, she was quite capable of ringing to check up on things. However, it proved to be another wasted journey. There was no sign of the son having been in and no messages or letters.

When Jo returned home, she found Lydia waiting to ask if she would like to make up a foursome with her and a couple of friends. They were going to see a film and have dinner afterwards. Jo was glad to go and enjoyed her evening though she could have done without the party continuing afterwards back at the flat. It was clear that the two men were hoping for more than just the pleasure of their company for dinner. Jo announced that she had to get up early for work the following day, even if they didn't, and wished them goodnight. Their drunken laughter kept her awake until the small hours. At about two a.m. she heard Lydia shooing them out and finally fell asleep.

When she got up the following morning, Lydia had already gone. On the hall table there was a video camera with a note pushed under the strap.

'Dear Jo, I forgot to ask you last night if you would be very kind and take this to the shop where I bought it and ask them to repair it. I hoped you wouldn't mind as the shop's in Victoria Street, not far from your office. I didn't have time and won't get a chance for another couple of weeks. It would be great if you could do it. Love, Lydia.' She'd pinned the invoice to the back of the note.

Jo sighed. Well I'm not doing it today, she thought, putting the note and invoice in her bag. It can wait till next week. But when Monday came, she forgot the camera. It was a grey, oppressive morning and she was depressed by the prospect of the inevitable mountain of paperwork.

She collected her mail and called in at the Whips' Office to ask Harry when he would like to see her. She opened the door to see Roy Phillips standing in the middle of the room, reading aloud from a newspaper, with Charlie Culver standing next to him, looking at the article. Andrew Oxley and Steve Lisle who were sitting at their desks were facing them, listening. Andrew Oxley was leaning forward, scowling.

'"The government must be made to come clean—"'

Roy looked up and saw Jo. No-one spoke. It was obvious they had been talking about the latest news, the pollution of a river and reservoir with a highly toxic chemical that was threatening the water supply of thousands of people. Several newspapers had accused the government of having prior knowledge of the risk and of doing nothing about it because of the involvement of one of their MPs in the company, a multinational that now controlled several utilities and was rumoured to have donated hundreds of thousands of pounds to the Party.

'Good morning,' said Jo, with exaggerated cheeriness. 'Don't let me interrupt you. Is Harry in?'

'Jack's with him at the moment, but you can go on in,' said Steve.

Harry's door was open and Jack was standing in the doorway, with his back to Jo, his hand on the edge of the door. Jo heard Harry say, 'It won't be easy, but we'll have to give it a try, or he could end up inside.'

Jack must have heard Jo approaching. He glanced over his shoulder, saw Jo and turned back to Harry. 'Jo's here,' he said. Jo heard Harry respond but he had lowered his voice and she couldn't make out the words.

'You can go in,' said Jack, standing back to let Jo pass. 'I'll have a word with him and report back shortly,' he said to Harry and shut the door behind him.

Harry folded up a piece of paper he had been reading and placed it in his inside jacket pocket. He was frowning. 'Good morning, Jo,' he said.

'I only came to ask when you would like to see me today.' He stared at her, clearly thinking about something else.

'Oh yes.' He looked at his watch. 'Come over at half-past twelve, would you. I can't do anything now.' He picked up the phone and started to dial a number. Jo left him to it. It looked as if all the Whips were now in the main office. There was a hubbub of conversation and Jo heard Andrew Oxley saying, 'Another health scare is all we need right now!' and Eddie Mallins said, 'This one will be harder to get away with than the last.'

As she walked back to her office, she wondered who it was that Harry thought could end up in prison. An MP? How her feelings about the place had changed in just a few weeks! The trappings and traditions of Parliament which she had found so intriguing at the beginning now seemed an elaborate façade to a diseased and crumbling institution. She had a growing feeling of unease about working for Harry, a sense of a squalid, even sinister undercurrent to his activities.

These thoughts depressed her further. It would be a relief when the time came to go home. She was about to make a start on her work when Laura telephoned.

'Ann's not feeling well, and I'm snowed under, so we've decided to give lunch a miss tomorrow and perhaps meet up on Thursday. What do you think?'

'That's fine by me,' said Jo.

'You sound a bit down. Anything wrong?'

Jo felt unequal to the task of explaining. 'I'm not cut out for this kind of work, as I suspected at the outset.'

'You're probably just having a bad day and you'll feel differently tomorrow.'

'Maybe.'

'Well, see how it goes. If I can do anything, ring me,' said Laura. She was about to hang up when she had an idea. 'I'll tell you what, Jo. Why don't we meet for a drink this evening, when you've finished your work? I shall be staying quite late today.'

'OK,' said Jo. 'Thanks. Shall I meet you in Central Lobby? I don't know where your room is.'

'You've not been over here yet, have you? And you haven't met Charles either. You'll like him. He's a sweetie,' said Laura. 'Why don't you give me a ring when you're ready, or you could ring me from the barrier when you come over to Central Lobby, and I'll come and get you. If Charles is about you can come and meet him. If not, we'll go off and have a drink in the staff bar. How about it?'

'Thanks, Laura. I'll see you later.'

Jo went over to the Whips' Office again at half-past twelve and found Jack alone, sitting on a sofa with a glass beside him and a cigarette in his hand. 'Hello, Jo. What can I do for you?'

'Harry asked me to come over,' said Jo.

'Well he's not here and there's no point in waiting.' Jack sounded as if he had had a lot to drink. 'He's over at Number Ten and won't be back for some time. Would you care for a drink?'

'No thanks, Jack.'

'You run along, my dear, and enjoy yourself. You're much too good for this place.' He smiled at her and raised his glass in salute before putting it to his lips and swigging the contents. 'I'll tell him you were here.'

When Laura met Jo in Central Lobby that evening she said, 'Let's go up to my room. Charles is in the Chamber at the moment but he'll be taking a break soon and we'll go and look in on him.'

She took Jo up to Ian Swift's room. As they reached the door, she pointed along the corridor. 'The Ways and Means Office is along there. Charles has a room next door. He'll be up in a few minutes and we'll go and see him briefly. Come on in here and sit down.' She made Jo sit in a comfortable armchair and put her feet up while she put her papers away.

'What do you think of my room?' asked Laura.

'Not bad. It's pretty small, isn't it? And isn't it quiet up here? Don't you feel a bit cut off?'

'Not a bit of it. Quite the opposite in fact.' At that moment, the door opened and a man looked into the room. 'Hello Laura,' he said, then saw Jo, 'Oh I didn't realize you had company. I'll come back another time.'

'OK, John,' said Laura and the visitor disappeared. 'See what I mean? That's one of the nice things about being here. People look in on me from time to time. Various friends drop in for a gossip.'

She replaced files in the cabinet behind her, tidied her desk, then checked the time on the television screen in the corner of the room.

'Let's go and see if Charles is in his room,' said Laura

and led the way along the corridor. She knocked on a door and opened it.

'Can we come in?' she said. 'Of course,' replied the man sitting at the desk at the far end of the room. Jo followed Laura into the room and shut the door behind her.

'I brought Jo up to see where I work and thought I'd bring her in to say hello. D'you remember, I mentioned she was standing in for Harry Hunter's secretary.' She turned to Jo, 'This is Sir Charles Donaldson. Jo Delvere.'

He was not prepossessing: average height and build, a pale, rather tired, round face and receding silvery-grey hair, dark-brown eyes; but an alert, keen look. He got up and came round from behind his desk to shake hands with Jo. He had a soft, mellow voice and an attractive smile. 'I remember. Laura disappeared for a morning, supposedly looking after a constituent, several mornings in fact, when you started. How d'you do, Jo.'

'Jo's finding it all a bit much, poor girl. I'm about to take her down to the staff bar in the Lords for a drink, to cheer her up,' said Laura.

'I'm just about to have a sherry,' said Sir Charles. 'Would you care to join me?'

'We'd love to,' said Laura, flopping into an armchair, 'wouldn't we, Jo?'

'Certainly,' she replied, still standing. Sir Charles went to a cupboard at the side of the room and got out a decanter and glasses. He poured three drinks and handed a glass to Jo. 'Why don't you sit down over here, Jo?' He pointed to another armchair. He handed a glass to Laura and took one for himself. 'Your good health.'

'Cheers,' said Laura. 'This is just what I need.'

'I haven't got long, I'm afraid,' said Sir Charles, walking round behind his desk and sitting down again. 'I've got a meeting in about ten minutes' time.' A clerk came into the room with a folder, which he handed across the desk to Sir Charles. He went out again.

'Laura's been running my life here for years, haven't you?' He looked appreciatively at Laura, 'And I think she knows as much about Parliament and about my constituency as I do.'

'Slight exaggeration,' said Laura, evidently not meaning it. 'I wanted Jo to meet you, to prove to her that there are some nice people in this place, doing the job for the right reasons.'

He laughed. 'What are the right reasons, Laura?'

'Doing it for the good of the country rather than personal advantage.'

'Meet the Charles Donaldson fan club: membership one,' he said and laughed again. He leaned back in his chair. He looked at Laura who smiled back at him. Jo caught the warmth of the exchange. Clearly he was fond of her and she of him. She wondered if there was more to it than that.

Sir Charles looked at Jo. 'The thing about Parliament is that many of the people who come here arrive full of zeal and ambition and determination to change the world. They quickly find that their personal impact is limited and after a year or two, they've settled for a lesser role. People find they have different reasons for doing things.'

'I find that rather disappointing,' said Jo.

'People run out of energy as they get older. The unexpected happens: personal problems, health problems. Only a few individuals, perhaps through luck as much as talent, make a difference. Most of us manage to make a contribution only by acting collectively.'

'Do people act collectively?' asked Jo. 'You get the impression, certainly from the outside, that some people are in it for what they can get out of it personally, just looking after their own interests.'

'People make the mistake of generalizing about

140

politicians,' he replied. 'That's partly our own fault of course and partly the effect of televising the proceedings – not that I'm against that. But if you were to study the place for some time you'd see that there's every kind of personality here: good, bad and indifferent, just like society at large.'

'Except that there are hardly any women,' said Laura acidly. 'And as for acting collectively, the only time we see that happen is in the annual vote to increase MPs' salaries.'

'Oh come now, Laura, that's not really fair, is it?' he said mildly.

They sat in silence for a moment, sipping their sherry.

'So you're not very happy here, Jo?' asked Sir Charles.

'It's not that exactly,' she replied. 'I enjoy some aspects of the job. It's just that it seems there are quite a lot of people whom the system fails completely and I'm not sure anyone cares too much about that.'

'You sound like Laura,' he said.

'You said just now there are good, bad and indifferent here,' said Jo. 'The good and the indifferent I can take. But if they're bad – I mean in a moral sense – should they be here?' asked Jo. 'And if they do anything bad, are they punished, or do they get away with it? Take this pollution scandal. If what the media are saying is true, will anyone be punished?'

'It remains to be seen whether it's true,' said Sir Charles cautiously. 'If it is, I agree with you, something should be done about it and those responsible should be punished. It would be very damaging to public confidence if they weren't.'

They were silent again, then Sir Charles said, 'You know, you two girls are rather alike in a number of ways. Has anyone ever told you?'

'It's funny you should say that,' said Laura, 'as a matter of fact Jo's—' but before she could continue the door opened and the clerk came in again. He said, 'I'm afraid you're going to be late for your appointment, Sir Charles.'

He stood up. 'I'm sorry we can't continue our conversation. You must bring Jo to see me again, Laura.'

Jo stood up. 'You two don't have to rush off,' he said motioning to her to sit down again. 'Finish your drinks.' He left the room.

Laura stretched out in her armchair and looked at Jo. 'See what I mean? Not a bad old stick, I think you'll agree.' She got up and poured them each a little more sherry. 'He'll probably notice, but he won't mind,' she said and sat down again. 'What would you say to a meal?'

'I don't usually say anything to my food: I eat it.'

'Very funny. I've got my car downstairs. Why don't we trundle down to it and go somewhere for something to eat?'

'Good idea,' said Jo. Three-quarters of an hour later they were sitting in an Italian restaurant not far from Laura's house. They consumed rather too much wine with their meal, swapping stories about work, friends and lovers, though Jo noticed that Laura spoke only of past relationships. Jo balked at asking outright whether she was involved with anyone now.

'I think you'll agree I couldn't drive you home,' said Laura. 'Why don't you stay the night?'

'Good idea.' It was after midnight by the time they got back to Laura's, but instead of going to bed, they had another bottle of wine and talked into the small hours.

CHAPTER SEVENTEEN

When Laura's alarm clock went off at a quarter to eight Jo was deeply asleep. She dragged herself reluctantly from her bed, her head aching and her mouth dry. She found Laura in the kitchen, looking puffy-eyed but cheerful.

Jo groaned. 'How on earth do you manage to look so amazingly energetic? Don't you have a hangover?'

'No. I feel quite good, as a matter of fact, though I could do with about ten hours' sleep. What about you?'

'I feel awful,' said Jo.

'I have to say you look it too,' said Laura heartlessly, 'but I'm afraid if you want a lift with me you're going to have to get a move on. Help yourself to some toast or something. I'm going to have a shower.'

Jo's headache persisted and she was glad to have a lift from Laura. She sat in silence for most of the journey, feeling queasy and wondering how she would get through the day. Laura was maddeningly cheerful.

'I can only conclude from your air of well-being that you must do this sort of thing regularly,' said Jo.

As they walked into Members' Lobby, heading for the

Post Office, Laura nudged Jo. 'There you are. I'll bet they're arranging a date.' Jo followed her gaze across the Lobby and saw Harry Hunter in close conversation with Jane Templeman. Harry was asking her something. Jane looked at her watch and smiled at him. She said something, made a small gesture with her hand, a private goodbye, and hurried away. He turned to go into the Whips' Office, unaware of Laura and Jo watching him.

'Maybe it's my hangover,' said Jo, 'but the very thought of a date with him makes me feel sick.'

'I don't think it's likely to happen, somehow,' said Laura with a laugh. She looked at Jo in concern. 'I'll find you an aspirin or paracetamol or something after we've collected our mail.'

She was as good as her word and by the time Jo had made herself a coffee she was feeling slightly better. She felt better still when Harry rang and said he wouldn't be able to see her until late afternoon. The sky had been overcast earlier in the morning, but now sunlight streamed through the window next to her. She opened her mail, starting as usual with the letters and putting the newspapers, magazines and circulars to one side. Having assembled all the correspondence for Harry's attention and got out various files to take over to his office, she decided to open the rest of the mail. Usually she left the magazines and circulars until she had finished her typing, but she didn't feel like making a start on that yet.

She tore the wrapper off the copy of the local newspaper from Harry's constituency and was about to place it, unread, next to the pile of correspondence when her eye was caught by the words 'TRAGIC DEATH . . .' She couldn't see the rest of the headline, because the newspaper was folded in half. She opened it out flat. The full headline was 'TRAGIC DEATH OF YOUNG MOTHER'. Jo read the article, feeling herself go cold. She put her hands up to the sides of her head and groaned, 'Oh God! No, not Rita!'

Rita had killed herself with an overdose of paracetamol. The article said, 'Mrs Hanssen was known to have been suffering from depression since losing custody of her children . . .' No wonder Jo hadn't heard from her. A coroner's inquest had recorded her death as suicide. Jo rested her elbows on her desk, her head in her hands. She could see Rita clearly in her mind's eye. If only I'd spoken to her, she thought. I should have spoken to her. I should have found some way to get hold of her. I should have asked the name of her solicitor and spoken to him.

She was overwhelmed with regret and sadness. Poor Rita. Her poor children. What a stinking system!

Mary came into the room. 'Good morning, Jo,' she said cheerily. Then she saw the expression on Jo's face.

'Jo. What's up? Are you all right?'

Jo felt unable to talk about Rita. 'I don't feel very well,' she said.

'I think you ought to go home,' said Mary.

'I think I will.' Jo rang Fred in the Whips' Messengers' Office. 'I can't get through to Mr Hunter,' she lied. 'Could you put a note on his desk saying that I'm not well and I've had to go home?'

By the time she got home, her grief for Rita had been supplanted by fury at Harry's callous indifference to her case, mingled with anger at herself for colluding with it. I can't go on with this. I must go back to doing something worthwhile.

She opened her wardrobe and looked at her clothes. I'm glad I didn't bring much with me. It wouldn't take long to pack. I could just go and get on a plane today and to hell with the lot of them. She took her passport out of her bedside table, stood with it in her hand, thinking. She put it in her handbag, then sat down again. What am I doing? I can't just walk out. It wouldn't be fair to Laura. And what would it achieve?

She decided to lie down for a while. She got into bed and tried to read, but sleep overcame her within a short time.

She awoke much later. It was that time of day which often made her feel nostalgic. There was a hint of sunset behind the clouds and the yellowing evening light cast long, low beams into the darkened room. How could she have slept so long? Then the morning's events came back to her. She rolled onto her back and lay still, staring at the ceiling and thinking of Rita's shattered life, trying to imagine what her feelings and thoughts must have been as she set about swallowing a lethal dose of tablets. She thought of Donald, his life cut short. Not many weeks ago she had felt that life had no more purpose for her. Now she was not so sure. She was certain she could not do what Rita had done. Supposing my life were to be cut short, as Donald's was, maybe in a traffic accident? Would it matter? 'I don't want to die,' she said out loud and sat up, swinging her legs out of bed. 'I want to go on living, but not like this.'

The phone rang and she went out into the hall to answer it. Lydia's video camera was still on the table. I must do something about that tomorrow, without fail, she thought as she reached for the phone.

'Hi, Jo, it's only me,' said Laura's voice, 'are you all right?'

'Much better now, thanks. I've been asleep most of the day.'

'I rang your office and when I couldn't get you I spoke to Vic. He said you'd gone home looking very unwell.'

'It wasn't just a hangover,' said Jo. She told Laura about Rita.

'Oh, Jo, how terrible. The poor woman. How dreadful. Those poor children.'

'I keep thinking that I could have done something to prevent it if I'd tried a bit harder,' said Jo.

'You mustn't blame yourself,' Laura protested. 'Didn't you say she'd had a breakdown before? She may have been headed for this for a long time. If anyone's to blame, it's the judge, maybe Harry too, but not you. You tried. Look, Jo – God, what on earth's that racket?' Laura was being deafened by a siren. It was so loud that Jo could hear it over the phone.

'What's going on?'

'I'm not sure,' Laura was puzzled. 'It sounds a bit like an air-raid warning doesn't it? No, come to think of it, it's more like a flood alert. But it can't be.' Laura paused. 'Now the division bell's ringing as well.' She turned to look at the television screen behind her. 'It says "Sitting suspended" on the screen. That's unusual.'

'Why? What does it mean?'

'The Speaker has suspended the sitting of the House. The debate's interrupted. Everything stops until he decides it can start again. I wonder what's going on?'

'Isn't it time you were going home, anyway, Laura?' asked Jo.

'Soon, I suppose. Now what! I've never seen that before!'

'What?'

'Now it says "ALERT" on the screen. One thing I'm definitely not. I'd better go and find out what's up. I'll talk to you later. You take it easy.'

Laura grabbed her coat and bag and emerged from her room to find the corridor full of people heading for the stairs. It transpired that the entire Houses of Parliament were being evacuated because of a bomb warning. There had been bomb scares lots of times over the years but this was different. Laura could recall occasions when the police had received warnings and had had to close St Stephen's Entrance and check the building minutely, only to find that the call had been a hoax. She couldn't remember the entire building ever having been evacuated.

They were directed away from the Chamber and Lobbies, down a back staircase into Speaker's Court, in front of the Speaker's House where they were told to walk through New Palace Yard into Parliament Square.

In the Government Whips' Office, as elsewhere, Members were hastily putting things away, grabbing papers and possessions of importance or value and heading for the door. Harry had been listening to Charlie Culver's report on a Backbench Committee meeting that had just finished. After Charlie had left him, he had opened the safe behind his desk and removed a book. He was in the process of writing an entry in it when Jack Bendall put his head round the door and said, 'Bomb scare. A big one apparently. We've got to clear the building. Bowerbridge thinks it could be somewhere near the Chamber, so no hanging about and bring anything really important with you.'

He hadn't waited for Harry's response. Harry had hesitated for a moment, then swivelled round in his chair and locked the safe, picked up the book and various files from his desk, thrust them hurriedly into his black briefcase and joined the throng of Members walking down the staircase to Members' Entrance.

Emerging into New Palace Yard, Laura could see groups of MPs hurrying out of Members' Entrance and turning to look back at the building as if they expected it to disintegrate before their eyes. Laura saw the Chief Whip and a group of Ministers, all carrying papers and briefcases, talking earnestly as they hurried in the direction of Ten Downing Street.

Sirens could be heard all around as fire engines converged on the Palace of Westminster from all directions. They roared into New Palace Yard and lined up along the Embankment. Laura, standing outside on the pavement with an ever growing crowd of secretaries and Palace staff, counted eleven fire engines. Army bomb-squad vehicles drove into New Palace Yard and soldiers ran into the building. More sirens could be heard in the distance. Ambulances arrived. Crowds of sightseers grew on both sides of Parliament Square and the police put up barricades to hold them back.

'Can I go down to the car-park to get my car?' Laura asked a young constable on duty at the gates to New Palace Yard.

'No, madam, I'm afraid you can't. Not yet anyway.'

'What's happened exactly?'

'There's been a tip-off that there's a bomb actually in the Houses of Parliament – a big one, so they say. So we can't take any chances.' Laura shivered.

'I wouldn't hang about here, madam,' the young constable added. Laura smiled at him. Funny how the old ones always call me miss and the young ones always call me madam, she thought. As she walked through the gateway she saw Ann on the other side of the road and went over to her.

'I'm just off to meet Tim,' said Ann, looking worried. 'Why don't you come too, Laura? We can't stay here. Perhaps we could all go for a drink somewhere.'

Tim was waiting for them at the entrance to the Cabinet Office. Whitehall was cordoned off so the three of them walked round to a pub in Victoria Street.

'I'm surprised the place is so empty,' said Tim, 'I'd have thought it would be busy at this time of day.' There was only one other customer at the bar. 'I suppose people have either joined the crowd in Parliament Square or cleared off home. Are you all right, darling?' He looked anxiously at Ann.

'I took the call from the Palace exchange that they'd had a warning about a bomb. They rang the police of course and our office too so that the Speaker could be informed immediately. The Deputy Serjeant had to rush through to the Chamber and tell the Serjeant-at-Arms.

After I'd told him and he'd gone haring out, I felt quite peculiar. Awful actually. I suddenly imagined hundreds of people being injured, not being able to get out.'

'Poor darling. I'm not surprised. I would have done too, I'm sure.' He held her hand. 'Let's get you something to drink.' He got drinks for the three of them and they sat down at a small table at the side of the room.

'I feel fine now,' said Ann. 'I just hate waiting for the bang. When I was a child, I always hated people shooting. I'd cover my ears, but I'd still jump when a gun went off. I feel the same now. Silly, isn't it?'

'We probably wouldn't hear it from here anyway,' said Laura, knowing that this wasn't strictly true. 'Try to forget about it. How's everything going with you, Tim?' she asked, to change the subject. 'Are you still doing your James Bond bit for the Cabinet Office?'

'More like a stand-in for Miss Moneypenny,' said Tim. 'Actually, strictly between ourselves, we've been expecting trouble for a few days now.'

'Really? That doesn't exactly inspire confidence. I would have thought if you were expecting trouble, security would have been tightened up and no-one would have been able to get a bomb near the Houses of Parliament.'

'Who says they have? This is probably just a hoax. An attempt to give the Government the jitters.'

'Who's supposed to be behind it?' asked Ann.

'I can't really tell you very much, but we've been expecting an attempt to interfere with the arrangements for the peace conference.'

They were silent for a while. All three of them listening, waiting. Twice they heard sirens in Victoria Street as yet more emergency vehicles raced towards Parliament Square.

Laura looked at her watch. 'Do you think the sitting will be resumed, Ann?' she asked. 'I'm wondering whether I should bother to go back to my office or just go on home from here. What do you think?'

'The Serjeant-at-Arms said it wouldn't be resumed because it would take so long to do a complete check of the building. I wouldn't bother to go back if I were you.'

'I was hoping to get my car. I shall miss it tomorrow morning.'

'Me too,' said Ann. 'I had to leave ours. Just think how good the exercise will be for us.'

They finished their drinks and walked out into Victoria Street.

'Isn't that Harry Hunter crossing the road?' said Tim. 'I wonder where he's off to in such a hurry.' It was indeed the Government Chief Whip, rolled umbrella in one hand, briefcase in the other, striding purposefully across the road. 'You'd think he'd be using a government car, especially on a night like tonight.'

'I suppose he's going to his flat in Ashdon Gardens,' said Laura.

'I didn't know he had a flat in Ashdon Gardens,' said Tim in surprise. 'I thought he and his wife lived at Number Twelve?'

'According to Jo, they've got a flat there which their son and daughter use. I rather think our Harry uses it too. Would you say he looks like a man on his way to a lover's tryst?'

'Complete with brolly and briefcase,' said Ann. 'Not my idea of a romantic figure, but it takes all sorts, I suppose.'

'What suspicious minds you women have,' said Tim. 'Come on, let's get home.' He took Ann's hand. 'Goodbye, Laura, it was good to see you.' He and Ann set off at a brisk pace up Victoria Street. Laura paused on the corner and flagged the first taxi that came along. To hell with exercise, she said to herself.

★   ★   ★

Just after nine o'clock that night a massive explosion rocked Westminster.

In Ashdon Gardens the explosion sounded very loud: a terrifying sound, so deep as to be felt as much as heard. Harry rolled away from Jane and sat up in bed. 'Christ! Listen to that,' he exclaimed. 'We must get out of here. They'll be expecting me to be at Number Twelve. Quick! Get up!'

He was out of bed, dragging on his clothes. Jane said, peevishly, 'What about the rest of our food? I was looking forward to it.'

'Well you can't have it here. I'll have to get back. You can take it with you, but for God's sake get a move on.'

She got out of bed unhurriedly and was dressed before him. At times like this he really infuriated her. He was great in bed, generous when he had a mind to be and good company when he was on form. But the minute his responsibilities overawed him and he switched into his statesman role he became maddening to her. She felt tempted to say, 'World War Three will start whether you're there or not,' but decided against it. She went into the kitchen, retrieved the carrier bag in which she had brought their supper, and packed up the remains of their meal. He can clear up the mess himself, she thought and turned out the kitchen light as he appeared behind her.

'Ready?'

'Yes.' He was so anxious about his job and his status that she felt sorry for him. She smiled at him.

'Thanks for being so nice about it, Jane.' He leant forward and kissed her. 'I'll make it up to you another time. Promise.'

He had his keys in one hand. He took his umbrella from the coat stand and opened the door for her, carefully locking up while she waited on the landing.

'Usual drill?' he murmured.

'OK. Bye,' she whispered. He left ahead of her, hurrying down the stairs. She waited until she heard the street door close behind him before she too descended the staircase and left. Who does he think he's kidding? she thought, bored and irritated by his petty attempt at secrecy.

Laura had just climbed out of a hot bath and wrapped herself in a towel when Jo rang her.

'Have you heard the news?'

'No. What news?'

'It was just on television.' Jo sounded breathless. 'A bomb's gone off in Westminster. I don't know whether it was in the Houses of Parliament, or where it was. I just wanted to make sure you weren't there when it happened.'

'No, I'm fine thanks, Jo. I've been here for ages.' She reached across to turn on her television. She watched for a moment.

'They're just saying that it was in the new Parliamentary block. I think I'll watch for a while and see what's happened if you don't mind. Thanks for letting me know.'

'That's OK, Laura. I'll talk to you tomorrow.'

'OK, Jo. Are you all right?'

'I'm fine, thanks. Bye.'

CHAPTER EIGHTEEN

Jo woke very early the next morning. It was still dark. She turned on her bedside light and looked at her alarm clock: a quarter to five. She turned out the light and lay in the dark, thinking of Donald's death, of last night's bomb explosion, of the needless suffering everywhere and the cruelty of mankind. Her thoughts returned to Rita. She had felt a profound sympathy with her over the loss of her children, perhaps because of her own continuing sorrow at not having had Donald's children. In a curious way, Rita's and Donald's deaths had become linked in her mind. Both had been cut down by an uncaring and cruel world.

She tried to banish such thoughts by turning on the light and reading for a while, but when she switched the light off again sleep evaded her, so she got up and killed time by cleaning the flat. Dusting the hall table, she noticed Lydia's video camera again. If she didn't take it to be repaired soon Lydia would have to take it herself. She went to her bedroom cupboard, got out her large shoulder bag and put the camera inside it. She couldn't be bothered to transfer everything from her handbag so as to have just one bag to carry. In any case, when she'd dropped the camera off she could fold up the big bag and put it inside her handbag. She had a shower and dressed and listened to the seven o'clock news on the radio. The new Parliamentary block had been severely damaged. Two security guards and a police officer had been injured but it was believed their injuries were not serious.

Jo decided she might as well go to work. She closed the front door behind her and hesitated, her face tingling in the cold air. Should she walk to the tube? Take a bus? It was bitterly cold. The cobblestones and the row of cars parked in the mews were rimed with frost. It was very quiet. There was a hard, expectant stillness in the air. Each breath she took materialized before her, wavered and reluctantly dissolved to nothing, as if to emphasize her indecision. It's not like a spring morning, more like December, she thought, remembering Christmas mornings in childhood. I'll walk to work, she decided, and set off for the Embankment.

The stillness and quiet were an illusion which vanished the moment she left the mews; the morning roar of traffic was just as it always was. Her morbid thoughts persisted. She found herself remembering suffering she had seen. Was I stronger then? she wondered. It seems harder to bear as I get older, not easier. She tried to imagine the streets of London silenced by war, without traffic save for occasional military vehicles, the silence shattered only by artillery bombardment, or sniper fire, or people crying.

When she reached the Embankment, she started to feel better, even though the roar of traffic was as oppressive as before. The sight of the river was soothing. The morning sky was full of promise: the layers of low dark cloud above the eastern horizon were streaked with glowing reds and pinks. As she walked along the Embankment, the distant clouds slowly lifted, separated and darkened as a blazing light spread out beneath them, making the river shimmer and dazzle. By the time she reached Lambeth Bridge, the city was bright with pale sunlight, the clouds far above.

The traffic was even worse than usual. It was barely crawling along the Embankment below Chelsea Bridge and Jo noted with satisfaction that she was making more rapid progress on foot than all these people in their cars and coaches. At the Lambeth Bridge roundabout the reason for the traffic jams became apparent. There was a police barricade across the Embankment and traffic was being diverted down Horseferry Road. Of course, there would be very tight security because of the bomb, she realized.

Her walk had given her an appetite and she was still so early for work she decided to stop for some breakfast. She turned down Horseferry Road, heading for a little café not far from her office. Its windows were steamed up but she could make out the figures of people sitting at tables. She opened the door and stepped into a cosy fug. A waiter ushered her to a table and lent her a morning paper to read over her coffee and croissant. It told her little more than had been given out on the news, but had spectacular and disturbing photographs of the damage to the new Parliamentary block. There was to be a special Cabinet meeting that morning to discuss security.

As she was paying her bill, she noticed Patricia Hunter's flat keys in her purse. She ought to go round and check the flat at some stage. She hesitated, wondering whether to go straight there now. It wouldn't take long. No, Harry might be trying to get hold of her. She'd better go in to work first.

'You're an early bird,' said Dave as she entered the building. He and Vic were sitting together in their room by the hallway. 'But you're not the first in. Lord

Hemsley's secretary's downstairs.'

'I suppose you were here last night, weren't you, Dave?' said Jo. 'What was it like? The bomb, I mean. Was it very loud?'

'It certainly was. Massive. The whole building shook. I'm glad I wasn't any nearer. It must have been terrible for the people on duty over there.'

'Some of them were hurt, weren't they?'

'Yes, but we don't know how bad yet,' said Vic.

'Well I'm glad we've got you keeping an eye on things for us – and it's nice to have that security camera too,' said Jo, looking at the screen behind the two men, which gave a view of the street. 'I'd better be going. See you later.'

Jo went down to her room, determined to catch up on some of the work she had missed the previous day. At half-past nine she got her security pass out of her bag and walked over to the House. She didn't bother with her coat. The day was turning out quite mild and she was cheered by the warmth of the sunlight.

After collecting her post, she went into the Whips' Office. Jack was the only person in the room. He greeted her enthusiastically.

'You're looking terrific, Joanna, a sight for sore eyes.'

'Thanks, Jack. Is Harry about?'

'No, he's over at Number Ten.'

'I was wondering whether he'd need to see me this morning.'

'No chance of that. He'll be in a Cabinet meeting this morning. What with one thing and another he won't have time for you until much later on, I shouldn't think.'

'Thanks. I'll give him a ring later.'

As she left the Whips' Office she almost collided with Geoff Harper.

'Sorry, Geoff. How are you?' She was determined to make up for her rudeness of the other evening.

'Not as well as you, I think.' He stopped himself. I sound just like all the other phoneys in this place, he thought. My God, she's as changeable as the weather, unpredictable but exciting. Jo was wearing a straight dark-blue skirt, dark tights, low-heeled shoes and a scarlet sweater over a white blouse. No jewellery, hardly any make-up. The slight shadows of fatigue beneath her eyes seemed to enhance rather than detract from their shape and colour. What beautiful eyes, he thought. She looks so serious, more unapproachable than ever.

Jo surprised him by saying, 'I hope you were nowhere close at hand when the bomb went off.'

'As a matter of fact I was at a press conference at Number Ten. It felt as if it had gone off almost beneath our feet.'

'How awful,' said Jo with feeling. 'But I suppose you've been in enough trouble spots not to have been frightened. I would have been petrified.'

For a moment he was afraid she was being sarcastic, then he saw the anxiety in her expression.

'Who wouldn't be? I don't think you can ever get used to that kind of thing. I've heard some big bangs in my time but that took some beating. There was absolute silence immediately afterwards. There's a kind of deafening, ringing silence as if your whole body is resounding from the explosion. We all just stared at each other. I had to suppress an awful desire to laugh because we'd just been told how wonderful our security measures were, that the Palace of Westminster had been searched and it would be business as usual today, when the thing went off. The PM's Press Secretary was totally at a loss for a while, which for him is quite something.'

Jo was smiling at him. He said, 'I'm not going to ask you to come and have a coffee with me because I know you'd refuse.'

'I'd love to another time,' she replied, 'but I've got to run some errands and get some work done by lunchtime.' I wonder if she really means it, he thought. 'I can see you don't believe me,' she added. 'I can't say I blame you.'

CHAPTER NINETEEN

At eleven-thirty, Jo stopped work again, picked up her bags and set off for Victoria Street. She would call at the Hunters' flat on the way to the camera shop.

She paid no attention to the vehicles parked in Ashdon Gardens, but one would have been of great interest to her had she been aware of its purpose. It was a blue van with signs on the sides advertising an electrical repairs and general maintenance service. There was a sliding ladder on a roof-rack and a tall radio aerial emerged from the front of the vehicle, just above the windscreen, and swayed slightly in the breeze. A man in blue overalls was sitting in the driver's seat. If Jo had looked round as she entered the building, she might have noticed him talking into a radio, but would have thought nothing of it. Of greater interest would have been the man in the Hunters' flat. He too was dressed in blue overalls with various tools hanging from his belt. He had a small metal toolbox which he had placed on Harry's desk. Somewhat unusually for a maintenance man, he was wearing very thin, flesh-coloured rubber gloves. At first glance his activities might have seemed harmless enough: a workman checking electrical appliances perhaps, or wiring. In fact he had been replacing the three-pin plugs on various appliances in the flat with plugs which looked identical to the ones he removed but which contained minute radio transmitters. It had been a quick and simple task to fit such plugs to the appliances which were permanently switched on in each room: the radio alarm in the main bedroom and the fax machine in the sitting room. He had just finished replacing the plug of the kitchen clock when, returning to Harry's desk, he brushed against a newspaper which had been left lying open over the desk blotter. The paper had slid to the floor, revealing what looked like a large address book. The maintenance man was standing over this, reading, when his radio crackled and he was informed by his colleague in the street below that a young woman had just entered the building and might be headed his way. 'Could be the daughter,' the man below said. With rapid but unflustered movements the man in the flat produced a small camera from his tool-box and photographed the book just as it lay on the desk, without touching it. Then he carefully picked up the newspaper from the floor and replaced it, leaving it more or less as it had been before, carelessly opened. He picked up his tool-box, looked carefully round the room to make sure he had left nothing behind and walked over to the French window which he had unlocked earlier as a precaution. He opened it and paused, listening. Sure enough, he could hear the chink of a key in the lock. He stepped onto the balcony, closing the window behind him. He moved to one side, so as to be out of view to anyone in the room, pressed the transmit button on his radio rapidly to signal to his colleague to maintain radio silence and put down his tool-box on the floor of the balcony. He took a small clipboard from his belt and looked up at the building, as if examining some feature.

Jo was surprised to find that the door was not locked,

but opened at one turn of the key. Perhaps Johnny Hunter was at home. She rang the bell. No-one appeared so she swung the door open. As she entered, she had to step over two letters which lay on the floor where they had been pushed through the letter box. She picked them up. They were both addressed to John Hunter so she placed them on the hall table. She glanced into the living room, called out, 'Anyone at home?' just to be on the safe side, then hastily checked the rooms. In the main bedroom the bed was unmade and there was unwashed crockery and some plates of food on the worktop in the kitchen. In the sitting room there was an ashtray with a half-smoked cigar stubbed out and two sofa cushions on the floor in front of the television. Johnny must have gone out in something of a hurry. She walked over to the desk, to check the answering machine and fax. No flashing light, no waiting sheets of messages. As she turned away her bag brushed the newspaper, which slid slowly off the desk. She bent to pick it up and saw a black briefcase on the floor in the footwell of the desk. She put down her bag and retrieved the pages of the newspaper, which had separated as it fell to the floor. She rearranged them, folded the paper and was about to replace it on the desk when she noticed the book lying open on the blotter. She glanced at it incuriously and a name caught her eye: Parrie. Parrie! She caught her breath, leant forward, all attention. It wasn't an address book. What was it? She stood over it frowning, unaware of the man watching her through the window.

She placed her right hand on the book to mark the page and half closed it with the other hand so as to look at the cover. It was bound in plain black leather. Inside the front cover on the first page were the letters AVT written in elaborate capitals in black ink. Inside the back cover was a leather flap covering two screws. The book was a kind of file, with two metal rods through the spine which could be unscrewed, presumably to add or remove pages. It looked at first glance like an address book because of the alphabetical tags to the pages. There were many entries, each one dated. They seemed mostly to have been written by the same hand. She let the book fall open again as it had lain on the desk. It had been open at the 'M' section. She turned back a few pages.

The first entry was 'MAUNTON, John. ?coke addict' then some initials and a date. There was a symbol alongside this in red, a kind of diamond shape like a 'V' with another inverted 'V' above it. Or perhaps it was a double X. Underneath was a later entry: 'Caused trouble (with Wiste) on Parly. visit to ASEAN countries (his second South East Asia trip). Arrested buying cocaine but police records and photos bought in arms/aid deal. (Kingborne)'. There were various letters and dates after this and a red line diagonally through the whole entry with a later date in red ink underneath.

The next entry said 'MILLINGS, Arthur. Gave us Hudson. Would like K, or something for eldest son (Robert) ? FCO or Treasury.' Again there were initials and a date, then underneath the letter 'K' another date, 2 years later.

She returned to the entry which had caught her eye: 'MORETON, Geoffrey.' There were various entries under this name, with different initials and dates. Once again there was the red diamond shape. Alongside this was a capital 'P' in red. Underneath it said, 'Chmn Moreton Micro. Large donations. ?K. Violent. Kingborne says he beat up a prostitute. He'll see to it she keeps quiet. Wife has left him.? Prefers boys. See PARRIE.' The last entry said 'Caught in drugs raid but Kingborne dealt with it. Confirmed coke addict. Told him he'll get no more protection if he's caught again.'

The next entry was headed 'MOWBERRY, Heyton' but she didn't stop to read it. She leafed through the book, looking for the entry for 'Parrie'. Amongst several items in the 'P' section she found: 'PARRIE, Alban. Enders's brother-in-law.' This had been amended later with the insertion of 'ex-' before 'brother-in-law'. There was a succession of entries over a period of several years, starting, 'Close friend of Wiste. Suspect interest in children extends beyond Family Division.' Then there was the red diamond shape again and below that some numbers, initials and dates. Further down it said: 'Known to take children to Kistrington'. Then, at a later date: 'Problem with Filipino maid. Kingborne will deal.' Below this it said, 'Staffer says Wiste and Enders regular visitors to Kistrington for video parties'. And finally, 'Staffer reports Moreton at Parrie party'.

Jo stood over Harry's desk, staring down at this page for some time. The reference to the Family Division and legal matters meant it *had* to be about the same man, Rita Hanssen's judge. But it couldn't be, surely? A High Court judge abusing children? A paedophile? The thought was so horrifying that she couldn't take it in. She kept rereading the page, thinking of Rita and her description of the judge. But the more she read it, the more convinced she became. This *must* be the same man! She burned with fury at the thought of such a man destroying Rita and ruining the lives of her children. And of how many other children?

Once again she looked at the covers of the book. She riffled through the pages. Could this be Harry's property? Some dossier he had compiled, full of sordid information about people he knew? A lot of the entries seemed to be in his handwriting. Or were they? She wasn't sure. Perhaps it belonged to his son. No, with that reference to Parrie, it must be Harry's. She leafed through the book again. There were so many names. Some of the entries went back years and seemed to be in a different handwriting.

She remained leaning on the desk, staring at the book and wondering what she should do. Having found it, she felt she had to do something about it. She must, for Rita's sake. She was still leaning on the desk, frowning. Suddenly decisive, she closed the book. She bent down for her large bag and placed it on the desk, then she pushed the book inside it, next to Lydia's video camera. She picked up both her bags and looked carefully round the room. There were no messages. There was nothing she need do here.

Her every move had been observed by the man on the balcony who had radioed his colleague below. Immediately, he got out of the van, reached for the ladder and erected it against the wall of the building so that the watcher could climb down to the street.

Jo glanced into the kitchen then walked to the door and stepped out into the hall. As she pulled the door shut behind her, the window to the balcony opened, just a crack. Jo double-locked the door and descended the stairs.

In the street she scarcely noticed the two men who were looking up at the building, apparently arguing about some job that needed to be done. They kept their backs to Jo and did not look round as she walked past. Almost immediately, however, the driver replaced the ladder on top of the van, while the other removed his overalls to reveal a pair of jeans and a dark-blue sweatshirt. He tossed the overalls into the back of the van, lifted out a small leather pouch and sauntered off down the street after Jo, whistling as he went. He clipped his radio to his belt. The other man resumed the driving seat of the van and made a call on a mobile phone.

Jo had abandoned her plan to take Lydia's camera to be repaired. All she could think about was the book. She hurried back to her office, deep in thought, unaware that she was being followed.

The man kept well behind her, but never let her get completely out of sight. After they had been walking for about five minutes he received a call on his radio from his colleague in the van.

'We think she must be his secretary. Name of Lois Young. Where are you headed?'

'Parliament, I think. I'll keep you posted. You'd better not call me from now on. I'm closing in.'

As Jo approached her office, the man behind her quickened his pace so that he was alongside her as she approached the door. He overtook her, to her right, and looked back at her so that his face would be away from the camera he had noted above the door. He said, 'Say! It's Lois, isn't it?'

'Lois? No,' she frowned at him. She was totally preoccupied with her thoughts.

'Harry's secretary?'

'Why, yes, but I'm not Lois. She's away. I'm just standing in for her.'

He was thinking fast. He plucked a name from the air.

'Fred pointed you out to me. When he said you were Harry's secretary, I assumed you must be the famous Lois.' He chuckled. He had a faintly American accent, Jo noticed. She pushed her security pass through the machine and reached for the door. He leant forward with a smile and pushed it open for her, following her in.

'When's Lois due back?' he asked, looking at her, so as to avoid the gaze of the attendant he knew to be close beside them.

'Some time in April, I think,' she replied. They were passing the attendants' room. Jo paused and looked past the stranger.

'Any messages for me, Vic?' she said. The stranger glanced round with a fleeting but intent look and memorized Vic's face.

166

Vic shook his head at Jo and she continued towards the staircase. The stranger accompanied her and paused at the stairs to see which way Jo would go.

'Tell Lois Andy was asking after her,' he said. Jo started down the stairs. He turned away as if heading for the first floor. He went up one step and turned back to her.

'Say! What's your name, if you don't mind my asking?' Jo paused and looked up at him. 'Joanna Delvere.'

'Thanks, Joanna. See you.' He gave her a wave and continued up the stairs. When he reached the turn he stopped and glanced up to make sure there was no-one above him. He stood still and listened. He heard voices below. He waited two minutes longer then sauntered back down the stairs, gave a nod and a smile to Vic and left the building. Then he called his colleague as he walked towards the Embankment and a few minutes later the blue van pulled up beside him. The driver got out and walked round to the passenger door so that he could take the wheel. They took up a vantage point some distance from Jo's building and waited, the engine running, apparently studying a map. Andy called up a number on the mobile phone. When he got an answer he gave Joanna's name and description. 'I'm not sure of the surname. It sounds like D-e-l-l-v-e-e-r. Try whatever variants you can think of. See if we've got anything. And see if you can find out what they've got on file for her security pass. Call me back.'

'If she comes out with the bag, you'd better follow on foot,' he said to his companion. 'I'll tag along behind in the van. She might recognize me now. If she comes out without it, you follow her on foot. I'll park and go back inside and see if I can get it.'

'What if she's switched the thing to something else, a briefcase maybe?'

'Just make sure you don't lose her,' said Andy.

'And if she goes in there?' said the other, jerking his

thumb towards the Houses of Parliament.

'You've got one of these haven't you?' asked the first, showing him a security pass for the Palace of Westminster.

'Sure, I have.'

'If she goes in there, one of us had better go after her. But if you get held up at the checkpoint, you've had it. You'll never keep track of her.'

'I'm not sure it's such a good idea us going in there. You know the rules. What makes you think this damn book is so important?'

'Gut feeling. You should have seen her reaction to it. We need to know who she is and why she's got it.'

When Jo had not appeared after a quarter of an hour, the second man, who had peeled off his overalls and emerged from them in slacks and a jacket, climbed out of the van and strolled down the street, glancing about him. He had a camera slung around his neck and a London A-Z and a guidebook in his hand, dark glasses pushed up onto the top of his head. Anyone who was interested would assume he was a tourist.

His colleague had driven away and disappeared into the next street. When he found somewhere to park, he pulled in, switched off the engine and waited. The other man was standing at the corner of the street, where he had a view of Jo's office. From time to time he glanced at his watch and looked around him as if waiting for someone. He leafed through his guidebook, took a few photographs. After waiting about twenty minutes, he pulled his mobile phone from his pocket and called his colleague, then strolled to the end of the street. As he rounded the corner, the blue van came into sight and pulled up so that the driver could take over the watch.

Joanna had got back to her room to find Mary and Bella both hard at work. She put the big bag on the floor behind her desk and tried to work but could not concentrate.

Walking back to her office she had resolved to look more carefully at the book, copy some of it perhaps and then take it straight back. Before she'd reached the next street she'd started wishing she hadn't taken the thing. Her feelings swung back and forth between resolution and indecision, anger at her discovery and fear at what she had done.

Now she was sitting at her desk, she couldn't even take the thing from her bag in case Mary or Bella noticed it. The longer she had it in her possession the more nervous she became. If only Mary and Bella weren't there.

At a quarter to one Mary announced that she was going over to the House for lunch and asked the others if they would care to join her.

Jo said, 'Not today, thanks, Mary. I've got too much to do. I may get myself something later on if I'm hungry.'

Bella said, 'I've brought something in with me, thanks, Mary.'

Jo's heart sank. So she was going to be stuck with Bella. About twenty minutes later, however, Frank appeared and Bella went out of the room to talk to him. A moment or two later she reappeared, took her coat and bag and said to Jo, 'I'm popping out for a while. Would you like me to get you a sandwich? I'll be back in about an hour.'

'That's very kind of you, Bella,' said Jo, 'but I don't think I'll have anything at the moment thanks.'

As soon as Bella and Frank had gone, she went to Andrea's room and looked in. It was empty. She couldn't believe her luck. Her resolve returned. She hadn't got time to look at the book now: Mary might be back very soon. She would copy the thing and then look at the copies later, when the coast was well and truly clear.

She went back to her desk and removed the black book from the bag. She took a large brown, A4-sized envelope from the bottom drawer of her desk, then selected a lever arch file from the top of the filing cabinet behind her desk. The file had only a few documents in it. She tucked the book inside it and took it out to the photocopier in the hallway. Then she set to work copying each page. It took some time. Not every page contained an entry but the book was too large for her to copy two facing pages simultaneously without scaling the copy down to fit A4 sheets. She wanted the entries to be legible so she had to copy each page individually. She was very nervous lest someone should come down the stairs while she was using the copier. Every few minutes she lifted the finished copies from the machine and tucked them into the large brown envelope.

At last the job was finished. She checked the machine carefully to make sure she'd left no tell-tale sheets behind, then hurried back to her room and put the book back into the big bag on the floor. She sat down and put the brown envelope in the bottom drawer of her desk in the middle of the pile of empty envelopes. Then she sat motionless for a while, thinking. It wasn't a good place to leave it. She bent down and took out the envelope again. She looked around her. Where should she put it? There was a shelf with a row of weekly *Hansards* on it. They looked as if no-one had touched them for months. She stood up and pulled the whole row of books forward very slightly, making sure they were all level, and dropped her brown envelope behind them lengthways so that it was completely hidden. She sat down again and looked at her watch. She must take the book back as soon as possible. When should she go? Supposing Harry were there? If he were there and had found his book missing and she turned up with the big bag, he might suspect her of taking it. Perhaps she could get it into her shoulder bag, if she took out some of the junk she carried around with her. She opened it and took out her little make-up pouch, her hairbrush, address book. She was surprised to see that she had her passport tucked inside her wallet. Then she remembered putting it in the previous morning when she'd felt so desperate. That seems ages ago, she thought.

She bent down and removed the book from the large bag, then pushed it down into her shoulder bag. She could just draw the zip across. It was a soft bag with various zips and a large flap that covered all of them. It was pushed slightly out of shape by the book inside it, but she didn't think anyone would notice. She hung it over the back of her chair as usual and looked at her watch again. It was two o'clock. She was feeling more nervous than ever. She got to her feet and went out to the copier again to make absolutely sure she hadn't left any copies in the tray. Having reassured herself again she returned to her desk. She was sitting there, wondering when to return to Ashdon Gardens when Mary reappeared.

'Haven't you had any lunch yet, Jo?' she asked.

'No, I'm not hungry. I might get something later. I'll have to go out some time, I expect.'

What should she do about Harry? How could she be sure he wouldn't go to the flat to pick up his briefcase? What if he'd already been? She decided to ring the Whips' Messengers. Fred answered.

'Oh Fred, it's Jo here. Is Mr Hunter back yet?'

'Not yet.'

'Do you know when he'll be back? Is there a Whips' meeting this afternoon?'

'He should be here in about twenty minutes to half an hour, I should think, if not sooner. And yes, there is a meeting, at three o'clock.'

'Thanks, Fred, I'll give him a ring later.'

CHAPTER TWENTY

Harry always liked to have his umbrella with him when walking any distance, even on days like this when there was no likelihood of rain. The umbrella always heightened his enjoyment of his walk. He liked to swing it up and forward and strike it smartly on the pavement with every other stride. He felt brisk and energetic and the umbrella emphasized that feeling. He thought it suited his style, gave him a slightly military bearing. He tried hard to keep himself looking trim and fit to make up for his disappointment at not being taller. The umbrella made up for that somehow.

It seemed to him that this was one of the best days he had had in years, though he could think of no particular reason why it should be. Indeed it was surprising in view of his acute shortage of sleep and the disruption of his usual timetable by the bomb explosion. He would not have admitted it to anyone, even Patricia, but he secretly relished the drama caused by the explosion, the briefing sessions, the special Cabinet meeting. He had just had a good lunch at his club with a couple of journalists and had enjoyed being in possession of secrets they would have loved to pry from him. He loved the tactics of the information trade: purchasing new data from the best sources with snippets from his own substantial store. He was pleased with the information he had just acquired. As he strode through St James's Park, the daffodils and crocuses struck him as even more beautiful than they had seemed that morning, the air fresher and cleaner, the sky a crisper blue. A number of passers-by recognized him, heightening his sense of satisfaction with his lot.

His only regret was that he had had to cut short his enjoyment of his time with Jane. He had just been getting going when that damned bomb went off. Jane hadn't seemed to mind. He puzzled over that for a few moments. He was never really sure what she felt about anything, but the sex must be as good for her as it was for him or she wouldn't go on seeing him, would she? He couldn't answer that to his satisfaction. What did it matter anyway? It would be great if she could make it tonight. It would be their last opportunity for some time because Patricia would be back tomorrow.

He decided to ring Jane from his flat rather than from Number Twelve where you could never be sure who was listening in. He looked at his watch. He would do it now. There was plenty of time before the meeting.

He quickened his pace, and headed for Ashdon Gardens. Coming into the block of flats from the bright spring sunshine, he found the building gloomy, even sinister. He opened the door of his flat and felt instant disquiet. It increased as he crossed the hall into his study. He couldn't identify the cause of his unease. Everything looked same as when he had left that morning. Then he saw that the French window to the balcony was open, just a crack. Suddenly, with the recollection of yesterday's events, came an instantaneous awareness of impending disaster which hit him like a massive blow. The window was *open*. Neither he nor Jane had been near the window. He hardly dared to look at his desk. He knew with a terrifying certainty that the Black Book was gone. He could see the corner of his briefcase beneath the desk. He could see the newspaper lying on his desk blotter. But the paper was folded. There was *nothing* else on the desk.

He stood stock-still. How *could* I have forgotten it? he thought. I must be mad! What came over me? He was almost overcome with fury at himself, at Jane, at that bloody bomb.

He remembered everything. They'd had some white wine and olives. He'd been sitting on the sofa, intending to watch something on television. She'd put some cushions on the floor. She wouldn't leave him alone. His appetiser, she liked to call it. He got no pleasure now from the recollection. Then she'd disappeared into the kitchen to cook the steaks and he'd gone to his desk and taken the Black Book out of his briefcase. He'd gone into the kitchen to borrow her newspaper. She'd mentioned an article about Heyton Mowberry and he'd wanted to check it. In the kitchen Jane had handed him a glass of red wine. He'd stood next to her, drinking it while she cooked. Then he'd gone back to his desk and sat down with the newspaper. He was still reading it when Jane had announced dinner was ready and he had joined her at the table, leaving the newspaper open on top of the book. Jane was a great cook. The steak had been delicious. Afterwards, she had made her usual joke: 'Instead of a little sorbet between courses, what about a little sex?' He'd gone back to his desk and was reading the paper when Jane had appeared in the doorway, stark naked. He'd said, 'For God's sake, Jane. I haven't drawn the curtains.'

'Then you'd better come into the bedroom,' she'd said, disappearing from view. He'd followed her to bed immediately and there they'd stayed until the bomb went off.

If only he'd taken the book to Number Twelve after his meeting with the PM! But no, he'd gone back to the House, intending to put it back in his safe, only to be stopped at Members' Entrance by Commander Bowerbridge, who wasn't letting anyone inside until they were absolutely certain they could give the all-clear. He'd said they'd need another half an hour or so. But Harry couldn't wait half an hour. He had a date with Jane. She didn't have a key to the flat. If he wasn't there, she wouldn't hang around in the street, waiting for him. She'd go.

He hadn't been able to get a taxi because Parliament Square, Whitehall and the Embankment were still closed to traffic, so he had hurried up Victoria Street on foot.

I shall have to tell the PM! But what do I tell him? He'll want to know what's in it. What *am* I going to do?

He walked slowly towards the desk. Who could have taken the thing? Patricia was still in America with Alison. Johnny was still in Hong Kong, he was sure. In any case, none of them would have taken it. There was no-one else.

Perhaps it was a common or garden burglary. The window was open. Perhaps someone had broken into the flat via the balcony. He walked over to the window and looked at it. The window had been closed. He was certain of that. How could anyone break in from the outside without smashing the glass? There wasn't so much as a scratch on the outside of the window. He closed it carefully. He looked around the room. There were a number of items that would appeal to a thief but nothing seemed to have been taken. He went back to his desk and walked round behind it. Everything looked the same. He sat down, thinking hard. Had someone been planting a bug? Or removing one? No, it wouldn't be that, surely. But you never knew at times like this. You couldn't feel private anywhere, he thought angrily.

He checked the other rooms but could detect no signs of disturbance and nothing appeared to be missing. He shrugged and turned to leave the flat, then saw the two letters on the table in the hall. The sight of them caused a fresh wave of fear to sweep over him. Whoever had been into the flat had been so confident as to pick up the mail and place it on the table. Who the hell could it be? It was as if they wanted him to know they'd been there, to rub his nose in what they'd done to him.

He went back to his desk and sat down, feeling weak. Then an idea came to him, ludicrous but nevertheless capable of filling him with desperate hope: perhaps the person who had so thoughtfully picked up the mail had been equally thoughtful about the Black Book and had put it away somewhere for him. He knew that it was laughable but he opened each of his desk drawers in turn. Then he leapt to his feet and yanked open the drawers of his filing cabinet, one after another. He searched every drawer and cupboard in the flat, knowing that his actions were idiotic, even pathetic. He knew it was hopeless. He even unlocked the special government-issue safe in his bedroom, although he knew it would be empty. If only he had put it there. He returned to his desk and sat down again. He put his head in his hands. His forehead was clammy with sweat, his shirt clung to him. He felt cold. What am I going to do? Christ, why do we have to do it? Why was it ever started? He recalled some of the entries in the book imagining the reaction should they ever become public. The thing would be denounced. He would be made personally responsible for the practice of keeping the Black Book. He would be the scapegoat. A blackmailer. His thoughts started to race away in mounting terror as the possible consequences occurred to him. He shuddered.

He sat for some time, staring into space, thinking, remembering some of the entries, struggling to remember others. He was still sitting there, when the phone rang. He jumped, reached for it, then changed his mind. He let it ring four times, hesitating over what to do. Then he answered it. He was relieved to hear Patricia's voice. 'Harry. What on earth are you doing there?'

He pulled himself together. 'Where are you? You sound very close.'

'I'm at home.'

'What? I thought you weren't coming until tomorrow.'

'Don't sound so thrilled to have me back,' she said sarcastically. 'I was just beginning to think you might have missed me.'

'Don't, Pat, I'm not in the mood for it.'

'Well what *are* you doing there?'

She noticed the tiny hesitation before he answered, 'Oh I just wanted something out of one of my files.'

He was irritated now. He counter-attacked. 'If you're so surprised at my being here, why are you ringing?'

She was prepared for that. 'Alison had a card from Johnny saying he was going to be in London this weekend.' This wasn't a complete lie. Alison had indeed had a card but Johnny had said only that he was coming 'some time soon, maybe next month'. 'I was just ringing to see if he was there yet.'

'Oh. Right.'

'Are you all right? You don't sound too good.'

'Oh, I'm – I'm fine, Pat, just a bit weary for some reason.'

'Are you coming home tomorrow? I was going to ask the new neighbours for drinks. What do you think?'

'OK. If you want to. I'll get the usual train.' He couldn't concentrate on what she was saying. She thought she could tell from his tone of voice the kind of expression he was wearing: indifferent, bored probably. She knew he wasn't attending to her but stifled her irritation. She'd find out what was going on in due course.

Patricia's call had brought him to his senses. It was no good sitting here, feeling helpless. He must get back to the House. He wouldn't tell anyone anything just yet. He'd wait and see what happened. He got up and left the flat, locking the door behind him and pocketing the keys. He felt exhausted and hailed the first cab he saw. A few minutes later it dropped him at Members' Entrance and he braced himself for the catastrophe he felt certain was about to engulf him.

Not far from Jo's office, the second of the two watchers was on another stint, though at a slightly different vantage point. Now that the lunch-time crowds had disappeared he felt very conspicuous. He called up his colleague on his mobile phone and was making this point when he suddenly said, 'I've been spotted by one of the locals.' He switched off his phone and walked away down the street. Randall Myers stopped and watched him, waiting for the man to look round. He didn't, but Randall saw the blue van appear round the corner. Now who could they be waiting for? Were they keeping tabs on someone, or waiting for a rendezvous? He strolled to the building, inserted his pass in the machine and went inside, nodding to Vic as he passed. At that moment, Jo appeared from downstairs. She was in a hurry. She had just phoned Fred again and was relieved to hear that Harry had gone in to his meeting. Randall felt certain that she was the person awaited by the man outside.

'Hello, Jo,' he said. 'Going over to the House? I'll walk over with you.'

Some instinct told Jo that if she had said she was not going to the House, Randall would have found an excuse to accompanay her wherever she was going. She tried to look unconcerned.

'How are you, Randall?' she enquired.

'Pretty good, thank you, Jo.' They left the building.

How can I get rid of him? she thought frantically. She had her pass in her coat pocket. It would be a disaster if her bag was searched. But they don't search bags, do they? she thought with relief. They put them through those scanning machines. Thank God for that.

'I trust you weren't working late yesterday, Jo,' said Randall. For a moment Jo couldn't think why he should say such a thing.

'You mean when the bomb went off? No, I wasn't here, I'm glad to say. I was at home watching television when it was announced on the nine o'clock news. Where were you?'

'Oh I wasn't here either.' She noticed he didn't say where he'd been.

She was relieved that she didn't have to open her bag but simply put it through the machine. Randall was sticking close to her and she was still trying to think how to shake him off as they entered Central Lobby. Then she saw that the police officer on duty at the barrier was the one who had talked to her about Rita. She ought to tell him what had happened to her. And she might also succeed in shaking Randall off. She continued walking straight ahead, as if going to Lower Waiting Hall then, after they had passed through the swing doors, she stopped suddenly and said, 'Oh, I've just remembered something. See you, Randall. Bye.' She hurried back and walked over to the barrier.

'Do you remember me?' she said to the officer.

'Yes, indeed I do. Miss Delvere, isn't it? How are you?'

She turned slightly and out of the corner of her eye she saw Randall come back into Central Lobby and pause, watching her.

'I'm all right, thanks. I just wanted to tell you about Mr Hunter's constituent.' said Jo. 'Do you remember?'

'Yes. Certainly I do. I can't recollect her name offhand, but I remember she was in quite a state.'

'Well, she killed herself. Isn't that awful? All because no-one cared enough to help her.' She could have added, and right now, in my bag, I've got this book which shows that the judge should never have been allowed near children, let alone to sit in judgement on their parents and decide their fate.

'That's terrible. And I can see you're upset about it too.'

'Not as upset as her children must be,' said Jo and walked away. She knew Randall was close behind her. She went into Members' Lobby and cut across to the Whips' Messengers' Office but instead of going in she went past and straight out through the doorway and out of the Lobby. Then she turned left and raced along the corridor, past Admission Order Office, ignoring the stares of members of the public who were walking towards the stairs to Strangers' Gallery. She turned the corner and disappeared out of sight before Randall reached the corridor. She went back into Central Lobby and hurried down the corridor to Peers' Lobby, wondering whether the police officer had seen her reappear. He would think her very odd if he had.

Inside Peers' Lobby she was stopped by a police officer. 'I wanted to see George Gunn. Is he there?' As she spoke she saw George appear in the doorway of his room. She signalled to him and he came over.

'Come to see me, have you? How nice.' He chaperoned her across Peers' Lobby to his little room. 'What's the matter? You look upset.'

'You'll think it's silly, I'm sure. It's just that there's someone in Central Lobby whom I want to avoid. Is there any way of getting out of this place without going back that way?'

'Just come with me.' He led her out of Peers' Lobby, along a red-carpeted corridor and down a staircase.

Then they walked along a series of corridors and emerged into a courtyard. 'Do you remember, I told you that you could walk from one end of the Palace to the other through these courtyards?'

'Yes I do, now you mention it,' said Jo. 'I can manage now, I think, George.'

'That's all right. I'll come with you.' They walked slowly towards New Palace Yard, Jo looking round anxiously from time to time, fearful that Randall might appear again at any moment.

'You can get out into these courtyards from various places, the doors at each end of the terrace corridor, for example. Then there's a staircase beyond the Chamber, near the Serjeant-at-Arms's quarters, that brings you out over there.' He pointed to another doorway in the corner of the next courtyard.

They reached New Palace Yard. 'If you want a taxi, you can get one there, at Members' Entrance, if you like. Or you could walk out through New Palace Yard. The exit to the tube is closed because of the bomb attack. Here comes a taxi now, if you want it.'

'I'll walk I think, George. Thank you so much.'

'Don't mention it. You look after yourself.' He went in through Members' Entrance and disappeared from view.

Jo hurried through New Palace Yard and set off up Victoria Street. When she reached Ashdon Gardens her heart was pounding with anxiety. She rang the doorbell of the Hunters' flat. No-one came. She unlocked the door and stepped inside, paused and listened. Silence. She hurried into the sitting room. She couldn't tell whether anyone had been in or not. Should she put the book back as she had found it, open at 'MORETON', with the paper over it, or just leave it there on the desk? She hesitated. If anyone had been back, they would have seen the newspaper had been folded up. She decided just to leave the book on the desk, closed. She extricated it from her handbag and placed it on the blotter. She turned and walked to the door and was about to leave when it occurred to her that the book must be covered with her fingerprints. Would that matter? She couldn't see how it could, but having thought of it, it seemed silly not to do something about it. She returned to the desk. She had nothing to wipe it with anyway. She felt in her coat pocket and found her gloves. She put them on. She picked up the book with her left hand and hastily rubbed the covers and outer pages with the corner of her coat, feeling somewhat foolish. You've watched too many thrillers, she said to herself. You must have left fingerprints on every page, but you can't stay here and wipe them all off. So she put the book down again and hurried out of the flat. I'm never coming to this wretched place again, she resolved as she reached the street and her tension eased.

Walking back to her office she felt suddenly famished. She made a detour to the sandwich bar but it was closed. She would get a bit of work done and then get herself something to eat in the Strangers' Cafeteria. Both Mary and Bella had gone by the time she got back. She hung up her coat and looped her shoulder bag over the back of her chair. She was just about to sit down when she realized that her big bag had gone. She had left it behind her desk. She walked about the room, looking for it, thinking that perhaps Mary or Bella had moved it for some reason. It was nowhere to be seen.

CHAPTER TWENTY-ONE

Jo went upstairs to the attendants' room. Vic had gone off duty and the man who shared shifts with him during the day, Alan, was sitting at the desk, head on hand, reading a newspaper and eating an apple. He sat up as Jo went into the room and swallowed his mouthful of apple.

'Yes, miss?'

'Sorry to disturb you, Alan. I was wondering whether anyone had seen a big black and purple bag that I had down in my room. I can't find it.'

'Oh dear. Your handbag is it?'

'Not exactly. I mean I wasn't using it as a handbag. It's quite big. About the size of a carrier bag, made of canvas and leather. You can use it as a kind of shoulder bag, but I don't usually because it's a bit large.'

'Where did you leave it?'

'In my room. Behind my desk. The point is, it's got a video camera in it and it's gone.'

'I don't like the sound of that.'

He got to his feet and accompanied Jo downstairs. 'Vic might know something about it,' he said. 'Normally he'd be on duty, but he asked me to cover for him. I think his mum's been taken ill. I'll see if I can get him on the phone in a minute.'

Jo showed him where she had left the bag. Together they looked in vain around the room. They went into Andrea's room, but she knew nothing about the bag. She hadn't been into Jo's room so she hadn't seen it. 'I'm afraid I've been going flat out all day. I haven't noticed anyone or anything. Sorry I can't help.'

They walked back upstairs.

'Surely no-one could have walked in off the street and stolen it, could they?' asked Jo.

'I don't see how they could. The door's closed all the time and there's a camera so we'd see them on our screen.'

'But that would mean that someone who works here took it,' said Jo in a disbelieving tone.

'A lot of people do come in and out of the building, of course,' said Alan, 'but they're usually with Members or their staff.' He picked up his telephone. 'I'll just try Vic. See if he knows anything about it.' But there was no answer from Vic's number.

'I'd better report it to the police, I suppose,' said Jo. 'Or do I have to tell the Serjeant-at-Arms's Office, or something? Who should I speak to do you think?'

'The Chief of Police in the House. Someone in his office. Shall I report it for you?'

'Would you? Thanks, Alan.'

He looked worried. 'They'll be wanting to talk to Vic and me about it anyway. They'll give us a going over, I reckon, what with the bomb and everything. We're going to be in real trouble. You don't suppose you could have left it somewhere else and have forgotten, do you?' he looked at her hopefully.

'I'm sure I didn't. I brought it in with me this morning and haven't taken it out since. I wish I had.' If only I'd taken it to the camera shop first thing this morning, she thought. Lydia's going to be so annoyed. I'll have to tell her. Sorry, Lydia, I had to go and nick something from my boss's flat first. Forgot about the camera. That'll go down well.

Jo went downstairs again and sat at her desk. There were piles of paper in front of her. The light on her answering machine was flashing and she could see several sheets of messages in the fax machine. She didn't feel like working. She was longing to have a closer look at the copies she had made of Harry's book, but she daren't take them out now in case someone came in. She swung round in her chair and looked up at the shelves. The *Hansards* were just as she had left them. She stood up and tried to reach down behind them. She had to stretch but she couldn't reach low enough. For a nasty moment she thought perhaps the envelope had gone, but when she slid one volume of *Hansard* out she could see part of it through the gap. She sat down again and set to work.

A few minutes later Alan appeared in the doorway. 'I've reported your bag missing,' he said. 'Someone will come over to see you shortly, if you wouldn't mind staying.'

'Thanks, Alan. No, I don't mind staying, I've got such a lot to do, but I may have to go and see my boss later.'

Harry was beside himself with anxiety. Throughout the meeting he had been impatient, absent-minded, rude. Everyone had noticed. Jack was enjoying Harry's discomfiture. His assumptions about its cause were entirely wrong, but very pleasurable. He indulged in a little fanciful speculation. The cocky little sod has come a cropper at last, he thought with satisfaction. The PM must have given him a dressing down over Monday's vote. He made a real balls-up of that. Perhaps he's for the chop . . . Perhaps I'll get my chance at last. He tipped his head back and looked at Harry.

'So that's agreed, then, is it?' he said. 'You'll tell the PM?' Harry was looking at the floor, tapping nervously with his foot.

'What?' Harry almost jumped. He'd been agonizing over what to tell the PM about the Black Book. He came to his senses. 'Of course I will. I'll be seeing him shortly. I'll tell him. We did our homework and it was Number Ten and the department who cocked it up, not us.' What *am* I going to say to him? That I was screwing Jane when the bomb went off and forgot the thing! Christ! I can't tell him that!

He made himself concentrate again on the meeting. Why's Jack making such a fuss about that frigging vote? he thought irritably. That's the least of our worries. If he only knew! Aloud he said, 'OK. Let's leave it there.'

Everyone got up except Harry, who remained seated for a moment longer, deep in thought. His gaze followed Roy Phillips, who went over to his desk and put some papers into his briefcase. His briefcase! The recollection of it had the effect on Harry of an electric shock. He felt as if his hair must be standing on end. His briefcase! Perhaps the book was in it! He had no recollection of putting it there but still, it was *possible*. These thoughts were swiftly followed by fury at his forgetfulness. What's coming over me? Am I going off my head? How could I forget the briefcase too? Or perhaps I didn't? He had to restrain himself from running into his room to check whether he'd brought it back to the House. He pulled himself together and walked to his room. No. No briefcase. I knew I didn't bring it of course. It's in the flat, under the desk. He glanced at his watch. There was just time for him to go round to the flat and still get to Number Ten for his meeting with the PM, if he took a cab. He could get it to wait while he went up to the flat. He hurried down to Members' Entrance and was relieved to see a taxi just coming into New Palace Yard. Minutes later he was racing up the stairs to his flat, and fumbling with the key. He stepped inside, walked over to the sitting room and stopped dead in the doorway. The book was on the desk. *On the desk!*

'Pat! Johnny!' he shouted, stepping backwards into the hall and looking towards the bedrooms, then the kitchen. There's no-one here. But *someone's* been here. What the hell's going on? He could see the corner of his briefcase in the footwell of the desk. Why hadn't he noticed it before? He became aware of his keys digging into the palm of his hand, where he had his fist clenched so tightly. He felt cold all over. He walked carefully across to the desk, stopped again, looked at the window. It was closed. He hurried over to it and checked the handle. It was locked. You couldn't open it without pressing hard on the two button locks – one above and one below the catch – and twisting the handle at the same time. It was difficult enough to do from inside the room. He was sure it would be extremely difficult from outside. And in any case they'd have to smash the double glazing first and no-one had done that. No. Nobody could have come in that way. So how the hell did they get in here in the first place? He turned back to face the room. The door to the flat had been double-locked. Whoever had been in had come through the front door and had had a key. He walked carefully round the entire flat, looking into all the rooms. There was no clue as to who had been there. The bed was still in disarray from his and Jane's hasty departure last night. If Pat has been here – or Johnny – they'll have seen that, and the mess in the kitchen, and the sofa cushions on the floor of the sitting room. I should have got Jane to clear up before we left. Why didn't I? How could I be so stupid! We were expecting to come back today of course. That bloody bomb! He raced round the bedroom, straightening the sheets, plumping up the pillows, replacing the duvet. He hastily tidied the room then rushed into the sitting room where he replaced the sofa cushions, straightened items on the coffee table. Finally, the kitchen. Then he returned to the sitting room and stopped in the middle of the room, looking once more at his desk. It couldn't be Jane who'd been here. She's never had a key. Jane . . . How did I leave things with her? I was meant to ring her. She'll be wondering why she hasn't heard from me. I must phone her. But first things first . . .

He walked over to his desk. It had to have been Pat, or Johnny. One of them must have taken the book and put it back. He didn't like that at all. He'd never told Pat about it. The less she knew about such things the better. She wouldn't understand and though he didn't like to have to admit it, he'd behaved so badly towards her over the years that, well, he couldn't be sure what she might do about something like that. As for Johnny, what would he make of it? He'd ask a lot of questions, that's for sure. He wouldn't let it drop, either, if I didn't explain it. Still, I'll deal with it somehow.

He went round behind his desk and stood looking down at the book. He put his hand on the cover. It was cool to his touch. What a thing it was. He handled it with care, almost reverently. He sat down and opened the cover. AVT. He'd written that there. The Masons' motto. *Audi, vide, tace.* Hear, see and be silent. Well he'd be silent about this. What a relief he didn't have to tell the PM. He relaxed a little and started to leaf through the book to remind himself of his lucky escape. Some of the pages were faintly discoloured. They were much older than the rest. Those were the ones he'd inherited from his predecessors. Quite a few of those entries were crossed through. Those ones were dead, but the information had to be kept. Its effect lingered on like the spores of some deadly fungus, lying dormant under the leaves, awaiting a propitious wind to expose them to light and growth.

There were times when he'd toyed with the idea of transferring the contents of the Black Book to a pocket computer which would be so much smaller, so much more convenient. He could carry it with him everywhere and jot things down as soon as he heard them, instead of having to wait until he was back at his desk. But there had never been time to do this. It would take hours to enter all the data and he couldn't possibly entrust such a task to anyone else, not even one of the Whips, not even Jack. No-one else had *all* the information. Each Whip had whatever bits he had passed on to Harry. But only Harry himself had the whole picture. That was the source of his enormous power. And that was the reason he would pitch into the abyss before anyone else, should the Black Book get into the wrong hands. His relief that it was not missing after all was immense and he leant back in his chair, stretching his head back to ease his tension. He sat forward again, a satisfied expression on his face.

Of course, there were some who were invulnerable. He leafed through the book. Arnold Hobbs was one. There was the entry, made many years ago.

'Troublemaker. Risk that he will establish a following. Suggest DA attempts to compromise him.' I wonder who DA is, or was? thought Harry. Before my time.

The next entry under Hobbs said, 'Anti-nuclear. Will vote against us next week. Says he'll expose us on Porton unless we meet him at least halfway.' Then further down, 'Told him he'll get nothing if he doesn't co-operate. DA.'

Then, 'Impregnable. Freezer.'

Arnold Hobbs didn't mind, thought Harry. He'd seen them off. They had had to climb down. So then they froze him out, made sure he never got anywhere, no promotion, ostracized within the Party. No knighthood.

And the bastard doesn't care. Just carries on doing his own thing. Revered by his constituents. And no matter how much he was run down by the Party and its media sympathizers, you could always hear a pin drop when Arnold spoke in the House. Everyone wanted to hear what he had to say. Harry was almost envious of Arnold Hobbs.

There were those at the other extreme, who would do *anything* Harry asked, anything to stay in his good books, under his protection. Protection. Hah! That's a good one. The corners of his mouth turned down in a wry half-smile. You pay me in kind, and I'll see you're protected. That was exactly the approach he used with Philip Filer. Harry didn't need to turn to Philip's entry to refresh his memory. Only two weeks ago he'd leant on him, just a little bit more. Got him to 'entertain' that chap Wesker from the State Department. Disgusting little pervert, thought Harry. But he has his uses. The Yanks have been trying to put one over on us and now we've got their chief European policy maker right where we want him thanks to our obliging little in-House bondage freak. Our poor little Philip has been begging to be released from his misery, but he never will be. I wonder when I'll see that bit of film? Those films do something to me. He stirred in his chair.

He flipped through the pages. There's even an entry for that poor sod Templeman. He looked at it. 'JB says Templeman screwing Henderson's wife. Jane T getting it from? Peter Hemsley.' Not any more she isn't, said Harry to himself. Then there was another entry: 'EM says Jane betrayed her source for anthrax article. Edwards, doing five years, was whistle-blower not perpetrator who escaped and is believed now to be in Germany'. Jane would be ruined as a journalist if it ever got out that she not only betrayed a source but allowed an innocent man to go to jail when she could have exposed the real villain. Harry looked grim. It just might come in handy for his own protection, should Jane ever move on and threaten to talk. It never occurred to him that he himself could have helped clear the man who had been wrongfully imprisoned. His thoughts turned to when he could see her again. He'd ring her as soon as he'd seen the PM.

Suddenly he remembered the taxi was waiting for him. He leapt to his feet, grabbed his briefcase and put the Black Book inside it. He pushed the clasp firmly home and hurried out of the flat, stopping for one last anxious look round. Then he locked the door carefully behind him and ran down the stairs to the taxi.

Harry wasn't going to make the same mistake twice, even if it meant being late for his meeting with the Prime Minister. He told the taxi driver to take him back to Members' Entrance at the House of Commons.

'I thought you'd gone to Number Ten, Harry,' said Jack in surprise when he saw him returning to his room. He noticed Harry was carrying his briefcase. He hadn't had it with him when he left. What's he up to now? he wondered.

'I just had to come back for something,' said Harry and shut his door behind him. His relief when he had locked the Black Book once more in its accustomed hiding place was immense. He felt exhausted, utterly drained. He had to sit for a moment in his swivel chair to collect himself. His telephone rang. He leaned forward and answered it.

'Harry?'

'Yes, Pat, what is it?' He made no attempt to conceal his impatience.

'Could you bring home some of our personal stationery? I seem to have run out.' She sounds far away, he thought. A germ of doubt crept into his mind.

'Where are you? Aren't you at Number Twelve?'

'Of course I'm not. You know I'm at home.' She sounded offended. 'I rang you this afternoon, remember? I know what I do is of little enough interest to you, but I wouldn't have thought even you'd have forgotten that quickly.' The creeping doubt was growing. He controlled himself with an effort.

'Sorry. I'm getting muddled. When you rang before I assumed for some reason you were in London.'

She didn't believe him. She wondered what on earth he was up to.

'Of course I wasn't in London. I came straight here from the airport.'

'Where's Johnny?' asked Harry abruptly.

'Johnny? Oh, he's not back yet.'

The doubt ballooned, burst in his mind, leaving him aghast.

'Harry? Are you still there?'

'I thought you said he was back in London.'

'I said I thought he was expecting to be here this weekend. In fact I gather he won't be here for at least another week, maybe longer.'

His heart was pounding as if he had been running. So Pat hadn't been in London at all today and Johnny was in Hong Kong. Neither of them could have been in the flat. He was back at square one. *Who* could have got into the flat, taken the book and then come back and returned it? His hand gripping the phone was shaking. He was sweating, but cold.

'I've got to go now, Pat. Bye.' He hung up before she could say anything else. He looked round at the cupboard behind him, opened the door and double checked the safe. He got to his feet feeling dizzy with anxiety and walked out of the room. Jack looked up as he went through the Whips' Office. Harry avoided his gaze.

The walk to Number Ten calmed him down. There was no point in being hasty. The Black Book was safely back where it belonged. No-one need know anything about what had happened, unless . . . He stopped himself from thinking about what might happen. I'll cross that bridge when I get to it. There's no need for the PM to know anything about it. Not yet anyway. And with a bit of luck, no-one need ever know. No-one, that is, other than the person who took it . . .

He managed to get his anxiety under control by the time he reached the door of Number Ten. As usual, it was opened by an unseen minion as he approached and he was wearing his usual self-confident expression by the time he crossed the threshold.

CHAPTER TWENTY-TWO

Joanna was typing fast on her word-processor when two police officers entered her room, accompanied by Alan.

'Good evening. Miss Delvere?' said the first.

'Yes. Is it about my bag?'

'That's right.' He turned to Alan, who was standing a little behind them, looking anxious. 'We'll come and see you in a minute.'

'The night man will be coming in soon,' said Alan.

'Well don't you leave. We'll be up shortly,' said the officer. Alan withdrew.

The officers were extremely thorough. They took a description of the bag and its contents from Jo and questioned her extensively about the time of her arrival at the office and subsequent comings and goings. These were not difficult to provide. Every detail of the day from the moment she awoke was etched on Jo's memory.

'And there was just the camera in the bag, nothing else? You've still got your pass?'

'Yes, I keep that in my handbag. I was using the other one as a carrier bag. There was nothing else in it. Just the camera.'

The two men looked around the room, and then went into Andrea's room, which was now empty.

'We'll look into the matter. Let us know if anything else untoward happens.' They disappeared upstairs to question Alan.

A little later, Jo went over to the House with a folder of letters for Harry to sign. Passing the attendants' room she saw Alan, deep in conversation with the two officers.

As she went into the Whips' Office she met Jack coming out.

'Is Harry here, Jack?'

'No, he's over at Number Ten at the moment.' Jo was relieved. She couldn't face seeing him now.

'It's probably just as well if you don't hang around,' said Jack. 'He's in a foul mood. Positively distracted this afternoon. He went flying out of here as if the hounds of hell were after him, then came tearing back a little while later saying he'd forgotten something.' Jack smiled at Jo. 'He looked like death warmed up. He even made himself late for an appointment with the PM, which is not like him at all,' he added maliciously.

'I don't want to see him,' said Jo, 'just to leave some letters for him to sign.' Could Harry have been back to his flat and discovered the book missing before she returned it? she wondered. So what if he has? Loathsome man. I wonder if he knows about Rita, if he's even given her a thought.

As she returned to Central Lobby she met Ann and Tim.

'You're here late,' said Ann.

'I could say the same about you,' Jo replied.

'I'm terribly behind with everything because of the bomb,' said Ann. 'Tim and I are just going to have some supper downstairs. He's got to go back to work later. Why don't you join us?'

'I've still got a lot to do,' said Jo, 'but I'd love to join you for a little while.'

They went down to the Strangers' Cafeteria. It was full of people and Jo found the heat and noise oppressive. There was a queue of people waiting at the counter and most of the tables were already occupied.

'Is it always this crowded in the evening?' Jo asked Ann.

'Frequently. In fact the quietest place these days is the Chamber itself. Everyone is busy elsewhere, in committees, seeing visitors, briefing the press, working in their rooms and so on.'

'That's partly the result of televising the proceedings,' said Tim. 'Now they can see what's going on in the Chamber just by looking at the television screens in their rooms, or wherever they are, Members don't need to spend so much time in the Chamber. But of course, the public sees the TV pictures too. They see the Chamber's practically empty and wonder what they're all up to.'

They got their trays of food at last and sat down at a table.

'Do you often have to work late?' Jo asked Tim.

'No. Only when something out of the ordinary happens, or is coming up, like the preparations for this European peace conference. And last night's bomb hasn't helped.'

'Do they know who's behind it?' asked Jo.

'No-one's claimed responsibility,' he replied, 'so it doesn't look like the IRA. It looks as if it was something to do with the conference, maybe an attempt to delay it, or force a change of venue. The Americans would love to get it moved to the US.'

'They couldn't be responsible for it, surely?' said Jo.

'No, but they might be beneficiaries in more ways than one. Mind you that could apply to various countries. The French and the Germans would like it to be in Bonn or Paris. They want it to be European rather than dominated by NATO or the UN. The anti-federalists want the opposite. The Russians probably don't want a settlement. The Chinese would be happy to see Europe falling out with America and the Israelis are glad of anything that takes the pressure off them, especially as they think American support may be weakening.'

'Things are never as they seem, are they?' said Ann.

'Too true,' said Jo with feeling. She was thinking of Harry and his squalid dossier. She longed to tell them about it but how could she? How could she justify having taken it, let alone having copied its contents? They simply wouldn't understand.

'What sort of a day have you had, Ann?' asked Tim.

'Hectic. Everyone going mad about security here and what can be done to tighten it up. Bolting the stable door after the horse has gone.'

'I don't suppose very much more can be done,' said Tim. 'There's closed-circuit television everywhere, we're probably being watched even now.'

'I wouldn't be surprised,' said Ann. 'Some of the cameras are very well concealed.'

'Nowadays none of them needs to be visible,' said Tim. 'You can have them in TV screens like that one up there, for example.' They all looked up at the monitor on the wall, which had a white caption on a black screen showing the subject of the debate, the time and the name of the Member speaking at that moment. As they looked, they heard a faint chime and saw the caption change to show the name of the next speaker. Tim continued, 'There could be a lens behind that screen and a camera filming us right now, as we look at it.'

'Perhaps we should wave?' said Ann.

'You don't believe me, do you?' said Tim. 'She never takes anything I say too seriously.' Ann was smiling at him. Jo saw her reach out under the table to take hold of his hand.

'If they were filming us,' said Jo looking up at the screen again, 'they'd either have to have armies of people checking through all those miles of totally useless film, or people sitting somewhere watching us on a screen right now.'

'No, they don't have to do either of those things nowadays,' he replied. 'The film can be digitized and stored on computer, or even go straight from camera to computer. That's already done with photos of terrorists and known criminals and new images can be checked against the stored records in a matter of seconds.'

'So they could be checking our mug-shots against files of terrorists as we eat our scrambled egg on toast. What a charming thought!' said Jo. 'Is that really true, or are you kidding us?'

'No, that's a fact,' said Tim.

'So there could be hundreds of closed-circuit TVs like that in this building,' said Jo. 'It makes me think of Dave, the night watchman in my building,' she added. 'He says he knows he's being watched when he goes down to my room at night. He says he can *feel* it. It sounds from what you're saying as if he's probably right.' Jo laughed as she said this, but she was feeling uneasy. Supposing I was being watched while I copied Harry's book? Or while I was hiding it?

'Apparently there are even one or two people working in this place whose real job is to keep an eye on everyone else,' said Ann. 'I wouldn't be surprised if that creepy fellow Randall Myers wasn't one of them.'

'What do you mean?' Jo was amazed. 'That he works for MI5 or something?'

'Ask Tim. Wasn't that why you invited him to our party, darling?'

'I didn't invite him. I thought you must have done. He came with those two MPs – Scott Chambers and Philip Filer. Don't you remember? He just turned up. I don't know anything about the man.'

Jo was thinking how ironic it was that, now she did have something to hide, Randall appeared to have lost interest in her.

Tim looked at his watch. 'I must get back to my office,' he said and stood up. 'It was nice to see you again, Jo. Don't work too hard.'

'You too,' said Jo.

'I'll walk some of the way with you,' said Ann to Tim, 'then I'll go down for the car.' She turned to Jo. 'I expect I'll see you tomorrow. We're meant to be meeting for lunch.'

'Right, I'll see you then. Bye. Bye, Tim.'

Ann and Tim turned to the right, heading for the courtyard, so as to walk through to New Palace Yard. Jo went the other way, along the Terrace Corridor and up the stairs to Lower Waiting Hall, then through to Central Lobby.

Outside it was nearly dark. As they stepped out into the courtyard, Tim put his arm round Ann's waist, drew her close and kissed her.

'I wish I didn't have to go back to work. What will you do this evening, my darling?' he asked.

'I'll slip into something exotic and wait for you.'

'You will?' They started walking again.

'Well, no, not immediately, I won't. There's the washing to be done and I must write some letters. Don't worry, I won't be sitting there pining for you. I've got plenty to do.'

'I shall be pining for you,' he said softly, still holding his arm around her, 'reading turgid civil service minutes and watching the clock go round.'

'Shall I sit at my window, like Penelope, weaving my tapestry and awaiting your return? Or shall I get into bed and watch the box?'

'I expect you'll be asleep when I get home.'

The air was cold and damp with a fine drizzle. Light from the windows high above them was reflected in patches of moisture in the uneven surface of the road.

'Listen,' he said, making her stop beside him for a moment. There wasn't a sound. 'You can't hear the traffic at all. Isn't it amazing?' He found it mysterious and romantic.

'Maybe there isn't any traffic,' said Ann, walking on again, apparently unmoved by their surroundings. 'Maybe another bomb's gone off and Central London is deserted and we're the only people who don't know. Or maybe it's just about to go off.'

Their footsteps sounded loud. He noticed that they were not quite in step, hers made a lighter, softer sound, fractionally after his, a reluctant echo. They passed through a dark archway into the next courtyard, where two men were loading sacks of mail into a large Post Office van. As they approached, the van doors were slammed shut and its engine started. Reluctantly Tim withdrew his arm from around Ann and they stepped to one side to allow the vehicle to reverse out into the road.

They walked through New Palace Yard and crossed the corner of Parliament Square. Whitehall was still cordoned off and Tim had to get out his pass to get them through.

'I like your friend, Jo,' said Tim, 'but she looks rather sad, don't you think?'

'Maybe she has reason to.'

'She looks to me like someone who's seen a lot. Your mother would say she's "a deep one".'

'We'll have to invite her round, so that you can get to the bottom of it, my angel,' said Ann. 'Perhaps next weekend.'

'Good idea. Invite her for Sunday lunch, why don't you?'

They reached the corner of Downing Street. 'I'll leave you here.' She stopped and he turned to face her. 'See you later,' she said and kissed him. He watched her for a moment as she walked back towards Parliament Square, then continued on his way.

CHAPTER TWENTY-THREE

On entering Central Lobby, Jo was spotted by the policeman at the barrier. He waved and started to walk towards
her, clearly intending to intercept her. She recognized
him as the officer she had talked to about Rita.

'Hello there,' he said. 'How are you?'

'I'm fine, thanks. And you?'

'I'm glad to see you're all right now. I was worried
about you earlier. You looked so upset.'

'I was feeling upset.' Now she felt embarrassed. Her
behaviour earlier must have seemed odd, to say the least.

'You seemed to be angry with me,' he said.

'I'm sorry. I wasn't, really,' she said looking up at him.
There was something very likeable about him. She could
well imagine visitors pouring out their life stories to him.
'I was feeling terribly sad about Mrs Hanssen – I still am
– and angry that there was no-one to help her. And I'm
angry with myself, I suppose, because maybe I could
have done something to prevent her feeling so desperate
and she might still be alive.'

'There's no point in thinking like that. You won't
achieve anything. It's right that you care and next time

you meet a really desperate soul you might be able to help. But it's not your fault you know. It's the result of many different things, lots of people's faults if you like, probably going back years.'

'Thank you,' she said.

'Don't mention it,' he said with a smile. 'What I really wanted to know is what you were doing disappearing down there one minute' – he jerked his thumb towards Members' Lobby – 'and reappearing over there seconds later,' he nodded towards the archway by Admission Order Office. 'I could scarcely believe my eyes. I thought you must be on roller-skates – or have a double.'

She blushed. 'I wondered if you'd see me. I knew you'd think I was crazy if you did. I was trying to avoid someone who was being a nuisance, a real creep.'

'Do you mean Mr Myers? He was with you when you came through here, wasn't he?'

'You don't miss much do you?' said Jo, surprised that he'd noticed them in the crowd.

'Well some people make more of an impression on me than others,' he smiled at her again.

'Yes, Randall is memorable, isn't he? What a jerk!'

'You know that's not what I meant.'

'Thanks.'

'He wanted to know what you'd been talking about to me.'

'What a nerve! What business was it of his, I'd like to know?' exclaimed Jo. 'What did you tell him?'

'I said, "Miss Delvere was enquiring about a constituent". Was that all right?' He lowered his voice and added confidentially, 'I don't much care for his type myself.'

'Thank you very much,' said Jo warmly. She could see a man and a woman standing a little way from them, looking at him expectantly, evidently waiting to talk to him. 'You're wanted,' she said, 'and I'd better be getting back to my office.' He glanced round and nodded to the couple. He turned back to Jo.

'If you ever find this place getting to you again, or just feel like talking to someone, you know where to come. All right?'

'Yes,' – she glanced at the sleeve of his uniform – 'Sergeant?'

'Yes – Jamieson. But call me Bill, please. Everyone does.'

'Thanks, Bill. And please call me Jo. Bye.'

When she returned to her office, Dave was on duty.

'Good evening, Jo.'

'Hello, Dave, how are you?'

'I'm very well, thank you. Sorry to hear about your bag. I hope you get it back.'

'Me too,' Jo had forgotten about the bag while she was with Tim and Ann. The recollection lowered her spirits.

'It's rather worrying,' Dave continued. 'The police will be after us for not keeping the place secure.' This made Jo feel worse. 'Oh dear, I'm sorry. I thought Alan looked worried.'

'He's afraid he'll lose his job.'

'That's terrible,' said Jo. 'In any case, I thought from what he said, it would have had to be someone in the building and that could hardly be his fault, surely.'

She went downstairs feeling gloomy. If only I'd taken the damned thing straight to the shop, she thought, none of this would have happened. Maybe I wouldn't have seen that book, either. Back once more at her desk, her anxieties about her discovery returned with a vengeance. What should she do about it? She had to do something. Now that she was in possession of this knowledge she was bound to do something about it. Or was she? She was locked once more into the circular pattern of thoughts that had preoccupied her earlier in the day.

She found herself thinking about what Tim and Ann

had said and couldn't help looking round for concealed cameras. She looked in the hallway outside her room. There was nothing which could possibly have contained a camera, she decided. She wasn't so sure about her room. There was a television set on the far side of the room from her desk. She wasn't sure whether it was an ordinary TV, or a Commons monitor. She thought it didn't look quite like the other monitors. Anyway, it wasn't switched on, so what was the worry? She turned away from it and eyed the shelf of *Hansards*.

I'm being ridiculous, she thought, and reached up, removed a couple of volumes and took out her envelope. She replaced the *Hansards* and sat down. Nevertheless, she swivelled her chair around so that her back would be to the screen before she removed the sheaf of papers from the envelope.

It occurred to her that it wasn't very wise to have the copies in a loose bundle: it would be so easy to lose a sheet. So she pulled out the sliding extension to the right side of her desk, put the papers down and used her large desk punch to make ring binder holes in the papers. Then she took a couple of Treasury tags from the tray on her desk and threaded them through the holes. Now there was less risk of losing a sheet and they would stay in the right order. While she was doing this she realized for the first time the scale of the dossier. There were dozens of entries, maybe even hundreds, far more than she had realized when she was copying the thing. Then she'd been concentrating on completing the task and hadn't been able to look at what she was copying. Now she could look at it at her leisure she was surprised to find that some of the entries went back many years; one was dated more than twenty years ago. She couldn't be sure without checking very carefully, but she thought that there were at least four different lots of handwriting. So it wasn't all Harry's work, though a lot of it seemed to be in his writing. She put the punch away and sat back in her chair to look at the papers, still keeping her back to the television screen. Ridiculous maybe, but she just couldn't be sure. She felt nervous enough to believe anything at the moment.

The very first entry was 'ALLARDE, James. Avoids disclosing payments from directorships and consultancies (est 300K) by having these made to own management company which owns all his assets, houses, cars etc. and pays all running costs. Conceals his ownership of management co. behind nominees. Warned him that if we could find out, so could media. Donates 50K p.a. through Filter.'

Below this a later entry with different initials said, 'His management company apparently owns property firm running dubious housing schemes. Complaints re debt collectors and enforcers. Could cause us serious problems, esp. in local elections.'

The most recent entry for Allarde said, 'EM says Allarde's involvement with pharmaceutical co. could be highly damaging. He's heard it's marketing an inadequately tested drug in Third World with rumours of serious side-effects. Allarde denies this. Says if he's to give up shareholding and directorship he expects compensation.' There were several incomprehensible entries after this with names, symbols and letters, dates and sums of money.

Jo was leafing through the pages when the bundle slipped in her hands and fell open at 'F'. She found herself looking at an entry which read: 'FILER, Philip. See PARSIMMER. ?lovers. ?kept by Parsimmer.'

Philip Filer was the MP Tim and Ann had been talking about who'd been at their party. Jo didn't meet him and hadn't come across the name before. There was quite a lot entered for Filer: 'On list. Parsimmer determined to help him.' Then, another entry: 'Since

Parsimmer died, Filer has been taken over by Bamber.'
Or was it 'Barber'? Jo couldn't read the handwriting very
easily. The next entry looked like Harry's handwriting
and said, 'JB thinks Filer is being blackmailed by Enders.
See Enders.' The next entry said, 'RP says Filer now
Enders' fag. Promoting him for Secretary of European
Affairs Committee. Told Enders if he wanted the com-
mittee post he'd better give me what he had on Filer.
Handed over letters and photos. Says he bought them off
Staffer but I doubt it. Suspect he has more. ?Parsimmer's
diaries.'

Suddenly Jo's eye leapt to the last line of Filer's entry
which was dated the day before Ann and Tim's party:
'Made Filer promise to set Wesker up for a Kistrington
party this weekend.' Wesker! The name on Harry's
notepad. The man from the State Department. What did
it mean? And what was this about film? She flipped
through to the entry for Parrie again. Yes, there it was, a
reference to videos. I wonder if Hank knows about this?
she thought. Should I tell him? What is the purpose of
the book?

She turned to the entry for 'ENDERS, Carl.' There
were numbers, sums of money and dates. Various
initials. Jo couldn't make any sense of it. Below this was:
'JB believes he has scheme with Geoffrey Moreton and
Philip Wiste. They won't admit to it. ?joint company
shelter to avoid disclosure of payments.' At the end it
said, 'With Wiste on Thailand trip. Photographed with
?child prostitute R B-A took care of it and bought the
prints and negs.'

As she turned the pages, it dawned on her that a lot of
the people named in it were MPs. Perhaps it was purely
political, to do with Harry's job as Chief Whip and not
some private activity of his after all. She reached for her
Palace of Westminster directory and started checking the
names against it. Sure enough, most of them were MPs.

Some were Peers. Some she couldn't find in the directory at all. Well Parrie wouldn't be in the directory. Could it be that some of the others she couldn't identify as MPs or Peers were judges too? There was one name, SANDERELL, Will, which she was sure she had come across somewhere before.

And there was another one, which cropped up several times: Kingborne.

She turned to the 'K' section. There she found an old entry for 'KINGBORNE, Dean, Chief Insp. Believed to be applying pressure to Gerald Peterson. GP's secretary told OC that Kingborne came to see GP re his daughter's involvement in drugs party in which teenager died. Kingborne arranged to keep her name out of it.' At a later date it said 'Kingborne definitely blackmailing Gerry Peterson. Better if we take him on board. OC will approach him.'

Next it said, 'P. will arrange promotion and additional pay, plus a QPM. Garden Party list.'

A later entry showed that he had been promoted to Commander at a London police station. Beneath this, it said, 'Bought Maunton's records for us.' Next to that was a large 'P'. Jo recollected seeing a large red capital 'P' at intervals in the book. The last entry said, 'Dealt with Fairbrand problem. Wants something for son, Darren. ?Stock Exch. transactions monitor could be useful.'

Jo got up and went to a bookshelf which contained some reference books and selected *Whitaker's Almanac*. Yes, sure enough Commander Kingborne was a top police officer with the Metropolitan Police.

Next she turned to the 'P' section. There was Parrie again and various other names. She continued to turn through these and then found the last page under 'P' contained just a list of names with no details. They were not in alphabetical order. Amongst them she saw the names of the Prime Minister and the Home Secretary. Kingborne's name was there too. And Geoffrey Moreton, for whom she had read an entry elsewhere. She looked back through the dossier and found that every name which had a large 'P' alongside it was also in the list. There were also some names she didn't recognize, which weren't to be found in the list of MPs and Peers in the Palace of Westminster and for whom she could find no entry elsewhere in the dossier. There was one name, Robin Brook-Ainlee, she'd seen somewhere. But there was nothing else on this page, nothing to indicate what linked these names together.

She went on leafing through the pages. What would Donald have thought about all this? What would he have done? What would he have thought of her for taking the book and copying it? Would he have approved? She was dismayed to find that she wasn't sure. She thought he would have felt just as strongly as she did about its contents, but what would he have thought about her taking it, stealing it, because that was what it was, even though she had put it back later? She felt isolated and unsure of herself. There was no-one she could talk to about it, except Laura, of course, though Jo wasn't sure she would approve of her actions either. She thought, as she had from time to time throughout her life, how nice it must be to have a brother or sister to confide in at such a moment. She could have talked easily enough to her mother about it, had she been in England, but it was hardly the sort of topic you could raise over the phone. No, there was only Laura. She would talk to her as soon as a suitable opportunity arose. Jo toyed with the idea of telephoning Laura straight away and seeing if she could call on her tonight but decided that it was too late. And while talking to Laura would be helpful, in the end Jo would have to decide for herself what she should do with the information now in her possession. She was going to do something about it, for Rita's sake. She thought that she really ought to give it to someone in the media, or tell a journalist about it. Her thoughts turned to Geoff. Could she tell him? Could she trust him?

She returned to her sheaf of papers and found herself reading Harry's words about Jane Templeman. She was astonished and repelled. Could he have written this while having an affair with the woman?

Further on she came to 'UNDERWOOD, James.' He was that seedy-looking drunk she'd seen in Laura's room upstairs. It seemed ages ago now. What did it say about him? 'Potential troublemaker. FG will keep an eye on him.' Then a later entry: 'May have financial difficulties. Daughter with severe anorexia.' And later again: 'Trying to organize rebellion on benefit cuts. Succeeded in forcing amendment.' With a much later date there was the following: 'Suspected of embezzling company funds. Nothing proved – no action taken against him.' Then lower down, 'Leading rebellion on Soc. Sec. Benefits Bill. Potentially serious problem. Took him to see PM who told him co-operation would be rewarded in next re-shuffle. He'd like Social Services or Treasury. Bin.' Finally, a year later: 'Complaining about being passed over. I said we knew he'd milked his company and will expose him if he makes trouble again. Said he'd needed money for daughter's treatment abroad and he'd now paid it back. Should have used NHS!'

Jo remembered the pathetic figure who'd avoided shaking hands with her. Now she understood why. She felt sorry for him. How he must hate Harry Hunter. She felt much the same about Harry herself.

She turned the page and was shocked to see 'WALLINGBURY, Michael.' Alongside it said, 'Unknown quantity. Not official candidate. Elected by popular local vote.' Then below that: 'Potential problem on foreign policy. Loner. No Clubs. Hasn't sought committee posts. Intellectual. Nothing in background apparently. Suggested to PM he's safest on board.'

What on earth would Barbara think if she knew about this? For that matter, what would Michael think?

Jo felt suddenly very tired. She had lost track of the time and it was very late. She really ought to go home. She put the sheaf of papers back into the envelope and carefully replaced it behind the row of *Hansards*. She would look at the rest of it tomorrow and try to find a better hiding place for it while she decided what to do about it. She cleared her desk and a few minutes later left her office, pausing only to say goodnight to Dave on her way out of the building.

CHAPTER TWENTY-FOUR

Jo awoke early the next day and once again she walked to work. It gave her time to think and the exercise made her feel good. It was a perfect spring morning, the air clear, crisp and invigorating. It would be quite mild later in the day. As before, she called at the little café near her office for coffee and croissants and stepped out afterwards full of energy, but no nearer a decision about what to do about her find or, for that matter, about her job.

She wondered how she could face being in the same room with Harry, let alone talk to him, now that she possessed his sordid secrets, but she could hardly give up her job when she had only a few weeks more to do. What excuse could she make for leaving early? In any case, there was no going back now. She'd seen the book, taken the copies: she'd have to do something about it. The die was cast. The question was, *what* should she do?

When she reached her office she glanced into Vic's room to say good morning to him. He was sitting at his desk, talking to someone on the telephone. He covered the mouthpiece, 'Can you stop a moment? I've got something for you.' Jo waited. He hastily finished his conversation, replaced the receiver and stood up.

'Your friend called earlier and left your bag,' he said with the look of satisfaction of one who has solved a problem that has defeated everyone else. Jo was so taken aback she said nothing. Vic reached behind the door of his room and brought out the missing bag with a flourish. 'There you are,' he said, smiling at her. Astonished, Jo took it from him.

'My friend?' she asked. Vic's telephone had started to ring again. He returned to his desk, put his hand on the phone in readiness to answer it and facing Jo, he said, 'The man who picked it up yesterday.' Jo was frowning, so he added, 'You know, the chap who came in with you in the morning. He forgot to take it away with him and you were out when he called back for it in the afternoon.'

'He's not a friend of mine. He's Lois's friend,' said Jo. The phone was still ringing, so Vic hurried to explain. 'That's right. He explained that it was Lois's and that she'd asked him to get it fixed. He described it to me, so I went down and got it for him. I think you were over at the House.' Before Jo could say anything, Vic picked up his phone. Now he had his back to her.

'Yes, sir. Just let me make a note of that.' He was taking a message. Jo's mind was racing. She remembered the man who'd come into the building behind her, who'd asked after Lois. What did he say his name was? Andy? So he'd come back and asked Vic for her bag. Who the hell was he? He'd walked in, cool as you please and asked for her bag! And having kept it overnight, now he'd brought it back! Jo's astonishment was giving way to fear. She looked cautiously inside the bag. The camera was still there. Nothing had been added, as far as she could see. She closed it again. Vic was still talking on the phone with his back to her. Could this man Andy have known what Jo had had in the bag? Surely not. How could he possibly have known? Jo relived her visit to Harry's flat, reviewing every second of it. She'd seen no-one in the building. No-one could have seen her going in or out of the flat, surely. Her mind raced on, remembering her conversation with Ann and Tim. Had someone seen her somehow, on some hidden camera? And this man who'd brought the bag back? Who was he? What did he know? Her anxieties erupted into one overwhelming thought. Had he gone downstairs to her room? Vic finished his call and put the phone down. He was smiling as he turned towards Jo.

'What a relief to find it wasn't stolen, isn't it?'

'It certainly is,' said Jo. 'Thank you.' It was a relief to be able to return Lydia's camera too, but it had brought a whole lot of worries with it, for Jo if for nobody else.

'Dave had just been telling me about it when your – when Lois's friend called,' Vic went on. 'I must ring Alan in a minute and tell him the good news. He was very worried. Thought he might lose his job, poor chap. Of course if I hadn't asked him to cover for me yesterday afternoon, I'd have been here to explain and there'd have been no need to call the police. Hadn't Lois told you he was coming?'

'No, she hadn't,' said Jo, feeling weak. She was at a loss what to say to Vic. If she told him that it was her bag, not Lois's, that she didn't know this man from a hole in the ground and Vic had had no business letting him into the building, let alone take her bag, she'd have to tell the police too. Vic would probably get the sack and she'd have to answer a lot more questions. She could just imagine them: 'Why would this man want your bag, Miss Delvere and why do you think he brought it back?' And she'd have to say, 'I suppose he didn't find what he was looking for.' 'What was he looking for, Miss Delvere?' No, the least said the better. For the moment anyway.

'Did he leave a message for me?' she asked. 'Did he go downstairs?'

'No, he didn't. He asked if he could go down to your desk to write you a note, but I said he'd better do it up here. He said he'd give you a ring in a while. I asked if he wanted to leave a number and he gave me this.' He opened the top drawer of his desk, took out a card and gave it to Jo. It was a business card, with the name A. G. McGovern printed on it. 'He's written his number on the back,' Vic added. She turned it over and sure enough there was a London number written on the back.

'Thanks, Vic.' Jo was relieved that this alarming visitor had not gone down to her room. 'Will you tell the police, or shall I? I don't know what number Alan called for them yesterday.' The last thing Jo wanted was to have to speak to the police herself.

'Oh I'll ring them, shall I?' said Vic obligingly. He was only too glad of the opportunity of ensuring that neither he nor Alan was in any way to blame.

'That would be very kind. Thank you.' Jo hurried downstairs and finding, to her relief, that the room was empty, she immediately checked her hiding place. Her envelope was still there. She checked inside it. Everything as it should be. She replaced it, took off her coat and hung it up and sat down at her desk. Then she remembered that she had not yet collected her post, so she put on her coat again and hurried over to the House. Vic was on the telephone as she went out and gave her a smile and a wave as she passed his office.

When she returned she was dismayed to see Randall standing in Vic's office. He glanced round, then turned his back on her. He did not acknowledge her. Jo was relieved. Evidently he did not want to talk to her, and that suited her fine. She was developing a hearty dislike for the man. She went downstairs to find both Bella and Mary chatting over coffee. Jo, however, found it difficult to join in the conversation. Her thoughts kept reverting to Randall. What was he talking to Vic about? She waited until she had finished opening her post then went up to Vic's office. Randall had gone and Vic was once more on the telephone. Jo studied the rows of telephone directories on the wall beside his desk as if she were searching for the right one. There were dozens of them, copies of all the telephone directories for the whole of the United Kingdom. After a moment, she picked one out and pretended to be looking up a number, leafing slowly through the pages, waiting for Vic's call to end. At last he put the phone down.

'Excuse me, Vic, have you got a pen and paper I could use to note a number down?'

'Certainly.' He handed her what she required and she copied a number out of the book, closed it and handed back the pen.

'Thanks.' Should she ask about Randall? No, better not. Instead she said, 'Did you have a word with the police, Vic?'

'Yes, I told them you'd got it back.'

'Thanks very much. And Alan? I bet he was relieved.'

'I'll say. It's a load off his mind all right. Me too,' said Vic. 'I think everybody's relieved, because of all the worry about that bomb. I had Mr Myers in here just now, saying what a good job it was you'd got it back.'

'How did he know about it?' asked Jo.

'Oh, I don't know. I thought you must have told him.' Vic was unconcerned. 'He was asking what had happened. Thought it was quite funny when I told him that a friend of Lois's had been in for it and brought it back. "How like a woman to make an arrangement like that and forget about it," he said or something like that,' said Vic with a smile.

'Did he now?' said Jo.

'Oh, no offence mind,' said Vic hastily. 'Anyway he didn't mean you. I think he thought it was a bit odd that Lois should arrange for her friend to collect a bag with your camera in it. Alan said you had a camera in it and that's what you were so worried about, isn't that right?'

This is getting complicated, thought Jo. 'It's just a mix-up, not important,' she said with a nonchalance she was very far from feeling. 'Thanks anyway, Vic.' Jo was increasingly anxious about her hiding place downstairs. Randall is capable of anything, she thought. I wouldn't put it past him to search my office. She went back downstairs, wondering how long it would be before she had the room to herself and could retrieve her envelope. And then what? Where should she put it? Mary and Bella were both typing now and Jo sat at her desk, thinking hard, trying to come up with a hiding place. She must take Lydia's camera to the shop and get it mended. Perhaps she should take the envelope with her and post it somewhere. But where? To her flat? No, she must find a hiding place which couldn't be linked with her. Then she had an idea. Vic's room. No-one would think of looking there and if the envelope were found, no-one could link it with her. No, that won't do either. If it's found, it might get Vic or Alan into trouble.

She racked her brains but could think of nowhere else. She walked up to Vic's room again and found it empty. Somewhere in here would do, she thought. After all, it will only be for two or three days, while I decide what to do, and so many people are in and out all the time, if it were found, it could be anybody's, not necessarily Vic's or Alan's. But where exactly to put it? She was standing in the doorway, looking round the room, when the answer came to her. She stepped over to the shelves of reference books and telephone directories and reached up to the topmost shelf. She ran her finger along the edge of it. Thick dust. The directories were tall enough to conceal an envelope. The ones on the top shelf were for Scotland. They looked as if they'd never been used. She didn't think there were any Scottish Members in the building, or secretaries who worked for Scottish MPs, so if she chose a directory for the Highlands and Islands, she could be reasonably certain it would remain untouched. All she needed now was an opportunity to remove the envelope from its present resting place and bring it up here, preferably when Vic was out of the room.

She went back to her room. Now she had decided to move it she was increasingly anxious to get the job done. Harry might summon her at any moment and she wanted to have dealt with it before she saw him. Fortunately Harry didn't ring her. However, Mary and Bella showed no signs of moving from their desks and Jo had to force herself to concentrate on her work. Her telephone rang frequently and she was glad of the distraction. Halfway through the morning, Mary got up and went out to the photocopier in the hall with a pile of papers and files. If only Bella would leave the room too, but as usual she was bent over her typewriter, hard at work.

Then a few minutes later she pushed back her chair and got to her feet, stretched and walked out of the room. Jo waited a few seconds, then leapt to her feet, and hastily retrieved the envelope from behind the *Hansards*. She was none too quick for she was just sitting down again when Bella reappeared. Next, Jo reached down into one of her desk drawers for a plain buff folder and placed the envelope inside it, together with a handful of letters from her desk. She waited a few minutes, then got to her feet, picked up her folder and walked upstairs.

As she reached the top of the stairs she saw Vic emerging from his room. Perfect! He was going to the hall to meet a visitor. She stepped into his room and looked at the row of telephone directories. She felt sure that the first two or three on the top shelf hadn't been moved for years. Would anyone notice if she got one down now?

She glanced involuntarily at the television screen on Vic's desk, thinking of Ann's concealed cameras. Nonsense, there couldn't be one there. Why should they want to watch the attendants? She looked round the room. There couldn't be any such device in here, she thought. She took a directory from the bottom shelf and placed it on the table on top of her folder. Then she quickly stretched up to the topmost shelf, which she could just reach, and pulled out the second directory. She was pleased to see that the top edge was thick with undisturbed dust. She could still hear Vic's voice in the hall just a few feet from her. She must hurry. He could return at any moment. She placed the directory on top of the first one, then reached underneath the pile for the envelope, slid it out of its folder and tucked it into the middle of the directory. Then she reached up to slide it back into its accustomed place. This proved difficult because the directory was now thicker than before and worse still, the envelope tended to slide out as she was on the point of trying to push the directory into its slot. Twice she had to withdraw it again and push the envelope back into place. She was beginning to feel desperate when, at the third attempt and using both hands, she managed to slide the directory into place. Her exertions had made her hot and flushed. She had just bent forward again over the first directory when Vic came back into the room. Jo remained looking down, carefully turning the pages as if searching for a number and giving herself time to regain her composure. She slipped the folder out from underneath the directory and got out a letter, as if checking an address, then replaced the directory and straightened up. She glanced down at the table, in case she had left dust on it. It looked as clean as before. She glanced surreptitiously at the top shelf, nervous lest she had left her new hiding place sticking out slightly, but it looked just like all the other directories and she was confident that no-one would be able to detect any sign of its having been moved. She relaxed, letting out her breath in a long sigh of relief.

'Tired, are you?' asked Vic sympathetically.

'A bit, yes,' said Jo. 'I worked rather late last night.'

'So Dave was saying.'

'It's very easy to get so behind with the work as to be completely swamped,' said Jo. 'I find it pays to stay late sometimes to catch up.' She looked at her watch. 'I'd better get back to my treadmill. I've got to go out in a while to take that camera to be mended.' She went back to her desk. As she reached it her telephone started to ring.

'Hi, Jo,' it was Laura. 'Just checking to make sure you haven't forgotten our lunch date.'

'It's just as well you rang,' said Jo. 'It had gone right out of my mind.' She decided to say nothing of any significance over the phone from now on. She would wait until she saw Laura in private. She arranged to meet in Central Lobby just before one and hung up, deciding to go immediately to the camera shop to get Lydia's camera fixed before any further unforeseen problems occurred. She looked into Vic's room once more.

'I'm going out now to the camera shop and depending how long I take, I may not be back until after lunch.'

'Right.'

'I haven't spoken to Harry yet today and he may ring.'

'Don't worry. I'll tell him you've popped out.'

'Thanks, Vic. Bye.'

When she emerged from the building it was raining: a fine, soft, penetrating spring rain. She paused on the doorstep and reached into her coat pocket for her beret. She put this on, tucking her hair up inside it, turned up her coat collar and hurried away, head bent down against the rain.

At the camera shop, she was told that it would be

difficult to have the camera repaired by Monday, but they would do their best. As she left the shop she checked her watch and regretted not having arranged to meet Laura at the restaurant. She would have to hurry to meet her in Central Lobby on time.

Jo had set out on her walk to the camera shop, happily unaware of the keen interest being taken in her activities by at least three people. If she thought Randall Myers's activities to date were surprising, she would have been astonished had she known that he had been sitting in a car in the street outside her office, waiting for her to emerge. When she had gone some distance, but was still in sight, Randall had got out with an umbrella in his hand, locked the car, put up his umbrella, a large and conspicuous blue and white affair, and walked briskly up the street after her. Nor had he been the only watcher. Andy McGovern and his colleague, the driver of the electrical maintenance van, were also waiting for her, this time in a dark-blue car. They observed Randall dogging her footsteps.

When Randall was some distance away, Andy emerged from the blue car and followed him at a discreet distance. The driver remained where he was, with the engine running.

Randall had followed Jo all the way to her destination, observed her entering the shop and continued past until he reached a bus stop, where he joined the queue. When a bus pulled up a few minutes later, he stepped aside so as to be able to keep the shop Jo had entered well in view. The bus pulled away and Randall was now alone beneath the bus shelter. He folded his umbrella and waited. A few minutes later Jo reappeared and retraced her steps down Victoria Street in the direction of Parliament Square. He emerged from the bus shelter, put up his umbrella once more and set off in Jo's wake.

Andy for his part had observed Jo entering the shop

and Randall taking up his observation post. He had summoned his colleague on his radio and within a few minutes the blue car picked him up, well down the street from Randall's bus stop. He would not have noticed them. They saw Jo emerge from the shop without her bag and Randall set off after her down Victoria Street. They had seen all they wanted and turned off down a side street.

Jo was relieved to see Laura again. She felt as if she had undergone a profound and irreversible change in the forty-eight hours since she last saw Laura. Her whole outlook on life had altered. When Donald had died, she had felt as if her existence had been compressed into a single terrible moment, as if the passage of time had been rendered meaningless. The opposite had happened now: time was suddenly expanded, filled and drawn out. Every passing second seemed significant, and she had the sense of events surging past her while her own life felt suspended, as if she had been immobilized by her lack of purpose and indecision.

'Are you all right, Jo?' asked Laura, who was struggling with her umbrella.

'I've had better days,' said Jo. Laura got her umbrella up at last and held it aloft. She gave Jo a searching look. 'I was worried about you on Tuesday. Are you feeling better now?'

'Not too bad, thanks. Does it seem strange that I'm so devastated by the news about Rita, when I only met her once?'

'No,' she sounded unconvincing, 'I can understand you being upset, but you aren't responsible for what happened to her.'

'I know that. Even so, I can't get her out of my thoughts. It's like Donald's death – so pointless and so unnecessary. Nothing is achieved and the same problems continue. Whether it's the fighting in Europe or the misery in a family like Rita's, for all the politicians' claims about justice and fairness, nothing is changed: individuals are destroyed and they don't give a damn. What happened to Rita seems to me to sum up the hypocrisy of it all.'

'You've got the blues really badly, haven't you?' said Laura. 'I sympathize, but I think you've got to make an effort to fight it, not let it get you down so much. If work's not a strong enough antidote, we must think of something else, don't you think? Some useful activity, perhaps at weekends, which will help you to feel more positive about things.'

Dear Laura, thought Jo. The work as an antidote! If she only knew! But now was not the time to start telling her.

'It's good to see you smiling,' said Laura and proceeded to entertain her with a description of the scene outside the Palace of Westminster on Tuesday evening, following the bomb alert. Jo thought how confident Laura always seemed and how unruffled, even by the most dramatic events. What would she make of Jo's find? They were nearing the restaurant. Jo said, 'There's something I'd like to talk to you about, when you've got some time and we can talk privately.'

Laura glanced at her. 'This sounds serious. What's up?'

'I think perhaps it is rather serious and I'd like your advice, but we'd need a bit of time if I'm to explain everything properly.'

'I'm agog,' said Laura. 'The suspense will kill me. The trouble is I'm doing something tonight. Can it wait until tomorrow?'

'Oh yes, it'll keep.'

'Then why don't you come home with me for the weekend. We'd have the place to ourselves and plenty of time to talk. And we could have a restful time, some good walks. It'll be looking great now, with the trees coming into leaf. How about it?'

'I'd love that. Thanks.'

'We might even be able to get away early, with a bit of luck. Will you have to see Harry tomorrow?'

'It depends on his schedule. The way I'm feeling, I wouldn't care if I never saw him again. Come to think of it, I think he feels the same way. He seems to have gone into hibernation as far as I'm concerned.'

'He's probably afraid of you,' said Laura with a chuckle. There may be more truth in that than you realize, thought Jo, but said nothing. They reached the restaurant.

'Why don't you bring a bag in with you tomorrow morning, with the stuff you need for the weekend, and we can go straight from work? Charles won't be around in the afternoon, or not for long, and I dare say Harry will disappear early too.'

Randall had been following them at a distance. He had seen Laura emerge from St Stephen's Entrance as Jo approached the door. When they walked together to the edge of the pavement and stood, waiting to cross the road, Randall had been standing at the corner of Parliament Square. He tipped his umbrella forward, apparently to shelter his face from the rain, but really to conceal himself from their view, and drew out a notebook from inside his coat, which he then studied for some moments. When Jo and Laura had crossed the road and gone on their way, he straightened and followed them to the restaurant. He lingered on the doorstep for a minute or two after they had disappeared inside, then entered the building and glanced into the restaurant from the hallway for just long enough to note where Jo and Laura were sitting and identify their companions. Had anyone taken notice, they would have thought he was looking round the room for a friend. He nodded to the waiter and withdrew without having been spotted by Jo or her companions. He paused in the hallway to make a note of the names in his little book then stepped into the street and started retracing his steps. A few minutes later he hailed a passing taxi and returned to the camera shop, where he told the manager that he was a plain clothes police officer investigating terrorist activities and produced an official-looking document and pass to support his demand that the camera left with them by Miss Delvere be handed over to him forthwith. It would be returned to the shop, unharmed, within a few hours. The manager complied without demur and having signed a receipt in a name other than his own, Randall Myers left the shop with Lydia's camera in a plain plastic carrier bag. Not long afterwards he handed it over to a man in an office in Whitehall and for the second time in less than twenty-four hours the camera was subjected to a minute but fruitless examination, inside and out.

In handing the camera over to his colleagues, Randall did not expect anything significant to be revealed, especially if the CIA had got there first, but you could never be sure. His superiors were unaware, as yet, of the CIA involvement and would approve of his initiative. More importantly, it might lead to some opportunity for private enterprise and advancement. His diligent observation of people in the Palace of Westminster, his cultivation of friendships amongst MPs and Peers and his willingness to do the 'dirty' jobs his superiors preferred to avoid, had enabled him to accumulate a wealth of information with which he had amassed riches beyond all his expectations in a series of overseas bank accounts in various names. This video camera was unlikely to produce any information at all, but he might pick up some useful gossip from the forensic people and he was confident that continued observation of Jo and her American watchers would produce information of value to his department and opportunities for his personal advancement. He was not concerned whether or not such information was of value to the country. In his experience, intelligence-gathering was rarely of benefit to the nation, whereas it was sometimes of benefit to his superiors and more frequently to himself, offering a path to either influence or affluence, sometimes both. However, he had always to be careful about how long he held on to information for his personal use before passing it up the line. He had to be particularly careful if he withheld any part of it. If anyone else was following the same line of inquiry he could get caught out. If those above him thought he was becoming too powerful, or acquiring an edge over them, he would be doomed. He had almost always to share, to a greater or lesser extent, the opportunities which came his way. Only occasionally could he run a scheme entirely on his own.

As he walked back to the restaurant to resume his observation of Jo and her friends, he indulged in a little pleasurable speculation about the possible explanations for Jo's activities and the Americans' interest in her.

CHAPTER TWENTY-FIVE

As usual, Barbara and Ann were at the restaurant ahead of them. Barbara was wearing a violet wool dress with a broad black patent-leather belt. She was leaning forward, arms folded, both elbows on the table, talking in a confidential manner to Ann. Her thick dark hair swung forward as she moved her head, emphasizing something she was saying. Ann looked very pale next to her. Her hair was drawn back into a loose pony-tail at the nape of her neck. She was sitting at an angle to the window and the light fell in such a way as to emphasize the hollows of her eyes, temples and cheeks, making her look thin and delicate. She looked up and waved to Jo and Laura. Barbara turned her head, saw them and smiled.

'Hello, you two,' said Laura, sitting down opposite Ann. 'You look very pleased with yourself, Barbara. Have you won the lottery or something?'

'No, nothing like that.' Barbara looked smug. 'Try again.' Jo took the last chair, so that she had Ann on her left and Barbara opposite her. Like Ann, she was at an angle to the window, and had a view of most of the room, which she liked. When it came to eating in restaurants,

Jo believed people fell into two distinct groups: those who liked to watch the room and those who cheerfully ignored it. She always liked to be able to see her surroundings and the other diners. Barbara and Laura, she decided, were definitely the other type. They plunged straight into a conversation; their surroundings were of little interest. Laura was facing the window. Outside, pale sunlight was breaking through the clouds. The rain droplets on the window sparkled and a shaft of sunlight fell across their table. Laura pushed up the sleeves of her dark-green roll-neck top in an impatient gesture and looked round to catch a waiter's eye. There were reddish glints in her hair where the sunlight caught it. She turned back to the table and looked at Barbara with a smile. Laura had a natural authority and seemed always to dominate the group, Jo realized. She was assured, cheerful and good-natured. Jo felt great affection and admiration for her cousin, feelings which at that moment were also slightly tinged with envy.

'Michael's been promoted?' said Laura.

'No.' Barbara sat back in her chair and laughed.

'Out with it Barbara,' said Laura. 'What secret are you bursting to share with us?'

'I was on the point of telling Ann. Now I won't need to repeat myself. There are five of us for lunch today.'

'What's that? Is someone else joining us?' asked Ann, who hadn't been properly paying attention but had been reading the menu.

'He or she's already here,' said Barbara, 'but won't be needing a chair. I'm pregnant.'

This was met by a chorus of approval and delight from the others. Laura ordered champagne and they toasted Barbara and her baby. Jo couldn't help thinking about Donald and the family they might have had. The deep sadness which was always there, underneath all her thoughts, welled up once more. The effort of trying to suppress it produced a dull ache beneath her ribs. Laura gave her a sympathetic, understanding look and reached over to Jo's glass and moved it towards her. Have something to drink, her eyes were saying to Jo.

'Let's order some food,' she said and they studied the menu.

'I don't know why we bother to read this,' said Ann. 'We must know it by heart by now.'

'Don't you ever go anywhere else for these lunches?' asked Jo. 'Don't you get fed up with this place, always having the same things?' She was filled with an intense longing to get away from everyone and everything she had ever known, to start completely afresh where no-one knew her and she could perhaps build a new life and shake off her feeling of despair. She'd enjoyed this interlude and in many ways it had helped her, but she still felt like an outsider. She would miss her new friends. She envied them their contentment. She looked at Barbara, sitting opposite her. She's totally happy with her lot in life. She's fulfilled, she thought.

'Oh, I like this place,' said Barbara, 'but then I probably don't come here as often as you three.'

'There isn't anywhere else close to the House that isn't fearfully expensive,' said Laura. 'Believe me, we've checked out all the possibilities over the years.'

The conversation turned to family and domestic matters for some time, Laura and Barbara swapping jokes and vying with each other with strings of portentous-sounding names for the infant. Jo thought Ann seemed rather preoccupied and wondered whether she too found this talk of babies disconcerting for some reason.

'Did you work very late last night, Ann?' she asked.

'Oh no, I went straight home after our supper. What about you?'

'It must have been after nine o'clock when I left, but I didn't get on top of my work, unfortunately.'

'You wouldn't catch me working late,' said Ann, 'not if I could help it. Fortunately there's not much call for it in the Serjeant-at-Arms's department. Talking of which, I heard this morning that you'd had a bag stolen from your office.'

'Goodness, news gets round fast! How did you hear about that?'

'Anything that causes concern about security always comes through to our office – and to Black Rod too, of course – because if changes have to be made, the Serjeant and Black Rod have to take care of it. Especially after Tuesday night's bomb. What happened exactly?'

'The panic's over. My bag was returned this morning.' Jo felt uneasy about the turn the conversation had taken. She didn't want to lie to Ann but couldn't tell her the whole story either. She would have to go along with what Vic had said and leave it at that.

'That's amazing. Did the police find it?'

'No. The doorman said that a friend of Lois's took it by mistake and brought it back this morning. So no harm done.'

'What a relief,' said Ann.

Jo was anxious to reach safer conversational ground, so she said, 'Tell me Ann, do you get involved in Tim's work at all? I mean, do you have to do a lot of entertaining and that sort of thing?'

'Not as much as if we were overseas. I'm going to have to do a certain amount when this peace conference is on. Some of us will have to look after the spouses of the delegates, taking them sightseeing and shopping. By the way,' she added, 'Tim and I were wondering if you would be free the weekend after next to come to Sunday lunch. Not a lunch party, just us.'

'I'd like that very much. Thanks.'

'If you came over during the morning, we could go for a walk, if the weather's nice, or laze over the Sunday papers. Just come when you feel like it. What's the matter?' She had noticed the change in Jo's expression. Jo was staring across the room.

'It's that creep, Randall.' Ann followed her gaze and saw Randall on the far side of the room, walking towards a table already occupied by another man.

'It's a free country, Jo. If he wants to meet someone here for lunch, you can't object, surely?'

'Of course not. It's just the sight of him reminded me—' she stopped. She couldn't possibly say what she was reminded of. 'It's just that he's such a creep.'

Laura was listening. She glanced round at Randall.

Randall was sure he had been observed by Jo but was careful not to look in her direction. He would have been content to eat alone, but was pleased to see a man from the Committee Office, whom he knew slightly, sitting by himself. 'Hello, James,' he said, 'are you eating alone?'

'I would have thought that was fairly obvious,' said the other, who was on his dessert course. Randall was un-ruffled by this unfriendly response. 'Mind if I join you?' That the man minded was plain from his expression but he said nothing and carried on eating. Randall could have sat opposite the man, but took the chair next to him, so that he could observe Jo's table out of the corner of his eye, and obtain a more direct view simply by turn-ing his head slightly to face his companion. He kept up a flow of trifling conversation, much to the irritation of his reluctant fellow diner, who vowed to himself never to eat alone again without bringing a book or newspaper in which to bury himself and who finished his meal as quickly as possible. Randall, however, was determined to delay him long enough to convey the impression that they had had a date and insisted on pouring him a glass of wine, which the other drank in gloomy silence, while Randall consumed a plateful of pasta.

Jo found it difficult to take her eyes off Randall. She

231

wondered who his lunch companion was. She could see from Randall's expression and gestures that he was conducting an animated conversation. What the other man felt about this she could not tell as he had his back to her.

'You seem rather down, Jo,' said Barbara, who had felt ever since her marriage that no-one could be quite as fortunate as she. Her pregnancy seemed to have enhanced all her senses and had heightened her feeling of being somehow privileged compared with everyone she knew. She could not have put these feelings into words but she felt a strong desire to see her friends as happy as she was. She had shared her secret with them. Now was the time for them to do the same. 'Tell us what's wrong,' she urged. Why not? thought Jo, emboldened by the champagne.

'If you found out something really awful about someone through your job, what would you do about it?' was Jo's reply.

'That would depend on what it was I'd found out,' said Barbara. 'I suppose if someone had committed a crime, one should tell the police. Of course, if *I* found out something like that, I'd tell Michael. You should tell Harry. What have you discovered?'

Jo was losing her nerve almost as quickly as she had found it. This conversation might take her where she did not yet feel ready to go.

'I wasn't saying I'd discovered anything. It was a hypothetical question.'

'Was it?' Barbara sounded disbelieving. 'What prompted it?'

'Oh, just something I – something I overheard,' said Jo.

'I wouldn't set too much store by what you hear in the Whips' Office. They're a terrible lot of old gossips,' said Laura. 'D'you know,' she added, warming to her subject, 'I believe that men are just as much inclined to gossip as women, more so perhaps, certainly in Parliament.'

'Do you? Why?' asked Barbara.

'Just think of any occasion when you have two or more MPs standing about with nothing to do, except talk. You should have heard them in the Whips' Office when I used to work for Ben Radstone. Admittedly that was years ago, but I'm sure they're just as bad now: taking people apart, banging on about who's screwing whom, who's gay, who's up to their hocks in debt and so on. They *loved* it, picking over scandal, particularly people's affairs. Not that I'd be sitting in on these conversations mind, but you'd hear the tail end of it as you came into the room, that sort of thing.'

'Well, I don't believe they are all constantly having affairs. This idea that they're a lot of randy Lotharios, looking for sex all the time, is garbage,' said Barbara, indignantly. 'I just don't think it happens, at least not on the scale the media would have everyone believe. I mean to say, half of them no sane woman would touch with a bargepole and most of them are so busy that they just wouldn't have the time.'

'I agree,' said Laura. 'In any case, most of them are much more interested in fame than sex. They'd much rather be on television than in bed with a gorgeous girl.'

This rather stumped Barbara, who didn't care to agree with either assertion. She was saved from comment by Ann, who said, 'They certainly flock to the chamber for the bits of debate which will be shown at peak viewing time and you can see them adjusting their posture and expressions for the benefit of the cameras.'

'Vanity thy name is politician,' said Laura. She noticed Barbara looking disapproving. 'Do you remember Budgie?' she asked.

'I certainly do,' said Barbara. 'Claude Parsimmer,' she said to Jo, who recognized the name from Harry's dossier and was trying to remember what it had said about him.

'He's dead now and not widely mourned, I should say,' Barbara continued. 'We used to call him Budgie because he was so vain. He could never pass a mirror without pausing to look at himself and to pat his hair in a satisfied kind of a way. Eventually someone said – probably you, Laura – "One of these days he'll kiss the mirror," and that's how he got his name.'

'He was repellent,' said Laura. 'He'd stand much too close to you or brush against you as he passed your desk.'

Jo had been secretly relieved that Laura and Barbara had taken over the conversation and was somewhat taken aback when Ann said, 'You haven't told us what you heard, Jo.'

She wasn't going to let herself be put on the spot again. She said, 'I'm sure Laura's right and one shouldn't pay attention to gossip.'

Laura was looking at Jo intently. She had noticed her watching Randall's table earlier.

'I think it's something to do with Randall,' she said. She immediately sensed Jo's unease and regretted her words.

'It wasn't, as a matter of fact, though frankly nothing about him would surprise me,' said Jo. 'It really doesn't matter too much,' she added, before anyone could pursue the point, 'because I shall be leaving soon.'

'Will you?' said Barbara in a tone of disappointment.

'Lois will be coming back very soon,' said Jo. 'Either during or just after the Easter Recess.'

'You're not going to leave, are you, Jo?' asked Ann.

''Fraid so. Unless one of you has a bright idea about some really desirable job here for a woman of my talents. Not another Harry, please.'

'We'll have to cast about and see who's going. Would you like to stay in the House?' asked Barbara.

'I'm not sure that I would, actually. I'm in two minds about whether to go back to Geneva or not.'

'Why's that?' asked Ann.

'I've got a flat there. I'm letting it at the moment, but it takes a long time to get a resident's permit for Switzerland and I don't think I want to lose mine. I'll probably go back.'

'When?' asked Barbara.

'Straight after this job ends, if nothing better comes up in the meantime. I may take a holiday first, visit Australia and New Zealand. After that I'll probably go back to the UN. There's an assignment for me in the Middle East, provided I make up my mind soon.'

'I feel quite envious,' said Laura.

'Why don't you come on holiday with me?' said Jo. 'Why don't we all go?' She paused, then added, 'It seems to me that the secretaries have to work much harder than the Members most of the time and I don't think they're really appreciated. It would shake the place up if everyone downed tools. Just imagine if all the secretaries walked out. The whole place would grind to a halt.'

'They're not all total wasters, you know, Jo. Michael works very hard. In fact I worry about him. He needs a holiday,' said Barbara.

Her companions laughed, causing other diners in the restaurant to look round at them. Barbara blushed. Laura said acidly, 'I reckon he'll be getting one soon. They all will, the Government's in such a mess.'

'It's all right, Barbara,' said Ann, 'we all know that Michael's one of the best.'

'I was just saying that the secretaries seem to me to work terribly hard – a lot of the time, anyway,' Jo explained.

'Barbara was always burning the midnight oil,' said Laura.

'Well we know why that was, don't we?' said Ann.

Barbara smiled at her. 'Now you do. Don't tell me you knew at the time, I won't believe you.'

'Michael's a lucky man,' said Laura warmly, regretting her earlier tone.

'I must get going,' said Jo. 'I'm so behind with everything, I'll not have got on top of the situation before the job comes to an end.' She turned to Laura.

'Can you take care of my share and I'll settle up with you tomorrow?'

'Sure thing,' said Laura.

'Don't let me break up the party. Thanks everyone. I'll see you anon.' Jo stood up.

Barbara said, 'I must be going soon. I'm meeting Mike shortly.'

'Hang on a minute,' said Ann, 'I haven't finished my coffee.'

Jo noticed Randall glance quickly in their direction and look away. She saw that he was now alone. She had not noticed his companion leave. She put on her coat. 'See you tomorrow, Laura. Bye everyone.'

As Jo threaded her way between the tables, heading for the door, Ann said in a low voice, 'Hang on a minute, you two. Just wait a bit. Watch Randall.'

Randall was folding his table napkin in a nonchalant manner and getting to his feet.

'He must have paid his bill already,' said Ann thoughtfully. 'There goes, Jo,' she said, seeing Jo hurry past the window. Randall left the restaurant and a moment later he too passed the window.

Ann said, 'It's rather peculiar, but I'm beginning to wonder if Jo isn't right.'

'About what?' asked Laura.

'About Randall. She's convinced he's following her. She said that she was sure he was trying to eavesdrop her conversations at our party the other day. It's most peculiar because I could swear he was watching her during lunch and that he got up to leave as soon as he saw her do so.'

'Oh come off it, Ann,' said Barbara, 'why on earth would he be following her?'

'Perhaps he's a stalker,' said Laura, 'obsessed with her every move. I can just see it, can't you?' she said to Barbara.

'It's not a joke, Laura. I'm serious,' said Ann. Laura felt it was anything but a joke, but wished to conceal her feelings on the matter, at least until she and Jo had had a chance to talk.

'Sorry, Ann. I must be going,' she said briskly, signalling to a waiter for the bill. 'Are you two walking back to the House?'

'Yes, I'm going back to my office,' said Ann.

'I'm meeting Mike in Central Lobby,' said Barbara.

'What about next week?' asked Laura.

'I can't make Tuesday,' said Barbara. 'Thursday OK for you?'

Thursday was agreed upon and Laura said she would tell Jo.

'I hope it's OK for Jo,' said Ann as they left the restaurant, 'it sounds as if she won't be with us much longer.'

'Goodness, Ann,' exclaimed Barbara, 'you make it sound as if she's dying, or something.'

'No, I don't.' Ann was indignant. 'She'll be leaving us soon. She said so herself.'

CHAPTER TWENTY-SIX

Jo did not go straight back to work. She wanted to spend a few minutes alone, so instead of turning off towards her office, she walked on until she reached the Embankment, intending to carry on towards Lambeth Bridge. The sight of the river was soothing, in spite of the traffic roaring past her. The sun was shining and after a few moments she stopped to gaze out across the river. Two massive red and white barges were moving slowly upstream. She was standing under the trees and there was a cold current of air rising up from the water. It carried a faint but not unpleasant smell from the river. She was reminded of holiday places of childhood, of harbours and canals. She placed her hands on the wall and felt the cold gritty texture against her palms. She let herself lean against the parapet wall and relaxed, bringing her arms up and folding them in front of her on top of the wall.

She wondered if she would ever do the things she'd always expected to do when she first came to London years before, like a trip to Greenwich for a picnic in the park, seeing the galleries and museums she'd not visited since she was a schoolgirl. Then there was the Palace of

Westminster. She'd not yet looked really closely at the place and taken it all in. I must look at the pictures and explore some of the nooks and crannies before I go, she thought.

She was unaware of Geoff Harper striding towards her along the pavement from the direction of Lambeth Bridge. He had spotted her from some distance away. His spirits rose at the sight of her and he wondered what to say to her that wouldn't cause her to hurry away as she so often did. He wouldn't have long, but he wanted so much to talk to her. He admired her profile, her luxuriant hair, wisps of which were blowing out above the collar of her coat which she had just pulled up around her neck and was holding together under her chin. As he drew closer he could see that her lips were compressed, her jaw tense. He wondered what she was thinking about. He stopped beside her.

'Not thinking of jumping, I hope?' As soon as he uttered the words he regretted them. They sounded so silly. She turned towards him and he read a succession of different expressions in her face. She was pleased to see him, but irritated by his words. She immediately suppressed this reaction, fearing that he would think she was always irritable. He looked so unsure of himself she felt quite sorry for him. Should she confide in him? Yesterday it had seemed like a good idea. Now she was unsure again.

'What a stupid thing to say!' he said, drawing his head back and giving an embarrassed little laugh. 'I don't know why I said it.' She smiled at him and he relaxed. 'Actually I was wondering what you were thinking about as you watched the river. It's good to look at, isn't it?'

'I was just thinking of all the things I've never done and places I've never seen in London. It's always the way when you're about to leave somewhere, don't you find?'

'You're not leaving are you?' He was deeply disappointed. 'When? Why are you leaving?'

'It's only a temporary job. I thought you must know that. Harry's secretary will be coming back soon, probably in the Easter Recess.'

'I don't really know Harry's secretary. She's not my type.' He smiled a little as he said this. Jo was wondering what his type was. She found the remark off-putting, but she liked his smile.

'Aren't you going to stay on? Why don't you work for another Member?' he asked. She has such a sombre look, he thought. Perhaps she's sad to be going.

'Another Member? I don't think so.'

'If you don't mind my saying so, you look rather down. Are you OK?'

The sympathy in his voice and his eyes was too much for her. It was strange that she could confide in Laura, even to the extent of talking about Donald's death, and yet stay in control of herself, but at the sound of Geoff's voice, her emotions suddenly lurched out of control. She was unprepared for his sympathy. In another moment her feelings would get the better of her. She turned away and leant against the wall, clasping her hands together tightly. Instantly he realized she was in the grip of powerful emotion. He would have liked to put his arm around her shoulders. He was glad he had said what he did. He felt he was on the point of becoming close to her at last. He turned to face the river too and rested his arms on the wall.

'I'm sorry,' he said. They stood together in companionable silence and she was pleased to find that it wasn't necessary to speak and he wouldn't put any pressure on her. After a moment or two the crisis passed. She sighed.

'Are you all right?' He was careful not to look at her.

'I'm fine, really, but I do feel depressed about my job.' She proceeded to tell him about Rita. She was calm and matter of fact and he realized that she had moved on to

240

something else and was not going to confide in him. He had lost his chance. He was trying to think of a way back and did not realize the importance of what she was telling him. 'What a tragedy,' he said when Jo told him of Rita's suicide. 'Her poor children.' But his response sounded mechanical and she wrongly attributed his detached tone to cynicism. What's another tragedy to him after the things he's seen around the world? she thought. Nevertheless, for Rita's sake, she decided to persist with her narrative in spite of this and was about to continue when she saw him glance at his watch. He had hoped she wouldn't notice. She was irritated. He wasn't touched by Rita's death. There was no point in telling him about Parrie after all.

'Don't let me keep you,' she said. 'I must get back to work myself.'

'You're not keeping me. I want to talk to you.' There was a note of urgency in his voice. 'It's just that I should have been back for Question Time. I'm supposed to cover it. Part of the job, you know. But so long as I'm back for Prime Minister's Questions, it doesn't matter too much about the rest. It's all such a charade anyway.'

'How true,' said Jo, and you're part of it, she thought. You're ready to indulge your own whims, chat me up when you feel like it, but someone like Rita is of no importance. She turned away from the river and started to walk towards the road. He accompanied her, furious with himself for having spoiled his chance of getting to know her better.

'I'd love to talk to you when we've both got more time,' he began.

'Would you?' she said. 'We'll see.' She saw a gap in the traffic and ran across the road. He watched her for a moment and went on his way disconsolately. Neither of them was aware that Randall Myers had been watching them from a side street on the far side of the

241

Embankment. After Geoff had gone a little way, Randall set off and followed Jo until he saw her enter her office building. Then he turned back towards the Palace of Westminster, entering by St Stephen's Entrance a few minutes after Geoff.

Jo returned to her desk feeling disappointed not to have been able to confide in Geoff and wondering who she could turn to. Perhaps Laura would have some suggestions tomorrow.

She was surprised but pleased to find a message from Harry saying that he would not have time to see her that afternoon and asking her to leave any letters for his signature when she had finished. She settled to her work, resolved to get on top of the backlog before she went home, so that she would have a better chance of leaving early on Friday and enjoying her weekend with Laura. It would be good to get out into the country after so many weeks in London.

At about four o'clock Mary announced that she was putting the kettle on and asked Jo and Bella if they would like something to drink. Bella said, 'Nothing for me thanks,' and continued to rattle away at her keyboard. Jo opted for black coffee and sat back in her chair, marvelling at Bella's capacity for work. Mary had just handed her a mug of coffee when Patricia Hunter walked into the room.

'Hello, everybody,' she said and walked over to Jo's desk. 'How are you, Jo?'

'I'm very well, thank you. How was your trip to America?'

'Most enjoyable. I didn't want to come back.' She put a small parcel down on Jo's desk. 'This is a little something by way of a thank you for keeping an eye on things for me. I hope it wasn't too much trouble.'

'Not at all.' Jo felt guilty and prayed she wouldn't blush. She hardly ever did so, but on those rare occasions when it did happen, she would go scarlet to the roots of her hair. She was afraid it would happen now. 'It's very kind of you to bring me a present. You really shouldn't have. I haven't done anything very much.' What a liar you are, she told herself. Not done anything! 'Can I get you something to drink? A cup of tea?'

'No thanks, I can't stop. Were there any messages at the flat? When did you last go?'

'Tuesday morning, I think it was. No it wasn't. It was Wednesday morning,' Jo corrected herself hastily. 'No, there weren't any messages. Just some mail for your son.'

Mrs Hunter could see Jo was ill at ease and sensed that any minute now her suspicions about Harry would be confirmed. She baited her trap: 'Oh, Johnny must have left the day before, I suppose. Did you meet him?'

'No, he'd evidently stayed at least one night, but I missed him,' said Jo, unaware of the furious turmoil her words had caused in Mrs Hunter's thoughts.

'What a pity you didn't meet him. You'd like Johnny,' Mrs Hunter went on, concealing from Jo the huge effort she was making to sound calm.

Would I? I wonder, thought Jo. So it was Johnny who'd been at the flat. Did that mean it was *Johnny's* book that she had copied? Perhaps the son was collecting information through the father and using it to blackmail people. What a thought! And what a close shave I had. Just supposing he had come back while I was there, or when I was putting the thing back.

'Did he leave the place tidy? He's terribly lazy sometimes. Leaves the place in such a mess,' said Mrs Hunter with the indulgent smile of a doting mother. Inwardly she was seething. So Harry had been there. But who had he been with? She'd find out somehow.

'There were some dirty crocks in the kitchen I think,' said Jo, her words stoking the furnace of Mrs Hunter's fury.

'You're a dear to have gone round there at all,' said

Mrs Hunter, with supreme self-control. 'Thank you so much. I won't have to trouble you again because I shall be in London from now on until the Recess. And then Lois will be coming back, won't she?'

'I believe so,' said Jo.

'We'll be sorry to lose you,' said Mrs Hunter. 'Thank you again. Bye.' She was gone. Jo breathed a sigh of relief. She opened the little package and found three pretty enamelled bracelets. It was bad enough to have accepted Mrs Hunter's gratitude when her mind was full of plans to betray Harry. She couldn't bring herself to wear the bracelets. She slipped them back into their wrapper and put them in her bag.

Jo did not see Harry that afternoon, or on Friday. She couldn't stop thinking about his wretched book. With time to reflect, she had swung back to the view that it couldn't belong to Harry's son because she was sure some of the entries were in Harry's handwriting, although she had had no opportunity of retrieving her envelope to check.

She was beginning to wonder if Harry were avoiding her, if somehow he knew she had taken his dossier. It was so unusual not to see him all week. When she looked into the Whips' Office early in the afternoon, Jack told her that Harry had left for the day. Jo decided to follow his example and just before three she and Laura drove out of New Palace Yard and headed west out of London for Laura's family home in Wiltshire.

CHAPTER TWENTY-SEVEN

'Will any of the family be there?' asked Jo.

'No, we'll have the place to ourselves. Mum's away visiting an old friend and won't be back until Tuesday. Robert and Jamie usually visit only in the school holidays when they can bring their wives and all the little darlings with them. It's just as well, really, isn't it?'

'I suppose it is,' said Jo, who was actually very pleased no-one else would be there. Much as she loved her aunt and cousins, she didn't feel equal to seeing them at the moment.

She was anxious to talk to Laura but thought it better to wait until they reached their destination to broach the subject of Harry's book. Laura for her part was dying to talk to Jo about Randall, but decided she ought to let Jo say what she had on her mind first. She didn't want to make her anxious. Laura had speculated at length about Randall and his interest in Jo, but remained puzzled. After all, if Randall were keen on Jo he was hardly the man to be reticent about saying so. There had to be some other reason for his behaviour.

So neither woman said much during the journey. After

a while Jo dozed off and awoke when Laura slowed the car to turn in at the gateway to her mother's cottage. It was a charming place, secluded, peaceful and unchanged in all the years Jo had known it. It was several years since she had stayed there and the sight of the white cottage, with its low slate roof, and the luxuriant garden filled her with nostalgia.

The house had been unoccupied for several days so Jo carried things in from the car and went round opening shutters, while Laura turned on the central heating and lit a log fire in the sitting room. Then they drove to the nearby village for provisions. Having stocked the larder for the weekend, they thought they might as well cook themselves supper and it was nearly nine o'clock when they dropped into comfortable armchairs in front of the fire. Laura switched on the television and they watched the nine o'clock news, which was preoccupied with the agenda for the European peace conference, due to start in just over a week's time. There was an item about the various officials and delegates arriving in London, including a clip showing David Wesker talking with his opposite number at the Foreign Office. Jo sat up in her chair. Then there was an interview with the Prime Minister, who talked about the need for forbearance and patience, for openness, frankness and trust, about European unity and the need for total commitment to the search for peace. The effect of this on Jo was that of a cork being drawn from a champagne bottle which has been vigorously shaken. She fizzed with anger and poured out what was on her mind.

'Damned hypocrite!' She turned to Laura. 'Do you want to watch any more of this or can I tell you something?' She didn't wait for Laura's answer. 'Don't say anything until I've explained the whole thing,' she began. 'I've got to tell you everything so you'll understand.' And she told Laura the whole story, beginning with Rita's first telephone call and the words scribbled on Harry's notepad.

She got to the point where she saw the book on Harry's desk. 'But for Rita, I probably wouldn't have noticed it at all, or wouldn't have paid any attention to it,' she said. She described how Parrie's name had caught her eye and what she had read about him. 'How about that?'

'It *must* be the same man. It's appalling!' said Laura.

'And that's just one entry,' said Jo. 'You should see the rest of it. There are references to drug addicts and prostitutes, blackmail and bribes.'

'What can it be, I wonder?' Laura looked puzzled. 'You know, you're pretty amazing to be able to absorb all that detail in just a few minutes,' she added.

'I didn't.'

'What do you mean? Did you sit down, make yourself at home and read it from cover to cover?'

'Not exactly.' Jo hesitated. 'This is the bit you're not going to approve of. I was afraid someone would come in and find me reading it.'

'Oh Jo, what have you done?'

'I brought it away with me and photocopied it,' Jo said in a rush. 'Then I put it back.'

'You did *what*? Are you *mad*?'

'You don't understand, Laura. I was so horrified when I saw what was in it. When I think of Rita and others like her, their lives ruined by a man who *abuses children*, who's not fit for human company let alone to be a judge – I couldn't *bear* it. I felt I was going to burst I was so revolted and angry. And so, well, I took it. I thought, I'm going to do something about this and I stuffed it in my bag and bolted. Then later on, after I'd copied it I took it back. I only had it for two or three hours at the most. But I can see you don't approve.'

'Don't approve! I'm staggered. No, don't get me wrong. It's not that I don't approve. If the things in it are true, then it's absolutely terrible and I'd probably have

247

done the same thing. I'm just very worried. Suppose you were seen taking it? And sometimes it's possible to tell when a book's been photocopied because it flattens the spine. Sometimes it's never quite the same again. Supposing . . . Well you must have left fingerprints all over it, for example.'

'But it's not that kind of book. It's more like a file. And I did try to wipe my fingerprints off it.'

'Are you sure nobody saw you?' said Laura.

'What if they did? After all Mrs Hunter had asked me to go round there. Anyway I was terribly careful going back. I must have looked very furtive, if anyone did see me. I had a nasty moment because that dreadful fellow Randall Myers followed me over to the House. He stuck to me like a plaster and I had to resort to various devious moves to shake him off.' She smiled at the recollection and told Laura how George had helped her.

Laura was looking thoughtful. She decided to say nothing about Randall for the moment. Instead she said, 'Tell me more about the thing.'

'Well, it was indexed, with the letters of the alphabet down the side, so the entries were in alphabetical order. There seem to be quite a lot of cross-references. There would be an entry under one name and then "See so and so". So some of them link up with each other. I checked the Commons directory and a lot of them are MPs. It began with Allarde and ended with Wiste. There are lots of initials and dates.' Jo started to describe as many of the entries as she could remember.

'Good God!' Laura sat bolt upright. 'I've just realized what you found.'

'What?'

'The Black Book!'

'It was black as a matter of fact,' said Jo. 'What is it?'

'The Chief Whip's Black Book. It must be! There have been lots of rumours about it over the years but its existence was never really confirmed.'

'What's it supposed to be?'

'Any talk about it was always terribly vague, and certainly never gave the slightest inkling of the sort of things you've described. No, the impression was always given that it was just the Whips' notes about any MPs who were letting the side down.'

'You make it sound as if there's nothing unusual or bad about it.'

'Well, on the rare occasions there was ever talk of it, it was always treated as something that all political parties do: a legitimate means of keeping tabs on things that might cause embarrassment.'

'Like what sort of things?' asked Jo. 'Not the kind of things I've been telling you about, surely?'

'Certainly not. No, it was always said it was things like someone having an affair with someone else's wife or husband, or continually failing to show up for important votes, or behaving badly on overseas trips, getting drunk, that kind of thing. But it was rumoured the Whips used the information they had to put pressure on people to make them toe the line, vote the right way when it matters, that sort of thing.'

'Well they do that all right.' She told Laura what it said about Jimmy Underwood. 'It puts him in a new light doesn't it? But it's *much* worse than that, I can tell you. The sort of things in this book would cause more than embarrassment, if they got out. I think some people would end up behind bars.' She paused. 'Now I think of it, that's exactly what Harry was saying to Jack about this pollution scandal: "He'll end up inside, if this gets out."'

'Who was he talking about, d'you know?'

'No. I didn't hear a name. But whoever it was, he's not the only one. The more I looked at that book the more obvious it became that a number of the people listed in it are child abusers – paedophiles, as they're called.'

'I hate that word,' said Laura. 'I've always felt that it's used to make what they do sound excusable in some way. Don't you agree? It makes it sound like some kind of illness or something, as if they can't help themselves.'

'I agree,' said Jo. She was silent for a moment, thinking.

'Go on,' said Laura.

'There were dozens of entries,' said Jo, 'some of them going back years. There was a reference to blackmail. And drugs. And something about some secret report being suppressed, the Vector report I think it was called. What was the name? Sanderell.'

'Sanderell. He's a top civil servant at the Department of Health,' said Laura. 'Can you remember any other names?'

'Seeing the news reminded me of one of them. There are these references to this place Kistrington and sexual perversions and videos. *And* there's something about that chap Wesker we saw being interviewed just now, about taking him there and setting him up. Maybe he's a pervert too. Or maybe he's being blackmailed by Harry or something. It's absolutely sickening. I keep thinking about Donald and all the other people who've died – for nothing! – at the instigation of politicians who are so corrupt and so hypocritical.'

'It's appalling!' said Laura. 'I'll never be able to feel the same way again about working there. The financial scandals have been bad enough but *this*! To think this sort of thing is happening, and the Whips cover it up! It's terrible.'

'There were quite a lot of things that didn't make any sense to me,' said Jo. 'Symbols and letters. Amounts of money and dates. And some of the names didn't feature anywhere in the Palace of Westminster directory. Some of the figures must be donations to Party funds. There were references to insider dealing, undeclared gifts, currency dealing and tax evasion. And getting knight-hoods for people, and directorships. And someone receiving payments from overseas in gems. And to think there was that inquiry into MPs' outside interests and disclosure of fees. All that was supposed to have been cleaned up, wasn't it?'

'That's a joke, isn't it?' said Laura sarcastically. 'Self-regulation never worked anywhere. The ones doing those things are hardly going to turn themselves in, are they? People like Allarde and Wiste just wave two fingers at them and carry on feathering their nests.'

They sat in silence for a while, then Laura said, 'Can you remember anything else. Any other names?'

Jo leaned back in her armchair and closed her eyes for a moment, 'Let me think.' She opened her eyes and looked at Laura. 'I wish I could have brought the photo-copies with me to show you.'

'I was going to ask you just now,' said Laura. 'Where have you left them?'

'Oh, they're quite safe, I think. I put them in an en-velope in the top row of telephone directories in Vic's room, second one from the left.'

'You did what?' Laura was aghast. 'Someone'll find it!'

'No they won't,' said Jo calmly. 'I looked very care-fully and I can assure you no-one's touched any of those directories in *years*.'

'But supposing they do now?'

'So what if they did? There's nothing to connect it with me.'

'I suppose not,' said Laura.

'I wanted to bring them to show you, but didn't get an opportunity to retrieve them. Vic was there all the time.'

'Did you see anything in the book about Charles?' asked Laura.

'No, not that I noticed. No, I'm sure there wasn't. I

don't think I saw Ian Swift's name in it either.'

'Good,' said Laura.

Laura sat in silence, waiting for Jo to come out with more. Jo sat and thought for a few moments. 'Brandon. Dick Brandon, I think it was. There was something about him having changed his name to conceal some offence from a long time ago.'

'Dick Brandon? I don't believe it. What did he do?'

'I can't remember. Sorry.'

'Never mind. Who else?'

'There was Fairbrand.'

'Fairbrand. What does it say about her?'

'I forget. And Camborough. I'm just trying to remember what it said about him.'

'Camborough. The Foreign Secretary?'

'Must be,' said Jo. 'And there was someone called Brook-Ainlee. That mean anything to you Laura?'

'Robin Brook-Ainlee. He's a television journalist. A Lobby correspondent. Terribly pleased with himself. What did it say about him? I can't stand the fellow.'

'I don't remember what it said about him, I'm afraid,' said Jo and yawned.

'The Whips are suspected of using Lobby correspondents to do hatchet jobs on people. He's the kind of person they'd use,' said Laura.

'Lots of them had this peculiar sign written in alongside them. It was a bit like two capital Vs, one inverted over the other, sort of crossing over each other in a diamond shape.'

'I wonder what that is,' said Laura. 'Perhaps it's a Masonic sign. I wouldn't be surprised. An awful lot of MPs are Masons. Men who like secret rituals and prancing about in leather aprons probably enjoy kinky sex too.'

Jo yawned again.

'Let's continue this riveting conversation tomorrow, shall we?' said Laura. 'I'm happy to stay up if you want to. But if you feel like turning in, we could get a good night's sleep and maybe go for a walk tomorrow and you can tell me more.'

'Good idea,' said Jo. As they were going upstairs, she said, 'One of the worst things was to find there's a senior police officer involved, called Kingborne. He's been covering things up for them for years and is now a big noise in Scotland Yard.'

They returned to the subject of the Black Book as soon as they got up the following morning. In fact they talked of little else all weekend. They were walking in the wood near the house the following day when Laura said, 'I didn't tell you last night because I didn't want to spoil your sleep by alarming you, but Ann seemed to think that fellow Randall followed you out of the restaurant on Thursday and I must say, after everything you've told me, I think she was right. Though why he should follow you, I don't understand.'

Jo repeated what Ann and Tim had said on the Wednesday evening. 'Perhaps he is a spy or agent or whatever they like to call themselves. But why should he have been snooping on me almost from the outset? I don't understand it.'

'Maybe he checks up on all newcomers,' said Laura, 'though I've never heard of such a thing in all the years I've worked in the place. I find it hard to believe.'

'Did Ann tell you about my bag?' asked Jo.

'No. What about it?' Laura's reaction to Jo's tale the previous evening was nothing to her reaction when she heard about Andy McGovern. She was horrified. 'But we've got to tell the police!'

'What can I tell them? That I stole Harry's book and someone stole my bag – possibly someone who knew what I had done, though God knows how – and that having made illicit copies I put it back? What does that make me look like?'

253

'Well we've got to do something about both of them, Randall and this man McGovern. I'll see what I can find out.'

'How can you find anything out?' asked Jo.

'There are various people I could ask, I think,' said Laura. 'There's George, for a start. He'd help us, I'm sure. He's a mine of information. He'll have a good idea what to do.'

'I'm not sure I want you to tell anybody what I've done, Laura. Not yet, at least. I've got to decide what to do first.'

'I won't do anything without your say-so. Don't worry about it. Let's enjoy our weekend.'

It was easier said than done. Neither of them could let the matter alone. Jo couldn't remember everything she'd read. 'There was such a lot of it anyway. I didn't read it all. I was going to have another look at it, but then all these strange things happened and I got nervous.' Laura questioned Jo minutely until she had extracted every detail Jo could remember. She thought that some of the names Jo had seen were those of Opposition MPs.

'So Harry keeps tabs on them too. I wonder what he does to them?' she said.

Laura decided that the initials sprinkled throughout the book were the initials of various Whips. 'Harry probably puts in the initials of the Whip who provided him with the information. Each one is supposed to keep an eye on the MPs in his area and no doubt reports everything he learns to the Chief Whip, who writes it all down in his book.'

'There's something revolting about it, don't you think?' asked Jo. 'They think they're above the law.'

'And they *make* the law. It's appalling,' said Laura sadly.

'And Harry allows it to go on happening,' said Jo.

'Maybe he benefits,' said Laura. 'The scope for blackmail must be enormous.'

'And the Prime Minister must know about it too. And the rest of the Cabinet,' said Jo. 'And that reminds me.' She told Laura about the letter 'P' beside some of the names and the plain list of names in the 'P' section. 'What do you think that is?' But Laura couldn't throw any light on it.

'I've just remembered something else,' exclaimed Jo and told her what Harry had written down about Jane Templeman.

'God! How revolting! He does that and has an affair with her. And as for her – she's prepared to let an innocent man rot in jail. I don't know which of them is worse,' said Laura.

'Well,' said Jo finally, 'what should I do about the Black Book, do you think?'

This was the question that exercised them for the rest of the weekend. 'I think we've got to be terribly careful,' said Laura. 'There is so much at stake and the people involved are so powerful that I think they'll stop at nothing to cover it up, and us too.' She saw the expression on Jo's face. 'I'm deadly serious. Just think about it. It would seem from everything you've told me that it's not just scandals that have been covered up but criminal activities. And then there's Randall and this strange fellow, McGovern. We don't know what they're up to. You must be very careful Jo and if *anything* out of the ordinary happens, you must let me know and you must tell the police.'

They decided that the first thing to do was to make at least two more copies of the dossier and leave one either in a bank vault or with someone trustworthy, like a solicitor, and then decide what to do with the others. Laura suggested that one should go to the Speaker of the House of Commons and, because of the involvement of a judge, the other should go to the Lord Chancellor as head of the judiciary. Jo wasn't so sure about the wisdom of this. She favoured giving one to a journalist. Laura pointed out that there was a senior journalist included in the book and maybe there were media and newspaper proprietors as well.

'There's another thing,' said Laura. 'We don't know how reliable everything in this book is. After all, if the Whips get the information from other MPs, it might not be true. Think how tempting it must be for some of them to do down their rivals and prevent them from getting promotion or whatever by feeding lies about them to the Whips. It seems to me that whoever we give it to may well say that.'

Their efforts to put the matter aside and enjoy the rest of their weekend were rather spoilt by the Sunday newspaper which carried a long article about Mr Justice Parrie's imminent appointment to the Court of Appeal. Jo was beside herself with fury.

'Look at the picture of him!' she exclaimed. Laura came and looked over her shoulder. 'He looks so pleased with himself, standing there with his wife. I wonder if she has any idea what he gets up to.'

'I don't see how you could live with someone for years and not have *some* idea,' said Laura.

Jo said, 'It says here he was divorced and remarried a year later, so she's his second wife.' She read on. 'Listen to this! "A devoted family man, Mr Justice Parrie is highly regarded for his ability to handle a bitter divorce or a sensitive case involving a child." I can't stand it.' She pushed the paper away from her and stood up. 'We've got to do something about him.'

CHAPTER TWENTY-EIGHT

While Laura and Jo were reading their Sunday paper, a heated discussion was going on between Andy McGovern and two of his colleagues, in a room in the American Embassy. The man who had acted as McGovern's driver was annoyed.

'Why the hell didn't you do the job properly?' He brandished a photograph in his right hand. It was a picture of the two pages of Harry's book which had been visible as it lay open on his desk and which Andy had photographed. 'This isn't nearly enough to go on. Didn't you get any other details?'

'That's easy for you to say, Lew. We were told the place was going to be empty, for Christ's sake. Are you saying I should have stayed there and let her find me?' Andy protested. 'We didn't have a clue who she was. Supposing it had been the daughter? Next thing we'd have had the cops turning up and we'd probably both have been arrested. Are you nuts?'

'It would have been better if you'd taken the book. We could have put it back later,' Lew insisted.

'Oh yeah? And what if Hunter had come back?'

'Well this is worse than useless,' said Lew sarcastically.

The third man spoke. He had been sitting in silence for some time, listening to the others. They both looked at him.

'We haven't got time for recriminations. Let's just run through the checks we've made so far, shall we?'

'OK, Jerry,' said Lew. 'We've had very little time, so for the moment we haven't got much. One of our contacts in Parliament said Delvere had worked for NATO and the UN. We've checked our records for both organizations to see what we could get on her and her husband Donald Hammond, but didn't come up with anything significant. However, there are two important points: first, we can't find out what she did for at least two years between the NATO and UN jobs. We know she went from Brussels to Australia and then she seems to have disappeared. And second, after he gets killed, she drops out of sight for a while, then just as the European conference is agreed, she gets this job at the House of Commons. We can't find out very much about her here, except that the father's dead and the mother remarried and lives in New Zealand, but we can't locate her. The lack of detail could be significant. And where was she during those missing two years?

'What do you think, Andy?' asked Jerry.

'We know she's not working for the Israelis,' said Andy, 'and we're almost certain she's not working for the Brits. I think we should tip our hand to the Brits and if she's one of theirs that'll let them know we're wise to them.' He sat back in his chair.

'We'll come back to that in a minute,' said Jerry. 'Just let's finish going through what we have.'

'OK,' said Lew. 'None of the people we've talked to in Parliament knows anything about her. She plays her cards very close to her chest, never talks about her past to anyone. We know she's friendly with this woman,

Laura James. It seems James got her the job. It's a temporary job – ideal cover for a short-term assignment. She appeared on the scene just as the peace conference was being agreed. On the other hand, she couldn't have known that the woman she was replacing would have a skiing accident – unless that was arranged of course, but that seems unlikely. So the job *appears* fortuitous. And there's nothing on the James woman at all. She's very highly thought of in Parliament. Delvere got the job on her say-so apparently. So either James has been duped, or she's in league with her. Delvere could have been looking for a temporary post and this one just came up, but that doesn't quite fit either, because apparently temporary jobs in the Commons are usually done by people who work there already filling in for each other. For someone as important as the Government Chief Whip to take an outsider for a short-term job like this is very unusual.'

Andy interrupted, 'Let's get one of our British contacts, like Myers, to find out more about her.'

'We'll come back to that in a minute,' said Jerry. 'Carry on, Lew.'

'We've searched her apartment and found nothing of any use at all. Her passport's not there so she must be carrying it with her. She's sharing with a woman called Lydia Rowe who's away at the moment. She's an airline stewardess. We've checked her out but there doesn't seem to be any long-standing connection. Delvere's only been staying with her since the New Year. And another thing: Delvere's got hardly anything there. One suitcase and not many clothes. So she's clearly here on a short-term assignment. She's also moved out of her apartment in Geneva, but where to? We haven't been able to find out.'

'So we're left with the book,' said Jerry.

'Yes,' said Lew. 'The thing is, did she stumble across

it or was she sent to get it? This doesn't help us much, as I was saying.' He tapped the photo.

Jerry reached across and took it from him. He placed it on the table in front of him and looked down at it for a moment. Then he spoke, 'OK. Let's see what we've got. One name, Geoffrey Moreton. We know quite a lot about him already in fact. These dates and sums of money don't tell us anything. Perhaps someone's putting the bite on him. There's a diamond shape here. We can't get anything on that. Unfortunately there must have been a shine on the page, or a fault on the camera to make the image fade out like that down the right side of the page.' Andy grimaced. 'It's just bad luck,' said Jerry calmly. 'This capital "P" could be a single letter, part of some initials or a word beginning with P. There are no clues further down the page. Then we have "Chairman Moreton Micro." An electronics firm. They make components for the arms industry and have had some big, top-secret contracts for the MoD. They had a spot of trouble over export licences a year or two back but have friends in the right places. What's next? "Violent. Kingborne." There's a senior police officer called Kingborne. The rest of it's too faint to make out. Can you remember anything else, Andy?'

'There wasn't time, I think it was an address book of some kind. It had an alphabetical index.'

'OK,' said Jerry, 'we've got these questions: who is she working for? What's her assignment? What's the significance of this book? Why did she take it? And finally, what's she done with it, or what's she going to do with it? The video camera she was carrying can be safely discounted. Our guys say they couldn't get anything from it at all. No film, no useful prints and the damn thing didn't even work properly. So we think she really was taking it to get it mended. Maybe she intends to use it later, but it's hardly state of the art for concealed camera work. More like something for home movies.'

'Yeah, that's why I took it back,' said Andy. 'Myers had spotted me and I didn't want to give the Brits any opportunity to make trouble for us, saying we'd stolen it.'

Jerry resumed his assessment, 'So, the only solid bit of information we've got is this guy Moreton, who works in the arms trade. She could be after information that Moreton or his company has.'

'Hang on a minute,' said Lew. 'Why was this thing where she found it? Who does it belong to?'

'We can eliminate the wife and the daughter, I think,' said Jerry. 'That leaves Harry Hunter and his son. OK, so Hunter's a member of the Cabinet, but it's not as if he's Foreign Office or Defence.' He looked down at the photo again. 'We've checked this against a sample of his writing and we're pretty certain he didn't write it. We haven't been able to get anything in the son's writing yet, but we do know he brokers deals between banks and governments for large infrastructure projects on the Pacific rim. He helped put together a big fund, some of which is being used in China at the moment. It could well be his. On the other hand he's out of the country at the moment and if this is of any importance he'd hardly leave it open on his desk for weeks on end. So we come back to Hunter Senior. We know he goes to this flat with his mistress, which was why you were there in the first place. She's the last possibility, Jane Templeman. It could be hers. In fact this could be the most interesting connection. She's a journalist. She's separated from her husband. He's a Cabinet Minister *and* he's Defence Secretary.'

'Yeah, but it still doesn't add up,' said Andy dejectedly. 'We've been monitoring the place since Wednesday and she hasn't been near it. If the book's hers, why hasn't she been back for it?'

'Could be she left it there for Delvere to collect,' said Lew thoughtfully.

'Strange kind of drop if you ask me,' said Andy. 'She left the book open. Hunter could have seen it.'

'You said it was covered with a newspaper,' said Lew. 'And don't forget the bomb explosion. That would have thrown them into a panic and could explain a lot. Also the wife's back and we know she was there on Friday afternoon. We heard her talking to herself. She was pretty mad with someone, you should have heard her language,' he added with a chuckle.

'The bomb is the other thing we should keep in mind, in case there's some connection,' said Jerry thoughtfully. 'The Brits haven't come up with anything on that yet, or else they're keeping it quiet.'

They were all silent for a moment. Then Jerry said, 'I think we should do as Andy suggested and let the Brits know what Delvere's up to. We can either let them think we've got the book – show them that – ' he gestured towards the photo, 'it's not much good, but we can let them think we've cut it – or we can tell them she's got it. We'll be seen to be doing them a favour, warning them about her, and we can let them think we got the photo at her apartment. Agreed?' The other two nodded. 'But first, we must put some pressure on her and see if we can't get some information out of her,' Jerry continued. 'Andy, I think you should see her and say we're going to tell the Brits about her if she doesn't co-operate, but if she tells us who she's working for and what they're up to and we'll buy what she's got and get her safely out of the country. What do you think?'

There was silence for a while after he finished speaking, then Andy said, 'It works for me.'

'Me too,' said Lew.

'If the Brits don't want her we can take her ourselves,' said Jerry. 'The main thing is, whatever she's up to we should be able to prevent her interfering with Washington's plans.'

'Unless she's a decoy,' said Lew. Another silence followed this. Then Jerry said, 'It's the best we can do for the time being. We'll have to see what pans out. Now what about this contact of yours, Andy?'

'Randall Myers. He's the obvious choice because he spotted us on Wednesday,' said Andy. 'I wouldn't be surprised if he contacted me to find out what we were doing. We know he followed her on Thursday and impounded the camera.'

'OK. Get on to him straight away and see what you can find out. Show him the photo.' Jerry got to his feet. 'Report back to me this evening.'

Randall was not surprised to receive a call from Andy and agreed to meet him at lunch-time at a pub in Kennington. They were friendly but cautious with one another.

'You were overstepping the mark on Thursday, weren't you?' said Randall. 'There could be a complaint about you coming on to the premises. You know that, don't you?'

'Exceptional circumstances require exceptional measures,' replied Andy.

'What was so exceptional about the circumstances?' asked Randall. Andy just grinned at him.

'You didn't get anything from that camera, did you?' said Randall.

'No, and neither did you,' said Andy, 'but I bet you'd like to know why we were interested.'

'I dare say you'll tell me when you're ready.' Randall was indeed very keen to know why the Americans were so interested in Jo. He had his own suspicions but whether they coincided with theirs remained to be seen.

'We're interested in a trade,' said Andy.

'Maybe what you've got isn't worth having,' said Randall.

Andy produced the photograph. 'We took this in Delvere's apartment last night. She was away, naturally.' He grinned at Randall. 'It's a sample of what she's got. You'll get the rest provided you tell us what you know about her and why she wanted this.'

Randall looked closely at the photograph. 'How much more is there?' he asked.

'Quite a lot. It's a book, in fact,' said Andy. 'But we're more interested in her. It's not what's in the book that interests us as much as the use she has in mind for it. We think she may be out to sabotage the peace conference and we want to know who she's working for. We feel confident your people either know that already or can find out. Tell us that and you'll get the rest of it.'

'First I need to know where she got this.' Randall tapped the photograph.

'You haven't given me anything yet,' said Andy. 'What do you know about her?'

'Very little,' said Randall. The Americans can't know anything either, he thought, or they wouldn't be asking me, but I'm not going to queer my pitch by sharing everything I know with them, not for a while anyway.

'She's told no-one anything about her past,' said Randall, 'which is unusual, especially in that place. She's got no family, apart from a mother in New Zealand with whom she doesn't seem to have been in contact recently. We haven't been able to track the mother down because she's travelling apparently.' Randall said 'we' but his researches had been entirely his own idea and he had not so far shared his findings with anyone else. 'We know she worked for NATO some years ago and was working for the UN before she came here. That's all we've been able to find out, so far.'

'You haven't told me anything we didn't already

know,' said McGovern. 'We want to know who she's working for.'

'I might be able to let you have something more shortly. First I need to know where she obtained this.'

'Why don't we talk again tomorrow?' said Andy. 'I'll come to the House of Commons.' Randall frowned. 'You can't object,' Andy continued. 'I'm coming to meet you, after all. Official business. I'll see you in Central Lobby at, let's see, a quarter of three – two forty-five to you.'

Randall thought long and hard about McGovern's photograph. He knew a certain amount about Sir Geoffrey Moreton and wondered why Jo was interested in him. It wasn't long before he was on the right track. Andy McGovern had referred to a book. What kind of book? And how would Joanna Delvere have it in her possession? She worked for the Government Chief Whip and Randall knew quite a lot about *his* activities. It was most likely to be something to do with him.

The longer he considered the matter, the more convinced Randall became that Joanna had the Government Chief Whip's secret dossier in her possession. Randall had heard talk of this in the past. What wouldn't he give to know what it contained. But why had Jo taken it? And who was she working for? Surely if she had taken it, the Chief Whip would have had to notify the Prime Minister and the security service. Randall's boss, Mackie, would have had him and others keeping an eye on her and her contacts, if she hadn't actually been arrested. But Mackie hadn't said anything to him. So did she really have it? He ought to go and see Mackie about it himself. It would look bad if he didn't pass this information on quickly. Clearly that was what the Americans expected him to do. However, he would leave it for a few hours, maybe until tomorrow, as there was a distinct possibility of turning this latest development to his own advantage. Sir

Geoffrey Moreton would no doubt pay substantial sums to prevent disclosure of certain activities. But first things first. He must go to Joanna's office tonight and search it thoroughly. There was always a possibility she would have left something there.

CHAPTER TWENTY-NINE

'I'm glad that's over,' said Laura, as they turned in at last to New Palace Yard and drove down into the underground car-park. 'We were crazy not to come back last night. I won't make that mistake again in a hurry.'

Jo was equally glad that the journey was over. They were both feeling apprehensive. Laura had hardly spoken since they left home and had fretted and sighed and complained about the traffic and made little attempt to conceal her anxiety. Over breakfast they had had a disagreement about the course of action they should follow. Laura was anxious to do something quickly. She was convinced that delay could be dangerous to Jo in some way. Jo had resolved not to discuss the matter further for the time being. She didn't regret telling Laura; she trusted her completely and was glad to have shared the burden of her knowledge with her, but the problem was of her making and she would have to decide for herself what to do with it.

They got out of the car and Jo retrieved her overnight bag from the back seat. Laura locked the car then paused for a moment, looking at Jo across the roof of the vehicle.

Then she slapped her hand down on the car. 'I don't know what's come over me!' she exclaimed. 'I'm sorry, Jo.' She walked round in front of the car and hugged her. 'Of course it's up to you, not *me* what should be done about it. I've been a pain, haven't I? It's because I feel it's my doing that you're in this situation at all. I should never have persuaded you to take the job.'

'Don't be silly. I'm glad you did. It's been good for me.'

'Has it? I hope so.'

'It's been a revelation,' said Jo.

'Hasn't it just? For me too. Anyway, I'm glad you told me about it.'

'Same here,' said Jo. 'Don't worry, Laura. I won't do anything rash, I promise. And I'll let you know first. That's if you want me to, of course.'

'Of course I do! I don't want you getting into any difficulty because of this sordid business and I'll back you up, no matter what happens. Just be careful who you talk to about it.'

'I don't propose to talk to anyone about it other than whoever I decide to hand it over to, maybe the Lord Chancellor, or the Speaker – I've just got to give it a bit more thought.' They left the car-park and started up the stairs. 'I have to decide whether to do something now, or wait until just before I leave, but I think it ought to be soon, this week probably.'

'Careful,' said Laura, lowering her voice, 'you never know who's listening in this place. There always seems to be someone coming up behind you, or just around the corner. The place is stuffed with inquisitive gossips.'

They parted company in Members' Lobby, after collecting their bundles of mail from the Post Office. Jo started towards the Whips' Office, intending to check whether Harry was in and ask when he wanted to see her, but changed her mind. She would go over to her office and open the mail and wait for him to ring her. As she hurried towards Central Lobby she met Ann.

'Hello, Jo,' she said. 'I tried to get you on Friday but you must have gone early for a change. You'll find a message on your answering machine. I'm afraid we want to change lunch next weekend from Sunday to Saturday, if that's all right with you.'

'That's fine by me,' said Jo. 'Or would you prefer to leave it to another time?'

'No. We're looking forward to it. Tim wondered if you might like a game of tennis.'

'Great, but I should warn you I'm not very good.'

'Same here. Don't worry about that. We'll see if we can rope someone in for doubles. Anyway, bring a racquet and come over about ten-thirty, why don't you?'

Unusually, there was no-one in Jo's room when she hurried in and dropped her bundle of mail on the desk. Mary was usually in early, especially on a Monday, but neither she nor Bella had arrived. The central heating was going full blast, even though the weather was much milder, and the room was hot and stuffy. Jo took off her coat and opened the window by her desk. She sat down and reached for the playback button on her answering machine and was surprised to see that the light wasn't flashing. There were *always* messages on her machine. Hadn't Ann just told her she'd left one on Friday? Jo played back the tape and sure enough there were half a dozen messages waiting for her, including Ann's. There must have been a power cut during the weekend.

She took the cover off her word-processor and noticed that the keyboard was not in the position in which she usually left it. This did not strike her as particularly odd, however, because the cleaners came in very early each morning and there was one who was particularly thorough with her dusting. Jo was glad of this because the static charges generated by all the office machinery attracted a great deal of dust. But a moment later, when she reached inside a desk drawer for her shorthand note-book, she realized with a shock that someone had been through her desk. Her thoughts raced. She experienced a turmoil of different sensations. Surprise, anger, fear swept over her in rapid succesion. She sat motionless, thinking hard. Who could have done this? The person who sprang to mind was Randall and she felt furious at the thought of him poking around amongst her belong-ings. After a moment she stood up and looked at the row of *Hansards* on the shelf. Yes, they looked different. She went over to them and tried to reach behind them, but found they had all been pushed back against the wall. She sat down. Again she looked at the *Hansards*. Of course, it could have been the cleaner who'd done that, just as it could have been the cleaner who'd moved her keyboard. But she knew it wasn't. She shivered slightly. Thank God she had moved the envelope. This thought was instantly replaced by another. Supposing it's been found. She had to stop herself from racing upstairs to look. I must be calm and sensible about this. How can I find out who has been in here? I probably can't. I won-der whether there is a doorman on duty over the week-end? Probably not. Randall. It had to be him. What is he up to? Who does he work for? She clenched her teeth. But supposing it wasn't Randall? Supposing it was that man Andy McGovern? Jo stood up. She *had* to check whether her envelope was still there. She picked up her notebook and a felt pen and walked up to Vic's room. He smiled at her.

'How are you today, Jo? Good weekend?'

'I had a great weekend thanks, Vic. What about you?'

'Pretty good, thanks.'

'Do you have to work weekends ever?'

'Oh no, hardly ever.'

'Alan told me last week that your mother had been

taken ill. How's she getting on? Is she better?'

'She's much better now, thank you. She did give us a scare, though. We thought she'd had a heart attack but they checked her out and she's OK.'

An MP came into the room behind Jo and Vic said, 'Yes, sir, can I help you?'

'It's about the heating in my room.' Vic got up and accompanied the man out of the room. Jo could hear them talking as they went upstairs. Now was her chance! She stretched to reach up to her hiding place and fumbled for the directory. It wouldn't move. She hooked her thumbnail under the spine and tweaked it out a little. Now she was able to grip it between finger and thumb and tilt it back towards her. What a relief! The envelope was still there. She could just see the top edge of the directory and make out a small gap in the middle where the pages were parted by the thickness of the envelope. She let the directory drop back and pushed it into line with its fellows. She would leave it where it was for a little while longer.

As she left Vic's room she could hear a telephone ringing in the distance. She raced downstairs. Sure enough it was her phone and it was Harry wanting her to go over straight away with the mail.

The Whips' Office was full of people. Most of the Whips were in, some sitting at their desks, others standing about in groups, talking with various MPs who had looked in to enquire about voting arrangements and other matters. Jo threaded her way through the knots of people. She found her path blocked by Charlie Culver, Roy Phillips, and Eddie Mallins. They were in jovial mood and effusive in their welcome. Even Eddie Mallins, who had hitherto always seemed so dour, smiled at her and joined in the banter.

'Hello, Jo!' boomed Charlie. 'How *are* you?' Before she could answer, Roy said, 'You're a breath of fresh air in this place, I can tell you.'

'Thanks.'

'Good weekend, Jo?' asked Eddie.

'Yes, great weekend. How about you?'

'I had to do rather a lot of constituency work, being the dutiful Member.'

'The upright Member,' said Charlie Culver with a snigger, 'when he's wanted, he comes.' He moved so close to Jo as to be almost pressing against her. She could not move away from him without colliding with Eddie Mallins. 'Which kind of member do you prefer, Jo? Hard-working or up-and-coming?' said Charlie with a sly look. He had his hands in his pockets. He glanced downwards, then up at her.

'Not your kind, that's for sure,' said Jo scornfully. 'Can I come through? Harry's waiting for me.'

'Lucky Harry,' said Charlie, making no effort to move out of her way. She pushed past him. He sniggered again.

'Christ, Charlie, you're drooling,' said Roy.

Jo opened the door of Harry's room and went in. He looked up and said, 'Good morning, Jo' in a cheerful and friendly tone which she could not match. He pushed a chair into place for her next to his desk. She sat down and handed him the folder of letters and messages.

'Good weekend?'

'Yes, thanks.

'I'm afraid we've got a lot to do, Jo. I was under a lot of pressure last week, so there's a bit of a backlog.' He proceeded to work his way through a mound of case notes, correspondence, and messages. She found it difficult to concentrate. As he handed her a page of notes he had made concerning a constituent's housing problem and she looked at his handwriting, she was reminded of his notes in the Black Book. She looked at him, wondering what he thought about the entries he made. What did he think about the people whose misdeeds he recorded in such detail? There was very little of his own feelings to be found in it. Did he enjoy doing it or did it revolt him? Perhaps he didn't care one way or the other. It was very hard to tell what he really thought about anything. He had never given any indication that he cared about his constituents. She had never heard any expression of emotion, as she had heard, for example, from Arnold Hobbs to Mary, about the plight of a constituent.

Her thoughts were interrupted by the telephone ringing. Harry answered it.

'Yes, Pat,' he said. She could hear the sound of Mrs Hunter's voice very faintly. What does Mrs Hunter think about the Black Book? she wondered. What did she think about Rita Hanssen? Maybe she didn't even know about her. Jo had not said anything to Harry about Rita. What was the point? There was no point in saying anything to *him*. She was going to *do* something, though what exactly she hadn't yet decided. She let her thoughts run on. She would do something about Parrie, that was for sure. But would that make any difference to anything? It wouldn't make any difference to Rita's children, would it? Their mother was dead, so perhaps it would be best for them to stay with their father. Poor Rita. Nothing could right the wrong done to her. But there were all the others. All the foul practices so faithfully recorded in Harry's book. Something should be done about them.

Harry put the phone down. 'Penny for your thoughts, Jo,' he said. 'Not worth it,' said Jo. There's a lie, she thought. If I were a blackmailer like you, my thoughts might be worth a fortune.

At that moment, the fax machine next to Harry's desk started to disgorge a message. He reached over and lifted the page from the machine. 'Great!' he said when he had read it. He drew out his diary from his jacket pocket, checked something and said, 'I wonder when Johnny left?' Jo wasn't sure whether he was addressing her or thinking aloud, but replied, 'Your son?'

'Yes,' he was still holding his diary.

'Mrs Hunter said he left last week. Tuesday, I think.'

Harry looked at her with a puzzled frown.

'So when's he due back, do you know?' he asked.

'Well he would have arrived in Hong Kong the next day, wouldn't he?' said Jo. 'Mind you I don't know whether he left London on the Tuesday or the Wednesday.'

Harry was staring at her. 'London?'

Jo read something in his look which made her uneasy. 'I don't know,' she said hastily. 'I'm probably just confusing matters, but your wife would know.'

'Yes, I dare say she would,' said Harry grimly. He put his diary away and stared at the fax.

The door opened and Jack Bendall leant into the room to say, 'We need to have a word with you about tonight.'

Harry pushed his papers into a pile and got to his feet. 'I'll be back in a moment, if you wouldn't mind waiting,' he said to Jo and left the room.

When he had gone, Jo stood up, leaned over Harry's desk and looked through his pile of papers until she'd found the fax he had just read. It was from a Hong Kong number and said:

'Dear Mr Hunter,

John left in such a rush he didn't have time to ring you. He asked me to fax you to say he's sorry not to have been in touch but was in Japan for most of the past three weeks. He is spending three days in Frankfurt on his way back to London but will ring to let you know when he is expecting to arrive.

Best wishes,

Trudy'

Jo sat down. It was her turn to look puzzled. According to this fax, Johnny Hunter had been in Hong Kong and Japan, yet Mrs Hunter had told Jo he had been in London. Why should she do that? She went over the conversation Mrs Hunter had had with her on Thursday and suddenly it dawned on her what she had been up to. Jo gave a disgusted groan.

A minute or two later the door opened and Harry reappeared, followed by Jack and a couple of the Whips. 'I won't be doing any more now, after all,' he said to Jo. 'You may go.' It was a curt dismissal.

On her way back through Central Lobby Jo saw Geoff and Alicia. They were walking towards Lower Waiting Hall deep in conversation. Geoff glanced up and saw Jo, but did not acknowledge her. Be like that! she said to herself. Only too ready to chat me up when your wife's not around. Then you cut me when she is.

She decided not to bother with lunch. There was too much to do. She had a feeling of impending disaster, brought on by Harry's sudden change of manner just now and enhanced by passing Vic's office and being reminded of the envelope and the difficult and unpleasant task she had set herself. Somehow she had to find the opportunity of retrieving it and making two more copies. She would have to do it when the coast was clear, probably in the evening.

CHAPTER THIRTY

At two o'clock Andy McGovern arrived at St Stephen's Entrance. He had chosen the time of his arrival with care. He wanted his presence to be noted by as many of the right people – people who would know who or what he was – as possible. He was certain he had achieved this with the plain clothes police officer standing near the security checkpoint inside St Stephen's Entrance and, if he hadn't, there were always the closed-circuit televisions. More important, if he hung about for a while in Central Lobby, he was bound to be spotted by one or two appropriate people.

He told the man at the security check that he had an appointment with Mr Harry Hunter's secretary and went on through to Central Lobby. However, he did not immediately go to the barrier and ask the police officer to call Jo. Instead he joined the throng of people waiting to see the Speaker's procession. At half-past two the police officer called, 'Hats off, Strangers!' and a hush fell over the Lobby. All heads turned as the Serjeant-at-Arms, resplendent in sword, knee-breeches, and buckled shoes appeared in the doorway from Lower Waiting Hall bearing the mace against his shoulder. He strode into the Lobby, turned smartly to his right and proceeded towards Members' Lobby. Behind him walked the Speaker, a rather frail-looking elderly figure, in his wig and gown, followed by his train-bearer and chaplain. Andy had witnessed this archaic ritual on other occasions. As a staunch republican he felt he ought to find it ridiculous but instead was always secretly impressed.

As soon as the procession had disappeared from view, the hubbub of conversation was resumed. Andy strolled over to the police officer at the barrier and asked if he would kindly telephone Mr Hunter's secretary to ask if she could spare some time to see him.

'Would you care to speak to her on the telephone, sir?'

'I'd much prefer it if she could come over and just give me a few minutes of her time. Would you mind asking her?'

The police officer dialled the number. When Jo answered he told her that 'A Mr McGovern would like to see you, miss. He's here in Central Lobby and wonders if you could spare him a few minutes.'

Jo was astonished by this enquiry. She was beginning to wonder how the day was going to end if it carried on like this. The police officer said, 'Are you there?'

'Yes. I'll be over in a few minutes,' she said, and put the phone down. She sat and stared at it. What can this man McGovern want? She felt decidedly anxious. She picked up the phone again to call Laura then decided against it. There just might be someone listening. There's nothing for it, she thought, I'll have to go and see what he wants.

She spotted him as soon as she entered Central Lobby. He looked bigger than she remembered. He was dressed differently too. She seemed to recollect that he had been wearing jeans and a sweatshirt when he followed her into the building, but she couldn't be sure.

Now he was wearing a checked jacket: Air Force blue and grey checks. Not loud but eye-catching. Dark-blue slacks. He was chatting to the police officer but had his eye on the doorway from St Stephen's Hall and saw Jo immediately.

'Hello, Joanna,' he called. A marked American accent. A loud, carrying voice. He strode towards her. 'Good to see you. Thanks for coming over.' Joanna said nothing. She would let him make the moves.

'Why don't we sit down over there?' He led the way to the bench seat at the side of the Lobby. There was a Post Office and letter box at the side of the Lobby, just behind their bench, which were regularly used by staff and visitors. Andy judged this to be the most conspicuous place to sit. They would be visible to anyone entering or leaving the Lobby. They sat down. Jo turned slightly towards her visitor and looked at him. He was powerfully built and had a confident, good-humoured expression. His voice did not match his look.

'Remember me?' he said in a threatening tone.

'You're the person who was passing himself off as a friend of Lois Young's in order to steal my bag.'

'Borrow, not steal. You got it back, remember?'

'You don't have a camera of your own, is that it?' said Jo sarcastically.

He tipped his head back very slightly. His chin jutted towards her. 'If I were you I'd think carefully before accusing other people of stealing. What do you people call it? The pot calling the kettle black? Yeah. How would you explain what you were doing in the Hunters' flat?'

Jo stared at him. How could he possibly know about that? Or did he? What could he know? But he took my bag. Did he know what I'd had in it? Her thoughts were in a turmoil. Surely no-one could have seen her at the Hunters' flat?

278

'What are you talking about?' Attack was the best means of defence. 'I go there for Mrs Hunter. And what business is it of yours, might I ask?'

'Nice try.' He grinned at her. 'We know what you're up to and things are going to get very hot for you quite soon,' he continued.

'What's that supposed to mean?' said Jo. Whatever he was up to, she wasn't going to let him intimidate her. Nevertheless, she straightened perceptibly and clasped her hands in front of her – a defensive reaction which he noticed with satisfaction. He ignored her question. 'It's quite simple. Either you co-operate with us, or we'll make sure the British know too. Then you'll be arrested.'

She leapt to her feet.

'I don't know who you are, or what you're talking about, but if you threaten me I shall – I'll—'

'Call the police? Hah!' He laughed loudly and a group of people standing near the barrier looked round at them. 'Go ahead. There's one over there. He's looking at you now, as a matter of fact.' With difficulty, Jo stopped herself from looking round at the police officer. She continued to stare at the American. She was very pale. She could feel herself trembling with anger and hoped it didn't show. She was facing him and didn't notice Geoff and Alicia entering Central Lobby from Lower Waiting Hall, though if she had turned her head a fraction she would have seen them.

'Now what's Jo doing with him?' said Geoff in surprise.

'Isn't he one of the heavies from the American Embassy?' said Alicia. Geoff stopped.

'What's he want with her, I wonder? Talk to me, for a moment, 'Lissie, I want to watch this.' Alicia turned slightly towards him and they stood chatting, while Geoff watched Jo and her visitor with narrowed eyes. If only he could hear what they were saying. He could tell Jo was angry. He'd seen that look before.

The American stood up. 'We know what you've got and we'll make sure the British know too. Unless you hand it over to us, that is. If you don't, we'll see to it that they lock you up and throw away the key. Or maybe you'll just disappear. All sorts of unpleasant things could happen to an attractive young woman like you.'

'I don't know what you're talking about. The only person round here who's done anything wrong is you. You've got a nerve, coming here and threatening me.'

Geoff was frowning. 'He seems very pleased with himself, wouldn't you say?' Alicia looked round.

'He does indeed. And she's not too happy about it, by the look of things. But I'm sorry, Sherlock, I've got to go. Let me know what you find out.'

'OK. Bye.' Alicia walked out of Central Lobby, unnoticed by Jo, who continued to stare angrily at her unwanted visitor. He was unmoved and grinned at her again. 'You know what we want and you've got my card, haven't you? I left it with that trusting guy, Vic. I'm surprised you haven't called me already.' He gave another derisive laugh. 'You co-operate and we'll make it worth your while. You've got until – let's see – you haven't been home yet, have you? No,' he grinned again. He was enjoying this. 'You've got until noon tomorrow. If you haven't contacted me by then, we'll turn you in.'

Jo drew herself up and said, icily, 'I don't know what you're playing at, but you won't get anywhere by threatening me. Now I suggest you leave.' She stared at him. He gave a short laugh and turned away. As he did so, he caught sight of Randall, who was sauntering towards them. Jo hadn't noticed Randall before. Perhaps he had come from the doorway by Admission Order Office. Or maybe he had been standing watching them.

'Randall. Hi!' said Andy. Randall nodded to him and waited for the man to join him. Then the two of them walked out of the Lobby in the direction of St Stephen's Entrance.

So they're in league, thought Jo. That shouldn't surprise me. Two thugs together. She was in a turmoil. She was burning hot and could feel perspiration on her forehead and neck, yet her face was pale. She felt furiously angry and frightened at the same time. She was at a total loss what to do next. She stayed rooted to the spot for a moment.

She turned away, intending to go and find Laura and almost collided with Geoff Harper.

'Friend of yours, is he?' said Geoff.

'No, he is not,' said Jo coldly. She was in no mood for silly chat.

'I'm glad to hear it. What did he want?'

'What do you mean, "You're glad to hear it"?' asked Jo. 'You know him do you?'

'No I don't, and I have no wish to. But I know a bit about him. What did he want?'

'Listen to you! What do *you* want? I don't know what *he* wanted!' said Jo angrily. 'Satisfied?'

'God, you're touchy. You ought to be careful who you mix with, that's all,' he said. He was annoyed now.

'And what business is it of yours who I mix with, might I ask?'

'OK, OK. It's the journalist in me, I suppose. I can't help but be puzzled when I see you having what looked like a row with an American agent.'

'American agent! I don't know what you're talking about and I don't know him from a hole in the ground! I wish you'd all leave me alone!' She knew she was being unreasonable, but all her pent-up fury and anxiety had burst out and she couldn't stop herself. 'Call yourself a journalist! Why don't you investigate some of the things in this rotten place which are crying out for investigation?'

'Like what, for example?' he asked quietly.

'I tried to tell you about one of them on Friday, but you weren't interested.'

'That's not true,' he protested.

'Oh yes it is. I started to tell you about Harry's constituent, Rita Hanssen, and you looked at your watch. You were too busy.'

'That's not fair and you know it.'

'Well, you should be checking out this damned judge, Parrie, who shouldn't have anything to *do* with children, let alone lay down the law about them in court. You should be finding out what he gets up to at this place Kistrington, not giving *me* a hard time! Or investigate Sir Geoffrey Moreton, why don't you? Ask *him* about Parrie. Better still, why don't you ask Harry Hunter?'

She turned and hurried away towards Admission Order Office, hoping that Geoff wouldn't follow her. There was no likelihood of that. Once again, Geoff found himself watching her walk away, their relations more strained than ever. He felt a mixture of regret and irritation. Why was he wasting his time with her? She didn't like him and didn't want to have anything to do with him, that was clear. These thoughts were quickly banished by his mounting astonishment at her final remarks. What was she trying to suggest about Moreton? And Parrie? She'd asked him about Parrie at the Fenchurchs' drinks party. He wished he could remember now exactly what she'd said, but he'd been more interested in getting the better of that jerk Randall Myers, who'd been following her about – or so she'd said. And now I've just seen him going off with that self-satisfied Yank who'd apparently been giving her a hard time. What on earth's going on? Whatever it was, it merited investigation and he wanted to be the one to investigate it. He walked slowly across the Lobby, deep in thought. Then he stopped, looked at his watch and made up his mind. What was happening in

282

the Commons Chamber could wait. The first thing he wanted to do was investigate this place Kistrington. He went to the library, studied a map and left the building as Big Ben was striking three o'clock.

Randall's conversation with McGovern was a waste of time. He felt McGovern had used him and was annoyed with himself for failing to anticipate it. He should have known the Americans would be playing some complicated game. Clearly McGovern had gone to the House either to warn Jo or to intimidate her, but he refused to explain or to add anything to what he'd told Randall the previous day. 'We had a deal remember? You haven't told me anything yet?'

If that was the way they were going to play it, Randall certainly wasn't going to enlighten them about Moreton and Harry's dossier. But he'd better not wait any longer to report to Mackie. If Mackie's opposite number were to tell him about Jo before he made his report, he'd be in trouble. He hadn't been able to see Moreton yet, but that would keep.

He went to see Mackie at four o'clock and told him everything he'd learned from the Americans, everything, that is, except the fact that they had shown him a photograph and that he had a shrewd idea what Jo had done.

Mackie wanted to know why Randall hadn't reported his concerns about Joanna sooner, especially McGovern's removal of the camera from Jo's office.

'I wanted to see if there was anyone else involved and I also thought it was likely McGovern would get in touch with me, as he knew that I'd spotted him.'

'That was probably all part of some devious scheme,' said Mackie scornfully.

'They seem to be convinced she's an agent and hope we can help them find out what she's up to,' said Randall. 'They say she's not working for them, but I'm not so sure,' said Randall.

When the meeting ended, Randall was confident that he could safely withhold the information about the photograph a little longer, at least until he had had a crack at Moreton.

Jo had a miserable afternoon. She had gone in search of Laura, only to find her room empty. It looked to Jo as if Laura had already left for the day, which was surprising. Then she remembered that Laura had said she had a dental appointment that afternoon. Maybe she would be back later on.

Jo went back to her room and tried to work. Her mood wasn't helped by Mary's innocent enquiry as to whether she had heard from Lois at all and when she was due back. I may be gone even sooner than I expected, thought Jo. That man made it sound as if someone's going to do me in. And I'll hardly be missed. If she didn't feel so frightened she could almost find the situation funny. She hadn't actually *done* anything except read some damned book which she didn't really understand and now she was being followed about and threatened.

At around six o'clock she went out into the hall to photocopy something and bumped into Andrea.

'Hello, Jo. I haven't seen you to talk to for ages. How's everything?'

'Not very good, as a matter of fact. What about you?'

'Very busy. What are you doing about supper this evening?'

'Nothing much. Going home, I suppose,' said Jo.

'Would you like to come and have a bite with me?'

'I'd like that very much. Thanks, Andrea. What time are you leaving?'

'In about three-quarters of an hour.'

'I'm just going to take some things over for Harry to sign. I'll look in on you on my way back, shall I?'

Jo was pleased to find there was no sign of Harry when she went over to his room at a quarter past six. The Whips' Office was deserted and she had a strong desire to find a cloth and wipe from their board all their records of how often their MPs turned up and which way they voted. But that would be a futile gesture. She would have to do something far more radical than that.

When she got back to her office, Andrea was still working. Jo went to her desk and telephoned Laura. There was no answer from her House of Commons number so she tried her at home. No answer there either. A few minutes later, Andrea appeared. 'Ready?'

CHAPTER THIRTY-ONE

Kistrington Hall was an imposing building, with a handsome Palladian façade. A large part of the extensive parkland which had once surrounded it had been sold for development over the years and the village of Kistrington was now threatened with absorption by the rapidly expanding nearby market town. Nevertheless, the village had maintained its identity and rural character, regarding itself as distinctly separate from its crowded, urban neighbour.

Geoff drove through the village a couple of times, getting the lie of the land, and paused at the gates of Kistrington Hall. Many of the windows were shuttered and there were no vehicles to be seen, but he glimpsed a man in the distance cutting the grass with a tractor and mower.

He parked his car in the centre of the village and commenced his enquiries at the local Post Office, explaining that he was researching historic buildings and their modern uses.

'I'm interested in the relationship between the Hall and village and how it compares with the old days,' he said to the postmistress.

'Relationship? Oh, they don't have much to do with the village. I suppose they reckon they're too good for the likes of us. We hardly see them really. Mostly they just come and go in their big cars.'

She was interrupted by the telephone. Geoff waited. He got out his wallet and when she came back he asked for some stamps. While she was giving him his change, she started talking about the Hall again, unprompted by Geoff.

'People round here get fed up with the place. It must cost a fortune to keep up. Taxpayers' money too. And hardly any of it gets spent in the village. We don't even get much mail for them. Everything comes by special delivery. You ask Mrs Oakes at the stores. They never buy anything locally. Not even in the town. Everything is brought in specially from London.'

'But I imagine it's closed up for a large part of the year, isn't it?' said Geoff. 'It's only open when its being used by visiting judges, isn't that right?'

'It's closed *some* of the time when the judges aren't here, but there still seem to be people coming and going most weeks. And then it's opened up sometimes for these big parties.'

'Big parties?' asked Geoff. 'What sort of parties?'

'They have these big dos for businessmen. Foreigners especially. And you should see some of the girls they bring down here too!' She gave a disapproving snort, more expressive than words.

'Is there a large staff?' asked Geoff. 'It must be maintained all year round, I should imagine.'

'I think there's a permanent staff of six. I'm not sure.'

'Don't they even employ local people?' asked Geoff.

'Not any more, they don't. A local chap used to do the maintenance work, Sam Rawlings, but he got the sack. He wasn't at all happy about the way he was treated. I think all women who work there are foreigners.' She stopped to serve a woman who had just come in so Geoff thanked her and left.

He found Mrs Oakes's shop and she confirmed everything the postmistress had said. She was a large, cheerful woman, who conducted a conversation with Geoff, while serving and chatting to a succession of customers, and calling to her husband at the back of the shop for confirmation of various of her assertions. There was nothing discreet about her conversation. She spoke in loud confident tones, designed to draw all-comers into the discussion. She was only too ready to talk about the Hall and to express her disapproval of its occupants for their failure to patronize her establishment.

'And it's not just here. They hardly ever buy anything locally. And the girls who work there look an unhappy lot. They don't come into the village much and when they do, they speak hardly any English, so you can't get much out of them.' She stopped to count out change for a customer.

'Isn't that right, Mary,' she said as the customer picked up her bag of purchases, 'about those girls at the Hall? And didn't someone say they were illegal immigrants?'

'There was some talk like that,' said the other, 'but I shouldn't think they could employ anyone illegal there, could they?' she said doubtfully, giving Geoff a suspicious look.

'There have been an awful lot of them over the years, haven't there?' Mrs Oakes persisted. 'They don't seem to last very long.'

'Probably don't like that man who runs the place,' said another customer.

'And I'll tell you another thing,' said Mrs Oakes to Geoff. 'One of them died a while back. And they didn't get the local doctor in. They brought some man down from London.'

Geoff went in search of Sam Rawlings, hoping he would find him as forthcoming as Mrs Oakes, but could get nothing out of him. As soon as Geoff mentioned Kistrington Hall the man stepped back inside his house and shut the door.

Other possible sources of information were the landlord of the local pub and the proprietor of the garage which Geoff had observed on the outskirts of the village. It would be a little while longer before the pub opened, so Geoff decided to go to the Hall. In view of what he had learned so far, he didn't expect any of the staff there to be forthcoming, but it was worth a try. He drove up to the Hall and parked close to the front door. There was a security camera above the door and he could hear a dog barking somewhere at the back of the house. He had to wait some moments for the doorbell to be answered.

The door was opened by a pretty, dark-skinned young woman of about twenty. She was wearing jeans and a sweatshirt. There was a large, dark bruise on her neck. She held the door open with her right hand and stood looking at him anxiously.

'Yes please?' she said. Geoff launched into his line about historic buildings but realized halfway through his sentence that she did not understand.

'You want Mr Staffer?' she asked.

'No, I—' but before Geoff could say another word the door was yanked back by a big man. The girl recoiled a step, as if afraid of him.

'You get back to your work,' said the man, stepping in front of her to confront Geoff. The girl turned and hurried away.

'Yes? What do you want?' He was thickset, heavy and had a sour expression. Geoff embarked on his patter again but before he'd finished the man had interrupted him.

'We're closed and I'm not an information service. You

289

can come back when the place is open to the public and buy yourself a guidebook. There's a board by the gate telling you when it's open, or didn't you notice?' he said accusingly. Geoff could detect a faint trace of an accent in his voice. German perhaps.

Geoff tried again. 'I just wondered whether you—'

'Are you deaf or something? Piss off!' He shut the door in Geoff's face.

Geoff restrained himself from waving two fingers at the security camera and returned to his car. He found the proprietor of the local garage was as talkative as Mrs Oakes and just as disapproving.

'No, they don't do much for the local community. They don't spend money in the village, although people come in here occasionally for petrol.'

'Who do, the judges?' asked Geoff.

'No, the chauffeurs. It's always chauffeur-driven cars. Must cost the taxpayer a packet. And they never hire cars locally but always use London firms. I think that's wrong myself.' As if concerned that he was being too critical, the man added, 'Of course they do let the kids go there sometimes, which must be quite a treat for them.'

'What kids?' asked Geoff.

'From the children's home down the road. I recognized one of them – used to be a local lad. They bring them over from time to time, just one or two.'

'Who brings them over?'

'The man who runs the Hall, Mr Staffer. Must be quite a treat for them, having outings like that.'

Geoff had been on the lookout for some confirmation of Jo's remarks. Nevertheless the implication of what the man was saying came as a shock and he had to make an effort to conceal it.

It was after seven when he returned to the Palace of Westminster. The first thing he did was go to Jo's office.

He was disappointed to learn from the attendant that she had left not long before with Lord Hemsley's secretary. Geoff hurried over to the House, hoping he might way-lay them, but there was no sign of them. As he walked in through St Stephen's Entrance he saw Randall Myers leaving the building with Geoffrey Moreton. He wanted to talk to Moreton. No doubt he'd be back for the vote at ten o'clock. Perhaps he'd be able to corner him then.

Geoff telephoned Laura, hoping to get Jo's number from her, but there was no answer from her phone. He even went up to her room but found the lights out, her desk clear. Evidently she had left for the day.

He went down to Members' Lobby. As he entered it, he saw Harry Hunter emerging from the Whips' Office. The sight of him clinched matters. Geoff raised his hand to catch his attention and Harry walked towards him.

'How are you, Geoff?' said Harry, who was always affable and helpful to journalists, especially Lobby correspondents, whom he regarded more as a useful adjunct to his job than an essential part of the body politic. He smiled amiably at Geoff, who came straight to the point, as usual, without unnecessary preliminaries.

'I happened to pick up a story concerning one of your constituents which interested me because of the legal side – custody of children in difficult cases – possible child abuse. I was interested in knowing more about it. The case of Rita Hanssen.'

'Oh yes,' said Harry, altering his expression to one of concern, eyebrows raised to a little peak in the middle, brow furrowed, lips pushed forward as if to contain the flow of emotion. 'A tragic case. Very sad. The poor young woman committed suicide. But I'm not aware there was any question of child abuse.'

'No? Maybe, I got that part wrong,' said Geoff. 'I was wondering whether you would let me have a look at the file.'

'The file?' Harry was surprised. He hesitated. 'Why

the interest in that case in particular?'

'I'm not so much interested in your constituent, more the general principles involved.'

'I see,' said Harry, though his tone and expression suggested that he did not.

'I'm looking into a number of similar cases. I'm particularly interested in the trial judge, Mr Justice Parrie.'

'Really? Well, he's not a constituent of mine, I'm afraid,' said Harry with a deprecating smile.

'So you wouldn't mind if I had a look at your file?' asked Geoff. 'I wouldn't need to take it away. I could give your secretary a call and have a look at it in her office.'

'By all means,' said Harry. He was about to turn away, when Geoff said, 'There's one other thing. Well, two really.'

'Yes?'

'I'm interested in the connection between Geoffrey Moreton and Parrie. And this place Kistrington. I wondered if you knew anything about it all?'

For a second or two Harry looked as if he might faint. He recovered himself quickly, but only by a supreme effort. Geoff could see the man was panic-stricken. He noticed the slight backward movement of the head, the sudden widening of the eyes, the pinpricks of sweat appearing in the little indentation above the upper lip, the rapid breathing. Harry looked down, blinking rapidly. He folded his arms across his chest, then raised his right hand to his mouth; an unsuccessful attempt to conceal his thoughts and anxiety. He frowned and said, 'Don't know the place. Moreton? Parrie?' He was still looking down, his voice puzzled. He glanced up at Geoff, 'What do you mean – connection?'

'There you have me,' said Geoff. 'I was told you would know.'

'Who by?' said Harry.

Geoff didn't answer. He just grinned at Harry.

'Well I'm afraid you've been misinformed.' Harry had recovered himself. He glanced at his watch and said, 'Sorry, must dash,' and hurried off into the Whips' Office. Well, well, thought Geoff. He'd just come out of there. Now he rushes back in. No doubt to confer with Jack Bendall or someone. You'd have thought he'd say, 'Why don't you ask Moreton yourself?' Maybe he's afraid I'll do just that. Perhaps he's trying to warn Moreton now. He won't find him, thought Geoff with satisfaction.

Harry had retreated to his room and was telephoning his wife.

'Do you know when Johnny's due back?' he demanded.

'Friday, I think. Why?'

Harry made an effort to keep his anger out of his voice. 'I was wondering why we haven't heard from him for some time,' he said.

'Didn't he go to Japan?' she replied. 'Maybe that was the reason.'

'If he went to Japan, why did you tell Jo he was in London?'

Silence. 'Well?' he demanded furiously.

'I had to tell her something,' she said.

'What *do* you mean? Why should you have to tell her anything?'

'Don't shout at me. I would have thought it was better that I tell her that, than have her start spreading it around that you've been having it off with some tart at our flat.'

'Have you had her snooping on me?'

Silence. 'Have you? Did you give her a key to the flat?'

'Why shouldn't I?' she said calmly. 'You're the one in the wrong, not me. And you don't even deny it. You make me sick,' she said. 'You don't give a damn do you? You don't even attempt to conceal what you've been up to?' But Harry had slammed the phone down. She could wait. He had a far more urgent problem to attend to. His heart was pounding. He sat leaning forward, his hands on the edge of his desk, as if to stop himself from falling. His thoughts were racing. So it was his secretary who had taken the book. She'd taken it from the flat and then returned it. What had she done with it in the meantime? Shown it to Harper? Copied it perhaps.

He got to his feet and paced about the room. What should he do? What *could* he do? He would have to speak to the Prime Minister. No doubt he'd have that security fellow, Mackie, in straight away. Harry couldn't stand Mackie, probably out of a kind of professional jealousy. After all, Mackie did officially and on an international scale, and with every kind of technological advantage, what Harry did by word of mouth, with the assistance of his little band of spies. He wondered how much Mackie knew about him and his unofficial duties.

What should he tell the Prime Minister? He couldn't say that he had had the Black Book at his flat. He couldn't say that it had been *taken* or he'd be asked why he hadn't reported this straight away. What *could* he say? He sat down at his desk again, remembering last Tuesday. If only he hadn't taken the thing out of his office. He must have been mad. He remembered the scene vividly. He'd had the thing in his hand when Jack had stuck his head round the door and said Bowerbridge wanted them to get out of the building and to take anything important with them. Yes, that was it. He took it because of what Bowerbridge said. But then they'd say, 'Why didn't you take it back immediately the all-clear was given?' How could he answer that one? He'd have to let them think that that was when it happened, not that she had taken it, but that she must have seen it then. He could say he must have left the safe open, but that sounded just as bad. Whichever way you cut it, it spelt catastrophe for him, probably for all of them.

He got up again. He *had* to tell the PM. He'd no choice. He'd just say that he had reason to believe it had been seen, that he didn't know how, but it must have been at the time of the bomb scare. That's it! They might think she had something to do with that. In any event something would be done about the woman.

He stuck his hands in his pockets and stood still. Who is she? I don't know a damn thing about her. I'll be criticized for that too. I took on some woman I know nothing about, without any references or anything. All on the say-so of that female Laura James. What's the connection with her I wonder?

Harry looked at his watch, went to his desk, rang Number Ten and learned that he couldn't see the PM until much later because he was speaking at a dinner. It was agreed that Harry could see him at the PM's room in the House after tonight's ten o'clock vote.

Sitting in the Chamber, listening to the closing speeches of the main debate, Harry's confidence in his story started to wane. The PM would be bound to ask what grounds he had for thinking this woman had taken the book. He'd want to know what had aroused his suspicions. If he said it had been Harper's questions, the PM would want to know why he thought the man had got his information from Joanna. How could he answer that? He couldn't. He'd have to say he found her in his office, that the book had been on the desk and that it was only now he'd realized what she'd been up to. But that wouldn't work either. He'd have to have a reason for thinking she'd copied it. She must have copied it, otherwise why take it away then put it back later? He'd have to say that he knew she was in league with Harper. How would he know that? Harper told him. No that wouldn't work. Journalists don't reveal their sources. But wait a minute, she obviously had told Harper, or shown it to him. So they'd both have to be dealt with. That was it. He'd have to include Harper. He'd just have to hope for the best. Maybe the confusion over the bomb scare would mean he wouldn't be asked too many questions. He knew this was a faint hope but there was still a chance he'd save his own skin. He drew a crumb of comfort from the fact that the PM couldn't get rid of him, for the moment at least, because only he knew exactly what was in the Black Book.

He sat on the front bench, looking about him. He even had quite a lot of stuff on some of the Members opposite. What would they think if they knew that? We could try to use that to limit the damage, he thought. If those bastards try to make trouble for us, we'll let them know what they're in for. That made him feel a little better. At that moment, the Prime Minister and the Chancellor of the Exchequer came into the Chamber and sat down. Not long to wait now, thought Harry.

CHAPTER THIRTY-TWO

The meeting with the PM was predictable. Harry could have written the script: 'How *could* you be so stupid as to leave it on your desk?'

'How indeed? But you've got to remember the bomb alert. The place was in chaos. I had to find the Serjeant-at-Arms.' This was not strictly true but the PM wouldn't know that. Harry had another idea. 'And in any case, I'm not sure that I did leave it on my desk. I've been wondering whether she hadn't taken it out of my safe and put it on the desk to look at it.'

'How would she know it was there? Or that there was a safe, for that matter?'

'How indeed?' said Harry. 'There are a lot of questions about this woman that need answering, but I haven't done anything to arouse her suspicions. I thought the priority was to let you know the position straight away.'

'You should have done that last week when you found her in your office!'

'As I said, we were all concerned about the bomb alert. That was our top priority.'

'That was Bowerbridge's top priority. Not yours,' the

PM snapped at him. 'Now what about this woman? Who is she and where does she come from?'

'She's a friend of Charles Donaldson's secretary, Laura James, and came highly recommended,' he said smoothly, 'good background: NATO, the UN.'

'I'd class that as a dubious background myself, but before we decide what to do about her, let's look at precisely what our problem is. What's in this Black Book of yours? What a name for it. It sounds terrible.' The Prime Minister could not number a stint in the Whips' Office amongst his credentials for office and felt at a decided disadvantage. Whilst this was, for the moment, a point in Harry's favour, it was also a major possible pitfall. If he concealed the truth about the book's contents and they became public, he was done for, not just in politics, but in every aspect of his life. The book would be treated as his personal property and he alone would be held responsible for its contents. He must tie as many of his colleagues to him as possible.

'It's not *mine*,' said Harry, 'it's the Whips' Office official record of matters which could be a possible source of embarrassment to the Party.'

'Come now, Harry. You keep the thing. It's your responsibility.'

'I was merely explaining that – well, of course, you will know this – it's standard practice for the Whips' Office to keep such a dossier, has been for – I don't know how long – generations.'

'And the outgoing Chief Whip takes it to his grave. Isn't that right?'

Harry looked wan. And I'm destined for an early one at this rate, he thought.

The Prime Minister didn't wait for a response. 'I want to know what's in the thing. How is it going to damage us?'

'Most of what is in it you already know,' said Harry.

'You know perfectly well what I mean. I want to know precisely what you have been so foolish as to commit to paper.'

'Some of it wouldn't mean anything to the average reader,' Harry began. 'Promises and pledges to the Party and what the person concerned hopes for in return.'

'I can't imagine why you think that wouldn't mean anything to your so-called average reader. To most people that would spell bribery and corruption. Go on.'

'I meant that there's not much detail to that kind of entry.'

'Well, what about the rest?' He was getting impatient. 'Everyone knows you keep tabs on who's screwing whom and what they'd rather their wives didn't know about. We could weather those things. I want to know what there is that's really destructive.'

'As you know, a number of our colleagues are drug users. And Kingborne has helped us – them – out on a number of occasions when there might have been trouble. And of course he's taken care of one or two drink-driving cases as well.'

'There's worse than that, isn't there?' said the Prime Minister grimly. 'As if that's not bad enough.'

Harry took the plunge. 'The potentially dangerous matters are first, the financial improprieties: the Filter slush fund, the big secret donations to the Party, particularly some of the recent ones from overseas, and the schemes set up to avoid disclosure of outside interests and incomes. There's one rather troublesome tax case which we hadn't quite sorted out: Vanett. We're stuck with him, unfortunately. And there's Camborough's currency dealing.' The Prime Minister winced. 'That would put his opposition to a single European currency in a new light, wouldn't it?'

'It's your fault we're in this mess, remember? Get on with it! What are the other "potentially dangerous matters" you were enumerating?'

'There are certain overseas connections which could prove embarrassing and which would come to light if some of the financial deals were exposed. Then there are all the other matters which Kingborne has dealt with for us. I don't know how reliable he would be if he were put under pressure. The Home Secretary would of course be implicated—'

'We'd *all* be implicated! Why on earth did you put such things on paper. It's madness!'

'You know perfectly well we have to keep an eye on these things,' said Harry, his confidence returning. 'There are matters going way back, as you know. A record of such things has to be kept. They could have come back to haunt us at any time.' Harry regretted this remark as soon as he'd made it.

'It's thanks to you and that damned book that they've come back to haunt us now!' the Prime Minister was in a fury. He made an effort to control himself. 'Go on! What else is there?' he asked in a defeated tone.

Harry paused, wondering how much to say, how little he could get away with, about the last category. 'And finally, there are the matters of, shall we say a sexual nature, the most potentially disastrous of which would be,' Harry hesitated, 'the recent entertainment of that chap from the State Department, Wesker.' He saw the expression on the other man's face and added hastily, 'Camborough said you wanted something that could be used to put pressure on him over the conference agenda.'

The Prime Minister groaned, but said nothing. Harry watched him. The worst was over and he got a certain satisfaction out of seeing the other man plunged into the nightmare he had had to contemplate alone for the last few hours. You won't blame me for practices you've happily gone along with up to now, thought Harry.

The Prime Minister reached for the phone and spoke

to a member of staff at Number Ten. 'Tell Mackie I want to see him in half an hour.' He hung up and said to Harry, 'You'd better come too. We'll have to take preventive measures straight away. I don't want to have to go through all of this twice, so you can save your explanations of how this happened until we see Mackie. However, I suggest you refer to it as a confidential file rather than a book. We don't want anyone to know what's really involved.'

Harry was anxious, but his situation was not entirely hopeless. He was aware that he was seen as being altogether too powerful for the liking of many of his colleagues and the ones he had had to force into line from time to time would delight in his downfall. However, he was reasonably confident that they would not have the satisfaction of seeing it, provided he could get that Delvere woman dealt with effectively. It was not as if she had the Black Book. She might have copies and that was not the same thing at all.

As he feared, Mackie was ruthless in his questioning. After about half an hour of grilling, Harry felt drained. Mackie said, 'So what it boils down to is this: the bomb warning was given. You were told to leave your office and you left your safe open—'

'Not open. Unlocked.'

'And this woman took the file out of the safe. You think she copied it. Or do you know she copied it?'

'How would I know that?'

'You think she may have copied it.'

'That's right.'

'And you think that because of what Harper knows about it. But you don't know whether he has seen it, or has copies.'

'Correct,' said Harry.

'Would you care to tell me what's in this thing that is causing so much anxiety?' asked Mackie.

'No,' said Harry flatly. Mackie looked at the Prime Minister.

'I don't think it's necessary to go into that kind of detail at this stage,' said the Prime Minister.

'You may revise that view when I tell you that we have reason to believe she may be a spy,' said Mackie.

Harry, who had been slowly recovering his confidence and composure, reacted as if he had been punched. 'A spy?' he gasped.

'Why didn't you say so straight away?' The Prime Minister was annoyed.

'I wanted to establish first exactly what Mr Hunter thought she had done.' The implication of this response seemed to be lost on Harry. The Prime Minister, however, understood exactly what the man meant: that Harry might have been less than honest with them. He had taken Harry's account of events at face value. Mackie on the other hand had more than a grain of suspicion that Harry's narrative was false, having learned from Tim Fenchurch that he had seen Harry, apparently on his way to the flat in Ashdon Gardens, shortly before the bomb went off.

Mackie made no mention of this, but relayed the information he had been given by Randall and the episode of the theft and return of her bag, which had automatically been reported by the Palace of Westminster police.

'We will need to check the file for fingerprints, of course,' said Mackie.

This was highly undesirable. The Prime Minister said, 'We'll come back to that later. What other action are you taking?'

'Delvere is now under surveillance. Harper too,' said Mackie. 'We will search her flat and office, but we have to decide whether to arrest her straight away, or wait and see what contacts she makes.'

'What's your own view?' asked the Prime Minister.

'I think we should leave things as they are for the moment. If she *is* a spy, we need to establish who she's working for. Whatever information she's acquired, it's likely that she transmitted it immediately, by fax or modem. We need to catch her red-handed, with something incriminating in her possession, copies of the file for example, if she made any that is, otherwise we won't have any evidence with which to charge her.'

'If that happens, our only hope of limiting any damage she may be intending to do will be by discrediting her,' said the Prime Minister. 'I agree with you that she should not be arrested for the moment. Above all, we do *not* want the media getting hold of any of this.'

'I can't believe she's a spy!' exclaimed Harry.

'That was my reaction too,' said Mackie. 'But for the interest of the Americans and given what we know about her, I would have said it was more likely she was intending to embarrass you in some way, perhaps for political or financial advantage, say by selling whatever information she acquired to a newspaper.' He recounted what had been established about Jo's background. 'We expect to have some more information on her shortly, but there are undoubtedly grounds for believing the Americans may be right.'

'She could be working for them,' said the Prime Minister. 'There's no doubt they have a hidden agenda of their own for the conference.'

He turned to Harry. 'I shall leave the two of you to discuss the next stage,' he said. 'I can't give any more time to it at the moment, but keep me informed.'

He was reluctant to be made party to any plans for Delvere that Mackie agreed with Harry in case anything went wrong. He still nursed a hope that he could avoid being involved, should anything really unpleasant become necessary. It was for the same reason that he had decided not to insist on Harry showing him the Black Book, much as he would like to know the full extent of the danger that faced him. If this thing blew up in their faces, Harry was going to be the one holding it.

Mackie said he would see Harry at Number Twelve in half an hour and left them.

'We can't allow him to have the file for fingerprinting,' said Harry. 'I don't think we could even allow them to do that in front of us.'

'I realize that,' said the Prime Minister. 'In any case, they can get her fingerprints off any number of other things, from her office, for example. No, I should say Mackie was hoping to see the thing and the less he knows about it, the better. Make sure you don't tell him any more than you have to.'

'There's no fear of that,' said Harry. 'I'm concerned about what we do if his men find anything when they search her flat and office. I wouldn't trust any of them further than I could throw them.'

When he returned to Number Twelve, Patricia was in the sitting room. He didn't speak to her but poured himself a Scotch.

'Sulking are we?' she said sweetly. 'Couldn't you get it up tonight?'

He ignored her and withdrew to his study. When he learned that Mackie had returned he went downstairs to see him.

'We can't search Delvere's flat as she is there at the moment, but there has been a surprising development.'

'What's that?'

'She rang the local police three-quarters of an hour ago to say that there had been a break-in. There are officers there at the moment and apparently the place has been gone over with a fine-tooth comb. What do you make of that?'

Harry was speechless with surprise. What could it

mean? His mind raced through the possibilities. She must have told someone about it and they wanted it for themselves.

'I don't know what to make of it,' he said. 'What do you think?'

'Either this is rather more complicated than you believe or you haven't told me everything.'

'I can assure you I have been totally frank with you,' said Harry frostily.

Mackie permitted himself a small but disbelieving smile and said nothing.

'Would you care for a drink?' asked Harry, recognizing the danger in antagonizing such a man. What a pity I don't have something on him, he thought.

Mackie accepted a drink and sat down. 'We've got one of our men there at the moment, checking things out, and he'll report back to me shortly. But it would seem that there's little point in searching the place again.'

Harry nodded and Mackie continued, 'We will seal her office – everyone will be told that there is a dangerous electrical fault which must be put right immediately – and go over it carefully. That'll be done very early tomorrow morning. And we'll be keeping a close watch on her. The same with Harper. Her phone at her flat is now out of order, so she can't contact him or anyone else. Once he's gone to work tomorrow we'll search his place. We'll also see what we can turn up at his office – we'll include one of our people amongst the cleaning staff – but we can't do much there and have to be very careful not to attract the attention.'

'I see,' said Harry.

'Once we've dealt with the housekeeping side of things, we need to decide what to do about her, and him.'

'What have you in mind?'

'We need, if possible, to find out more about her first,'

said Mackie. He proceeded to grill Harry about Joanna, but to little purpose. 'We've checked all our sources, using the information she supplied for her passes and have turned up the fact that she did a spell in NATO, which you'd told us about, of course. Otherwise very little. Her address in England still belongs to her mother, but has been let for the past two years. The father was a police officer. Ex-military intelligence. Interesting fact, wouldn't you say?'

'Very,' said Harry, wondering what further surprises lay in store for him. 'Unusual career. Very distinguished too. Various special overseas assignments. You don't remember the name? No? I didn't know him. He died ten years ago. The mother remarried and is living in New Zealand.'

'What are your thoughts about her?' asked Harry. 'What do you advise?'

'There are various options but it would help if we knew why she did what she did. Is she a spy, or a terrorist? If so, is she working alone or with others. If we had some idea what she was planning it would be easier to decide how to deal with her. If she's intending to spill the beans, she must either be stopped or discredited. There are so many risks with the former, that we generally find it is better to start with the latter. For example, we can arrest her and hold her under the Prevention of Terrorism Act. That way we can keep her out of circulation for several days, and while we've got her, let the world know that she's off her head, then let her go. Even get her certified, perhaps. We're bound to have some closed-circuit television footage we can use.' Harry nodded. He knew all about that trick. That was what we did with Fairbrand, he thought. 'Digitize it appropriately and she could be charged with holding up a building society, or planting a bomb,' Mackie continued. 'Now there's an idea. We could tie her into last week's bomb blast. Of course, she just might be something to do with it anyway, although it seems a bit over the top as a means of getting hold of your file.' Mackie enjoyed this thought and permitted himself a short laugh.

Harry had had enough. He suggested to Mackie that they could review matters in the morning and Mackie promised to report to him at nine o'clock, or sooner if something important turned up.

CHAPTER THIRTY-THREE

The last shock of the day had made Jo feel ill. She sat on the sofa in Lydia's flat, still in her overcoat, reluctant to move, reliving her return to the flat.

Supper with Andrea had taken her mind off her worries and she was feeling tired but calm when she arrived home at a quarter to eleven. When she opened the door of the flat, the hall was in darkness but there was a light on in the sitting room.

'Hi, Lydia,' she called. She pushed the door shut behind her with one hand and pulled off her beret with the other. 'Lydia?' There was no answer. Fear engulfed her. She remembered McGovern's smile as he said, 'You've not been home yet, have you?'

'Who's there?' she called. Her voice sounded wobbly. If it's someone out to get me they're hardly likely to answer, she thought. She pressed the hall light switch. The bright light made her feel a little better. The two bedroom doors were closed. She crept past them towards the sitting room. How could she look into the kitchen and the sitting room at the same time? They might be in either room. She pushed the door of the sitting room wide open so that she could see the whole room. She couldn't see behind the door. Her heart was beating so hard her ears were singing. She was terrified someone was going to leap on her from behind. She glanced round over her shoulder, turned her body sideways and flattened herself against the wall, then sidled into the room. There was no-one there. The room was in chaos. She felt weak. She stood still listening hard. The silence was overwhelming, terrifying. She stepped quietly out of the room and looked into the kitchen. It was empty. Back into the hall. The two closed doors were almost more than she could stand. She wanted to race out of the building and never return. She looked down. There was an umbrella lying at her feet. The contents of the hall table were strewn about. Strange that she hadn't noticed them when she came in. She stooped and picked up the umbrella, stepped across very quietly to the door facing her and flung it open. Umbrella aloft she stepped into Lydia's bedroom. It was barely recognizable. Everything Lydia possessed had been thrown about. But Jo couldn't stop for that now. She stepped out of the room, a little more bravely now, and repeated the exercise with her bedroom. The same again. Everything that could be moved and examined had been. She leaned against the door and slowly lowered the umbrella. She looked at it as if for the first time. What a weapon. She could have screamed with hysterical laughter. Instead she felt two cold tears roll slowly down her cheeks as if they had waited a long time to fall.

She went back into the sitting room, replaced the sofa cushions and sat down. She picked up the telephone and dialled Laura's number. It was engaged.

The police. I must phone the police. To hell with their questions. I shall tell them nothing. But Lydia could come back at any time. She'll be utterly devastated. And she'll expect me to have telephoned the police. And she'll expect me to have dealt with her camera, thought Jo. I should have collected it today. What a day.

The police investigation was exhausting but welcome. It was good to have people in the flat with her, to hear their strong, reassuring voices. Their questions and forensic checks seemed to take for ever. She could see surprise and disbelief in their eyes when she said that nothing had been taken and hastily retracted this. 'Of course, I could be wrong,' she added. 'You see, it's not my flat. I don't really know what the owner has here' – this was perfectly true, Jo hadn't really bothered to take it all in – 'so I can't really say whether anything has been taken.'

When she was asked why she thought the place had been searched so thoroughly she lied. 'I'm afraid I haven't the faintest idea,' she said. Then it dawned on her, when they asked for particulars of the owner and learned that she worked for an airline and travelled a great deal, that this could lead to yet more difficulties for Lydia. She could almost read the word 'drugs' in the eyes of the CID officer who was questioning her and was not surprised when a sniffer dog was brought to the flat a little while later. 'Why a dog?' she asked in an astonished tone. 'We have to try everything,' was the reply.

After they had gone, Jo tried Laura again but found that her telephone was no longer working. There was no dialling tone, just a faint crackling sound. How she wished she could talk to Laura. She toyed with the idea of going out to find a telephone box, but felt too frightened. It was dark in the mews. Just supposing there was someone waiting for her. So she stayed sitting where she was, feeling very alone and afraid.

After a while she got to her feet and went to her bedroom, dragged a chest of drawers out into the passage and pushed it up against the door. It was too bad if Lydia came back. Jo was sure she would understand how she felt. She poured herself a stiff drink, drank it and finally set to work to clear up the mess. It was nearly three a.m. when she finished. Then she had a bath and before lying down she carefully assembled the clothes she would need when she got up. If the burglar did come back, or anything else untoward happened, she wanted to be able to dress and leave at top speed.

When she awoke on Tuesday morning, she had a headache. She had woken before her alarm went off and felt instant fear. Had some sound woken her? She crept out of bed and stood in the hall listening. Nothing. She returned to her room, dressed and then sat in the kitchen, trying to eat some breakfast. Finally she pulled the chest of drawers away from the door and returned it to its usual place. It was a relief to leave the flat and go to work. She hesitated on the doorstep, debating what route and form of transport to take and decided she was probably safest travelling on foot along the busiest route she could find. So she repeated her journey of the previous week and walked along the Embankment. The walk made her feel better as did the prospect of confiding in Laura.

She did not go first to her office, as she usually did, but went straight to the House in search of Laura. To her dismay, Laura was not in her room, though it was evident she had been in. Perhaps she had gone over to Jo's office. Then she saw that Laura's coat and bag were there. She must be with Sir Charles. Jo felt too desperate to wait. She walked along the passage to his office, knocked and opened the door. Laura was sitting in an armchair, notebook in hand. Sir Charles was apparently in the middle of dictating something.

'I'm sorry to interrupt,' said Jo, 'but I must see you, Laura. It's terribly important.' Laura jumped up. 'Do you mind?' she said to Sir Charles but did not wait for

311

his answer. 'Don't mind me,' he said with a smile. She hurried across the room and out into the passage with Jo, pulling the door shut behind her.

'What is it? You look terrible. What's happened?'

'Don't let's talk here,' Jo whispered. They went into Laura's room and Jo sat down heavily in an armchair. 'You'll never believe the things that have happened since we parted company yesterday morning. I've been desperate to talk to you and you weren't here.' She almost wailed. Laura thought Jo was going to burst into tears.

'Hold on there, Jo, let's make you a coffee.' She put the kettle on and stood next to it, waiting for it to boil and watching Jo with a concerned expression. Jo launched into a vivid account of all that had happened the previous day. Laura was so thunderstruck that she forgot to make the coffee. When Jo finally drew breath, having described erecting the barricade to her front door, Laura said, 'Your poor thing! What a nightmare. How terrifying!'

'I'll have that coffee now, thanks,' said Jo, who was feeling a bit better, now that there was one person at least who would have some idea what had happened should disaster befall her.

'What *are* we going to do?' said Laura.

'Well I'm going over to my office now. I'm going to retrieve my envelope, make copies and do something straight away. I think we should go to the Speaker – if you don't mind coming with me – and the Lord Chancellor's Office and anyone else you think would be a good idea. But we should do it this morning, immediately.'

'We could take it to Sir Charles and ask him to take us to see the Speaker,' said Laura.

'OK,' said Jo, 'let's do that.'

'I can't help thinking,' said Laura slowly, 'that we ought to rope someone else in as well. The person I have in mind is Geoff Harper.'

'I don't think so,' said Jo icily.

'Why ever not? He's a terrific journalist. He's tough and courageous and extremely knowledgeable. *And* he likes you.'

'He's just out for what he can get, like so many married men,' said Jo, 'and I happen to like Alicia.'

'Married? He's not *married*!' exclaimed Laura. 'Did you think he was married to Alicia? What a hoot!' she rocked with laughter. 'That's hysterical.'

'He's not married?' asked Jo, incredulously.

'No, you dope! Alicia's his sister. Whatever gave you the idea they were married? Just wait till I tell him.'

'Don't you dare,' said Jo furiously. 'I don't know how I came to make such a mistake.' She blushed. She was remembering the occasions when she had rebuffed him.

Laura was enjoying herself hugely. Jo was in no mood for jokes, especially at her own expense.

'Anyway, I tried to tell him about Rita and that bastard Parrie before and he wasn't interested,' she said defensively.

'Has it occurred to you that you might just have been a trifle off-putting in your manner, my sweet?'

'Don't "my sweet" me,' said Jo, but was unable to sustain her injured look and broke into hysterical laughter.

'Shush,' said Laura. 'If we make too much noise people will come and investigate. We must be serious. What do you think? Shall we speak to Geoff?'

'OK, Laura, you win. I'll ring him from my office.'

'Why don't you ring him from here?' said Laura. 'I'd better be getting back to the boss.'

'Thanks for the coffee,' said Jo. 'I'm feeling better now.'

'It does you good to have a laugh occasionally, dearie,' said Laura. 'I won't be much longer with Charles. I'll expect you back here soon.'

'All right.' Laura left the room.

Jo looked up the number for the Press Gallery in Laura's Palace directory. Geoff was away from his desk and she got his answering machine instead. She decided to leave a message for him.

'Hello, Geoff. It's Jo Delvere. I'm sorry I was so poisonous yesterday. I was—' she hesitated, '—things were very difficult. I'd like to talk to you. I wondered if we could meet. Perhaps you could give me a ring.' She left her office number and hung up.

She left Laura's room and went down to Members' Post Office, collected her bundle of mail and walked along the corridor towards Central Lobby. The Lobby was deserted, save for Sergeant Jamieson who was standing at the barrier, smiling at her.

'Good morning, Jo. How are you?'

'I'm not too bad, thanks, Bill. How about you? You're usually on duty in the afternoons, aren't you?'

'Sometimes I am. This week I'm doing ten till two. Next week, I'll be on two till rise again.'

'Two till rise. What does that mean?' asked Jo.

'Two o'clock in the afternoon until the rising of the House. This shift is better because you know exactly when it'll end. If you do two till rise you could be here all night if the sitting runs on.'

'I see,' said Jo. 'That must be exhausting.'

'It is. If you don't mind my saying so, you look a bit exhausted yourself.'

'To tell the truth, Bill, I've had better days – and nights.' She told him about the ransacking of her flat and he was full of sympathy.

'You poor girl. Now, you mustn't let it frighten you. I know it can give you a terrible feeling, knowing that someone has been in your home, pawing over your belongings. It's horrible. A good tip is to rearrange the furniture and make the place look a bit different, or even freshen it up with a coat of paint, perhaps in a different

314

colour. That often makes people feel better after a burglary.'

'Thanks, Bill, I'll bear it in mind. Though I have to say that whoever did it rearranged everything so thoroughly that I couldn't remember where things were before anyway.'

'You may find you feel worse later on than you do now. Some people feel quite shocked some time after the event.'

'I felt pretty shocked last night, I can tell you.'

'Well, you look after yourself.'

'I will. See you later.'

Jo's new-found confidence deserted her when she saw a police car parked outside her office. She was reminded of the burglary and Andy McGovern's threats. Could they be about to arrest her? He had said she had until noon to give him the Black Book but perhaps it was all a sham, some kind of trap for her.

She opened the door and was greeted in the hall by Vic, who said cheerfully, 'No work for you this morning, I'm afraid, Jo. Your room is closed and no-one's allowed in there. There's some kind of electrical problem and they're taking the place apart looking for it.'

Jo stared at him. 'Electrical problem?' she said. She could guess exactly what was happening in her room. It wasn't an electrical problem they were looking for. She stood stock-still wondering what to do. She tried to sound nonchalant. 'Oh well, I'll just have to deal with some other chores, I suppose.' She *must* retrieve her envelope. Now! She had to do it immediately, no matter who was around. She heard the front door opening behind her and drew in her breath nervously. She looked round. It was Andrea.

'Hi, Jo,' she said.

'Hello, Andrea,' said Jo. 'How are you?'

'Fine thanks,' Andrea passed her, heading for the

stairs. I should have thanked her for last night, thought Jo, but then I'd have to tell her about the flat. There's no time.

'Vic, would you mind if I left my bundle of mail in your office, while I go over to the House for something?' asked Jo. 'I won't be long.'

'No problem,' said Vic. Jo walked into his room and put the bundle on the table. She hesitated.

Was Vic coming in? No, he was still in the office. She reached up, straining to get the directory from the top shelf. She couldn't grasp it. She pushed it upwards, hooked her thumb under the spine and yanked it out, breaking her nail. She pulled too hard and the directory shot out of the shelf and made a loud smack as it hit the floor. Jo bent to retrieve it as Vic came into the room. The envelope had fallen out of it. She picked it up, reached up and replaced the directory and turned to leave the room, aware of Vic giving her a puzzled look. 'I'll be back in a minute,' she said and hurried out of the building.

She did not look round at the police car but felt certain that its occupants were observing her closely. She started to run along the street, then thought better of it. I mustn't look as if I'm fleeing. She walked along, swinging her bag in one hand, the envelope in the other, trying to look nonchalant.

Bill was surprised to see her back in Central Lobby so soon.

'I just had to bring something over to the House,' said Jo.

'Oh well, it'll save you another journey,' said Bill. 'There were a couple of detectives asking for you just now. Special Branch, they said. I expect they've got some news for you about the burglary.' He looked past Jo. 'Oh, here they are again now.'

Jo looked round and saw two men entering the Lobby.

316

She thought furiously. She turned to Bill and said, as calmly as she could, 'Can you tell them I'll be back in a minute, please Bill? I've just got to take this to the Library.' She didn't wait for his answer but turned away and headed for Lower Waiting Hall. She heard a man's voice shout, 'Stop that woman!' and she broke into a run, racing through the swing doors, across Lower Waiting Hall, and into the Library corridor. She was aware of the surprised look of the police officer in Lower Waiting Hall as she tore past him. She didn't go into the Library, but raced past it, down the corridor. More swing doors ahead. She hesitated, glancing over her shoulder to see if she were being followed. Not a soul in sight. She stopped running as she turned left at the end of the corridor. There might be a police officer behind the Speaker's Chair, or outside the Table Office. It wouldn't do to attract attention by hurtling into view. She walked quietly along the corridor, breathing hard. There was no-one in sight. She was certain she would be apprehended at any moment. She *must* get rid of the envelope, but how? Then she had an inspiration. Of course, why didn't I think of it before? I'll post it to Laura. She fumbled in her bag for a pen and scribbled an address on the envelope, then walked round the Speaker's Chair and into the Chamber, intending to walk through into Members' Lobby and turn right into Members' Post Office. Disaster stared her in the face. The two men who'd tried to waylay her in Central Lobby were entering the Chamber by the far door. They spotted Jo. 'Hey, you!' shouted one. 'Stop!' Jo whirled round and raced out of the Chamber. She paused for a moment behind the Speaker's Chair, but by the time the two men got there, she had vanished.

CHAPTER THIRTY-FOUR

News travels fast in the Palace of Westminster. As George had told Jo, you had only to remain where you were and keep your eyes and ears open and you would hear any number of interesting things. Even George, who could safely be counted one of the most experienced news-gatherers in the building, rated the news about Jo as one of the most extraordinary things he had heard in all his years in Parliament. He had heard it from a Badge Messenger as he came out of the staff canteen. He kept his amazement to himself, however, and walked slowly up to Central Lobby in order to check the facts with Sergeant Jamieson. Bill gave a detailed account of what had happened. George said nothing for several moments but gazed at him with a thoughtful and disbelieving expression. Finally, he said, 'Stolen Cabinet documents, you say? I doubt it somehow.'

'That's what they said. Mind you, they gave me such a hard time for letting her go – said I could perfectly well have detained her – and I felt so annoyed that I didn't really take that part of it in. I dare say we'll hear more quite soon.'

'And I'd say there's a lot more to this than meets the eye. As for saying you should have detained her, that's nonsense. She's got a valid pass, hasn't she?'

'She must have if she works here.'

'Well then, she's allowed to come and go and you couldn't have been expected to stop her. I wouldn't worry about it.'

'Oh, I'm not worried,' said Bill. 'I wonder if they caught her before she left the building?'

'You'll let me know what you hear, will you, Bill?' asked George. 'Somehow it doesn't add up. I just can't see her doing something like that.'

'You know her do you?' asked Bill.

'Not particularly well, but I like her. She seems a good sort to me.'

'Me too,' said Bill. 'And she cares about her job, about helping people.' He told George about Rita.

'There you are,' said George. 'And another thing, she's a good friend of Laura James's. In fact, I think the job was Laura's idea.'

'Well, Laura'd never be mixed up in anything like that. It's very strange, there's no doubt about that.'

'I'd say there was something fishy about the whole thing,' George sighed heavily and walked slowly away towards the House of Lords.

The news of Jo's flight from the law spread like wildfire through Parliament, the story expanding and changing in the telling. Laura, who was still immersed in work with Sir Charles was unaware of it. So was Geoff, who hadn't come into the House of Commons but had embarked on a series of visits and telephone calls, making enquiries in the City and elsewhere about Sir Geoffrey Moreton and adding to the store of information he had gathered the previous day.

At ten-forty-five a.m. Geoff called his answering machine and, amongst other messages, heard Jo's voice apologizing for yesterday and saying she wanted to meet him. He immediately tried her number, but got no answer.

Shortly before eleven, Laura's answering machine clicked into action. The volume was turned right down, so no sound came from the machine, save its clicking as the outgoing and incoming message tapes switched themselves on and off. Then the red light started flashing. It was the first thing Laura saw when she came back to her room at a quarter past eleven. She hurried over to her desk, pressed the playback button and turned up the volume. In a moment she heard Jo's voice: 'Laura, it's Jo.' Her voice was breathless and she spoke rapidly. 'I'm sorry I couldn't come back to you. It was impossible. But you can relax, it's in the bag. I pulled it off. Just. So don't worry and I'll be in touch as soon as I – Oh God! I'll have to go.'

Laura was puzzled. So Jo had dealt with the problem, but why couldn't she come back? Laura thought she detected a note of panic in Jo's last words. She rang Jo's number, but got no answer. She dialled the recall code, hoping to find out where Jo had called from, but the number wasn't stored. Where could she have been? It didn't sound as if she had been in the Palace of Westminster. She played the message back again. There was a lot of background noise as Jo was speaking but Laura couldn't make out what it was. Perhaps it was traffic. What was it that had made her cut short her message? It seemed to Laura that Jo's voice sounded frightened.

She told herself she was being ridiculous. Thinking it over more calmly, she concluded that Jo must have retrieved her envelope and done something with its contents, having spoken to Geoff. Perhaps she was with him and they had gone somewhere together. Maybe his car was parked on a double-yellow line and they'd seen a traffic warden coming and that was the reason she had had to hang up suddenly. It was probably as simple as that.

Having thus reassured herself, Laura got on with her work. However, she found it difficult to concentrate and kept looking at her watch. Geoff and Jo would probably appear together shortly. She couldn't wait to hear what they had decided to do with Jo's find. After a while she rang Geoff's number, and heard his firm, confident voice on his answering machine, but thought it was unwise to leave a message in case someone else heard it.

By twelve o'clock, she was beginning to feel a little irritated that neither of them had bothered to ring her. It would be nice to be kept in the picture, she thought. I don't want to have to sit by my phone all day.

At twelve-thirty she tried Jo's number again. Still the answering machine. She sat at her desk, frowning, wondering what to do. She got up, thinking she would go over to Jo's office, then sat down again. There was no point if Jo wasn't there. If she left her desk, Jo might turn up, or ring her again. What should she do? She picked up the phone and rang Vic, only to learn that he hadn't seen Jo since about ten-fifteen when she had rushed out of the building, saying she was going over to the House. The unease which Laura felt at hearing this was nothing to the alarm she experienced at Vic's subsequent remarks.

'We've had some excitement over here, I can tell you. It's very strange, I must say. You wouldn't believe the things that have been going on.'

Oh wouldn't I? thought Laura, her fear mounting. She tried to sound normal.

'Really, Vic? What sort of things?'

'Well,' he paused, embarrassed, 'it's a bit awkward. I mean, you're a friend of Jo's aren't you?'

'I am indeed.'

'Well, we've had the police in, questioning me and

everybody else about her. They wanted to know what we knew about her, where she came from, that sort of thing. Very odd. Of course, I said I didn't know anything about her, except that she works for Mr Hunter and that she's a friend of yours. I hope that's all right.'

'Of course it is,' said Laura. 'Go on. What else?'

'This is the really strange part. It seems she had something hidden here, an envelope – well I don't know what it was exactly – anyway they asked me a lot of questions about it. I said I didn't know anything about it, just that I saw her take it from the shelf here and rush off with it. Goodness knows what it's about.'

'I see. Yes, it's certainly all very strange,' said Laura. 'Thank you very much, Vic.' She was about to hang up, but changed her mind. 'Oh Vic, I'd be very grateful if you'd let me know anything else that happens. Could you?'

'Of course. No problem.'

Laura hung up. So Jo had collected her envelope and rushed off. Had she gone to see Geoff? If the police were asking questions about her, perhaps they had waylaid her in the House. Perhaps she didn't get to see Geoff. But then if the police had stopped her, what was the meaning of her message? It could only mean that the problem was solved. Suddenly, the sound of panic in Jo's message had a new, frightening explanation. Perhaps it was McGovern who had caused her to cut her call short. 'Unpleasant things could happen to a young woman like you,' he'd said to Jo. Jo could have dealt with the problem of the envelope, taken it to someone in authority, but still be vulnerable. McGovern might take revenge for her refusal to hand over her find. Had something terrible happened to her? Laura shuddered. If only she knew where Jo had gone. She didn't know what to do. She got to her feet, thinking she would talk to Charles about it, then changed her mind and sat down again. Supposing Jo rang her again? It would be terrible if she weren't at her desk.

There was still a possibility Jo was with Geoff, of course. But supposing she hadn't been able to get hold of him, what would she have done? Where would she have gone? Laura could find no answer to this question, except to be certain that Jo would not have gone home, not after the burglary.

Suddenly decisive, she rang Geoff's number again and left a message on his answering machine.

'Geoff. Laura James here. I need to speak to you urgently. Please could you ring me as soon as possible. It's *very* important. Thanks.'

Next she rang Mary.

'Oh, Laura! Have you heard about Jo?' said Mary in awed tones.

'Only what Vic told me,' said Laura. 'Fill me in.'

'You'll never believe this. It was most peculiar,' said Mary. 'When I came in, I couldn't get into our room. It was locked and Vic said there were electricians checking a fault in the wiring. I could hear them moving about inside. So, anyway, I decided to go and do some shopping and when I got back at about a quarter to eleven, Vic told me that the police had been questioning everybody about Jo and that she had made off with some package. There are rumours flying round here, I can tell you.'

I'll bet there are, thought Laura. 'Like what?' she asked.

'Like that she's stolen some secret papers. Someone said she'd got hold of some Cabinet documents, but since then I've heard that she was spying for the Opposition and had got hold of the Government's draft election manifesto. Andrea said that was rubbish. Who's to know? Have you seen her?'

'No,' Laura lied, 'I was hoping you had.'

'No, I missed her. What an extraordinary business, don't you think?'

'I'll say.'

'And that's not all,' said Mary. 'I don't think any electricians had been in here. Well, that's to say, if they had been checking all the wiring, it didn't look to me as if they'd had the carpet back and the floorboards up, for example. But it did look as if they'd been searching the place, because everything looked slightly different. I didn't see them; they'd gone by the time I got back. I can't explain it exactly; it was just odd.'

'How strange,' said Laura.

'And, guess what?'

'What?'

'They've taken away everything of Jo's – I mean Lois's – all the files and books, the things in her desk. Jo told Vic that she was just going over to the House for something and left her bundle of post in his room. They took that too, so they evidently don't think she's coming back. Isn't it extraordinary?'

'It certainly is,' said Laura. And frightening too.

'Well you'd better brace yourself for a visit from the police, Laura,' said Mary. 'They'll be wanting to talk to you about her. Did Vic tell you?'

'He did say something, come to think of it,' said Laura.

'When they came to see me, they knew that you got her the job here – you introduced her to Harry didn't you? – so I'm sure they'll be wanting to talk to you.'

'Thanks for warning me, Mary. I'll be on my best behaviour.'

Laura's first action on putting the phone down was to remove the incoming message tape from her answering machine and replace it with a new one. She got up and looked around the room, the old tape in her hand, trying to think where she could hide it. The police might do more than question her. They might give her room a going-over too, especially if they learned that Jo had been to see her that morning. She'd better not take the tape home, either, for the same reason. She got up, put the tape in her bag. Before leaving her room she took the phone off the hook in case Jo or Geoff rang her. If they found the line engaged they would probably try again shortly. Then she walked along to Sir Charles's room, knocked and opened the door. The room was empty. She stepped inside, closed the door behind her and looked slowly round the room. Where could she hide the tape? She went over to the desk and opened the drawers. No, that wouldn't do. There were bookshelves. She toyed with the idea of putting it behind a book. Then she saw the shelf containing his collection of videos and cassette tapes of speeches he'd made, and television and radio programmes he'd taken part in before he became Deputy Speaker. She was sure he hadn't looked at them for years. The very place. She walked over to the book-case and selected a cassette case, removed the tape and replaced it with the tape from her answering machine, then slid the box back into its space on the bookshelf. Then she put Charles's tape into her handbag and returned to her own room, where she put the tape into a box and tossed it into the top drawer. That was a relief. She put the phone back on the hook and sat down at her desk.

Reflecting further on all that had happened, Laura was surprised that the police had not been to see her already. It was, according to Vic, an hour and a half since Jo had rushed off with her envelope. She sat at her desk trying in a half-hearted fashion to deal with some of her work, hoping for the phone to ring and to hear Jo's voice, but expecting the door to be opened at any moment by officers of the law. The minutes passed and Laura felt increasingly isolated and in need of news.

At one-fifteen she could stand it no longer and decided to go down in search of news. If she had waited only a minute or two minutes longer she would have spoken to Geoff, who had rung in once again to check the messages on his answering machine and had immediately dialled her number. When he got her answering machine he decided that perhaps her call hadn't been so urgent after all, or she would have stayed at her desk. He would see her in the House later on, or phone her again.

Walking through Central Lobby, Laura saw Bill at the barrier.

'Hello, Bill.'

'Hello, Laura, how are you?'

'I'm worried, if you must know. I was supposed to be meeting Jo Delvere – Harry Hunter's secretary – for lunch and she hasn't shown up. I suppose she hasn't been in, or left a message or anything?'

Laura thought Bill's look strange. He seemed to hesitate a moment, then change his mind.

'You're a good friend of hers, aren't you?'

'I certainly am. I'd like to think they don't come any better. Why?'

'Well I don't know what she's done, but apparently the police want to question her about something and when they came looking for her this morning, she did a runner. I think there may even be a warrant out for her arrest.' Bill told Laura what had happened. 'I've been criticized for not stopping her when I could have done.'

'I'm sorry to hear that, Bill,' said Laura, 'but I'm sure you did the right thing. Did you see her again after that?'

'No. And nor did anyone else, to judge from the questions I've been asked this morning. It's very strange. Do you know what's going on?'

'I'm afraid I don't,' said Laura. This was no less than the truth. 'I wish I did,' she added.

She walked back disconsolately to her room. She didn't know what to do. Jo might get in touch with her by telephone, so it would be better to wait at her desk. She gave lunch a miss, feeling too anxious to eat, and stayed at her desk, hoping that Jo would ring again and determined not to miss her this time. She tried to work, checking her watch at intervals and eyeing her telephone, willing Jo to ring her, unaware that her line was now being tapped and that, shortly after she went down to Central Lobby, a man had entered her room and placed a microphone behind a bookcase in the corner of the room near her desk. Fortunately for both Laura and Jo, these measures had been implemented just too late to net Jo's call and Laura's replaying of it so, for a while at least, Jo's pursuers would not pick up her trail.

CHAPTER THIRTY-FIVE

'She got away? How on earth did they manage to let her get away?' Harry was furious. What a pleasurable sensation it was to be able to indulge his anger, release all his pent-up anxiety in a burst of rage, to be the injured party for a change. He looked at Mackie with undisguised scorn.

'I would have thought, with the number of police officers on duty in the Palace of Westminster at any one time, that it should have been possible for them to stop one woman!'

'Indeed?' said Mackie. 'It may sound simple, but the place is a maze of passages and stairways.'

'Well, enough of excuses,' said Harry. 'What about the package she was carrying?'

'She had it in her hand when she was seen running out of the Chamber, but the officer outside who thinks he saw her running towards the underground swears she had no package in her hand, only a handbag. One of the men on the gate says the same thing.'

'So she must have left it somewhere in the building.'

'We think she must have slipped it into the post somehow. At first we thought she must have handed it in to the sorting office by Star Chamber Court but the men there don't remember anyone coming in with a package. She could just have tossed it into one of their skips, of course. We can't be sure what she did but we think she got it into the postal system somehow.'

'So what are you doing about it?' demanded Harry.

'Can you imagine the difficulty of finding a package like that in the post coming out of the Palace of Westminster? All movement of post out of the building has been halted and we're checking, but it's going to take hours. We can eliminate a huge quantity of course, because we know it was a large item. The attendant who saw her take it said it was a foolscap size, pre-paid, brown House of Commons envelope, printed with "On Her Majesty's Service". A nice touch, wouldn't you say?'

Harry found Mackie's willingness to indulge in humour at such a time almost more than he could stand, but said nothing. Mackie continued: 'He was convinced there was nothing written on it. If that's the case, we can assume that, if she did address it, the address would be handwritten rather than typed – unless she used a label of some kind. So we're looking for a large OHMS envelope addressed in her handwriting. We got a sample from her notebook. Matters are made more difficult by the fact that we don't know who she will have addressed it to.'

'Then you'll just have to open everything.'

'We can't do that. It's against the law.'

'Hah! Don't make me laugh. Since when have you people been concerned about breaking the law?'

Mackie ignored this remark. He paused a moment, then said, 'Has it occurred to you that your Parliamentary colleagues would have a thing or two to say about it if they knew what we were doing? There'd be questions to the Prime Minister this afternoon, for one thing. There may already be a question being put down about it as we speak.' Harry's anxiety reasserted itself and quickly supplanted his anger. What Mackie said was perfectly true. The prospect of the whole thing getting into the news made him feel sick with fear.

'Does the Prime Minister know about this?' he asked.

'I shall be reporting to him at two-fifteen,' said Mackie. 'I thought I would bring you up to date first and see if you had anything further to add to what you've already told us.'

'Of course not,' said Harry indignantly.

'I wondered whether you might have seen Delvere this morning, or heard from her.'

'Heard from her? Why should she get in touch with me?'

'Officially she's still your secretary,' said Mackie. 'She might have thought you'd expect her to be in touch, but that was not what I had in mind. It occurred to me she might try to blackmail you.'

'Oh, yes, I see,' said Harry.

'To get back to the envelope: we've narrowed it down to the three likeliest addresses: her own, that of the James woman, and that of the journalist she's been in touch with, Harper. But of course, she could have sent it anywhere. Overseas, for that matter. We'll have to see what we find. But there's another possibility of course.' He waited for the effect of this on Harry.

'What?' said Harry sharply.

'That the package she was carrying was nothing to do with your item at all, but something she happened to be carrying when she decided to bolt. After all, you said yourself that you didn't know whether she had made copies of your file.'

'It must have been something important because she had obviously hidden it. So why wasn't she carrying it when she left the building?' asked Harry.

'She may have dropped it, dumped it, or given it to someone.'

Harry did not pursue this point. He longed for the whole problem to be over. He looked at his watch.

'What about Laura James?' he asked. 'What have you done about her?' He'd like to see something really unpleasant done to her for landing him with this woman in the first place. But for her, none of this would have happened.

'We're not doing anything about her for the moment, except monitor her calls and movements very closely. We don't want to alarm her in case she turns out to be our only source of information.'

'What do you mean?'

'If we lose Delvere, our only hope of tracing her may be through James. Also, Delvere may contact her. We'll just have to wait and see. We'll be leaving Harper alone for the time being for the same reason. Unfortunately we don't know where he is at the moment. He hasn't been into the Palace of Westminster today, which is unusual for him, apparently.'

Harry was present when Mackie reported to the Prime Minister and stayed on after he had left the room.

The Prime Minister sat in silence for a moment then said, 'Well what do you think we should do, Harry?' His tone was angry. 'Have you any ideas?'

'Mackie seemed to think—'

'We must be wary of Mackie's ideas. He doesn't have to live with the consequences of his schemes: we do. We'll have to be able to explain them if something goes wrong. I'd like to hear *your* views.'

'I think we need to do something soon to discredit her, before she tries to make anything public, before anyone gets wind of what she did. In the House, I mean,' said Harry.

'The whole damn place is on fire with rumour and speculation already,' said the Prime Minister. 'We must agree a strategy. At the moment, only you and I know what the problem is. We've managed to escape having to tell the Cabinet anything yet, but they'll have to be told something very soon. The question is, what? I'm certain that the longer we keep the lid on this the better.'

'What do you propose to say if someone brings it up at Question Time this afternoon?' asked Harry.

'I shall say it's strictly a police matter, of course, and naturally no-one would expect me to say anything while they're pursuing their inquiries. The real problem's going to be the media. They're panting for information.'

Harry had been going to great lengths to avoid journalists. This was so unlike him as to be in itself worthy of comment. 'How do you think we should play it?' he asked. 'For the moment, there are two stories doing the rounds: one, that she stole some Cabinet documents; the other that she is an Opposition mole trying to get her hands on our election manifesto.'

'If only it were that simple!' the Prime Minister groaned. Silence reigned while both men struggled with their thoughts.

'Should we go with one of those rumours?' asked Harry cautiously.

The Prime Minister thought for a moment. 'I'm not sure. The manifesto story could backfire on us. I may well have a problem with it during Questions. As for the other story, if anything it's worse. It gives rise automatically to questions about security and then it's a short step to espionage. We'll be lucky to keep the lid on it for more than a few days.'

Harry felt defeated. The Prime Minister said, 'What have the Whips reported to you?'

'Nothing as yet because I haven't had a meeting with them today. I had to wait to hear from Mackie,' Harry lied. The truth of the matter was that he had avoided the Whips' Office because he didn't know how to handle the questions that would be coming thick and fast.

'It would be easier to decide what action to take if we knew exactly what, if anything, she's got,' he added cautiously.

'How true! Thanks to you we don't. But I think you could hazard a guess at the most likely form the danger will take, couldn't you?' He glared at Harry, waiting for his answer.

This was the moment Harry had wanted at all costs to avoid. He dared not go into too much detail, not as long as there was a chance of the Delvere woman being stopped in her tracks. If he revealed too much now and later it proved to have been unnecessary, he'd be done for. 'As I said yesterday, there's the problem of Wesker,' he began. 'Camborough wanted him compromised in case there were difficulties with the conference.'

'We've been over that already,' said the Prime Minister impatiently. 'What about Bamber? And Sanderell? If there is anything in your damn book about either of *them*, that really would spell catastrophe for us. Well?'

Harry didn't answer immediately. 'You stupid bastard!' exclaimed the Prime Minister furiously. 'You haven't got anything in it about them, have you? Christ, what have you done?'

'Steady on,' said Harry. 'It's not like that. There's just their names and some dates and figures. There's nothing about what was in the Vector report.'

'We'll be held responsible for every outbreak of unidentifiable disease and every food shortage in Europe if that gets out. We'll be blamed for every bloody disaster that's going, at this rate.' The Prime Minister got to his feet and went over to the window. He stood motionless for some minutes, staring out at the bright spring day, his figure a dark silhouette against the light.

He continued, still with his back to Harry. 'Even if that didn't get out, the Wesker business could be equally catastrophic for us. The Americans would exact a heavy penalty from us for undermining their position. They'd insist on taking the conference over and would probably pay us back with exposures of their own. We'd be international pariahs, especially after all we've said about Britain representing fair play and the reassurances we've given to the warring parties. None of them will trust us and the conference could well be called off. We'll be held responsible for further avoidable slaughter and suffering.'

He stopped speaking and continued to stare out of the window. Harry waited in silence, thinking about the other things that would emerge and the accusations that would be hurled at them from all sides, from petty dishonesty and chicanery to corruption and the cover-up of crimes. There would be months, even years of digging, investigation and exposure. Most damning of all would be the revelation of the extent of their hypocrisy, which would wipe out their credibility at home and abroad – hypocrisy from which none of them would ever recover.

The Prime Minister suddenly thrust his hands in his pockets and turned to face Harry again. 'We have to decide three things: first, what do we say about the Delvere woman. We have to say something to try to halt the rumours and keep the media happy. Second, we have to decide whether to make some pre-emptive move to neutralize anything damaging that might become public. Third, we have to decide what to do about Delvere and Harper. Right?'

Harry had been giving some thought to the first question already, being preoccupied with the damage done to him by the mere fact of having employed her, quite apart from what else might happen to him. He said, 'It has occurred to me that the best thing for the moment would be to put it around that she is deranged, that she had a breakdown some time ago and has had a relapse.'

'We still have to decide what to do about the documents angle,' said the Prime Minister. 'I think we will have to go with the rumours. Say that she didn't in fact take anything but had been seen looking at copies of secret, no, confidential, papers – belonging to the Party rather than the Government. We should run with the idea of her trying to find out our election plans. Yes, that's it. She's nuts and she became obsessed with the idea of obtaining a copy of our draft manifesto, something like that.'

'We could say that I took her on as a kindness, a favour to her family,' said Harry. 'She doesn't have any family on hand with whom the media could check this. If Mackie can't trace her mother in New Zealand, I can't believe the press will manage it either, not for a while anyway.' He was warming to his subject. 'We could say that she had a breakdown some years ago, and was supposed to have made a complete recovery, but suffered a major relapse this morning, say she suffers from delusions and persecution mania and ask them to be restrained for her sake. We could let them think she's been readmitted to hospital for treatment. I expect we could arrange for a helpful statement by a private clinic, implying that she's a patient there – can't say more because medical matters are confidential, that sort of thing.' Harry looked at the other expectantly as if hoping for praise.

'Yes. That would take care of that side of things for a while and would have the added advantage that the media here might treat any information she took to them as suspect,' said the Prime Minister. 'But they're bound to ask why the Government Chief Whip employed such a person in the first place.'

'We'd say I did it as a favour to her mother and stress

335

that it was only temporary, because my regular girl broke her leg skiing. I'd have thought we'd get away with that all right,' said Harry confidently.

'Unless the other woman, James, tries to put a spanner in the works.'

'But will she? We could get Charles Donaldson to scare the shit out of her: tell her that she will be exposed to maximum embarrassment in the media for landing us with this problem. After all we could say that she persuaded me to take her and concealed her mental history. Land her right in it and tell her if she doesn't keep her mouth shut she can say goodbye to her job and her pension.'

'I wonder,' said the Prime Minister thoughtfully. 'What kind of woman is she? She might tell us all to get stuffed.'

'But who would believe her if she did try to make trouble? So she tries to enlist sympathy for Delvere, or defend her in some way. We can say she's defending a lunatic or a thief, or however we want to play it,' said Harry.

The other man looked at him despairingly. 'I was forgetting that you do this sort of thing for a pastime, don't you Harry? That's what got us into this hole in the first place.'

'You asked for my suggestion and I gave it to you. If you have a better idea, please tell me,' said Harry defiantly.

'All right,' said the Prime Minister, 'we'll go ahead with that. Get on with it straight away. Tell the Whips, let them spread it around. And tell Mackie too. We may need him to do something as well because if she is caught, she can be put away out of reach in a secure mental hospital while we decide what to do with her.'

He paused, then continued: 'Right, now to number two: how to neutralize or limit the damage if anything *is* published anywhere.'

'The media here will be wary of publishing anything which could constitute a very serious libel, unless they're totally confident of its truth. That will tend to hold them up, for a time anyway,' said Harry.

'Yes. There's a much greater risk of something coming out overseas,' said the Prime Minister. 'Get on to Robin Brook-Ainlee and tell him we need to know the minute *anything* appears anywhere, in any newspaper or programme here or abroad. He must monitor it, without giving anything away. Do you think he can be trusted with that?'

'With what we've got on him, I've no doubts at all,' said Harry.

'As for neutralizing the damage, what are your thoughts on that?'

'Fight fire with fire,' replied Harry, his confidence increasing as the risk of having to detail the book's contents receded. 'Without bringing Delvere into it for the moment, let it be known a foreign agent has been attempting to damage the government by setting up an elaborate web of false accusations of financial and sexual misdemeanours. Suggest that attempts have been made to compromise ministers and others with gifts and damaging introductions to criminals and so on. Hint at invention of—'

The Prime Minister cut him short. 'Before you get too carried away, this is something we'll have to get Mackie and his colleagues to handle. Unless they establish who she's working for, we'll have to decide who we're going to make responsible for it. Do we point the finger at America, or Russia, or closer to home? France, or Germany? Of course, she could still turn out to be an American agent. It's just the sort of thing they go for. Mackie is certain she isn't, but we needn't let that deter us. We could accuse them of trying to interfere with the peace conference for domestic political reasons. They've

337

got a Presidential election coming up soon after all. Or we could pick one of the parties at the conference. And while we're about it, we might turn things to our own advantage. After all, with our own election not far away, we could take advantage of the build-up of xenophobia. From that standpoint, the Germans might be the best target. We'll have to tell Templeman and Camborough, but they can be relied on for discretion for obvious reasons.'

'Camborough can. I'm not so sure about Templeman,' said Harry, who was thinking about Jane.

'Before we do that, you and I have to decide what possible disclosures pose the greatest risk and tailor our plans accordingly.'

'I think Camborough is one of the biggest liabilities. Perhaps you ought to get rid of him,' replied Harry.

'Christ! I can hardly appoint a new Foreign Secretary days before the peace conference starts,' the Prime Minister groaned. Silence again. Then he looked at his watch. 'I've got Questions shortly and there's a queue of people waiting to speak to me. So let's get on with it. We'll leave the question of damage limitation a little longer. We'll give it another twenty-four hours. That leaves item three: what to do about Delvere and Harper? We can't do anything about her, apart from what we've already agreed, until she's caught. That leaves Harper. I'm certain a pre-emptive strike is called for. If he knows anything at all, we've got to do something to spike his guns.'

'He obviously knows *something*,' said Harry, 'the question is, how much? But what can we do about him?'

'We can't have him arrested, that would cause more problems than it would solve,' the Prime Minister continued. 'The media would never let go of the story if we did that and it would look much worse for us if something did come out later. No, we have to discredit him

somehow.' He thought for a while, then said, 'The proprietor of his newspaper owes us one. We need to get
him sacked and make sure that no-one else will employ
him. How can we achieve that?' He didn't wait for Harry
to answer, but said, 'It's for you to make sure he gets the
sack. Then tell Mackie to arrange things so that no-one
will touch him again as a journalist. Report back to me
this evening.'

Mackie grinned wolfishly when Harry passed on this
instruction to him. 'We'll make sure he's a journalistic
outcast all right, no trouble. And then we'll get the
Revenue to check all his tax returns for the last ten years
for false expenses claims. He'll be kept so busy he won't
even have the time to sign on for the dole!'

The Prime Minister got through Question Time
unscathed, the line about police inquiries proving a
successful fire blanket. How long his luck would hold
remained to be seen. The expense and risk involved in
the examination of the Palace of Westminster post
proved to have been wasted. There was no sign whatever
of Jo's envelope. And Jo herself had vanished without a
trace.

CHAPTER THIRTY-SIX

Alicia opened the door of Laura's room without knocking, looked in and saw that Laura was alone. She put her finger to her lips and beckoned. Laura followed her out of the room.

'D'you know where Geoff is?' said Laura as soon as they were in the corridor. 'I need to speak to him. It's terribly urgent.'

'Not here,' whispered Alicia and led the way along the corridor to the stairs where she stopped.

'We've got to be very careful,' she said in a low voice. 'I think you can be fairly certain your room is bugged, and your phone too.'

'Where is Geoff? I must speak to him. Have you heard about Jo?' asked Laura anxiously.

'Have I ever! No-one's talking about anything else. Do you know where she is?'

'I was about to ask you the same thing. I haven't the faintest idea,' said Laura, 'and I'm worried sick about her. I was hoping Geoff might know something.'

'I'm afraid not, but he's got a lot to tell you – and ask

you. He needs to talk to you, urgently.'

'And I need to talk to him!'

'Whatever you do, don't say anything in your room, or on the phone, or anywhere here where you might be overheard.'

'What makes you think my phone's bugged?' Laura was puzzled.

'I'll explain later. You probably will be followed when you leave here, too. Geoff's in the same boat and wants the three of us to get together, somewhere well away from the House.'

'Whatever you say,' said Laura.

'If you don't mind, I think it would be better if you didn't leave here in your car. I'd leave it in the underground car-park – that's where you usually park, isn't it? – and walk over towards Jo's office. I've got my car parked nearby. I'll go and get it and pull into Old Palace Yard and wait for you. Is that all right with you?'

'Certainly.'

'Can you get away soon?' asked Alicia. 'And meet me in Old Palace Yard in, say, three-quarters of an hour?'

'No problem. I would normally have left by now, but I've been sitting by my phone, hoping to hear from Jo. I'll go and shut up shop.'

'I'd leave it looking as if you were coming back,' suggested Alicia.

'Good idea.'

Laura switched off her computer, but left papers and files out on her desk, which she usually left tidy at the end of each day. She also left her coat hanging on the coat stand in the corner of the room and walked across the road from St Stephen's Entrance carrying only her shoulder bag. Alicia was waiting for her as arranged and they drove away feeling fairly confident that they were not being followed.

'We've decided to camp out with a friend of ours,

Murad. He's an Egyptian journalist. Lives in Islington. We're meeting Geoff there,' said Alicia. 'He's been nosing around, following up something Jo said to him. I got hold of him on his mobile eventually and told him the amazing news about Jo bolting from the building and the various wild theories about what she was supposed to have done.' Alicia looked at Laura. 'Do *you* know what she's done?'

'Do you mind if we wait till we see Geoff, so that I don't have to explain it all twice?' asked Laura, who was feeling worn out with anxiety. 'Tell me why you're so certain my office is bugged,' she added.

'Because the first thing I heard when I came in this morning was that Geoff's desk had been searched,' said Alicia. 'They must think we're pretty thick,' said Alicia. 'It was one of the cleaning ladies who tipped me off. These women have been doing the job for years. It's hardly surprising they smell a rat when they're suddenly joined by a newcomer and then see them rummaging through someone's desk when they're supposed to be dusting it.'

'It's not just Geoff's office,' said Laura and repeated what Mary had told her about Jo's room.

Laura was very glad to see Geoff, but bitterly disappointed that he had no news of Jo. He took them to a little restaurant nearby and insisted she have something to eat and drink. Gradually Laura felt calmer and more relaxed. It was a relief to be able to tell Geoff and Alicia about the extraordinary events of the past week. 'I tried to get hold of you all day today. I've been frantic with worry.'

She did almost all the talking to begin with, prompted with a question here and there from the others. She gave them a long and careful explanation of everything that had happened, beginning with who Jo was and how she came to be working in the House. She talked quietly, urgently, putting in every detail, fervently hoping that they would arrive at some idea where Jo might be and how she could be helped. When she came to Jo's discovery in Harry's flat, Geoff exclaimed, 'Now I understand what she was trying to tell me!'

'Last weekend we went home to my mother's – she was away – and had a long talk about it, but we couldn't decide what to do.'

'I wish she'd confided in me,' said Geoff. Laura said nothing. She was thinking of her conversation with Jo that morning and remembering their hilarity. It seemed so long ago. How she wished Jo had confided in Geoff too.

'What I don't understand is what this American agent was doing, talking to her yesterday,' said Geoff. 'She seemed to be having a disagreement with him about something. And when I asked her about it she was furious with me, but now I understand why, of course. And I understand why she wanted me to investigate Parrie and Moreton. But I'll tell you about that in a minute. Carry on, Laura.'

'I was just coming to McGovern next,' said Laura and explained how scared and puzzled Jo had been, how she couldn't get hold of Laura and then had gone home and found her flat ransacked and had turned up at work that morning, very frightened and determined to do something about the envelope immediately. She explained what she and Jo had decided to do, how she had waited for her to return.

'The last I saw of her was when I left her sitting at my desk, about to phone you,' said Laura.

'If only I'd gone into the House this morning!' exclaimed Geoff.

'All I know is that she retrieved the envelope and did something with it which she regarded as solving the problem. I assumed she'd given it to you,' said Laura.

'If only she had,' said Geoff ruefully.

'Then I got a message on my answering machine, but she had to break off. She sounded frightened. I'm so afraid that it was this man McGovern who caused her to cut short her call.'

'You mustn't get carried away with thoughts like that,' said Alicia reassuringly. 'She'll ring you up and you'll find there's a really simple explanation for that call. And another thing, whatever she did with her envelope, the authorities evidently haven't managed to get hold of it. They seem to think she put it in the post as she raced through the courtyards. One of the postmen told me the Post Office had been turned upside down while the authorities looked for it. But it looks as if she was too smart for them. I'm reliably informed that their searches turned up nothing.'

'Well that's something, anyway,' said Laura.

'I hope she didn't post her envelope to one of us,' said Geoff. 'It's bound to be intercepted if she did. If she could just get those photocopies to us, we could do something straight away. I've managed to acquire a certain amount of circumstantial evidence, but it's useless without Jo's material.'

'And when do you plan to share your findings with us?' asked Alicia. 'The suspense is killing me.'

'My inquiries might have been more productive if I had known exactly what it was that Jo had discovered. Unfortunately I didn't get a chance to ask her. The only detail I'd got from her was about this divorce and child custody case and possible child abuse. Otherwise it was just names.' He took a sip of wine and continued: 'The first thing I did was go to this place Kistrington Hall. It's a palatial pile. Used to belong to the Kistrington family until they couldn't cough up the death duties and sold it to the nation. Now it's used as a judges' lodgings for quite a large part of the year. When it's not being used to keep judges comfy and happy it's used for occasional official functions, banquets and bunfights like that, it seems it's used to entertain visiting potentates and to put heart into businessmen. And some of the time it's open to the public.'

'All very interesting,' said Alicia. 'Get on with it.'

'These judges certainly do themselves proud by all accounts. There's a permanent staff of six or seven, headed by a dubious-looking character called Staffer. There's a maintenance man, a housekeeper and three or four maids, at least that's all I managed to gather in the neighbourhood, where people knew precious little about the goings on at the Hall. I was told that the maids were all foreign, spoke little English and were hardly ever seen in the village. The locals thought it very strange that when one of the staff died a while back, the local doctor wasn't called in. They said some doctor was brought down from London instead. They take a dim view of the fact that the neighbourhood derives little or no financial benefit from the Hall, although it's run at the taxpayers' expense. Apparently hardly anything is bought locally but is brought from elsewhere by special delivery. It seems that the whole establishment is pretty much resented locally because they don't employ any local people. They had a local chap as the maintenance man but he got the sack because he asked too many questions. I tried to talk to him, but he was very nervous and refused to speak to me. He said, "I'm not taking any chances, mate," and shut the door in my face.'

'You poor dear. How very disheartening. They're normally so willing to unburden themselves to you, aren't they?'

'Be serious, 'Lissie. The man was scared, I tell you.'

'Go on with your story.'

'The landlord of the local pub said that he'd heard all sorts of weird rumours but didn't pay much attention to

345

them. He's an incomer and has a slightly superior attitude to the locals. He did say, however, that they seemed to have a lot of visitors to the place some evenings, even very late at night, in "swank cars", as he put it, and he resents the fact that none of them ever come to the pub for a drink.'

'I can imagine,' said Alicia. 'All that wealth passing him by.'

'My enquiries at the Hall itself didn't yield much. It was a pity it wasn't a day it was open to the public. Still, I rang the bell and after a long delay the door was opened by a girl who could have been Filipino and who was wearing jeans and a sweatshirt.'

'So? It's not unusual garb,' said Alicia.

'Not exactly maid-like.'

'Maybe she was off-duty. Maybe there weren't any judges at home.'

'That's not the point. I was about to tell you that she had a bad bruise on her neck. Really nasty. Almost as if someone had tried to throttle her. And she looked scared. I don't think she spoke much English. Either that, or she was afraid to talk. She didn't get a chance anyway because this man appeared behind her and said, "Get back to your work" in the kind of tones a gaoler might have used to a recalcitrant member of a chain-gang on Dartmoor a hundred years ago. He didn't exactly bellow at her, but she fled. And then he told me to piss off and come back when they were open to the public. There was a closed-circuit television camera staring at me from about two feet away while this little exchange took place, recording my image and words for posterity.'

'So what did you do then? Continue with this gripping tale,' said Alicia.

'I went back to the House and had another word with our Harry. I thought he would peg out on the spot. Then he rushed off, no doubt to warn Moreton because I couldn't track him down.'

'Did you find him today? I take it that's where you were all day, nosing around on his trail.'

'His and Parrie's. I checked Moreton first, but didn't get to see him. Oh and guess what? I saw Randall Myers walking out of St Stephen's Entrance with Moreton yesterday evening. Interesting, wouldn't you say?'

'I wonder what they were up to?' said Alicia.

'I tried to talk to people at Moreton Micro but got very little out of them,' said Geoff. 'One of the interesting things about Moreton and Parrie is how little I could find out about them. Usually people will tell you *something* about a person. The most interesting feature in both cases was people's reluctance to talk.'

'It could mean that they're respectable citizens, loved by one and all.'

'Then someone would have said that. No, it wasn't like that. I did everything I could: cashed in a lot of old favours and used all the contacts I could muster, but I couldn't find out anything about Parrie in the Law Courts or elsewhere. I said I was writing a piece about his promotion to the Court of Appeal. Generally the re-action was either "I'm far too busy," or "You'll get me into trouble if you persist with this." The few who did unbend tended to trot out the same response, "Of course, Mr Justice Parrie – sorry, Lord Justice Parrie, I should say – is very experienced, you know, very much the family man, very concerned about the welfare of children." The only positive – I should say negative – comment was made by a barrister who said he'd been surprised by Parrie's promotion. Unfortunately he wouldn't say why.'

'Even if you did manage to unearth anything, what would happen? Nothing,' said Alicia. 'There've been other scandals involving the judiciary, but they just get swept under the carpet. Have you ever heard of a judge being punished for anything? The worst that can happen is early retirement on a full pension.'

'Even that doesn't happen very often,' said Geoff. 'It has to be something pretty bad for the Lord Chancellor to insist on a judge standing down.'

'Yes,' said Alicia. 'Moral turpitude, for example.'

'The likes of Parrie probably think that's something you clean your paintbrush with,' said Laura.

Geoff laughed. 'Are you feeling a bit better, Laura?'

'It's a relief to talk to you two, but I'd feel better still if I knew what had happened to Jo.'

'I did have one stroke of luck,' said Geoff, who'd been saving it till last.

'I thought so!' said Alicia. 'I could tell you were holding something back. Go on. Out with it.'

'I showed a photograph of Moreton to the garage owner in Kistrington and he said he'd seen him there two or three times, driving a Rolls. He'd filled up at his garage. He said he thought the last time was a couple of weeks ago, when he'd had another man and a couple of children in the car.'

'Children,' said Laura. 'Do you think . . .'

'I do, I'm afraid,' said Geoff and recounted what the garage proprietor had said about outings from the children's home. Laura put her head in her hands. 'It's terrible. Somehow, until now, it's all been like some ghastly story, not real. Or maybe it just seemed too awful to be true. But now . . .'

'We've got to put a stop to it,' said Alicia grimly.

They were silent for a time. Then Geoff said, 'I'd like to go and interview Parrie. And Moreton. What do you think 'Lissie? With you there too. Put it on camera.'

'Good idea. We could maybe persuade Parrie we wanted to interview him about his appointment to the Court of Appeal and then ask him straight out what he gets up to at Kistrington. And we ought to get an MP lined up to ask a question in the House at the same time.'

'No-one will touch it, without some evidence,' said Laura. 'I don't think you'd find anyone who'd agree to put a question down for you without something to go on.'

'I realize that. But we'll do it. Soon. As soon as we hear from Jo. You'll see.'

While Laura, Geoff and Alicia were having supper together, Mackie was reporting to Harry Hunter that there was still no sign of Delvere or Harper but that they had identified her friends at the House of Commons, one of whom they already knew about of course – Laura James – the others being Ann Fenchurch and Barbara Wallingbury.

'We think it significant that she should have tried to cultivate those particular friendships,' said Mackie. 'It tends to support the view that she is a foreign agent.'

'Why's that?' asked Harry.

'Ann Fenchurch's husband works in the Cabinet Office, dealing with security matters amongst other things and his wife is well-placed to obtain information about security in the Palace of Westminster, being in the Serjeant-at-Arms's Office. Barbara Wallingbury's husband, as you know, is PPS to the Foreign Secretary. And of course, Laura James works for a Junior Home Office Minister, Ian Swift, in addition to working for Sir Charles Donaldson. It all adds up to a carefully laid plan. We will deal with Fenchurch, and we'll be monitoring their telephones – a temporary measure, of course – but it would be preferable if you were to have a word with Wallingbury and see what you can get him to find out about Delvere from his wife.'

Harry undertook to do so without delay.

CHAPTER THIRTY-SEVEN

Laura walked wearily up to Central Lobby. She had gone to bed very late the previous night. After leaving Geoff and Alicia she had gone to Lydia's flat, hoping to find some news of Jo, but there was no response to the doorbell.

As she emerged from Members' Post Office with her bundles of mail, Laura saw Ann, who looked pale and red-eyed.

'Hello, Laura,' said Ann, without a smile.

'Ann. Are you all right?'

'No, I'm not.' Ann started to walk away, then stopped. 'Have you got a moment, Laura?'

'Sure thing.'

'Have you got time to come downstairs and have a coffee so that we can talk?' Ann looked round her with an unhappy glance. There was a steady stream of people in and out of the Lobby and it was hardly the place to talk privately.

'Certainly,' said Laura and they went down to the Strangers' Cafeteria. 'What's wrong?' she asked as they walked along the terrace corridor.

'It's about Jo.'

'What about her?' asked Laura in alarm.

'You mean you don't know?' said Ann, astonished.

'Oh, I know there's some crazy story going round that she's run off with some Cabinet documents or something. I don't believe a word of it.'

Ann looked at Laura, but didn't say anything as they had reached the cafeteria and joined a short queue. When they had got their coffee and sat down, Ann said, 'I know she's your friend, but don't you think it's all a bit odd, Laura?'

'It's odd, all right, but I'll reserve judgement until I hear from Jo herself. Anyway, I know that the stories going round are a load of cobblers,' said Laura emphatically.

'How do you know? How can you be so certain?'

'Because I know Jo would never do a thing like that. And if she's disappeared she's got good reason. That's not to say I'm not worried. I am. Very.'

'Tim and I had a row about it this morning. We've never had one before. It was terrible.' Ann looked down at her coffee cup and leant her head on her hand.

'You poor girl. What a shame. But why did you have a row exactly?'

'We'd probably have another if Tim knew I was telling you this. But you know his present job has a certain amount to do with security matters, don't you?'

'Yes, he told me so himself.'

'Well yesterday he saw something, I don't know what exactly, some report or memo which said that Jo may be a foreign agent.'

'What?' Laura's astonished exclamation carried round the whole room and people looked round at her.

'Not so loud,' said Ann, looking embarrassed.

'A foreign agent! A *spy*. She's not a spy!' hissed Laura

at Ann. 'Good God! Whatever next? It would be hysterical if it weren't so serious. A spy! What a joke!'

Ann looked miserable.

'You can't be serious!' Laura continued, 'Does Tim believe that? Surely not. It's rubbish, dangerous rubbish and I'd like to know who's behind it,' she added furiously.

'Don't *you* start being angry with me, too.' Ann had tears in her eyes. 'It's not my fault!'

'I'm sorry, Ann, truly I am.' Laura calmed herself. 'Of course it's not your fault, nor Tim's for that matter. Let's both relax, shall we. Of course, it'll all come right soon, I know it will. It's too ridiculous for words.'

'Tim doesn't think it is.'

Laura let this pass. She looked at Ann for a moment. She could see she was very unhappy. 'I can see he's rather been put on the spot by his job,' she said. 'Tell me exactly why you had a row. Did you stick up for Jo, or what?'

'It wasn't like that exactly. No, it's all because I suggested we invite Jo round on the weekend. We were having breakfast this morning and I asked Tim what he thought we ought to have for lunch on Saturday for Jo and he said, "Oh, I meant to tell you last night, I don't want you to have anything to do with that woman from now on and you'll have to cancel Saturday."'

'What was happening on Saturday?' asked Laura.

'Oh, we'd invited her to lunch. In fact we'd already changed the date once, from Sunday to Saturday. The thing is, I hadn't talked to Tim about what happened here yesterday – Jo running off with some package – because he'd come in very late, after I'd gone to sleep.'

'What did you say to Tim?' asked Laura.

'I said, "What do you mean, I mustn't have anything to do with her?" He refused to say at first and said he couldn't talk about it. I was annoyed, as you can imagine. It's not as if I didn't know what happened yesterday. I can't stand it when he treats me like a child, as if I'm not old enough to know about these terribly important things he deals with at work – or maybe he thinks I can't be trusted.'

'Nonsense!' said Laura. 'Of course he trusts you. He *adores* you! You know that, don't you?'

Ann was silent. She couldn't talk to Laura about all the other things they had said. How she wished they hadn't said them. Tim had accused her of not taking his job seriously, of not valuing what he did and his achievements. She had said that his work was more important to him than their marriage, that he didn't value *her* work, that she'd choose her own friendships without having them vetted by him. He had been stung into further furious criticisms which she couldn't bring herself to remember. And she had given back in kind; she had been cruel. How she wished she could take all her words back, make it so that their row had never happened.

'We had a *terrible* row, Laura. Awful. I rounded things off nicely by saying that he didn't know what he was talking about, that I was sure Jo wasn't a spy, that it was a stupid idea and that I liked her and I'd choose my own friends without any help from him. And a lot more besides. He didn't say another word and left shortly afterwards. Things will never be the same again between us, even if we do make it up.'

'Of course, you'll make it up. And things will be *better* between you, you'll see. Sometimes it's necessary to say these things, better than having them as unspoken doubts between you, don't you see?' Ann was unconvinced and looked it.

'And there may be all sorts of reasons why he doesn't talk much about work,' Laura continued. 'He may be worried about his work. Perhaps they're giving him a hard time at his office. He may have been pumped for information on what you know about Jo. He may fear that you'll be questioned. Who knows? There could be lots of difficulties for him over something like this. He's not to know that he's been fed a lot of crap about Jo, is he?'

Ann smiled. 'I won't tell him you said that. But how can you be so certain that it's not true?'

It was Laura's turn to hesitate. She had been on the point of telling Ann but now she had doubts. Given Tim's responsibilities and the attitude he had adopted, there was a risk that anything she told Ann might get passed on to the authorities. Until she knew whether Jo was safe – and her information safe too – she felt reluctant to trust anyone.

'I just know it's not. *I* know Jo. OK?'

'OK, Laura. I can see you're upset about it too. It's awful, isn't it. Poor Jo. I wonder what's happened to her. I hope she's all right.'

'Same here,' said Laura gloomily. Then, determined to continue with the positive line she had taken over Tim, she said, 'We'll hear from her soon, you'll see. In the meantime, you ought to ring Tim and make it up, don't you think?'

'I'd like to but he said on no account was I to mention her over the phone, not just to him, to anybody. He begged me not to talk about her to anyone, anywhere in this place. And here we are talking about her at the first opportunity.'

'You can ring him up without mentioning Jo, surely?' Laura exclaimed. 'And don't worry, I won't tell him about our conversation, I promise,' she added, smiling. 'Come on, let's go back upstairs, shall we? I must put in an appearance or Charles will think I've quit.'

CHAPTER THIRTY-EIGHT

Sir Charles was indeed wondering what had become of
Laura. He had been preparing himself for the past hour
and a half for his conversation with her. He had been
sitting at his desk, but now he was pacing about his
room, adjusting the position of an ornament on a shelf
here, straightening a picture there, scarcely aware of
what he was doing. He was rehearsing the questions he
would have to put to Laura and wondering how she
would respond to them. When she entered the room, he
still had not made up his mind exactly how to handle the
matter and was feeling very uneasy.

'Hello, Charles. I'm sorry to be so late. Various things
came up that simply couldn't wait.' She sat down in an
armchair and put a folder of papers on the table next to
her. She looked up, waiting for him to sit down too.
Instead he stood in the middle of the room, looking at
her.

'Like the thing that came up yesterday morning, I suppose?'

'What do you mean?' she asked.

'You know perfectly well what I mean. When your friend Joanna came busting in here saying she needed to see you urgently.'

'Well she did.'

'What about?'

Laura was taken aback. She was not prepared for his hostile, angry tone.

'Whatever's the matter? Why are you angry?'

'Answer my question. What did she want to see you about?'

'No, I will not answer your question until you tell me why you're angry with me. What am *I* supposed to have done?'

'You know perfectly well why I am angry.'

'No, I don't. Clearly it has something to do with the rumours about Jo. But that doesn't explain why you're so angry with me.'

'I have had the Serjeant-at-Arms here and the police, asking all sorts of questions about her and about your involvement.'

'If they have any questions of me, they should come and see me,' said Laura. 'What did you tell them?'

'What could I tell them? I said that I didn't know anything about the woman. They wanted to know how well you knew her. Did I think you had had the wool pulled over your eyes by her? What did you really know about her? Did I know that you had persuaded the Chief Whip to employ her?'

'What a nerve! Why don't they speak to *me* if they want answers to such questions? I didn't *persuade* him. And he was lucky to get her. I can see he's responsible for all this, the gutless little—'

'He feels, quite rightly, that you were less than honest with him.'

'Oh he does, does he? What do you mean "quite rightly"? You agree with him, do you?'

'You haven't been honest with me.'

'Honest? You question *my* honesty? How about this for honesty? Your distinguished colleague, Harry, is now putting it about that Jo is a spy or a terrorist or some lunatic idea like that. How's that for honesty?'

'But perhaps it's true.'

'It's a pack of lies! Just now you were saying I'd persuaded him to employ her. Make up your mind.'

'You've put me in an embarrassing position.'

'How have *I* put you in an embarrassing position?'

'By not telling me about her. You even had the nerve to bring her here and introduce her to me the other evening. I'm surprised at you.'

'Oh you are are you? You've always been happy to meet friends of mine in the past.'

'You're being unreasonable.'

'No, I am not. It's *you* who's being unreasonable. This is me you're talking to remember. *Me.* The person you claim to care for. Your closest confidante.'

'But why didn't *you* confide in me?' he asked miserably.

'I was just about to tell you all about Jo the other evening, when I brought her here to meet you, only you had to go off to the Chamber, so I didn't get the chance.'

'Well tell me now.'

'How can I after what you've said?'

'What do you expect me to say? You've put me in an impossible position.'

Laura leapt to her feet. 'Your position! That's what this is all about. I thought you were different, but no, you're just the same as all the rest. You don't care about me! You only care about your position! Your career! Well I won't tell you a damn thing about Jo. And if the police come to you again, you'd better refer them to me. Not that it would do them any good.'

'What do you mean? So you don't know anything

about her either, is that it?' he asked hopefully.

'I know a great deal about her, all that I need to know to be able to assure you that these stories about her are madness, absolute garbage.' Laura was in a fury, tears in her eyes. 'I notice nobody is worried about *her*. Fantastic! Has it occurred to you, or anyone else, that we ought to be *worried* about her?' She rushed out of the room and back to her desk, where she buried her face in her hands and wept.

Laura was not the only person to be under a strain. Harry Hunter had just found Michael Wallingbury at last, having spent much of the past hour trying to track him down. The two men were walking slowly along the Committee Corridor.

'I'm glad to have this opportunity of a private word with you, Michael,' said Harry, by way of opening gambit. 'I dare say you heard all the commotion yesterday about this unfortunate young woman who's been working for me while Lois is away.'

'I did hear something, yes. Why is she unfortunate?' asked Michael politely, though what he was thinking was that it must have been something of a misfortune to have to work for an odious little creep like Harry.

'Oh, haven't you heard? Well, she was rather unwell in the past. Sad story. Had a breakdown. Her family thought she'd got over it, but she's had a major relapse. We'd noticed signs of trouble in the last few weeks, but didn't pay too much attention. You know how it is.' Michael didn't help him out.

Harry stopped walking and turned towards him and lowered his voice confidentially. 'We don't want it talked about too much, because it's rather embarrassing. Her family must be going through hell. Unfortunately she seems to have gone right off the rails. We caught her going through some of my papers. It seems she was obsessed with getting hold of our draft election manifesto. God knows what she thought she was going to do with it if she did!' He gave a short laugh, like the yap of a small dog. He looked up at Michael, clearly expecting him to share his amusement.

'I can see it must be rather embarrassing for you to have employed such a person,' said Michael.

'Oh, I took her on as a favour to her family, you know,' said Harry. 'Enough of that, what I wanted to say to you was – this is a little difficult – well, I know that Barbara has been rather chummy with her and I wondered if she knew anything – whether she had heard anything from Joanna, knows where she is, for example.'

'Don't you think you had better ask her yourself?' asked Michael.

'Well, I thought it would be better coming from you. I wouldn't want to offend her,' said Harry.

'How would it offend her?'

'I don't want to seem to be criticizing her choice of friends.'

'If it was all right for you to employ her, I would have thought it was all right for Barbara to be friends with her,' said Michael.

Harry did not like the way things were going. This was not what he had had in mind at all. He started again. 'You must understand, Michael, that we are in something of an embarrassing position. I would have thought you would appreciate it better than most, especially at this juncture.' Michael said nothing. What a pompous ass Harry is, he was thinking. A pompous little prick in platform shoes. Nicely alliterative, that phrase. He smiled faintly at the thought and enraged Harry.

'I don't know what there is to smile about,' he snapped. 'There's nothing funny about this situation. If you value your career, you'll have a word with your wife. I'm sure she'll see how important this is.'

'Are you threatening me, Harry?' asked Michael in a mild tone, though inwardly he was seething.

'I'm just trying to ensure that you and Barbara understand the seriousness of the situation.'

'If you've quite finished, I've a meeting to attend,' said Michael and walked away without waiting for his answer.

When Michael met Barbara at his office just before lunch he told her what Harry had said.

'You must be careful, darling,' she said, alarmed by the prospect of Michael falling out irretrievably with Harry. 'He can harm you, you know. Get on the wrong side of him and your career will be ruined.'

'If my career is dependent on his goodwill, then it's not worth it,' said Michael. 'I'd like to think that whatever success I have will be due to my ability, nothing else.'

'But Michael, be reasonable.'

'Reasonable? You sound like him. I'd have thought you'd object to criticism of your friend.'

'She's not a particularly close friend. I hardly know her in fact and you've got to admit her behaviour is pretty extraordinary. When I heard this morning that she'd gone off her head, I wasn't terribly surprised really.'

'Who told you that?' asked Michael.

'Jimmy Underwood. He was reeking of booze again. He said that the Whips were talking about it. "It's her turn now," he said to me. Is he nuts too, do you think?'

'No. He may be pathetic, but he's not nuts,' said Michael.

'She's awfully moody sometimes,' Barbara continued. 'Long silences, that kind of thing. That's what I told the police.'

'You what? When did you talk to them?'

'They came to see me this morning. I think they're talking to everyone who knew Jo.'

'Knew? You make it sound as if she'd died.'

'Died? Of course she hasn't. I don't know what's happened to her. Nobody does. She's vanished without a trace.'

'Don't you care? I'm surprised at you, Barbara,' said Michael. What he was actually feeling was disappointment and a nagging doubt. If she could abandon a friend so easily, could she abandon him if the going got too tough for her? It was a horrible thought and he buried it as quickly as it had surfaced, but the seed was sown.

'What do you mean, surprised at me? I'm on your side, remember? Of course I care. She'll turn up. The police will find her. But you're the only person I really care about. I couldn't bear to think of you being harmed as a result of some trifling disagreement with Harry Hunter. He's very powerful, you know.'

'He's too powerful, in my opinion,' said Michael and there they left the matter, for the moment.

A mile or two away across London, a discussion was taking place in the American Embassy between Andy and his colleagues, who were surprised that there had been no come-back whatsoever from the British about the information that had been passed to them.

'There are only two explanations, it seems to me,' said Jerry. 'One is that Myers hasn't passed it on to headquarters because he's planning to use the information himself. The other is that the British know all about Moreton and are keeping something from us. Either way, we may need to do something about it. First, just fill me in on what else you've got.'

'The most significant thing is this Delvere woman has vanished,' said Lew. 'No-one knows where she is. And there's several stories doing the rounds, all of them official, by all accounts. First, that she stole Cabinet documents, second that it wasn't Cabinet documents but the Government's election programme and third, today's version, that she's nuts and hasn't taken anything at all. What does that say to you?'

'It tells me that they're shit scared, that perhaps they don't know exactly what she's got and they can't find her,' said Lew.

'They're definitely holding the lid on tight on this one,' said Andy.

'Don't forget, they'll know you went and rattled her cage, Andy, so there's a risk they'll think we're involved,' said Jerry. 'We'll give it a bit longer, just in case we turn up anything else first. If we don't, I guess I'll just have to go straight to the top, ask them what they're playing at, maybe say we think the Delvere woman was investigating this guy Moreton. Or maybe ask them about the Templeman angle. It's odd they're holding out on us. I want you to use all your contacts and see what you can find out.'

'My best contact has dropped out of sight,' said Andy. 'No-one's seen Myers since Monday evening. I expected to hear from him, but no-one knows where he is.'

Laura's prediction that Ann and Tim would get over their row and be happier than before proved to be premature. Their argument had been too shattering for both of them, with the result that it had dominated their thoughts all day and they returned home still aggrieved and anxious. They were stuck in a chilly stand-off in which neither would admit to having got it wrong. Eventually Tim asked what sort of a day she had had.

'Not a very good one.'

He asked, foolishly, 'Why was that?'

'As if you didn't know.'

'Oh don't let's start that again.'

This stung Ann into saying, 'I think you're wrong about Jo. Laura says she'd never—'

'Laura says! So you talked to her, did you? After I told you not to!'

'Told! Yes, that's it. You *told* me. How dare you? You make it sound as if I don't know how to behave. What was I supposed to do? The whole place is talking of little else. Was I supposed to say *nothing*? Anyway I think Laura's right. I'm sure Jo hasn't done anything wrong and I'm worried about her.'

At this Tim stormed out of the flat, slamming the front door behind him. He did not return until hours later and Ann pretended to be asleep when he came into the bedroom. He looked at her, sighed, and removed himself to the spare room.

CHAPTER THIRTY-NINE

Laura didn't feel like meeting the others for lunch but Ann had rung her up and begged her to come. She had sounded so wretched that Laura didn't have the heart to say no, but she was not looking forward to the inevitable discussion of Jo and speculation as to what might have happened to her. She was trying not to think about yesterday and the misery she had felt after her conversation with Charles. She had felt deeply and irreparably hurt by his attitude and was suffering a loneliness she had not felt for years. For the past three-quarters of an hour, however, these thoughts had been supplanted by a new worry caused by her conversation with Alicia, who had come to her room with urgent news to impart. They had gone down to the staff bar, where Alicia told Laura that Geoff had been fired by his newspaper and his Commons security pass removed. On top of this, Alicia had noticed a marked reluctance on the part of Geoff's erstwhile colleagues in the House to have anything to do with either of them. People with whom she regularly exchanged information and views had suddenly become guarded in their conversation with her. Alicia could not find out why and was alarmed and angry.

'I've never come across anything like it before. It just goes to show what powerful enemies he and Jo have made. We must all be very careful,' she had warned Laura. Geoff had gone off on his own somewhere, pursuing his own investigations and she would feel anxious about him until she saw him again. In the meantime, she did not know quite what to do next. Laura was equally at a loss.

'I find it decidedly odd that the police haven't been to see me,' she said. 'Positively sinister, in fact. They've questioned everyone Jo could possibly have had dealings with, but they haven't been near me.'

'I dare say they'll get round to you in due course,' said Alicia grimly. 'In the meantime, keep in touch. And I'll look in to see you later, if I have anything to report.'

As soon as Laura sat down at the table with Ann and Barbara, she knew it was a mistake to have come. They were all much changed from the last time they had met and were all aware of it. Ann looked exhausted. Barbara, who had been so happy on the last occasion, made no attempt to conceal her irritation. Michael had left her with a vague feeling of failure which she did not understand. It made her uneasy and heightened her irritation towards Jo, whom she held responsible for getting her into a situation which was indefinably but unmistakably some kind of threat to her personally. They ordered their food and made a brief but unsustainable attempt at normality. They felt Jo's absence too keenly.

'Well, Laura,' Barbara demanded, 'have you heard anything about Jo?'

'Nothing except malicious rumour. I haven't heard from Jo, unfortunately,' Laura replied sadly.

'What an extraordinary thing to do, rush off like that!' exclaimed Barbara. 'You've got to admit it's a pretty strange thing to do.'

'It might not seem strange if we knew why she did it,' said Ann.

'Well I always thought she was a bit odd,' said Barbara.

'Did you now?' said Laura in a dangerous tone.

'Yes, I did, as a matter of fact. She was always so moody and unpredictable, you have to agree.'

'I'll agree nothing of the kind. You don't know what you're talking about,' said Laura angrily, 'you're just trotting out the garbage being put about by the Whips.'

'No, I'm not! Just think how heated she got the other day. And all that business about Harry's constituent. That was a bit over the top, wasn't it?'

'I don't think so,' said Ann. 'She was genuinely upset about it and I don't blame her.'

'Well, I bet Tim thinks her behaviour's strange, doesn't he? It makes her look guilty as hell!' said Barbara.

'Leave Tim out of this, will you?' said Ann quietly.

They ate in silence for a few minutes. Then Barbara said, 'Look what she's done to us. Why should we three be falling out over this? It's ridiculous.'

Neither Ann nor Laura responded to this, which annoyed Barbara even more. Her feeling of being in the wrong was increasing and she disliked it intensely.

'This is your doing, Laura. I think it's about time you came clean with us. You've never told us anything about Jo and I find that a bit odd, frankly. I think you're holding out on us.'

'It's no big deal, but I made a promise to Jo and I intend to keep it,' said Laura. That was not the reason for her refusal. She would like very much to explain things, to defend Jo and to enlist their sympathy. But she felt Barbara was even more of a liability than Ann, whose heart was at least in the right place.

'Well, what about Randall Myers?' demanded Barbara. 'Don't you remember last week, Ann, when you

366

said you thought he was following Jo? Don't tell me that that's not significant. And now she's vanished. The two things must be connected. That's what I told the police anyway.'

'You did what?' asked Laura.

'What was I supposed to do?' said Barbara, afraid of the look in Laura's eyes. 'They came to see me and asked me a lot of questions about her. Are you suggesting I should have lied?'

'You two. Keep it down, will you?' said Ann. 'People are staring at you.'

They sat in silence for a moment or two. When they seemed to have calmed down, Ann said, 'I've remembered something just now. Do you remember what Jo said at our last lunch? She said "What would you do if you found out something terrible?" or something like that. Didn't she?'

'She did,' said Laura.

'And when I asked her if she'd found something, she backtracked hard and said it was a hypothetical question,' said Barbara. They both looked at Laura.

'I can't tell you anything, not yet,' said Laura, 'except that Jo did indeed find out something terrible, and she hasn't done *anything* wrong, I swear to you she hasn't, and I'm *very* worried about her. I think she's in danger. Something may have happened to her already,' she couldn't continue, but stood up and got some money out of her handbag. 'I'm feeling too upset about all this. I can't stay. Take care of my share will you?' She handed the money to Ann and hurried out of the room.

The Prime Minister and Mackie were waiting for Harry and as soon as he saw them he had a feeling he was about to be put on the spot.

'Mackie tells me the Americans think we know something about Delvere which we ought to be sharing with them. They swear she's not working for them and are getting stroppy. As evidence of their good intentions they have offered to help us try to find Delvere, provided we tell them everything we know about her and what she was after. As you can imagine that presents us with a difficulty.'

'They're not being honest with us,' said Mackie. 'We know that one of their men came to the House on Monday and saw Delvere in Central Lobby. We've established that he took a bag belonging to her from her office and later returned it, no doubt after their people had examined its contents thoroughly. So it would seem that either they knew what she was up to and wanted a piece of the action, or they were trying to sabotage her in some way. We're also concerned that one of our agents has gone missing and may be involved with Delvere in some way.'

'I don't trust them,' said the Prime Minister. 'They say they're concerned about the conference, but we suspect it's really an attempt to embarrass us and upset all our plans.'

'In what way?' asked Harry.

The Prime Minister dropped his bombshell.

'Because they say they believe that Delvere was investigating Geoffrey Moreton's electronics business and his connections with the arms trade and they're hinting at some connection with Jane Templeman and an attempt to compromise David Templeman.'

'What!' Harry struggled to control his feelings. So the Americans knew about Moreton. They must have got the information from Harper and Delvere. But what was this about Jane? They *must* have seen the book. Maybe they had it. He was overcome by a feeling of helplessness. The more they tried to grapple with the problem, the more complicated it became.

'Whatever makes them say that?' gasped Harry.

'We've no idea. But it bodes ill for us, I fear. We have to do something and soon. The question is what. The House will rise next week for the Easter Recess, which is something. If we can hang on until then, we may yet deal with the problem satisfactorily, but we must avoid questions here at all costs.'

'If I might make a suggestion?' said Mackie.

'Yes?'

'I think we should build on what we've done so far. We could put out an official bulletin that Delvere has escaped from a secure mental hospital – that will give people the impression that she is violent and make them more likely to come forward. We have it said that she must be apprehended at all costs, that she's very sick, suffers from delusions, and put her picture out on television. That way we have a better chance of finding her and can further discredit her at the same time.'

'It's a bit soon, don't you think?' said the Prime Minister. 'After all she only disappeared on Tuesday morning. Could she have been caught and committed to hospital in two days? I doubt it somehow. We don't want to provoke further questions from the media.'

'We could leave it until the weekend,' said Harry. 'Saturday is always a better time for that sort of thing. The media are usually more interested in sporting matters on the weekend and we could put it out more unobtrusively.'

The result of this discussion was a news bulletin on Saturday evening about Jo that caused Laura and her mother great distress. She had gone to her mother's home hoping that she would have a telephone number for her sister, that might in turn lead to a number she could try for Jo. On hearing the news bulletin, Laura made her mother come out into the garden, in spite of the cold, so that she could tell her everything without any risk of being overheard by concealed microphones or some other unimaginable device. Her mother thought this far-fetched and fanciful, but went along with it when she saw how upset Laura was. Unfortunately, Mrs James had no telephone number for her sister and expressed the fervent hope that the news story about Jo would not reach New Zealand. Laura was in a fever of anxiety about Jo and returned to London soon afterwards.

On Sunday morning she went to her office in the House of Commons. The building was deserted, save for occasional security patrols. Of course, the Speaker and the Serjeant-at-Arms lived in the building, but she would be very unlikely to see them. The police officer on duty at the gates of New Palace Yard would have been bound to note her arrival, but she was fairly confident of being undisturbed, for some time at least.

She had been into the Palace of Westminster on weekends occasionally over the years, but only rarely. She was struck by the presence of the building, a kind of breathless, waiting silence. She found herself moving as quietly as possible. She was conscious of herself, imagining what she would look like if anyone had been able to see her, conspiratorial, furtive. How many people have come into this place on a mission of this kind? she wondered.

She was relieved to reach her office. Fortunately the day was bright and she had no need to turn on the lights. She did not wish to attract any more attention to herself than she already had. She sat down and switched on her word-processor and set to work to write down everything that had happened, in particular everything that Jo had told her about the Black Book and about Randall and McGovern. She worked for hours, pausing only briefly from time to time to make herself a cup of black coffee. When she was satisfied that she had it all down, she saved her text on a floppy disk, rather than on the hard disk of her computer. Then she made sure she had left nothing stored in her computer that could reveal what she had been up to. When she had decided what best to do, perhaps tomorrow, she would print out the text from the floppy disk. In the meantime, she had to hide the disk somewhere safe.

She left her room and walked noiselessly along the corridor to Charles's office and quietly opened the door. The room was empty. She looked slowly round wondering where to hide her disk. She checked the hiding place for the tape from her answering machine. It was still there. That had proved a safe choice so far. Why not do the same with her disk? It wouldn't fit into a cassette box, of course, but she could slide it in with one of Charles's videos of interviews he had done in the days before he became Deputy Speaker. There was a suitable one, an old late-night television debate. She'd put it there. She slid the disk in alongside the video and replaced the box in the shelf with the rest. It looked no different from the others. Satisfied, she returned to her room, collected her bag, and left. The police officer gave her a cheerful wave as she drove out of New Palace Yard and she waved back, feeling she had done something positive at last. It wasn't much, but it was a step in the right direction.

CHAPTER FORTY

Harry and the Prime Minister relaxed a little. There was no news whatsoever of Delvere or Harper, both of whom had sunk without trace. So far, they had managed to escape the political catastrophe that had loomed over them for the past week. With each day that passed, their confidence grew.

On the Wednesday morning it was shattered when Mackie sought an urgent meeting with the Prime Minister to inform him that Randall Myers's corpse had been found in an isolated stretch of woodland and that a careful search of his home had revealed a photograph featuring information about Sir Geoffrey Moreton. Did the Prime Minister think this might be part of Mr Hunter's file? He had consulted his American counterpart and established that they had given the photograph to Myers in the expectation that it would have been passed on to his superiors.

Mackie continued, relentlessly, with his assessment of the situation. 'We have established beyond question that Delvere was not in the House of Commons on the day of

372

the bomb explosion, other than for a brief period first thing in the morning. I have to say that I do not believe that she saw the file in question in Mr Hunter's office.'

Harry was summoned by the Prime Minister at ten a.m. and walked through from Number Twelve with a growing certainty that he had reached the end of the line in politics. He had had another arid, cruel conversation with his wife, in which they had inflicted the maximum verbal wounds on each other. She had some justification for feeling as she did. He had none and he knew it. He was conscious of having no remorse for something that should cause him to feel shame. I've reached the end of the line in more ways than one, he thought. Nevertheless, he was unprepared for the ordeal he was about to face.

The Prime Minister was standing at the window of his room, waiting for him. Mackie was there too. Mackie was sitting down, looking perfectly relaxed. Harry shut the door.

'Good morning, Prime Minister,' he said.

'There's nothing good about it,' said the Prime Minister as he turned round from the window to face Harry.

'Do you recognize this?' he asked, handing Harry a copy of the photograph which the Americans had decided that morning to pass to their British counterparts.

Harry took the photograph and looked at it. His hand shook so much that the end of the photograph quivered as if in a slight breeze.

'Do you?'

'Yes,' said Harry.

'Is it what I think it is?' asked the Prime Minister.

'It is. Yes. Where did you – where did it come from?'

'The Americans. Would you like to revise your story about your missing file, Harry? And I warn you to be careful.'

373

'What do you mean? I've told you what happened.'

'Think again. Where did you say this woman found it?'

Harry realized that total disaster had overtaken him. 'I must sit down,' he said weakly and lowered himself onto a chair. 'Since you seem to know where she found it, perhaps you'd enlighten me?' he said, in a feeble attempt to brazen things out.

'Let's not waste any more time, shall we? We know she took it from your flat. The Americans think she's still got it in fact and don't believe our protestations to the contrary. I take it you *do* have it.'

'Yes. It was returned. I didn't even know who'd taken it until—'

'I can guess.'

There was a heavy, threatening silence in the room. Eventually Harry spoke, 'You'd better have my resignation,' he said quietly.

'Oh no you don't, you bastard! If the ship's going down, you're going to be locked in the bloody hold, d'you hear? Don't think you're going to wriggle out of this now!'

Harry sat in silence, perspiration trickling down his temples and glinting on his upper lip. He seemed to be unaware of it.

'The problem you have left us with is so appalling that I hope it tortures you to your grave,' said the Prime Minister savagely. 'We're damn sure this woman was working for the Americans and that they set the whole thing up weeks ago in order to take over this conference, probably to sabotage it altogether. They've got some scheme under way, some anti-Russian ploy and they don't want the conference to go ahead. Either that or they've got some other lunatic scheme afoot to manipulate the Middle East problem in some way. They've as good as said they'll go public with what they've got if we don't cancel the conference. But we don't know *what* they've got, thanks to you, do we, Harry? So it's crunch time. I want you to hand over this damned book to me this afternoon, in my room in the House, at two o'clock. Is that understood?'

Harry stood up to go.

'You haven't asked how we know they've planned this for some time, have you?' said the Prime Minister.

'No. There didn't seem much point.'

'We've had your flat swept and discovered they had it bugged. I wonder why they did that, Harry? You're supposed to be living at Number Twelve aren't you? But that wasn't good enough, was it? You thought your grubby little book made you bulletproof, didn't you? Instead it may yet destroy you and all the rest of us with you.'

The Prime Minister made a statement to the House that afternoon expressing his deep regret that owing to difficulties that had arisen between some of the participating nations, the European peace conference was being postponed to allow these problems to be resolved. Fortunately for him and his government, a second bomb explosion in central London distracted the attention of the media sufficiently for him to escape further questioning and any remaining media coverage was hailed by the anti-Europeans as conclusive proof of their case against European union. Their claims went unchallenged, the House having risen at the end of the afternoon for the Easter Recess.

On Thursday morning, Laura arrived at work early, feeling a strong sense of impending disaster. Already the House was largely deserted, most MPs having left for their constituencies or their holidays the previous day, the moment the Recess began. Laura went into her room to find Alicia waiting for her. She looked exhausted. She was sitting, slumped in an armchair, as if she had been taking a nap, when Laura opened the door. She instantly leapt to her feet and beckoned Laura to follow her from the room.

'What's up?' Laura whispered. Alicia led the way to the staircase. They stood at the top of the stairs and talked quietly.

'Really bad news,' said Alicia. 'Geoff has been arrested and I can't find out where he's being held. They're using the Prevention of Terrorism Act as a pretext to hold him incommunicado. I'm frightened, Laura.'

'Me too,' said Laura.

'I think you and I may be arrested too. What are we going to do?'

'I'm not delaying another day,' said Laura. 'I've written down everything I can think of that Jo told me, everything that's happened, including what Geoff told me. It's on disk at the moment, safely hidden away. In a little while I'll retrieve it and print it out and then I'm going to take it to the Speaker. Is that all right with you?'

'It's fine by me, but do you think it will do any good? Without any hard evidence, will anyone believe us? If only Jo had let us have copies of what she had. If we had those, we'd be able to clear Jo and Geoff.'

'Well she didn't, so we'll just have to make the best of a bad job. I'm going to have a word with George Gunn, tell him what I'm going to do. He'll have some good advice, I'm sure. He may be able to help us. All right?'

'OK. Good luck.'

'You too. I'll keep you posted,' said Laura and ran downstairs to the Serjeant-at-Arms's Office. To her relief she found Ann alone in her office.

'Ann, I need to talk to you urgently. Can you get away for a little while?'

'Sure thing, Laura.'

'You know George Gunn's room in the Lords?' Ann

nodded. 'Meet me there as soon as you can. And do you think you could go and find Barbara and get her to come too?'

Laura walked through Peers' Corridor to Peers' Lobby. The place was deserted. She went into George's room and sat down, hoping that he would arrive soon. She didn't have long to wait. George came ambling across the lobby a few minutes later.

'This is a nice surprise. How are you, Laura?'

'I'm frantic, George, and I've come to ask your help.' She stopped. She could hear the sound of footsteps. 'I hope you don't mind, George, but I've asked Ann Fenchurch and Barbara Wallingbury to meet me here. Do you know them?'

Ann and Barbara appeared at that moment. There weren't enough chairs for everybody. George insisted on standing, his bulky figure filling the doorway. Ann perched on the desk. Laura didn't waste time on preliminaries.

'I'm about to do something to try to help Jo and I wanted you to know because there may be repercussions for you. Not because you've done anything,' she added hastily, seeing a look of alarm on Barbara's face, 'but because people know we're friends and you may be asked questions. I just wanted you to be prepared, that's all. Also I think you'll feel – I hope you will – that I'm doing the right thing when you hear what I have to say.'

'Can I say something, Laura?' said Ann. 'Before you tell us anything. I just want you to know that whatever you do to help Jo is fine by me. Tim and I had a long talk about this over the weekend. He says the whole thing stinks. He had a row with his superiors who were giving him a hard time about me. I hope he won't lose his job as a result. Anyway he said the truth is what matters and he doesn't think we're hearing it from the Government.'

'Thanks, Ann.'

'The same goes for me,' said Barbara and blushed. 'I know you must think I was awful the other day and I was, I admit it. Michael was really annoyed with me for swallowing the Whips' propaganda. We nearly fell out over it. I was only trying to do the right thing by him. Truly I was.'

'Don't worry, Barbara. It hasn't been easy for anyone, has it? And I owe you an explanation. I know I do.' Laura glanced up at George. 'I expect you've been wondering about all the rumours too, George.'

'I didn't pay too much attention to them. I thought it all sounded very fishy.'

'Well, I decided this morning that something has to be done to try to help Jo. And Geoff Harper too. He's been arrested. Alicia hadn't seen him for days and now finds he's being held under the Prevention of Terrorism Act. It's monstrous. Anyway I told Alicia that I was going to write down everything I know, everything Jo told me, and take it to the Speaker. But I want to show it to you first, George. I'd like to know what you think, whether I should take it to the police, and if so who exactly.'

Laura paused. No-one spoke. Then she said, 'I'm getting all this back to front really. The point is there are people in power who are trying to discredit Jo with all these terrible stories so that if she spills the beans about them they can say it's all the fantastical ravings of a deranged female. Any day now they'll twig that she's not Joanna Delvere but Joanna Hammond and that her husband was shot in the Balkans.'

'What?' Ann and Barbara looked at her in amazement.

'I know I should have told you. I'm sorry. She asked me not to tell anyone because she was finding it so hard to cope with his death. Delvere is her maiden name. And she's my cousin. She was married to this terrific guy, Donald. They'd been together for years. He worked for the UN. They got married last November and he was killed just before Christmas. I got her the job here to try to help her keep occupied and get to grips with things. And look what's happened.'

Laura stopped. Ann reached across and stroked her hand. 'I'm sure she's all right. You'll see.'

'There's a lot more to tell you, but there's no time now. I must go and get it all ready. I just wanted you to know what I was doing.'

'I'm glad you told us,' said Barbara. 'Me too,' said Ann.

They were all silent again. Laura gazed out at Peers' Lobby.

'*Dieu et mon droit*,' said Laura, 'what a joke!'

'What?' asked Barbara.

'It's written into the pattern on the floor out there, isn't it, George?'

'That's right.'

'Everyone walks over it all the time but no-one ever stops to think about it. In fact the whole building is full of the symbols and rituals of honour, chivalry and duty. It's a bit of a joke, isn't it? Like that bit in the prayer they say in both Houses about "laying aside all private interests, prejudices and partial affections".' She stood up. 'If anything's happened to Jo I'm never going to have anything to do with this place again.'

'Now, Laura,' said George, 'it's not like you to be defeatist. You'll hear from her soon.' He moved towards the door. 'I'm afraid I've got to go and meet a party of tourists, but you can stay here as long as you want.'

'Thanks, George, but I must get back to my room and print out this dossier. When can I bring it back to you? That's if you don't mind looking at it for me?'

'Of course I don't mind. I'll be glad to do what I can to help. Why don't you come back in about an hour and a half?'

Ann and Barbara went back to their offices, Laura

having promised to let them know when she had been to the Speaker. Then she went straight to Charles's room to retrieve her tape and floppy disk. Charles was sitting at his desk. She ignored him and went to the bookshelf.

'Laura, I'm glad you're here. I need to speak to you.'

'Not now, Charles. I'm sorry. I've got to deal with something really urgent.' She retrieved her tape and disk and left the room.

She was in the process of printing out her dossier when Sir Charles put his head round the door.

'I know you can't talk now. I can see that. I just wanted to say something.' Laura looked at him.

'Will you forgive me? Please? And whatever you're up to, I'll back you.' He left the room.

Laura wouldn't allow herself to stop and contemplate his words. Not now. She finished printing out her dossier and put it into a file. Finally she placed the file, tape and disk in a large brown envelope which she sealed carefully with sellotape. Then she wrote 'George Gunn, Esq.'on the front and returned to his room to wait for him. The sun had come out and was shining down into the Lobby and she felt calmer and more confident than she had felt for days. It was a relief to have told the others, but if only she knew where Jo was.

She was deep in thought when George came into the room.

'Don't despair,' he said, soothingly. 'I'm going to make you something to drink, then you can give me your parcel.'

Later that morning George rang Laura.

'Can you meet me in Members' Lobby? In, say, five minutes?' he asked. She raced downstairs.

'Have you read it, George? What did you think?

'I think it's shocking. Parliament's changed so much. There was always some rum types, but never anything like this. And in the old days, they saw themselves as serving the country rather than serving themselves. Nowadays there's such rich pickings that they'll do anything to hang on to their jobs.'

'If only we had some proof! Without Jo's photocopies, I think people may not believe us.'

'We'll talk about that in a minute. First, I want you to come with me, my girl.'

'What about my envelope? Where is it?'

'Don't you worry about that. It's quite safe. I'll give it back to you in a minute. Just come with me.'

Mystified, she accompanied him into the Chamber.

'Where are we going, George?'

'I thought it was time you had another guided tour.'

'What? That's all I need! What's got into you?'

He smiled at her.

'You look very pleased with yourself, if you don't mind my saying so,' said Laura.

He chuckled, 'You remember all those years ago when I showed you round the place for the first time, just as I did for your friend Jo not long ago?'

'I do indeed.'

They had reached the bar of the House and stood facing the Speaker's Chair.

'I think you've forgotten some of the details and it's time for a refresher.'

'Come on, George, what are you up to?'

'Just humour an old man,' he said, 'and tell me what you remember about Jo's message.'

She thought for a moment. 'She said "Relax, it's in the bag. I'll be in touch as soon as I can." I think that was it.' She paused.

'Do you mean to say you've forgotten the origin of the expression "It's in the bag"?' he asked. 'You don't remember what I told you all those years ago?'

'Good God!' Her eyes were shining. 'Of course! Why

didn't I think of it? The Petition Bag!'

'Shush. Keep your voice down.'

She raced past the table and the Speaker's Chair. The doors beyond the Chair were closed. She opened them and looked around her. No-one in sight. She stepped back into the Chamber, where George stood smiling at her. There was the Petition Bag hanging on the back of the Speaker's Chair.

'I hardly dare look.'

'I already did.' He beamed at her. 'But I didn't take anything out. I wanted to see your face.'

She put her hand into the green baize bag and drew out Jo's envelope. Scribbled on it in Jo's writing was 'Laura James, c/o Speaker's Office.'

Laura turned it over. On the back Jo had added, 'Ring Etienne Bernhardt, UNHCR.'